Praise for *BE*

"I recommend this book .... in

metaphysics, psychologic .... ~ge themes."

~Robin Gregory, Author of *The Improbable Wonders of Moojie Littleman.*

"[*Between Will and Surrender*] blends the standard elements of a good novel with the specific ingredients of visionary fiction (growth in consciousness, paranormal events, spirituality) to render a tale that entertains, mystifies and enlightens—and not necessarily in that order or in any order. The result is exquisite."

~Victor Smith, Author of *Channel of the Grail, A Novel of Cathars, Templars, and a Nazi Grail Hunter* and *The Anathemas, A Novel of Reincarnation and Restitution*

"Margaret Duarte has succeeded in telling an entertaining story, complete with characters worth caring about, whose motivations are clear and believable, and in the process, she revealed mystical truths in an organic way."

~Rea Nolan Martin, Author of *Mystic Tea* and *The Anesthesia Game.*

"Well-written work. Highly recommend to those who love stories of the paranormal-metaphysical at work in daily lives."

~Gini Grossenbacher, Author of *Madam of My Heart* and *Madam in Silk.*

ALSO BY MARGARET DUARTE

Between Darkness and Dawn
Between Yesterday and Tomorrow
Between Now and Forever

BETWEEN
WILL AND
SURRENDER
MARGARET DUARTE

Omie
PRESS

Book Cover design Yocla Designs by Clarissa

Publisher's Cataloging-in-Publication Data

Names: Duarte, Margaret.
Title: Between will and surrender / Margaret Duarte.
Description: Elk Grove, CA : Omie Press, 2015. | Series: Enter the between, bk. 1.
Identifiers: LCCN 2015920212 | ISBN 978-0-9860688-2-9 (pbk.) |
    ISBN 978-0-9860688-3-6 (ebook)
Subjects: LCSH: Women--Fiction. | Esselen Indians--Fiction. | Self-actualization (Psychology)--Fiction. | Spiritual life--Fiction. | Paranormal fiction. | BISAC: FICTION / Visionary & Metaphysical. | FICTION / Fantasy / Paranormal. | FICTION / Native American & Aboriginal. | FICTION / Occult & Supernatural. | GSAFD: Occult fiction.
Classification: LCC PS3604.U241 B48 2015 (print) | DDC: 813/.6--dc23.

For my husband, partner, and friend, John Duarte

Spring

2001

The path of initiation begins in the East,
the place of clarity and illumination.

Sometimes, quite suddenly, we are caught unaware, and a door opens, offering a new insight, a new path, and we hesitate at the threshold, reluctant to go through, because we know if we do, life will never be the same. In retrospect, I can safely say that Cliff Smotherman drove me straight to it.

BETWEEN
WILL AND
SURRENDER

Chapter One

L EAVE IT TO CLIFF to insist that we take a romantic day trip to Carmel on Ash Wednesday. I could have said no, of course. I could have suggested that we turn the car around and do this some other day. It's just that . . . Well, it had been so long since he'd asked. And it wasn't as if I would have been in church anyway. Five years ago, yes, I probably would have had ashes on my forehead by now, in the shape of a cross, a reminder of my earthy beginnings, of my dusty heart, of repentance, of death.

Vivaldi's "Winter" Concerto No. 4 surged through all eight speakers of the digital sound system in Cliff's Mercedes Benz, evoking in my fertile mind images of dark clouds, dripping fog, and violent storms. Instinctively, I sank deeper into the soft leather passenger seat, which, according to Cliff, had been adjusted in one of fourteen ways for my ultimate ease and comfort. I shivered against this luxury.

"Sulking?" Cliff asked.

I smiled. "Sort of."

"Well snap out of it, Marjorie. You've been bugging me for weeks to take you somewhere."

"I know, but—"

"Yeah, yeah, not on Ash Wednesday. I heard you the first time."

I closed my eyes and pressed my head back onto the seat, then wrapped my arms beneath my chest as if warding off a draft.

"Cold?" Cliff asked.

"No."

I heard the protest of leather as Cliff leaned forward and edged up the heat. "Better?"

"Sure."

"It's all filtered and controlled, you know."

"What is?"

"The air."

"Huh?"

"The temperature, the dust, the pollen, it's all monitored."

I sighed.

"And it tracks the sun."

"What does?"

"The climate control."

"Why?"

"To keep the temperature inside this baby at" —Again the sound of creaking leather— "sixty-eight degrees."

"Sounds like you've actually read the owner's manual," I said.

"Cover-to-cover."

I stifled a yawn. "I haven't even opened mine."

"That figures," he said.

I opened my eyes and focused on my fiancé. Like his Mercedes, Cliff was sleek and alluring, in an aluminum, magnesium, and steel sort of way. His front end was bold and riveting and was currently accented by reflective glasses that gave him a captivating look. His take-charge personality often rocketed me to places I didn't want to go. Like today.

We were cruising along the famous 17-mile stretch of California road that zigzagged through the Del Monte Forest of Pacific Grove and then picked its way along the coast to just north of Carmel. Yet Cliff hadn't slowed down even once to take in the view.

I felt the sudden, almost violent, urge to escape the cockpit of this technologically perfect machine. "Cliff, please pull over."

Mirrored glasses turned my way. "Why?"

"I need some fresh air."

"Then open the window."

Fighting the onslaught of a familiar ache in my head, I looked at the brochure on my lap and noticed the picture of a cypress tree on its cover. "I'd like to see the Lone Cypress. It's at the next stop."

Cliff fiddled with the buttons behind his steering wheel, re-adjusting the settings of the CD player for what seemed like the hundredth time, then smiled at me in a way I had once considered charming. "I'll buy you a post card when we get to the mission."

"I'm going to be sick, Cliff."

"Damn!" He hit the brakes and skidded into one of the parking spots lining the two-lane road.

"Want to come?" I asked.

Cliff tapped his fingers on the steering wheel. "Are you getting out or what?"

I reached behind me for the digital camera lying on the back seat and opened the door.

"Be careful," he said. "I paid a fortune for that camera."

Yeah, I'd heard it all before. A heavy, ruggedized, full-frame, digital camera, with 22.3 megapixels, autofocus, GPS capability, and a big telephoto zoom lens. "I don't know why. You haven't taken a single picture since we left Menlo Park."

Without waiting for his response, I strapped the camera around my neck and escaped into the unfiltered, unregulated outdoors.

Ocean waves crashed, smashed, and retreated. Gulls *kee-yahed*, *cow-cow-cowed*. Cool air brushed my cheeks and fingered through my hair.

On reaching the wooden observation deck, I un-slung the camera, steadied it on the platform railing, and zoomed in on the Lone Cypress standing some forty feet away.

Although miraculously born of a seed that had become stuck in a crevice of granite, the Pebble Beach icon was a disappointment— small, spindly, fenced in to protect its roots, supported by steel cables to keep it from falling. Yet . . .

While positioning the tree in the viewfinder, I noticed how it clung to the wave-washed rock, defying the elements that raged against it. "Defiant. Atta girl."

I half pressed the shutter to activate the autofocus.

Sunwalker.

Chills swelled over my neck and face like an army of unearthed garden ants. Who was that?

Sunwalker.

A voice. But where was it coming from?

You've come at last.

The camera clicked, whirred, and slipped from my shaking hands.

You must listen. Time is running out.

It had to be Cliff, playing tricks on me with one of his highfalutin technological gadgets. A hidden speaker, maybe. Like the ones used in haunted houses to induce artificial paranormal experiences.

Beeeep. The blast of a horn tore through me like a shaft of ice.

A door slammed. Feet pounded on wooden steps.

"What the hell?"

"Cliff! Oh, thank God. I just heard someone talking to me, but no one was there . . ."

Cliff picked up the camera, blew on it, and rubbed it with the tip of his shirt. "I knew I should've had it insured."

Part of me was relieved that the camera had tumbled onto the wooden deck instead of the rocks below. Another part of me didn't give a damn. "She called me *Sunwalker*, as if she knew me."

He pressed the power button and the shutter. *Click. Whir.* "It seems to be working okay."

"Cliff, please. Tell me you were messing with me. I won't be mad. Promise. Actually, I'd be relieved . . ."

"Damn it, I told you to be careful."

"Please listen. I think I'm losing my—"

"See what happens when I listen to you," he said. "Let's get out of here."

For a split second, I imagined my fiancé plunging over the edge of the deck railing, helpless, voiceless . . .

Sometimes I hate you, Cliff.

﹏ ﹏ ﹏

4

By the time we reached the Carmel Mission, it was nearly noon, and I felt numb. In contrast, Cliff projected a tinselly glow. He reached for his camera.

"Why, exactly, are we here?" I asked.

Several emotions played across Cliff's face before embarrassment appeared to take hold. He looked like he'd been caught cheating on his taxes, or, heaven forbid, cheating on me.

"Tell me," I said.

After a slight hesitation, he asked, "Did you build a model mission while in school?"

"Of course. Don't all kids in California?"

He smiled tightly. "My parents were furious when I asked them for help."

"Your parents?"

"They told me to do my own damn assignment. Trouble was I couldn't drive."

I shook my head, completely lost.

"Our teacher wanted us to build a scale model of an actual mission. I chose the Carmel Mission, but couldn't find a picture of it."

"We used empty milk cartons and Popsicle sticks," I said.

"Then obviously you weren't in an honors class."

"Well, no, I don't think our school had one."

A snort. "So which mission did you build?"

"I don't know. Just a mission."

His eyebrows rose above his sunglasses. "A generic mission?"

"Hey, what's the big deal? At least we had fun, more than I can say for you. Plus, I got an A. What did you get?"

"I got a C. But my classmates, with the help of their parents, built some incredible missions."

"So, what are you going to do? Go back for a better grade?"

"I just wanted to come here and see."

"And you're finally getting around to it . . . now?"

"Been too busy," he said.

This time, I snorted. Then, curiously, I began to sense things about Cliff I'd never sensed before. I could hardly believe it.

5

Something so trivial still bothered him after nineteen years. As a child, he hadn't been in control. And he needed to be in control—desperately. Over life. Over the world. Over me. But I could no longer give him my full attention, my adoration, and my submission. Today had changed all that. I'd suddenly come to realize that Cliff and I had nothing in common.

And that I didn't know my own mind.

"Are you coming?" he asked.

I wanted to tell him to quit leaning on me, that I wasn't there to lift him up, that the time we spent together was rare and precious, and that we should treat it as such. Instead, I said, "Take your time. I'll meet up with you later."

He nodded and took off, pressing the camera to his chest as though cradling glass.

Wow, I thought, as I got out of the car and headed for the mission entrance.

In exchange for the admission fee, the woman behind the gift shop counter handed me a shiny brochure. "Welcome to the Mission San Carlos Borromeo."

I entered the courtyard and immediately sensed a presence.

Marjorie Marie Veil.

A woman in white slacks and a blue striped top stood a short distance away, taking pictures.

There is something you must know.

Blood throbbed in my temples. Objects appeared larger, then smaller, larger, then smaller. I bumped into someone, startled, and turned. It was the woman with the camera. "Sorry," I said.

"Are you okay," she asked.

"Yes. Yes, I'm fine." I gave her a faint smile and then walked to the wooden bench in front of the courtyard fountain, sat, and pressed my face into my hands.

Chapter Two

WAS I LOSING MY MIND? The question plagued me for three weeks before I finally sought help. It felt like giving up though, which bothered me. I didn't see myself as a quitter.

Eventually, I convinced myself that I wasn't giving up, but giving in; a minor difference, true, but one that made a big difference to me. Anyway, I couldn't do this alone.

I eyed the plaque on the office door: PSYCHOLOGY, Tony Mendez, PsyD, and not for the first time wondered how a psychologist could relate to my deepest needs. Science simply didn't deal with issues of meaning and belonging. It was too separated from the mystery of life. Sure, the doctor could tell me if I was crazy or not, but what then?

Somehow, I didn't believe drugs would be the answer.

I'd considered going to a priest, of course, but in my experience, church was mostly about rules and rituals, sermons and homilies. Anyway, only saints and prophets were supposed to hear voices, and believe me, I was neither.

✗ ✗ ✗

The waiting room was nearly empty. Only a young boy looked up as I entered. Next to him sat a woman bent over a stack of papers, shifting and sorting, completely absorbed in her task. Under normal circumstances, I would have wondered what a mere child was doing in a psychologist's office, accompanied by someone who looked more like a caseworker than his mother, but today wasn't normal— not by a long shot. I'd lost track of normal three weeks ago.

For a few merciful moments, I found relief in the framed print hanging above the child's head. It was a Bev Doolittle: *The Spirit Takes Flight*. I had planned to buy one just like it at a seaside gallery along Highway 1. That is, until I'd shown it to my mother.

"Are you out of your mind?" she'd asked, with that in-your-face authority of the closed minded. "Why would you want to hang that disturbing picture anywhere in your house? A patch of ground with a bunch of leaves and rocks and . . . dear God, is that a snake?"

Torn between a desire to purchase the print and an equal desire to appease my mother, I'd opted for appeasement. Better to give in than immerse myself in the thick cloud of censure she wore around her like a cloak and was more than happy to share with the ones she loved.

Now, looking at the print with renewed longing, I counted the butterflies camouflaged in its midst. Camouflage, one of the techniques Doolittle is famous for, hidden pictures that speak to you; if only you take the time to look. And understand.

I remembered pointing this out to my mother and her immediate response. "All I see hidden in that picture is an Indian peering at me like he's about to scalp me."

So much for hidden messages. She'd come up with a doozy of her own, one that made sense to her, but missed my point entirely.

"If it's a signed limited edition you're after," she said, "why not a Thomas Kinkade? It's so much cozier."

"Cozier," I'd repeated, reading the quote by Chief Seattle etched on a plaque beneath the print. *We are part of the Earth, and the Earth is a part of us.* The images that made my spirit soar were obviously too pagan for her. She preferred a gingerbread cottage, surrounded by flowers and a white picket fence, with a church steeple highlighted in the background. How comforting was that? I was already living that scene, yet there was still something terribly important missing.

Funny how today, on one of the worst days of my life, I'd come across the print again, as though it were mocking me: *See what happens when you don't listen to your heart?* As before, I turned away. Too many butterflies; too many, hidden between the pine needles, pebbles, and plants.

I headed for the reception desk and then called on years of discipline and self-control to get through the ensuing questions and to a vacant chair. I sagged into it wearily; wanting nothing more than to forget, forget about the *Voice*, pretend it did not exist.

The fear, so familiar now, constricted my chest while a dull, pressing ache grew on both sides of my head. Desperately, I searched for a distraction and, again, noticed the boy. He sat to my right, unnaturally still, and appeared to be about seven years old. His blue-black hair fell over his forehead, thick and straight, and in his hands, he gripped something as if for protection.

I followed the direction of his gaze and was surprised to find him staring at the fire opal ring on my right hand. Unconsciously, I'd been rubbing the stone, drawing comfort from its smooth surface.

He looked up. Brown eyes met blue. And with sudden clarity, I realized that he'd perceived my dark mood. But how? He was just a child, too young for such depth, such sensitivity.

"Hello," I said, in part to cover my embarrassment at being caught out by a kid, but also to distract him from his sudden interest in my hair, my face, my hands. But all I gained, besides an intensification of his stare, was further discomfort, as his companion—suddenly as alert as a bodyguard spotting a paparazzo—looked at me, her eyes dark and disapproving.

I smiled, amazed at how a simple look could make me feel guilty, apologetic, want to say I'm sorry.

Instead of acknowledging my smile, the woman refocused on the stack of papers on her lap, which she proceeded to clasp in her hands and pound against her thighs to force them into line. While the papers thumped and her heavy floral scent wafted into the air, I wondered if she was sending me a silent message: *Don't mess with what you don't understand.*

My skin prickled. My face grew hot. If only it were that easy.

Pretending to be unaffected by the child's ill-tempered bodyguard and ignoring the inadvisability of speaking to someone obviously awaiting therapy, I decided to ask the boy his name. But before my decision could turn into deed, the receptionist stepped into the room. "The doctor's ready for you, Joshua."

Instead of acknowledging the newcomer, Joshua cocked his head and continued to stare at me.

Something cold rippled down the back of my neck. Those eyes. They drew me with a force that was stunning. This child had a story to tell, a story too big for someone his age. By rights, we should've had nothing in common. By rights, he should've experienced only love, joy, and understanding during his short time here on earth. So why did I get the feeling this wasn't the case?

Joshua's escort got up stiffly. She lifted her bulging briefcase and, with her free hand, gave the child a gentle shove. "Your turn, kiddo."

My first impulse was to look away. This was none of my business after all. I was a patient, too, a lost soul. Who was I to intervene?

Yet my attention remained riveted on the child, something stronger than force of will directing me. My chest ached with something familiar—something fierce. Time, space, all sense of self suddenly meant nothing. My only thought, my only need, was to comfort the young boy.

Why was it that no one seemed to notice that this was a big deal? An innocent child, no more than seven, was entering a psychologist's office, with a woman who appeared more concerned about the well-being of the papers in her briefcase than the state of his mind.

Where's your momma? Where's your papa?

Are you hearing voices, too?

Joshua halted and turned as if I had spoken out loud.

And then he smiled.

My scalp quivered, seemed to rise from the bone.

He reached out his hand, palm open, and I saw something brown resting there.

Tears burned the back of my eyes. *Joshua, I don't understand.*

He took a step toward me, but his companion, using her briefcase

10

in lieu of her hand, blocked his path and angled him toward the door. "Oh no, you don't. The doctor's waiting."

One more glance at the fire radiating from my opal ring and he disappeared into the hallway.

What had just happened here? I eliminated simple curiosity. It was more than that. Yet my mind refused to accept what every muscle, every bone, in my body seemed to know.

The child had read my mind.

Suddenly, out of nowhere, like a message from cyberspace, the *Voice* muscled its way into my head.

By avoiding the light, you destroy from within.

In my shivering, I lost track of time.

ℵ ℵ ℵ

The receptionist came out of the inner sanctuary once more. "Marjorie?"

By this time, I was perched on the edge of my chair, my muscles contracted, ready to unfurl like a taut spring.

"My name's Jane," the woman said. She was tall and angular, her graying hair cut short, and her eyes sparkled, as if a psychologist's office, of all places, was her favorite place to be. She shouldered the open door and motioned for me to enter the hallway, but instead of leading me to a room with a couch as I had expected, she ushered me into an office with a desk and two chairs. "Dr. Mendez prefers this room for first-time patients," she said. "Make yourself at home." Then she dropped the folder into a slot outside the door and was gone.

I focused on the magazines lying on a roll-cart next to my chair. *Sunset* and *Bon Appétit* were the first to catch my attention, but the one I picked up to study was *Central Coast Adventures*.

About to page through it, I had a depressing thought. You've taken a twenty-eight-year detour, and now you're lost.

With my eyes wide open, I looked inward and what I saw made my heart ache. I saw a lifeless creature with a frozen heart. But worst of all, thick, cold bars caged me in, with no means of escape.

The magazine dropped to my lap forgotten.

"What do you want?" I asked myself.

My chin came up. *I want my life back.*

"And?"

I want freedom.

Hope trickled back into my heart, and as if recovering from frost-bite, I felt its warmth incite my senses, particularly my sense of pain. But with the pain came awareness—that I was still alive and there was still time.

Time to fight the fear.

Time to face the *Voice* in my head.

Chapter Three

I WASN'T PREPARED FOR MY FIRST SIGHT of Dr. Tony Mendez. Never would I have pictured a psychologist wearing Wranglers and lizard-skin boots, with his hair pulled into a long, silver-striated ponytail. I stared at the middle-aged man as he entered. Then, as if viewing a silent movie and holding the remote, I froze the frame on pause. I needed time to digest this new development. The unexpected always threw me.

Reluctantly, the delete key in my mind erased my former image of a doctor in a white smock and rimless glasses. It also erased the pallid skin I had envisioned as befitting a man of medicine. My new image was tinted a natural brown, and all that framed his topaz eyes were thick, black lashes.

Dr. Mendez wore no ring or watch, his only embellishment, besides the boots, a large silver belt buckle with the image of a hawk taking off in flight. His shirt was denim, comfortably worn, and his proud bearing and bulk gave him the appearance of being tall; though I guessed, if I were standing, we'd meet eye-to-eye.

My carefully constructed world didn't allow for surprises. I liked everything neat and orderly. Careful planning was my trademark, my motto. Yet now, I was confronted by a shaman cowboy.

The doctor stepped forward and, in a voice pitched low enough to calm a panicked nation, said, "Good morning, Miss Veil."

I liked that voice, for once pleased by the unexpected. "Good morning," I said.

He tilted his head, let time pass. Another surprise. In my world, time was like money and never wasted, each quarter hour in my daily planner faithfully promised. Action ruled. Yet . . . This lapse was such a pleasurable sin.

"Do you have any questions before we begin?" the doctor asked.

"No," I said, although a thousand questions ballooned in my head—big questions, small questions, questions easy to answer, questions hard to answer, questions with no answers at all.

The doctor leaned against the corner of his desk and gave me a softened look. "Did you ask for references before you made your appointment, Ms. Veil?"

Not about to admit how desperate I'd been, I said, "While searching for a therapist, I came across a referral service here in Menlo Park for people experiencing . . . um . . ."

"Spiritual difficulties," the doctor finished for me.

"Yes . . . yes, the grad student who took my call actually seemed to know what I was going through. She called my condition a 'psychic opening' and referred me to you. I was so relieved that you had an opening the next day, I wasn't really concerned about anything else."

"And now?"

I started to slump in my chair but caught myself and straightened my spine. "You aren't a typical psychologist, are you?"

He opened the folder containing my new footprints in the medical system and scanned the top page. "If you had asked, you would have been advised that I do things rather unconventionally."

My face must have registered alarm because he winked before divulging conspiringly, "My methods are accepted by the forces that guide our profession, and I do have some degree of success, pony tail and all."

As this information churned in my mind, I glanced up and, behind the doctor's head, spotted a colorful illustration of a four-spoked wheel, denoting the four directions, the four seasons, and the four elements, bringing to mind the circle of life, where one can get lost and then find oneself again.

Dr. Mendez turned toward the framed poster. "Are you familiar with the Medicine Wheel?"

"There's one in Wyoming, at Big Horn. A sacred hoop, I think, once used by the Plains Indian tribes for some kind of ritual or ceremony."

The doctor sat on the tip of his desk like an instructor about to begin a lecture. "The Medicine Wheel is indeed ceremonial, but so much more. You could call it a mirror of sorts in that it helps you visualize where you are in life and what you need to work on to reach your potential."

He paused and then continued at such a slow pace that I clung to his every word like a trapeze artist reaching from fly bar to catcher to fly bar on her return to the takeoff board. "When Native Americans use the term 'medicine' they are not referring to drugs and herbal remedies, but to an inner, spiritual healing."

Energy surged through me, an endorphin rush. The very mention of inner, spiritual healing and reaching one's potential drew me like pain pills to an addict. But this particular type of healing would apparently not be part of my therapy. The doctor stood, walked to the other side of his desk, and sat in his chair. Lecture over.

"Now for the big question," he said. "Why are you here?"

Mesmerized by his topaz eyes and Morgan Freeman voice, I didn't answer immediately. I focused on my hands, surprised they lay flat and relaxed on the magazine's surface. "Actually, I don't know where to begin," I said, which was true. It was also a way of stalling. Though disillusioned by the negative results of my usual lock-jawed stance on all that mattered in life, opening my mouth and putting my foot into it sounded equally unappealing.

I glanced up, expecting the doctor to register annoyance or dismissal at my reluctance to share, but his face gave nothing away. "Go on," he said.

My muscles twitched. My palms began to sweat. I wanted to tell him my secret but feared nothing more than the possibility it might be true. That I was losing my mind.

15

"Tell me about yourself, Miss Veil," he said, offering yet another opportunity to sidestep the issue of my mental health.

I took up the offer like a perfect pitch. "Doctor, I'm confused. I mean, by today's standards, I'm sitting on top of the world. I have more money than I expected to make in five lifetimes, and it should be enough, but . . . I don't feel successful in all that counts."

"What counts?" His voice was so soft and low that I nearly missed the question.

"I don't know. Serenity. Peace-of-mind. Freedom." How could I explain? I had everything that was supposed to make me happy, yet . . .

"What kind of car do you drive?" he asked.

"A Jeep," I said.

"Why not a BMW, a Mercedes . . . a Toyota?"

I didn't answer. The referral service had been wrong in sending me here.

"Well?" he said.

Wrong question. Wrong therapist. My immediate impulse was to get up and walk out the door, offering an obscene hand gesture to boot. But, of course, I didn't. I had made it this far in life without a single scrape to the knuckles. Why start now? "I feel safe in my Jeep."

"A Mercedes is safe," he said.

"But I can't take it just anywhere."

"Where do you go that you cannot take a Mercedes?"

"Nowhere," I said. "I take it to work and back home. I take it to the grocery store."

Finally, he explained. "Sometimes you can learn about yourself through small things. Your choice of car, for instance."

"Maybe I love my Jeep because I can pack it full of stuff and make my great escape."

Dr. Mendez's smile—no more than a quick upturn of his lips— suggested that I'd revealed something significant, but before I could delve into what that might be, he asked, "What are your emotional outlets?"

"You mean what do I do for fun?"

A nod and a barely perceptible lift of his hands, like a participant at an auction, who doesn't want his competition to know he's bidding.

"My life has been pretty much all work and no play," I said, "which . . . until recently anyway . . . suited me just fine."

The doctor picked up a pen, reopened the folder containing the medical version of my new life story, and began to write.

"I like puzzles," I said, eyeing the pen. "Crossword puzzles, jigsaw puzzles, a game of solitaire. About five years ago, I realized that investing in the stock market was like a giant puzzle. Believe it or not, I actually got high on the research. I took all the bits and pieces of information—you know, the ticker symbols, PE ratios, earnings-per-share, risk and reward—and put them into graphs and charts until pictures formed in my head of companies to invest in. For once, I took off without a plan and didn't look back."

"All this in addition to work?"

"In addition to work *and* school."

"Very time consuming. Do you ever get lonely?"

"I like being alone," I blurted, then shifted in my chair as though I'd just admitted guilt during a polygraph test. Where were these outbursts coming from? And what were they revealing about me?

"I am not here to judge you, Miss Veil," the doctor said in a tone that matched his words.

What was he, a saint? Human beings judge. It's part of their nature. Plus, it's a psychologist's job to judge. In this case, my sanity.

"Investing in the stock market is risky," he said. "How do you handle the pressure?"

"I don't know . . . I guess investing makes me feel free in a way I've never felt before."

"And when you lose money?"

I smiled—couldn't help it. I took pride in accomplishing this one small feat without the imprint of Cliff or my mother. "So far, I haven't."

17

No expression on the doctor's face; a perfect soldier for the Queen's Guard.

"When I noticed how large my portfolio had become, I handed it over to a financial advisor. He suggested that I replace my high-risk stocks with less aggressive options, taking out much of the risk." I shook my head, feeling a familiar sadness. "He converted most of my portfolio into mutual funds, bonds, and CDs."

"With the recent market downturn, he kept you from losing a lot of money," the doctor said.

"Yeah."

"But you lost your taste of freedom as well."

I nodded, didn't meet his eyes.

He leaned back and tapped the pencil on his desk. "What about your job?"

The mention of my job caused a hollowing in my chest. I focused on the Medicine Wheel as though I'd find an answer there. "While attending San Jose State, I worked part-time as an administrative assistant to one of the partners in a large venture capital firm. Nothing big, just calendar scheduling and the editing of reports and presentation materials. Anyway, it seems I also have a knack for digging up buried information. You know, the kind of facts about private companies that live under the radar. Stuff that's invaluable to a VC looking for seed companies to invest in. Which led to a job doing company research."

"Are you still there?" Dr. Mendez asked.

"By the time I'd earned my teaching credential at San Jose State, I was making too much money to quit."

He nodded, took more notes, then asked, "Tell me about your family."

A family of three. This should be quick.

"Dad died of cancer two years ago, and I miss him."

"With tragedy comes humility," my father used to say while fighting the disease that killed him. Was this what he'd meant by humility, this loss of self?

18

"And your mother?"

"She's a good person, and I love her, but . . ." I shook my head, smiled. "There's always a 'but,' isn't there?"

When the doctor didn't respond, I said, "She wants to live my life for me, which makes her a bit hard to deal with."

"Unlike your father."

"Yeah, unlike my Dad." *If only he could see me now.*

"Do you have any siblings?"

"No."

Though Dr. Mendez had been taking notes throughout our conversation, he now wrote for what seemed a long time. I looked around in panic, sorry I had come.

"You said you like being alone," the doctor said, "but I need to ask. Are you in a relationship with someone?"

I swallowed hard, shook my head. "I was engaged to a guy named Cliff, but I broke it off. He didn't take it well."

The doctor waited, his gaze probing like a phlebotomist searching for the perfect blood-releasing vein.

"He was suffocating me."

"Back to freedom again," the doctor said, his tone so gentle that my throat clogged. "In order for me to help you, Miss Veil, I need to know . . . What have you not told me?"

He was right. I would gain nothing by holding back. I'd come here for guidance, which I wasn't about to get without sharing. And trusting.

"I'm hearing a *Voice*. As clear as if someone's standing right next to me. Except . . . no one's there. It's like ear buds are stuck in my ears, and I can't get them out."

I swabbed the moisture leaking from my eyes with the tip of a finger, ridiculously careful not to smear mascara all over my face, then used the sleeve of my jacket to wipe my dripping nose like some snot-nosed kid.

Chapter Four

WITH THE PEN PRESSED AGAINST HIS CHEEK, Dr. Mendez studied me. I, on the other hand, became aware of the ticking of a clock and wondered why I hadn't noticed it before.

"Can you pin-point when you first heard the voice?" he asked.

"Yes. Three weeks ago, yesterday."

"Where were you?"

"We were on the 17-Mile Drive near Pebble Beach."

"We?"

"Cliff and I."

"What part of the 17-Mile Drive?"

"Excuse me?"

"Huckleberry Hill?" he prompted. "Spanish Bay? Point Joe?"

"We stopped near the Lone Cypress."

"And . . ."

"I remember thinking the tree was disappointing."

"How so?"

"The way it was cabled and fenced in."

"To protect its roots," the doctor said, "and to keep it from falling."

"I know, but what's the use? I mean, one little tree among so many, beaten day after day by the elements. Why not leave it alone, let it out of its misery?"

"It's a symbol of strength, endurance, and stability to many," the doctor said, "a tough little tree, resisting near insurmountable forces."

"True," I said. "For a few seconds there, I actually felt as if the tree and I were united in some way and that we were surrounded by unconditional love. But then . . ."

I met the doctor's gaze and sent out a silent plea. *This is where I cross the line, where you'll decide if I'm crazy or not. Please listen. Please understand.*

"Then I heard someone say *Sunwalker* in what sounded like a normal voice talking to me in a normal way. But no one was there. At first, I thought that maybe I'd misheard, with the pounding of the surf and the gulls *kee-yahing*, or that maybe Cliff was playing a trick on me. But then I heard it again. *Sunwalker.* And again. *You have come at last.* And again. *You must listen. Time is running out.* Doctor, I'm scared. This kind of thing isn't supposed to happen. I believe in the invisible world of the spirit, when it comes to God and the angels and saints, but I can't handle this. It's like hearing someone else's thoughts."

"Male or female?"

"Female."

"So, you're hearing only one voice?"

"Yes."

"Does she tell you what to do?"

"Actually, she sounds like a preachy poet, spouting off warnings that can be interpreted in different ways, especially if you're scared half out of your wits."

After a short silence, Dr. Mendez said, "'By whom, and by what means, was this designed? The whispered incantation which allows free passage to the phantoms of the mind?'"

I recognized the lines from T.S. Eliot's tribute to Walter De La Mare, which reset a tripped breaker in my head and opened what felt like a new channel between the doctor and me. Maybe he could help after all.

"Did you tell Cliff?" he asked.

"Yes, but he didn't understand."

"What happened next?"

"We drove on to Carmel."

"Did you hear the voice again that day?"

"Yes. At the Carmel Mission."

"Can you recount what happened?"

"I felt a familiar presence, and then . . . I heard it again. *Sunwalker, there's something you must know.* Oh God, who is she? What does she want? How can I make her stop?"

"Let's leave the voice for now," Dr. Mendez said. "What do you know about the fire opal you're wearing?"

I glanced at my hands, now gripping the magazine on my lap. "I know Cliff hated it."

The abruptness of my outburst caught me off guard—again. "I'm sorry."

"No apology necessary."

"I fell in love with the ring the moment I spotted it at an estate sale, and when I put it on, something charged through me, like the spark you feel when you touch a doorknob during dry weather."

"How do you account for Cliff's reaction?"

"He wanted me to wear the sapphire ring he'd given me. But the stone left me cold." Guilt seeped into me like water filling the hollows of silica-rich lava, which, under heat and pressure, traps the water inside. "In ways like this, I was always hurting him."

"You did well."

Well? How could hurting someone add up to anything but selfish and mean?

"The fire opal has great harmonizing powers and may be your spirit helper," he said. "Native Americans would call it your gemstone totem. There are animal and plant totems as well."

I liked the sound of this and appraised the doctor with renewed interest.

"Can you get two or three weeks off work?" he asked.

"Three weeks? Yes, I think so. I've accumulated a lot of leave."

He touched the tips of his fingers together and looked over them at me, reminding me of the finger game I'd played as a child: *Here's the church; here's the steeple . . .*

"Miss Veil, my job is to assess danger. The rest is almost as scientific as using a crystal ball. The fact that you came here on your own is a good sign. It proves that you are still in charge of your life and want to keep it that way. Your answers to our registration questionnaire indicate that you have no past history with medical health professionals, no known medical conditions, and are not taking any drugs."

"How do you know my experience isn't" —schizophrenia came to mind, but I wasn't about to say it— "pathological?"

The doctor's eyes formed into slits. Not, it seemed, at the ridiculousness of my question, but of concentration. "I have worked with hundreds of patients with psychotic illnesses in my career and none have reported their experiences as being unitive or filled with unconditional love. True, they have reported auditory hallucinations, but the voices they hear generally tell them what to do. You show no signs of bizarre delusions or disorganized thinking, so my tentative diagnosis is that you do not have schizophrenia or paranoia. I am also eliminating manic depression."

I closed my eyes, took a deep breath.

"I believe you are experiencing a spiritual crisis, a reasonable and very human reaction to an encounter with a nonhuman entity, which puts you outside the scope of mainstream health care. People like you, at least the ones brave enough to talk about their ordeal, are not usually allowed to experience such mystical states. Instead they are put on massive doses of anti-psychotic medications to bring them back to normal."

To hell with experiencing mystical states. I *wanted* normal. I wanted my life back.

"I understand that you are upset and confused," the doctor said. "I would be, too, in your position. Rest assured. If I thought you required help from mainstream professionals, I would refer you immediately. I am sensitive to the spiritual dimensions of reality, one reason why I specialize in psychology that supports the transformative potential of spiritual emergencies, rather than treats them as mental diseases. In my opinion, all you need for now is nurturing and assistance in integrating your experience."

The doctor paused. And I waited, figuring the bad news was yet to come. The kind that usually starts with *However*.

"You expressed a need for peace, freedom, and something else that eludes you," he said. "I also noticed your restlessness and agitation, and I assume you are having headaches."

Yes, to all of the above. How did he know?

"In my opinion, you have not lost control of your mind. Nor do I think you are in danger of losing it anytime soon."

At my look of surprise, he raised his hand. "However—"

There it was, the word I'd been dreading.

"I believe your body is trying to tell you something, and ignoring the signs could lead to serious problems."

"What about the *Voice*?"

"The voice may be part of your wake-up call, otherwise known as 'The Dark Night of the Soul.' You would be surprised at how many people go through such a thing. They often end up using tranquilizers to cover it up."

"Will I need tranquilizers?"

"No. At least, I hope not. There is another route I would like you to try first. I would like you to take a retreat . . . away from this town, away from your home, and away from anything else that distracts you, including work, phones, and your mother. Somehow and for some reason, you are hearing with the ears that too many of us ignore."

At my look of confusion, he added. "Most of the time, we use only a small portion of our sensory equipment, and, in your case, your ordinary sense of hearing may have become fine-tuned. You may be more consciously aware than usual and may be experiencing a special insight into other realms of your existence."

I didn't want insight into other realms of my existence. I was having enough trouble with the realm I was in.

"Let me put it this way," Dr. Mendez said. "Do not be afraid of the voice just because you do not understand it. There is a lot in life we do not, and may never, understand. Just listen. I do not mean tolerate. I mean listen. Weigh the words and try to understand."

I'd never considered listening to the *Voice* before. I'd been too scared.

"You need to clear your mind and quiet your thoughts, enter the mystery and live the questions, rather than seek the answers."

"How do I know where to start?" I asked.

"How did you find me?" he countered.

"Let me get this straight. You want me to leave town and find my personal Walden Pond to clear my mind and quiet my thoughts."

A smile on the doctor's face at last. "And listen to the voice."

"But where will I go?"

"Let your heart lead you."

"I don't get it. Why leave what's familiar? Isn't that the last thing I should do?"

"You need to push past your perimeter of comfort and safety, slow down, follow some blind alleys, let the truth catch up to you."

"I'm afraid."

"Freedom comes at a price. Is your mother your protector or your keeper? Is your home your castle or your prison? How will you know unless you break the bonds for a while? Your heart has been silenced for too long. Let *it* be the expert."

"But the *Voice*."

"Can you truly listen to the voice while you are hiding it from your mother?'

Judging by the topaz light of intelligence streaming from his eyes, the doctor had caught my look of guilty surprise. "You must be free to listen," he said.

Currently, freedom seemed as elusive as the pot of gold at the end of a rainbow, though, according to physics, there's no end to a rainbow, thus no pot of gold. "This can't be all."

"I would also like you to keep a journal, starting today." He opened a desk drawer and retrieved a black notebook with an elastic band closure and satin marker. "Personal revelations can come as a whisper in the night, a fleeting thought, or, as in your case, a voice in your head. Record what you hear and see. Put the voice to the test. Ask her what she wants. Let her surprise you."

I didn't want another person telling me what to do. Even if she was dead.

"Share what you have been taught to keep to yourself. Later, we will try to decipher and understand."

In the past, when I'd heard the *Voice,* I'd been deaf with fear, but now I realized this wasn't the answer. Curiosity overtook me, and a new kind of excitement began to build inside. I put the journal into my purse and stood. "May I take this?" I asked, holding up the magazine I'd been cradling on my lap.

"Consider it yours," he said. "And when you get back, make an appointment to see me."

I slid the magazine next to the journal inside my purse.

Dr. Mendez opened the door and motioned for me to proceed, but Jane, the receptionist, blocked the exit.

"Doctor. I'm sorry. I didn't want to interrupt. It's about Joshua Alameda."

Chapter Five

JOSHUA STOOD AMIABLY IN THE HALLWAY next to his companion, the one who had seemed so impersonal in the waiting room and whose eyes now glistened with tears.

Jane, however, could hardly contain her excitement. "Joshua spoke!"

"When?" Dr. Mendez asked.

"During his drawing assignment, about twenty minutes after his controlled breathing exercise. In fact," —Jane's attention now focused on me, causing a wave of skin prickles to skitter across my scalp and neck— "it concerns Miss Veil."

The doctor knelt next to Joshua and tousled his hair. "How is that?"

"He called her 'Sunwalker.'"

A full body shiver. *Oh God. Not him, too.*

The doctor's eyes met mine. "How do you know he meant Miss Veil?"

"He drew a picture of her," Joshua's companion said, pointing at the sheet of paper dangling from the child's hand. "Show them, Joshua."

Joshua held up a drawing of a woman washed in sunlight, her blonde hair lifting in the wind and her hips cocked, with a leg thrust forward in superhero fashion and an orange-stoned ring flashing on her right hand like a DC Comic identity-usurpation weapon. She looked kinda silly, though, wearing khaki slacks and a blue blazer instead of a skintight, super-powered unitard.

"Did he say anything else, Mona?" the doctor asked.

"No, just 'Sunwalker.'"

Dr. Mendez draped his arm around Joshua's shoulders before turning his intense focus on me. "Our friend here has not spoken in over a year."

"Oh my God," I whispered as comprehension set in.

"Joshua likes you," Mona said, her switch from disapproving bodyguard to proactive fairy godmother so incongruous it brought to mind some kind of multiple personality disorder.

The boy walked up to me and held out his hand, revealing what appeared to be a tiny mouse made of smooth, brown stone.

"It's his totem," Mona said. "He wants to give it to you."

No way could I accept anything from this child when I had nothing to offer him in return, least of all something he would treasure enough to carry with him like a favored toy. "I don't think so . . ."

Joshua raised his hand and looked at me as if I were the superhero in his drawing.

I knelt in front of him. "Sweetie, I can't take your totem."

He caught my left hand and pressed the stone mouse into it.

I felt a wave of something I'd never felt before—a thawing that made me want to cry. As I reached to touch his totem, my opal ring attracted the hallway light and sparkled as if spitting out fire.

Joshua's eyes widened.

Fire opal, symbol of faithfulness, assists wearer with finding true love. I slid the ring from my finger and handed it to the child. "My totem."

His smile came so unexpectedly and so transformed his face that I was captivated. A fragile bubble of joy grew inside of me, quivering, shimmering, unpredictable as a kaleidoscope. But then Joshua cupped the fire opal in his palm, closed his eyes, and broke the spell.

I turned to the doctor. "What's he doing?"

"He is activating the stone by thinking and feeling love into it."

Joshua's lids flickered several times before parting. He then pointed at my hand, indicating it was my turn.

I shut my eyes and wished love into my new totem—his gift.

When I'd finished, Dr. Mendez escorted me to an exit door

opposite the one I'd entered. "Something important has just happened here," he said, "probably for you as well as for Joshua."

"What's wrong with him?" I asked, surprised by my concern. "Will he be okay?"

"I hope to have some answers upon your return." He opened the door, giving me no choice but to step through it. "Go taste the freedom you so desperately crave."

The sudden step from artificial lighting to bright sunlight was blinding. About to reach into my purse for my sunglasses, I realized that I still held the stone totem in my hand. Birds sang, insects hummed, and the scent of freshly mown grass wafted in the air. I scanned my surroundings, wondering what had changed.

◢ ◢ ◢

When I reached my Jeep, I didn't get inside, deciding instead to stay outdoors and more fully experience the first day of spring. Oak trees lined the street, and, even though their leaves were just forming, many still in bud, they created an enchanting canopy above my head. Sun filtered through the branches and sparkled off the new growth.

This time, when I sensed the *Voice* coming, I was ready. I sat on a narrow stretch of grass bordering the sidewalk and took out my journal and a pen.

Caged heart.
Shadowed soul.
You have so much to learn.

Time passed and darkness grew, yet I remained seated. Only when my jeans became uncomfortably damp due to the moist grass, did I head home to process what I'd learned.

Chapter Six

THE LAST TRACES OF DAYLIGHT had disappeared by the time I pulled into my driveway. But my house wasn't completely cloaked in shadowy gloom. A soft golden light glowed from my living room window. The source? A lamp hooked to a timer. I smiled, pleased by the simple effect I had rigged up to make it look like someone was home, when in fact nothing living or breathing awaited me, not even a pet.

A sweet, sugary smell greeted me as I opened the door, thanks to the vanilla-scented plug-ins spaced throughout the house, instead of anything yummy baking in the oven. "Welcome to your Thomas Kinkade cottage," I said, meaning it, though something ached within. I disengaged the security system, slung my purse over the ear of a dining room chair, and sprinted up the curved wooden staircase to the master bathroom. Unlike the rest of the house, which, with the help of my father, I had redesigned for comfort and warmth, this space allowed for glamour and extravagance. "Here's where you pamper yourself," my father had said when he shared his vision for the room: strips of Broadway lighting to illuminate an expansive mirror; cream built-in cabinets to support a countertop of shell-pink marble; and a high-efficiency whirlpool tub with foam insulation.

It was hard not to catch my reflection in all that mirrored space while I undressed and filled the tub, but I managed. The person looking back at me lately appeared haunted, and I didn't like seeing myself this way.

"Polish the mirror regularly," my father had instructed while stenciling "To thine own self be true . . ." above the mirror like a tattoo. "Face your imperfections and then wipe them away."

After inserting a vanilla-scented wicking strip into the aromatherapy canister on the deck of the whirlpool, I engaged the mood light and pulsing jets. I then eased into the warm, churning water, rested my head on the back of the tub, and let my body go limp.

Electronic control panel; eight jets; 600-Watt blower system; balanced airflow; aromatherapy; mood lights. And *I* had the gall to begrudge *Cliff* the luxury and performance of his Mercedes-Benz?

For fifteen theta-soaked minutes, the sound of pulsating jets and the scent of vanilla sedated my monkey brain into a state of rest. But gradually, Joshua's image—his intense brown eyes, his chubby and dimpled cheeks—formed behind my closed lids. How was he doing? Did he miss his mouse totem? Had my opal ring brought him comfort?

Damn.

I stood, pressed my face into a bath towel, and forced thoughts of the child from my mind. No way would I allow another complication into my life, no matter how sweet and innocent the source. The mouse totem, however, promised comfort without asking for anything in return. Bath towel wrapped around me like a sarong, I hurried downstairs to retrieve the small stone from my purse.

Back upstairs, I crawled into bed, adjusted my pillow, and curled into a ball; leaving the totem on the nightstand for easy access should the need for its comfort arise. In the morning, I'd decide where to go on my retreat. Or exile.

N N N

On waking, only fogginess weighed on my mind, a rather pleasant state of disorientation. I had forgotten to pre-set the coffee pot the night before, which meant no coffee aroma to jumpstart my brain; but that didn't matter. I had also neglected to eat lunch or dinner the day before; but that didn't matter either. What mattered was that I was still in bed at 8:00 a.m., quieting my thoughts and tasting freedom, just as the doctor had ordered.

Cool air rushed at me from all sides when I removed the down comforter, but the promise of coffee quelled the impulse to turn over and retreat into the warmth of my bed. I pulled on my robe and within minutes had the coffeemaker sputtering to life. I retrieved the newspaper from the porch step and glanced at the front page. The forecast was for partially cloudy skies with temperatures in the 60's. Another fine day in Menlo Park.

I dropped the paper onto the table and poured myself a mug of coffee, then took a cranberry scone out of the bakery bag on the counter and slid into my favorite spot at the breakfast nook facing the street. Out of habit, I flipped to the business section of the paper, belatedly remembering that I no longer controlled my portfolio. Not surprisingly, the market news lost its appeal. The headlines, full of the usual murders and fraud and political unrest, also failed to engage me. The comics lacked humor.

Then it hit me. My home phone hadn't rung all morning. The fact that I was usually at work at this hour accounted for the lack of personal calls, but since when did that stop the telemarketers? I folded the paper and checked for messages. The first a hang up, the second, yep, a telemarketer spamming me with a $1,000 gift card, and the third, my mother. "Marjorie? I stopped by, but you didn't answer the door. It's six o'clock. Why aren't you home? Call me. Bye."

As automatic as a yawn during late night prayer, my mother's words drew out a sigh. Truus Veil certainly hadn't lost *her* road map. She knew exactly where she was going and what she was doing, and last night at 6:00 p.m., she'd been checking on her only child.

In contrast, my current life path was full of pitfalls and barriers. I had enough money, but was alone; I had religion, but couldn't comprehend it; I had a job, but it no longer inspired me.

A buzzing in my ears and slight fogginess of vision, warned me that the *Voice* was about to speak. I hurried to retrieve my journal and pen.

It's in the bird's song.
The message. It's there.

The message is in the breeze.

I was disappointed that the *Voice* still scared me and that I felt anger when it spoke. But as I stared at the page, I lost myself in the words: *It's in the bird's song.*

◢ ◢ ◢

I wanted to touch my totem, Joshua's gift, but I'd left it on the nightstand next to my bed. I sprinted upstairs for the belted pouch I had stuffed into a drawer and long forgotten, then put the stone mouse inside, dressed, and clipped the belt into place. Totem close, I felt ready to take on the world. However, all that greeted me when I stepped into my backyard was a stray cat.

It came to see me nearly every day, sometimes in the morning and sometimes at night. I had ignored it as long as I could before finally relenting and feeding it scraps. Now, I was actually buying it food.

It was the most common of cats, a gray tabby with black stripes, too old and skinny for kitten cuteness. But there was something about its eyes. They appeared to look directly into a part of me that stored my secrets, my hopes, my fears.

I took in the warmth of the sun-drenched deck beneath my feet and the black birds' throaty, territorial chatter, while the cat sat still as a statue—watching me.

"Okay, okay." I headed back into the house for a can of food.

When I returned and emptied the slippery goop into tabby's bowl, it backed off. "Darn it, if you want my handouts, you could at least start trusting me. Come on sweetie, I won't hurt you."

As I continued to cajole, the cat inched closer, hesitating, staring, listening. Finally, it snatched a few bites and ran away.

"You'll never learn," I said, thinking it strange that I had a stone mouse and a stray cat as companions.

The cat halted and froze. Its ears twisted as if tuning into sounds beyond my hearing, reminding me of mini-satellite dishes rotating to catch invisible channel waves. Its stillness caused me to still. I drew in my breath, wondering why the birds had stopped their jabbering—their silence more noticeable than their thunderous chatter had been.

A breeze came up and, like a cool and invisible hand, tickled my cheek and stroked my hair. It was the lightest of sensations, not touching exactly, barely there, close as breath, like the touch of the sun, but cooler. I followed the cat's gaze and spotted a large bird soaring overhead, with its wings slightly raised. As it circled and swooped closer, I noticed that it was a hawk—a hawk looking directly at me. Goose bumps covered my skin, and a familiar buzzing filled my ears. The raptor's huge silhouette hovered above me for several seconds before shooting back up and out of sight.

As the birds resumed their dawn chorus, I remembered that the *Voice* had said there was a message in the breeze and in the bird's song. And just as I was beginning to break through the fog of understanding, I heard the *Voice* again.

Awaken child.

Discard the cloak of darkness.

Drop the shroud.

The cat shuddered and so did I. Then ever so slowly, it inched over and rubbed its body against my legs, the vibrations of its silent purr traveling through the fabric of my jeans. I didn't move or speak. The cat had never gotten this close before.

The phone rang, and the cat fled.

My first impulse was to answer the aggressive summons. Instead, I let the machine pick it up. Then I slapped on some makeup, grabbed my purse, and headed for the perfect place to get away from phones and uncalled for interruptions.

Chapter Seven

JAVA, MOCHA, AND ESPRESSO flavored the air as I walked through the double glass doors of the bookstore. The cash register rang. The espresso machine whirred, air surging, squirting, and steaming. How could such irritating noises sound so good?

Books, magazines, newspapers, journals, calendars, and CD's were stacked on tables and housed in shelves, treasures to excite any taste. Music played in the background, blending with the buzz of many conversations. I was grateful that the majority of shoppers preferred to browse in malls and large discount stores, leaving this space tranquil and crowd free. No one would bother me here.

I ordered a large white mocha with whipped cream. When I reached into my purse for my wallet, my hand brushed against the magazine I'd taken from Dr. Mendez's office—a reminder of what I still needed to do.

But where would I go armed with only a journal and a pen? It would be Easter soon. There would be vacationers on spring break, crowds of them. I thought fleetingly of calling a travel agency but discarded the idea. I didn't need brochures of sightseeing tours and didn't want misleading pictures.

After settling at a round table for two, I took the magazine from my purse. My heartbeat kicked up a notch, as though I were holding a tattered treasure map marked with X's for buried treasures, lost mines, and buried secrets. I ran my fingers over its glossy cover before paging to the table of contents. Under "Features," I found "The Complete Guide to Carmel Valley."

I flipped to the article, "Carmel Valley, Pastures of Heaven" and, under "What to Do," read about The Ventana Wilderness Ranch "with its trails meandering through oak-covered meadows and along fresh mountain streams." I checked the names, descriptions, and phone numbers of available lodging and then patted the magazine and kissed its cover, my destination decided.

Hungry after yesterday's fast, I returned to the coffee bar for a turkey sandwich, then sat back down and brought out my journal and pen—this time without prompting from the *Voice*.

I wrote: *She haunts me, demanding, relentless . . .*

"Marjorie?"

Distracted by my journal, I hadn't heard Cliff's approach. But I recognized his voice immediately. As did my heart, which lurched against the wall of my chest like a caged rabbit.

"Where have you been?" he demanded. "I called your house yesterday and again this morning, and all I got was the damn answering machine. And what the hell's the use of having a cell phone if you never turn it on?"

If I told him why I was averse to engaging my cell phone, namely to avoid calls from him and my mother (He was my ex, darn it!), it would hardly improve his mood. I motioned to the vacant chair at my table, wanting to scream for him to leave me alone. But I didn't, knowing he wouldn't—and likely never would—understand the changes going on inside of me.

Cliff slid his long legs under the table, nearly crowding out mine. "When I called your office, they said you'd taken three weeks off. What's going on?"

"Why aren't *you* at work, Cliff?"

"I took the afternoon off."

"You never take time off."

"It wasn't necessary before."

Pain inched into my chest as I thought of all the opportunities we had wasted, moments we could have shared. *Work before pleasure* had been our unspoken motto during our voyage to success.

Cliff jutted his chin and pouted his lower lip as though faking the royal Hapsburg jaw. "What are you doing here?"

He might as well have dosed me with pepper spray, considering how his question inflamed my insides and obstructed my airways and lungs. I put down my pen and fisted my hands on my lap, praying that this would be over soon.

"I've decided to give you the space you need," he said with the benign tolerance of a judge granting me a tremendous favor.

"As you're doing now?"

His gaze darted to mine in a quick contact and release. "What's that supposed to mean?"

"It's too late, Cliff."

"Did I wait too long to commit to a wedding date?"

"Cliff!" I said, slapping my hand on the table. "How can you even think of commitment and marriage?"

People turned to stare. No wonder. I sounded like a bitch, blowing off my engagement to an outwardly perfect man. I lowered my voice to a harsh whisper. "Think about it. There was something terribly wrong with our relationship."

Cliff stared at me as if I'd turned into a monster. Maybe, to him, I had. "I'm going away for a while," I said, not that I owed him an itinerary of my plans; but old habits die hard. "I have some personal discoveries to make."

When his face turned from hard lines to droopy curves, I felt a familiar sadness, but pressed on. "And you can't change my mind." *Not this time. Not anymore.*

His half smile registered disapproval so clearly that I knew, in spite of his promise, he would never have given me the space I needed. "What's the matter with you?" he asked. "Why can't you discover what you're looking for right here where it's safe and we can keep an eye on you?"

"We?"

"Your mother and me. Have you told her?"

I have an internal fuse switch easily thrown when provoked, and nothing does the trick like the questions "What are you doing here?" and "Have you told your mother?" My current reaction—likely linked to an instinct for self-preservation—was a full body shake. Why was he still talking to my mother? Did he—did she—actually think I would take him back?

"I'm not asking for permission, Cliff."

I took a deep breath to calm myself. When that didn't work, I waged a not-so-therapeutic rant. "Life is dangerous. Getting into my car and driving down the street is dangerous. I could get mugged going to the grocery store."

Staying here with you is dangerous, dangerous to my sanity.

His eyes turned into hard beads and his lips thinned, but it would take more than facial threats to stop me now. "Don't try to convince me that my plans are crazy, because that's your opinion and I don't agree."

I had never talked to Cliff with such confidence and determination, and I noticed his surprise. But before he had a chance to recover, I added, "And don't ask where I'm going either, because I won't tell you. Or Mom. Somehow I get the feeling she'd send you after me."

"At least your mother has some sense," he said. "I wish you were more like her."

And there was part of the problem. He wanted a duplicate of my mother, a woman who considered a life of self-denial and joylessness the pathway to heaven. Looking at his model-perfect face with a regret that felt like drowning, I said. "You're a good man with a tremendous need to protect, and I'm sure there are women who crave that kind of protection. But not me."

"I'll change," he said with a bit of a slur.

"You can't."

"For you, I would."

The walls of his obsessive protectiveness closed in on me, making it hard to breathe. "For me, you'd try, and maybe it would work, for a week or a month, but then we'd wear each other down. We'd end up fighting for the rest of our lives."

I paused to rally strength before leaning forward and gazing directly into Cliff's eyes. "It's over."

He looked at me as a parent looks at a naughty child, with a combination of disappointment and an awful need to control.

Instead of cringing under his stare, as I used to, I smiled at him with all the warmth I could muster. "You deserve to be happy, Cliff."

His eyes took on a silvery sheen as though melted by my unexpected kindness. A jolt coursed through me at the fuzzy realization that I'd been part of the problem, always retreating and turning a cold shoulder when he'd frowned at me rather than expressing my true feelings and standing up for myself. I'd gone into hiding, closing him out, and now, I didn't have the energy to start over again. I didn't love him enough for that.

"When you look at me, I sense censure and disappointment," I said, "like you're afraid that if you don't watch me every minute, I'll be gone."

"I love you, damn it," he said between clenched teeth.

Okay, maybe the silvery sheen of his eyes more closely resembled the color of duct tape, which brought to mind the jingle, "If it's not stuck and it's supposed to be, duct tape it."

"Is that why you're always criticizing me?" I asked.

"I can't believe this," was his reply.

We sat in silence until I became aware of the soft music and murmur of conversations. I slid my magazine, journal, and pen into my purse.

"You'll be sorry," Cliff warned.

I stood and walked away.

✎ ✎ ✎

Back home, I called my mother.

"Mom, I went to a psychologist."

"Marjorie?"

"I thought I was having a breakdown."

"A breakdown! What in God's name are you talking about?"

"Remember when I told you I was having headaches and my hands were shaking?"

"You probably just need a little rest. I'll come over and fix some tea."

"No, Mom, but thanks." No amount of *Celestial Seasonings* would help me now. "The doctor suggested I go away for a while."

She pulled in an oh-my-God breath. "Where?"

"Not far."

"Alone?"

"The point is for me to be alone, Mom."

"It isn't safe for a young woman to travel alone. You could get raped. Someone could cut off your arms and your legs and—"

"I promise I'll be careful."

"When are you leaving?"

"Monday."

"How can a doctor send you off by yourself? Did you check into his credentials? How do you know he's not a quack?"

It was always like this with my mother and Cliff, my protectors—my jailers. Both insisted that I call each day to report my comings and goings—step-by-step, minute-by-minute. Well, I was free of Cliff, but Mother was in my life to stay. I'd have to hold firm—stick to the plan—or there would be no chance of growth. "Can you keep an eye on my house while I'm gone?" I asked, giving her something solid to hold on to at least.

"Of course. Will you call me every day?"

Her question served as a reminder to change my cell number lickety-split.

"I'll call when I can."

"I love you, Marjorie," she said in the sad voice that usually succeeded in forcing my surrender under a white flag of guilt. "I just want what's best for you."

"Love you, too, Mom."

But you aren't going to change my mind. Not this time.

Tight with tension and a touch of fear, I gathered my writing

40

tools, settled at my desk, and allowed my thoughts to drift back to Joshua.

Who are you? Why did you call me *Sunwalker*?

My pen took off like the planchette on a Ouija board.

Little Otter.

Homeless offering.

What the hell did that mean? Could it have something to do with Joshua?

I dropped my pen as if it had burned me.

I had to forget about that child!

Chapter Eight

IT WAS SATURDAY AFTERNOON, and I prayed it wasn't too late to make reservations for a three-week stay in Carmel Valley, especially on the cusp of Easter week. I crossed my fingers and made the call.

A woman, who identified herself as Heather, assured me that there would be no problem in reserving a room. "Since you'll be staying for, like, three weeks and all, you bet we'll have a room available. A nice one, too. Your first week'll be kinda quiet, it not yet being Easter break and all."

"Just what I need," I said. "Peace and quiet."

"Then you've picked the right place," Heather said.

I hung up, relieved. Speaking to such a bubbly person made the trip seem less forbidding somehow.

I'd already alerted the bank of my travel plans, instructed the post office to hold my mail, changed my cell number, cleaned my house, and packed my bags. But instead of enjoying the temporary reprieve from pre-travel arrangements, panic threatened to turn my last hours at home into a nightmare of *what ifs* and *how comes*.

Why?

The answer that came to mind was not flattering. I saw myself wired into an unnatural world of constant stimulation, every minute filled with constructive things to do, leaving no room for contemplation, questions, or dreams. Heck, I'd quit dreaming a long time ago.

Then it hit me. I was obsessed with the same goals that drove the Silicon Valley company I worked for: speed, productivity, and the constant need to upgrade. And whenever I received a compliment from a co-worker or my boss, it only whetted my appetite for more. I was no more than a hollow-headed puppet, jumping to the tune of a crazy world.

And Cliff had been the same.

Almost from the start, after meeting through a mutual friend, we'd subsidized each other. Before too long, we began putting off romantic dinners and Sunday drives. We found ingenious ways to slip in a "Hello" and "See you soon," but work had always come first. Now, I saw this life as pathetic and oppressive, and I shuddered at the thought of returning to more of the same after my retreat.

I searched for something constructive to do, until my attention settled on the stone-veneer fireplace that my father had built for me, following a how-to video on a home-improvement channel: "Add rustic charm to any hearth for a fraction of the cost. Looks like the real thing. Just takes a few days to build." Usually, I only lit fires on holidays or when the power went out, but this *was* a holiday of sorts, and the power *was* out. Mine.

Once I got a blaze going, I settled on the couch, content to watch the flames flicker and leap within the frame of taupe, caramel, and sage stone. Gradually, my gaze lifted to the empty space above the fireplace mantle. I hadn't yet found the perfect mirror to fill the spot, aware of how the shape and quality of the mirror's surface would affect the image reflected back to me. "Don't look into the mirror blind," my dad used to say. "Let your mirror be the gateway to your truth."

I refocused on the fire. Moving images began to form in the flames, like the ones electronically displayed on my flat-screen TV. I saw burning brush, burning trees, and smoke spewing in all directions. And out of the thick gray mire stepped Joshua, his eyes wild, his mouth moving without making a sound.

I stood and leaned against the coffee table for support. This wasn't normal. This was crazy. Yet dared I ignore what I'd seen? What if Joshua was in trouble? What if he needed me?

All I had was Dr. Mendez's office number, but I tried it anyway, hoping to reach an on-call service for urgent care needs. What I hadn't expected was for the doctor himself to answer.

"Hello," he said, in a voice of deep calm.

"Oh, thank God."

"Marjorie?"

"This is going to sound crazy, but, oh my God, oh my God . . . I saw Joshua in a fire, is he okay?"

No response from the doctor.

"What I saw . . . it all seemed so real. He was dirty, and it looked like he'd been crying."

"Can you stop by my office Monday morning?" was his level reply.

Didn't anything rattle this man? I took a deep breath to calm myself. "I'm headed for Carmel Valley on Monday, but I can swing by before I leave."

"Carmel Valley? Why there?"

Who cares? I wanted to say. *Tell me about Joshua.* Instead, I said, "Remember the magazine I took from your office? It had a feature on Carmel Valley, and I figured it was as good a place as any for the retreat you advised."

Silence.

"Doctor?"

"See you on Monday," he said before ending the call.

It took several seconds for me to realize that he'd hung up on me.

I blinked at the phone.

It rang.

"Hello." My voice wobbled, as if I'd just stepped off a physical roller coaster rather than a mental one.

"Don't say anything until I'm done, okay?"

Jeez. What in blazes did my mother want now?

"I want you to go to Mass with me tomorrow."

Oh God. This can't be happening.

"You used to love to attend Mass, remember? The organ music, the hymns, the chanting . . ."

44

I'd give her that. The music, the ornate vestments, the gold vessels, the holy water, and the mysterious host had all fascinated me once. "You know I don't go to church anymore."

"Just one more time before you go."

"Oh, Mom."

"Do this and I promise to leave you alone."

"Okay," I said, though from experience I had good reason not to believe her.

"I'll be at your place at 11:30 sharp. We'll walk from there. Just like old times."

"Fine."

"God will help you, Marjorie, I'm sure of it."

"I hope so, Mom. I honestly hope so."

Chapter Nine

IT WAS SUNDAY MORNING, and because the alarm hadn't yet sounded, I drifted between two worlds. I saw brown eyes, green eyes, oak trees, and a circle of stones. Something important was about to happen, something pleasant, something relevant, but before I could discover what it was, the picture faded and withdrew to that mysterious place where dreams are stored. I tried to force my way back in, but all I could remember was that a door had been about to open, a door that was closed to me now.

Thoughts of the day ahead replaced longing for reentry into the world of dreams. I was going to Mass, something I hadn't done in five years. Could my mother be right? Was it possible to experience, once again, the sweetness of unity with God in His Church?

While dressing, I recalled attending Mass every Sunday with my parents. I'd been taught that missing even one weekly service was a mortal sin, for which I would be severely punished—by God. I had believed in the command and the consequences of disobedience with all my heart, as my mother still did today. The law didn't make sense, but it wasn't about making sense. It was about following the rules. At least that's how I had understood it at the time. God wanted me to follow the rules, and I didn't ask questions. That, too, would have been a sin.

Praying the rosary was another ritual my family never skipped, though we performed this sequence of prayers by choice rather than as obedience to a church-made law. Meditating on the *Sorrowful*

Mysteries had required special effort on my part. The *Agony in the Garden, Scourging at the Pillar,* and *Crucifixion* presented images that were too painful to internalize and understand. I, like the apostle Peter, would have denied knowing Jesus three times before the cock crowed. I, too, would have feared death by crucifixion.

There had been so many regulations and so many unanswered questions that, ultimately, church had no longer filled the void.

◢ ◢ ◢

Mother walked briskly, too briskly, in the way of someone heading to a post-Christmas sale rather than a pre-Easter sharing in the Holy Sacrifice of the Mass. "Today's the fourth Sunday of Lent, you know."

"Already?"

Lent, Holy Week, and Easter Sunday included enough rituals and symbols to fascinate any child: ashes, palms, incense, Stations-of-the-Cross, benedictions, lighted candles, and Easter lilies.

My mind flooded with visions of stained-glass windows, with the light and sparkle of transparent marbles, the solemn-eyed statues of St. Theresa and the Blessed Virgin Mary, and an altar covered with candles and starched linens like a table set for a special feast. I heard the steeple bell ring to announce the beginning of Mass and the peal of the Sacryn bells used during the Eucharistic prayer. I smelled the pungent aroma of incense, felt the padded kneelers, the wooden bench. Would my old spot next to the Sixth-Station-of-the-Cross be unoccupied? If so, I would sit there for old time's sake.

"Remember how you used to give up candy for Lent?" my mother asked. "You had such a hard time, loving sweets the way you did, but you usually stuck to it. You were such a good little girl."

The perfect child.

As we neared the church, my heart leapt in the same old way, my mood younger, clearer, lighter. The Gothic Revival building with its spired steeple stood ablaze in sunlight, so white, so pure that it appeared to illuminate from within.

Mother gripped my hand, and we took the red brick steps like new BFFs heading for the playground. When we reached the threshold, she took a raspy breath. "Ready?" Her face and cheeks were rosy, as though smartly rouged by a department store beauty consultant, her mood downright contagious.

Maybe this hadn't been such a bad idea after all.

I laughed. "Let's walk right through that door."

We made it as far as the vestibule.

That's when the dime life turns on flipped from heads to tails and my stab at happiness turned sour. Cliff stood between the pamphlet rack and the holy water font. The expression on his face resembled a smile, but no, my ex didn't smile. He smirked. His eyes were as lifeless as the eyes of the pedestalled statues inside, not the eyes of someone in love.

My heart jabbed against cartilage and muscle like a woodpecker foraging for food. Since when did Cliff start attending Mass?

Then realization struck.

"Mom!"

I backed out of the vestibule door and down the brick steps, my mother following as if attached by a string. "But Marjorie, he's such a good man."

I pressed the palm of my hand to my chest in an attempt to ease the swell of pain throbbing inside. The switch from exultation to deflation—from kindness to cruelty—had occurred so quickly that I was surprised I didn't get a nosebleed.

"Marjorie?"

"Go on without me, Mom."

"But—"

I looked up at the church and felt nothing.

The pipe organ burst into the first, deep notes of "How Great Thou Art," and the steeple bell tolled, but I walked away.

Some kind of magnetic force held me close to the church's perimeter, a force I didn't attempt to shake loose. In my current dark mood, the peaceful, park-like setting of the grounds offered some comfort at least. I walked to the fountain located on the east expanse of lawn and sat on its ledge. With my back to the trickling water, I faced the wood-framed church and wondered if God had it in His expansive heart to accept me, considering I was sitting on the wrong side of its walls. The parishioners celebrated the Mass, visited with their friends, and drove away. All the while, I sat, still as a statue.

I heard footsteps, but paid them no heed, expecting them to continue their leisurely stroll along the paved walkway. Instead, they stopped, and someone said my name.

Seeking out the speaker, my gaze settled on the youngest priest I'd ever seen. His blond hair was unruly and certainly too long, and his silver-blue eyes glinted with what looked like pleasure.

"Remember me?" he asked.

His face tugged at my memory, but I couldn't place him.

"John Phillip," he said.

"Oh my God, Morgan van Dyke's little brother?"

"In the flesh. But . . . is that all I was to you, Morgan's little brother?"

A rush of warmth rode the stored memories triggered by the mention of Morgan's name. "John Phillip, are you masquerading as a priest?"

He laughed and spread his arms wide. "What you see is what you get."

John Phillip had been a restless, mischievous young man, likely the reason I'd considered him less mature than I, though we'd been about the same age. His parents couldn't keep him still, yet he'd been too upbeat and friendly to punish.

My thoughts returned to Morgan, John Phillip's oldest brother. *Gorgeous Morgan*, I'd secretly called him. I hadn't known him well but had made it my business to find out all I could. He and his family lived on a dairy farm near Sacramento. They often attended Mass here because of its close proximity to St. Patrick's Seminary. David, another of John Phillip's brothers, was enrolled there in hopes of becoming a priest. So even though the family didn't belong to this parish, twelve-thirty Mass provided a convenient place for them all to meet.

"Did David become a priest, too?"

John Phillip chuckled in the same old boyish way. "Heavens no. David's married and has two sons. He and Morgan took over the dairy when Pop retired."

"How's Morgan? Is he married too?"

"No again. Big brother is too picky for his own good. Even Mom's given up on him."

"How about Teri?" The last I'd heard, John Phillip's sister worked freelance for *Sunset* magazine, while studying photography at night school.

The silver glint in John Phillip's eyes turned gray. "Wish I knew. We haven't heard from her in years."

Silence followed, during which our gazes settled on the water cascading from the platform that supported a stone statue of St Francis of Assisi.

"Morgan's looking for her," John Phillip said, "but I don't think he'll find her alive."

"I'm so sorry."

He gave a brief nod and smiled. "I had a crush on you, you know."

The quick change in subject confirmed that the old John Phillip was still alive and well.

"Church was never boring with you around," I said. "You used to rock and sway to the music and play an invisible drum."

"I was trying to impress you. Guess I did a pretty good job."

I closed my eyes and played back the memories from all those years ago.

"You looked rather contemplative sitting there all by yourself when I came walking by," John Phillip said. "Can I help in any way?"

I took in his boyish face, wondering if somehow, in his own mischievous way, he'd discovered the path to true happiness. "I don't think so."

He tossed up his arms as if breaking into a Hallelujah. "Why not try me? You may find I'm still full of surprises."

I liked his cheekiness, his irreverence to usual priestly seriousness. How had he made it through the seminary and into priesthood with such an upbeat attitude? I'd always thought that carefree spontaneity was quashed during a priest's reshaping as a seminarian. I patted the fountain ledge next to me. "If you're going to hear my confession, you might as well make yourself comfortable."

John Phillip sat, folded his hands, and gave me his full attention.

"I haven't been to Mass in years," I admitted, while taking in the church's pointed arches, pinnacles, and lancet windows. Great marketing tools for spiritual seekers like me. "Today I hoped to come back and feel something again, you know, like sneak in through a crack in the door and take up where I'd left off."

No use in mentioning Cliff or my mother. If I had really wanted to celebrate the Mass, no one could have stopped me.

"You always appeared so devout, so calm, so together," John Phillip said. "You were all I wasn't, and I believed you'd become a nun."

His words surprised me, though they shouldn't have, being so close to the truth. Entering the convent had crossed my mind on more occasions than I cared to admit, but more as a running from than a calling to, especially after Morgan had disappeared off my radar.

"You'd never guess what Morgan used to call you," John Phillip said.

"Out with it," I said. "I know you're dying to tell."

"The little nun."

So much for romantic fantasies. "Well, I called him *hottie*."

John Phillip hooted with laughter. "I didn't think the word, *hottie*, was in your vocabulary."

"Some prime examples of false appearances," I said. "You distracted me from my prayers, but so did Morgan, in a different way." It felt good letting go of past secrets like pieces that no longer fit the current puzzle. Wrong size, wrong shape, wrong color.

"We all had a crush on you," John Phillip said, "David, Morgan, and I. Of course, Morgan never admitted it. No cradle robbing for him, thank you. But I watched him watching you. In the name of brotherly rivalry, of course. All's fair in love and war."

"I never thought I'd say this to a priest," I said between giggles, "but you're full of it."

John Phillip snorted, not unlike the snorts he once shared in church, along with the whimpering puppy sounds that had driven his parents nuts and caused his sister, Teri, to cover her mouth in amusement. "Actually, you scared me to death," he said. "Whenever you favored me with a bit of attention, I got the shakes, wondering what I'd done wrong."

"Now *that* I believe."

"Enough about old times," he said. "What brings you here?"

Crystal white clouds drifted past the sun, causing light and shadow to vie for attention, while I told John Phillip about Cliff, Dr. Mendez, and the *Voice*. Then, unexpectedly, I told him something I hadn't put into words until then. "I think the Church has failed me." It came out like a whispered prayer, and Father John Phillip apparently took it as such, because where I had expected censure and judgment, I sensed only connection and love.

"I prayed for a messenger, but never guessed it would be you," I said.

John Phillip dipped his fingers into the fountain and crossed himself. "As the saying goes, 'God works in mysterious ways.'"

I couldn't argue with him there, considering all the unexplainable things that had been happening to me lately. "Talking to you seems appropriate somehow."

"I'll always be that prankish kid to you," he said, "which will make it difficult for you to value anything I offer."

"No, please. I want to hear what you have to say."

"Maybe it's not the Church that has failed you," he said, his eyes nearly the same color as Cliff's, though warmed by sunshine rather than frozen by ice.

I drew in my breath, about to tell John Phillip that this line of thinking solved nothing. I'd heard it before, that it wasn't the Church's fault, but my own, that I no longer felt a connection.

He stopped me with the shake of his head. "And neither have you failed the Church."

I felt caught between the urge to laugh and cry.

"You just aren't open to its message right now."

I stared at him, yet through him, realizing that he was right and had simply put into words what I should've known all along. Messages had been coming at me from all directions, but I hadn't been listening.

"Like millions of other people, you're trying to figure out who you are and why you're here on this earth. Sometimes, understanding comes slowly, when you least expect it." John Phillip studied me with the pensiveness of a priest rather than the levity of a prankster. "I happen to see a well-adjusted woman in front of me."

I nearly laughed out loud. Well-adjusted was not a term my mother and Cliff would have applied to me right now, but I let the thought pass. Father John Phillip's opinion came gift-wrapped with lightness and optimism and therefore carried more weight than the opinion of my detractors.

As we stood to go, I said, "I've never been able to talk to a priest before, but you made it easy. I predict you're going to help a lot of lost souls and misfits like me."

"Don't underestimate yourself," he said. "You'd be surprised how many souls you may touch along your journey. You've just touched mine." He paused and then added, "It reinforces my belief in miracles."

Miracles?

"I don't belong to this parish, Marjorie. I was only visiting for old time's sake, haven't been here in years."

"So, we both just happened to show up at the same place at the same time," I said, my inner skeptic betrayed by the noticeable edge to my voice. "It's probably just a coincidence."

"I don't believe in coincidences," he said.

I could think of nothing more to say.

"Where are you going on your getaway?" John Phillip asked.

Sunbeams streamed through gaps in the clouds and illuminated the white steepled church, just like in my mother's beloved Thomas Kinkade prints. "Carmel Valley," I said.

A quick glance at John Phillip revealed an odd expression on his face.

"*That* should be interesting," he said.

Chapter Ten

WITH MY BAGS STACKED in the back of the Jeep and my house secure, I was ready to set out on my journey. At least physically. Emotionally, I balked at the very idea of leaving the comfort and security of my home. I reminded myself that Carmel Valley was only a few hours away, and as I backed out of the driveway and drove down the street, I was careful not to look back.

As arranged, I made a detour to meet with Dr. Mendez. I parked on the curb next to the gray medical building, standing straight and unappealing against the drab morning sky. When I turned to grab my purse, I caught movement in the back seat. Goose bumps shot over my skin in the seconds it took me to recognize my stray cat.

"How'd you get in?" I snapped. My face and hands felt numb and tingly as if I were recovering from multiple injections of anesthesia. I didn't want to return home and repeat the process of leaving again. It had been hard enough the first time.

I slid out of the Jeep, fully intending to walk off without a second glance, until I realized that the windows were closed and the cat might suffer. "You owe me," I said as I cracked open the back windows for air to circulate through.

How had I managed to get involved with a homeless cat and a mute child? Each had approached me at a most inconvenient time, and each had a way of looking at me that prompted a response I wasn't prepared to offer. If they wanted help, they'd picked the wrong person. I was like a rock rolling downhill in need of a place to land before I could be of use to anyone.

Jane, looking crisp and cheerful in her teal quilted jacket and white-collared shirt, directed me to Dr. Mendez's office with a he's-expecting-you wave and a smile.

On locating the doctor sitting behind his desk, I started right in. "I know you're not supposed to discuss your patients with outsiders, but you've got to admit, there's something weird going on here, which makes this case an exception. Is it too much to ask if Joshua's okay? I mean, just tell me if I'm going crazy or hallucinating and we'll go from there. But if this vision was real . . . oh God, if it was real . . ."

"Sit down," the doctor said, indicating the chair I'd occupied during our first mindboggling chat.

"I'd prefer to stand, if you don't mind." By retaining a foothold on *terra firma*, I hoped to act less defensively than I felt; keep some semblance of normalcy; keep from falling apart. Besides, the carpet bolstered my feet like an anti-fatigue mat. A good thing in my current mood.

"No problem," the doctor said, and, after a quick glance at the notes in front of him, he finally addressed my concern. "First, let me assure you that I do not reveal information about my patients without their permission, except in special circumstances, such as probable abuse, suicide, or homicide. However, Joshua has granted me consent, through his caseworker Mona, to release certain details that I believe will serve both of your best interests. Understood?"

Why the need for a caseworker? Where is Joshua's mother? "Yes."

"Okay then, for starters, Joshua lives in Carmel Valley."

Great. Of all the places I could have chosen for my retreat, I ended up picking Joshua's hometown. "So, what was he doing all the way here in Menlo Park? Aren't there any psychologists locally?"

"Standard psychological diagnoses and routines were not working for him. His condition required support rather than suppression. Thus, the need for transpersonal psychology."

"What condition?" *What's wrong with him? What's wrong with me?*

"Let me start by sharing a bit of Joshua's history," Dr. Mendez said, "and I believe you may begin to understand. A year and a half ago, Joshua lived with his parents, Paul and Theresa Alameda, in the tiny settlement of Jamesburg near the Tassajara Hot Springs in the Ventana Wilderness of the Los Padres National Forest. Paul guided tourists on excursions through the area. There was a fire in the Jamesburg/Tassajara Hot Springs region that year, caused by a lightning storm. It consumed over 87,000 acres of the aboriginal homeland of the Esselen Tribe of Monterey County. Joshua and his parents became trapped in that fire. Only Joshua survived."

The floor seemed to rise and fall, then sway from side to side like the deck of a ferry broadsided by a sneaker wave. "Oh my God."

"By some miracle, Joshua walked out of the smoldering wilderness alive. The firefighters who found him reported that he was in shock and had a small stone gripped in his hand, the stone he gave to you."

Only then, did I realize how much the child had suffered and what a true sacrifice the gift of his totem had been. Giving up my opal ring had amounted to zilch in comparison.

"The child has not spoken since, except, of course, to call you 'Sunwalker.' We believe he is aware of what happened to his parents but have had no success in getting him to share."

"My vision" —I grabbed the back of the chair in front of me for support— "I saw him in a fire. But how? I'm not psychic."

"Are you familiar with the holographic model of the universe?" Dr. Mendez asked.

At my blank stare, he added, "The concept of the universe as a giant hologram?"

"Sounds like something straight out of *Star Wars*," I said.

The doctor smiled and shook his head. "Believing that the universe is an illusion, like the three-dimensional laser image of Princess Leia, is shocking and contrary to our current world view. However, the holographic model of the universe makes sense of many phenomena beyond scientific understanding, especially when it comes to experiences in which the consciousness transcends the customary boundaries of the personality."

"Boundaries my consciousness presumably transcended when I saw Joshua in the fire."

"Such non-ordinary experiences are beginning to be taken quite seriously by quantum physicists, as well as transpersonal psychologists and psychiatrists," the doctor said.

"And likely still trashed by the majority of doctors and scientists," I countered. "So, by most standards, I'd still be considered loco as a cuckoo bird, which includes you, too, in a Carlos Castaneda-ish sort of way."

"I wish I could disagree with you."

"So, can you explain in laymen's terms, just how my consciousness transcended the boundaries of my personality where Joshua is concerned? Are we talking clairvoyance here?"

"In a holographic universe all things, including consciousness, are interconnected, which makes us beings without borders. Our brains in such a universe operate as a holographic frequency analyzer, decoding projections from a dimension where even space and time may not exist as we perceive them."

"Sorry, Doctor, but that explanation isn't quite laymen enough for me."

"Let me put it this way. You may somehow have formed an extrasensory interconnectedness with Joshua. Possibly a moving picture or holographic memory of a past experience that he was reliving in vivid detail became accessible to your perception."

"But I saw him through my own eyes, like in a lucid dream, which means I wasn't in his head, but my own. Or" —I shivered at where my thoughts were taking me— "in the head of someone else with him at the time."

"The world out there and the world in here," the doctor said, touching his temple, "are not always clearly delineated. The holographic theory suggests that there is a fifth dimension or parallel reality, which most people do not possess the sensory skills to perceive. The holographic theory is also compatible with Carl Jung's theory of the collective unconscious, derived from our two-million-year-old collective history, which we may be able to tap into through our dreams."

"So why the connection between Joshua and me? I hardly know the child."

"You may be resonating at similar frequencies."

"You mean like tuning forks?"

"That is one way to look at it. When two people are in resonance, they create enormous energy, powerful enough to affect those around them. But for now, what is happening between the two of you remains a mystery."

And mystery it would probably remain.

"What I do know," the doctor said, "is that meeting you has been good for the child."

"Then why'd you practically kick me out of your office last week?"

"You were not ready."

Ready for what? "Does Joshua live in an orphanage?"

"He's in the custody of a Native American adoption service, in a group home."

"What about his relatives or his tribe?"

"His parents kept to themselves and apparently went by assumed names. Their belongings were few, no credit cards, no phones, no car, no bank accounts, no pictures of themselves, no personal records. In other words, they and their extended family have been nearly impossible to trace. Word has it that Joshua's father was Native American with links to the Esselen tribe, but, so far, that's all we know."

At the shake of my head, he added, "Unfortunately, the agency is reluctant to place a child who requires ongoing therapy. The emotional and financial and cost to adoptive parents can be prohibitive."

"Has he been back to where he lost his parents? Maybe if he returned . . ."

"Whenever we approach the subject, he becomes extremely agitated."

"So, what *can* be done for him?"

"This case has proven to be a difficult one. You precipitated our first breakthrough."

"So, what now?"

"That is up to you."

"Me?"

"Do you want to see Joshua again?"

I felt shamed at what I knew must be my answer. How could I help this precious child when I couldn't even help myself? I shook my head no.

"I understand," he said. "Have you started your journal?"

"There are some strange scribbles coming out of my pen," I said, my mind still on Joshua, the nightmare of his past, the loneliness of his present, the starkness of his future.

"Continue to write everything down and, if you feel threatened, call me." The doctor stood. "I'll have Jane send you my contact information to make it easier for you to reach me if you feel the need. I may not be in my office the next time you call."

I studied the man who I was beginning to consider a friend and said, "You're saving my life."

The shake of his head hardly registered as far as body gestures go, but I could tell by the slight uptick of the corners of his eyes that he was pleased. "You are saving your own."

Then, as previously, he escorted me to the door.

When I got back to the Jeep, the cat was asleep on the back seat. I started the engine and turned on the radio, but the tabby didn't stir. "Okay, wise guy. It's time I gave you a name."

Something tender blossomed inside of me that somehow bypassed the numbness surrounding my heart. I didn't even like cats. But for now, this was my only friend, a hitchhiker along for the ride. "And I'm not hauling you back home, buddy. You're coming with me."

What had inspired the stray to hitch a ride in my Jeep? Was it a messenger of some kind?

It opened its eyes, leapt into the front passenger seat, and curled up next to my purse.

"Since I don't know if you're male or female, I'll call you Gabriel. How does that sound?"

The cat yawned and shut its eyes.

"And since you're such a couch-potato, I'm going to assume you're male."

That said, I whispered a prayer to St. Christopher, the patron saint of travelers, and eased my Jeep onto the street.

Chapter Eleven

THE SUN STREAKED THROUGH THE CLOUDS over Highway101 as I drove south between the coast-hugging range of the Santa Lucia Mountains and the rugged Pacific Coast. The freeway stretched in front of me, busy but unclogged. I tuned into KCBS radio just in time to catch a weather update. The forecast was for temperatures into the low 60's with partly cloudy skies, when on this March morning, the first day of my journey, I had hoped to bask in the sun.

Swirls of fog shrouded the entry into Carmel like a permeable shield, but as I turned east onto Carmel Valley Road, I left its confining and concealing mist behind.

Gabriel hadn't stretched, purred, or opened an eyelid since we left Menlo Park, a good indication of the kind of companionship I could expect from my unfettered friend. He dozed in curled contentment, displaying a complete faith in my ability to protect him and a deft talent for preserving his strength—as well as his affection.

Soon he'd wake up, anxious for adventure, just about when I'd be anxious for a nap. Might as well be prepared. When I spotted a grocery store to my right, I made a quick detour into the parking lot. Time to buy Gabriel's favorite chow.

At checkout, I asked the clerk if he knew of a place where I could buy a shelter for my cat, knowing full well that Gabriel preferred his homeless state and would likely not appreciate the confinement of a house. The young man recommended a hardware store down the road that sold igloo-type shelters. When I asked for directions, he said, "You've probably passed it a hundred times. Actually, it's hard to miss."

"I'm not from around here," I said.

He presented me with a narrowed, Sherlock Holmes gaze. "Could've sworn I saw you here just last week."

The teenage girl bagging at our station said, "Except your hair was black."

"Nope," I said. "It wasn't me."

Embarrassed by their unconvinced stares, I wished them a nice day and headed for the exit.

At the hardware store, I bought an igloo, and, though it was small, I had to do some creative rearranging of the Jeep's contents to find space for it. When I finally repositioned myself behind the steering wheel, I wasn't surprised that Gabriel had slept through the entire ordeal.

Back on course, my attention shifted to the surrounding hills covered with oak trees, chaparral, and intense light. The sun had broken through the clouds just in time for my arrival.

Seven miles east of the hardware store, I pulled into the Carmel Valley Inn. The woman behind the registration desk looked about my age but was at least two inches shorter and had a mass of curly brown hair. Her initial smile of polite interest widened, and her hazel eyes took on the sparkle of recognition. "Well, hi again," she said.

When I didn't respond, she squinted at me as though contemplating an interactive Sudoku puzzle that she couldn't solve. "Like, we *have* met before, right?"

"Not in this lifetime."

My comment elicited a wink from the cheerful receptionist. "Oooh, I can already tell you're my kind of girl."

I set my purse on the counter and held out my hand. "You must be Heather. We spoke on the phone Saturday. I have reservations for three weeks."

She shook my hand, her expression cycling between confusion

and relief. "Marjorie from Menlo Park? Oops. Girl, you've got a twin in these parts."

"You have one, too," I said, noticing her resemblance to a child-model-turned-actress quite popular a while back.

Heather's laughter was so musical and full of joy that I wondered what I'd need to do to hear it again. "Brooke Shields, right? Except I'm, like, a foot shorter and not nearly as famous." She printed out a registration form and set it on the counter. "After you've settled in, come on back and I'll give you the scoop on things to do around here and places to eat."

I hesitated, thinking about Gabriel. Better fess up now rather than have it come out later that I sneaked a cat into my room. "Ummm."

While signing in, I told Heather about my stray.

"I'll keep him outside," I said. "He's so quiet you'll hardly know he's there."

"Ah hell," she said, probably afraid I'd burst into tears if she exiled my cat to some Carmel Valley pet sitter. "I'll alert maintenance, so they'll be prepared."

I was surprised at my relief at the news. Was I that hard up for a friend?

"Oh, I almost forgot," Heather said. "We serve wine and cheese in the dining room from six to nine."

✎ ✎ ✎

Bougainvillea vines weaved around the supporting posts of the covered walkway that led to my room, with shiny green leaves sprouting from their thorned and twisted stems. Hummingbird feeders, hanging between the columns, brought to mind brightly plumed birds, with their needle-like bills, probing and sipping the upcoming flowers.

Gabriel showed the beginning signs of life, but was still groggy, so I left him in the Jeep while I unloaded my bags and stacked them outside the room. When I stepped through the doorway, I sighed with relief. A comforter, patterned with clusters of pink cabbage roses and edged with lace, covered the queen bed. Matching shams leaned against a white wicker headboard, with shaded swivel lamps extending from the wall on each side.

Beyond the sliding glass door, I spotted a sitting area facing a pool, a perfect location for Gabriel's new home. I folded a picnic blanket from my Jeep's cargo into quarters, positioned it inside the igloo, and filled Gabriel's bowls with food and water. As expected, the cat was eager to leave the confines of the Jeep and eager for adventure. Also, as expected, he ignored the igloo. The food and water, however, received his full attention.

In spite of the cool weather, I was tempted to go for a swim, but decided instead to unpack my bags and take a nap, the first of what I hoped to be many during a quiet, restful, three-week retreat.

✂ ✂ ✂

Birdcalls, via my phone's "dreamer" alarm, woke me from my snooze. After a few minor touchups to my makeup and hair, I jogged to the Inn's dining room. Small round tables were scattered about the place, each covered with a flowered tablecloth and white topper. Ceramic rabbits, interspersed with cheerfully painted dishes, stood at attention in a hutch centered against the west wall, and a faux fire glowed in a rustic fireplace to the north. But what caught and held my attention was the southern bank of windows that framed a distant panorama of hills and trees made dream-like by the evening haze.

I filled a plate with crackers and cheese from the sideboard and sat facing the windows. Being the only current guest to enjoy the picturesque scene suited me just fine. I didn't have to worry about appearances; I didn't have to worry about safety; I didn't have to worry about anything at all. An elderly man with the serene look of a western yogi entered the room by way of a motorized wheelchair. A swing-away lap tray attached to the chair held a wineglass and two bottles of wine. "Hel-lo," he said, presenting me with a wide, lop-sided, smile. "W-ine?"

The sight of his kind face and perfectly trimmed white hair and beard triggered an influx of warmth inside of me, as if the wine were already flowing through my veins.

I wasn't much of a drinker. In fact, I was apparently one of the few people left on the planet still holding out on the fun. But I wasn't a teetotaler either and wasn't about to become one anytime soon. Anyway, there was no refusing this kind-faced man. "How nice. Thank you."

"Wh-ich?" he asked, indicating the two bottles.

"Surprise me," I said.

The Sauvignon Blanc the man selected tasted like nectar and blended perfectly with the crackers and cheese. While I sipped and munched and stared at the sherbet colors of the setting sun, I decided that everything about this place pleased me. When the man in the wheelchair returned to offer a refill, I was surprised that I'd finished the entire glass. I passed on a second. "It's quiet tonight."

"Yes," he said, considering me with eyes that shimmered like etched copper.

"Any suggestions for a good place to pick up dinner?" I asked, reluctant to leave the comfort of this room and the old man's company. "It's a bit late for exploring."

He pointed out a ring binder propped open on the podium next to the dining room entry. "You can call for res-erva-tions."

The thought of spending an evening alone in an unfamiliar restaurant felt suddenly unappealing. Especially after what I'd just experienced here with a man trying his best to make me feel comfortable. "You know, I think I'm in the mood for take-out. Maybe it's the wine."

"Pizza?" he said. "They de-liver."

"Sounds perfect."

I got up to leave, hesitated, and held out my hand. "My name's Marjorie."

He took hold of my hand, squeezed, and presented me with a

smile that matched photos I'd seen of the saintly Pope John. "Cor-nelio."

"Nice to meet you, Cornelio," I said.

"Con-tinen-tal breakfast . . . at seven-thirty," he said.

Something in his voice suggested a fatherly concern, a reluctance to let me go, which left me suddenly close to tears. "Sounds good," I said. Then I copied the number for pizza delivery out of the binder, wished Cornelio a good night, and headed for my room, using the landscape lighting along the road's perimeter to guide the way.

Once there, I searched for Gabriel.

He was gone.

I sank onto my bed, struck by the force of my disappointment. He's a stray, I reminded myself, not about to give up his freedom to be coddled, protected, and confined to an igloo. Let him be.

A picture of Joshua crowded out thoughts of my adventurous cat. I felt a familiar tug of guilt at my refusal to see him again and knew it would soon find nourishment in my soul.

Chapter Twelve

NEXT MORNING, I got up slow and easy, surprised, but not concerned, that it was already 8:00. I took a leisurely shower and, after slathering my face with moisturizer, decided to confront the day without makeup, something I hadn't done since high school.

I pulled on a pair of well-worn jeans and a loose pullover, then clipped on my belted pouch and put my wallet and mouse totem inside.

Croissants, sliced bagels, donuts, and an assortment of fruit, fruit juices, specialty teas, and gourmet coffee lay elegantly displayed on the sideboard in the dining room. I chose a blueberry bagel, poured a mug of coffee, and sat at the same table I'd occupied the night before. Within minutes, Heather breezed in with the morning paper and an energetic greeting. "Hope you slept well because I'm about to intrigue you with the highlights of our charming town."

I raised my mug in a give-it-to-me toast.

"For starters, the Carmel Valley Village center is within walking distance, that is, if you're in the mood for some exercise."

"Good," I said. "You just answered my first question."

"And what's the second?"

"Is there a fitness center in town?"

"Yep, and for, like, ten bucks, you can work out all day, but first you've got to check out the Village shops. One specializes in 17th and 18th century architectural antiques. Actually, it's more than a store. It's an experience. You'll thank me later, I promise. Another collects and sells authentic quality glassware, lamps, furniture, and . . ."

Encouraged by my rapt silence, Heather shared enough what-todos, what-to-eats, and what-to-buys to extend my stay by three weeks. "But to shop for clothes," she said, "your best bet is the Barn-yard Shopping Village off Highway 1. You won't find anything around here except for no-change-your-mind boutiques, if you know what I mean."

"Got it," I said. "No returns or exchanges."

"And if you're into books, our library is a three-minute walk from here, a great way to stretch your legs, if you don't mind a few missing sidewalks and pedestrian paths."

"Thanks for the heads up," I said, getting up to leave.

"Hey, what about the paper?"

"No thanks," I said. "It's time I start generating some of my own news."

Before heading out, I returned to my room to check on Gabriel. Still gone.

Deep breath. Hold. Blow out the crud.

Not about to spend the morning worrying about my errant stray (I knew from experience that he had an itinerary of his own), I headed for the Village down Carmel Valley Road. The traffic was heavy for a Tuesday morning, but concentrated and directed, as if composed primarily of locals running errands. I checked the menu posted inside the window of Bill's Dining House. The grilled salmon with shallots, mushrooms, and garlic prompted my decision to return later for dinner rather than spend another guilt-ridden evening alone in my room.

Across the street, I spotted the architectural antique store Heather had raved about. After a break in traffic, I sprinted across the road to its huge outdoor lot. One-of-a-kind doors, fireplace man-tels, fountains, vases, pillars, and Roman arches crowded the space, leaving only small paths in between on which to maneuver. I won-dered where all the ancient artifacts had come from. What sort of building, for instance, had once housed the glass door etched with the image of Saint Theresa? A church? A chapel? A convent? Sad-ness gripped me as I remembered that Theresa had been the name of Joshua's mother. Theresa, who along with Joshua's father, Paul, had died a fiery death and left her son an orphan.

I saw a statue that appeared to be hundreds of years old. It reminded me of the apostle Peter, hiding within the folds of his cloak after denying Jesus three times. The atmosphere turned liquid, and I leaned against the statue for support. The sound of a thousand cricket wings rubbing together announced that the *Voice* was about to speak.

You are not who you pretend to be.

I strained to hear more but experienced instead an eerie silence. The *Voice* hadn't spoken to me in two days, and I had hoped it was gone for good. I blinked and waited for my head to clear, automatically reaching for the mouse totem in my belted pouch. I could think of no reasonable explanation for the comfort I received from contact with the small smooth stone.

When my world steadied again, I left the lot. Later I would record the *Voice's* strange message in my journal, and hopefully someday I would understand.

On the other side of the street stood another antique shop. Something—call it intuition—urged me to hurry to its door.

The traffic running through the Village was alive and pulsing. The vibrating purr of a diesel truck barely registered in my mind as it slowed, allowed me to cross, and then sped up again.

A bell jingled when I opened the shop door. Furniture, paintings, linens, jewelry, glassware, and tools cramped the store in orderly disorder, and on the wall directly in front of me hung a mirror. My mirror. I knew this with a certainty not open to question.

It was oval, beveled, and adorned with a pink ribbon of carved satinwood that looped over the top and was gathered on each side by a sprig of roses also made of satinwood and painted a soft pink. A bit foofoo for the space above my stone fireplace, but I didn't care. With the right positioning, accessorizing, and lighting, I could make it work.

The mirror's surface appeared a bit wavy and tarnished near the edges, giving it a spooky feel, but its center, except for a sprinkling of small black spots, was clear as newly re-silvered glass. Catching my reflection gave me a start. My eyes sparkled with a child-like joy that I hadn't noticed in them for some time. "The mirror reflects what's going on inside," my father had said. "If you don't like what you see, it's time to make some changes. And I'm not talking about your makeup routine."

Slightly over my left shoulder, I caught sight of another set of eyes—deep green and familiar. *No. It can't be.*

What was Morgan van Dyke doing in *my* mirror?

I stared at his reflection, reluctant to turn around. Maybe it was an illusion or the result of a mirror tilt; or maybe my subconscious had conjured him up due to my recent conversation with John Phillip, which had awakened memories of my first serious crush.

"Marjorie?"

The image had a voice.

"Marjorie . . . is that you?"

I hadn't felt such an elastic, weightless sense of reality in years—ten to be exact—when I had last seen Morgan and last dreamed about those dancing green eyes. His hair was still thick, blond, and neatly trimmed and appeared to have been styled by the wind. I turned, unable to get words past the constriction in my throat.

"I can't believe it's you," he said, taking a step closer. "What brings you to Carmel Valley?"

"It's a long story…" Then, just like that, it struck me why Father John Phillip had reacted strangely when I told him where I was headed. "Ah, now I understand your brother's odd reaction."

"Brother?"

"Father John Phillip," I said. "The only person I know with two first names. We met after church last Sunday and spent some time catching up. Actually, it was more like a confession on my part, minus the 'Bless-me-Father-for-I-have-sinned' and 'mea culpas.' I can't believe he became a priest."

Morgan chuckled. "Mom called him by his first and middle name every time she chewed him out for something, and the name eventually stuck due to frequent use."

"He knew you'd be here and didn't tell me."

"Little brother must have had a good laugh on that one, figuring we'd meet up sooner or later." Morgan tilted his head and focused on me with what appeared to be genuine interest. "I'm glad we did, by the way."

"Glad to meet up with the 'little nun' again?" I said, the teasing note in my voice a cover up for the disappointment I felt at the chaste and virtuous portrayal of my teen-aged self he'd shared with John Phillip. My thoughts had never been chaste and virtuous where Morgan was concerned.

Quite the opposite.

"Guess I can thank my brother for spilling that particular can of beans," Morgan said. "What else did he say?"

"That David's married with two sons and that you're still single."

"Hope he's more discreet about sharing what he hears in the confessional."

"He also said that Teri was missing and that you're searching for her. I'm so sorry."

Morgan looked over my shoulder and shifted his feet. "Me too."

For a few seconds, neither of us spoke.

Then he asked, "Will you have lunch with me?"

"I'd be happy to, but first I have a mirror to buy. Do you have a lot of shopping to do?"

"Actually, I was just driving by when you crossed the street in front of me. I nearly wiped out a priceless statue or two while trying to find a place to park. But I had to know if it was you."

"When I saw your reflection in the mirror, I thought my imagination was playing tricks on me," I said.

"Likewise," he said.

The store clerk walked over obviously pleased. "This beauty just came in. Would you care to take a closer look?"

"Consider the mirror your spiritual doorway," my father once said. Well, I'd seen Morgan in this mirror and a new, happier me. Did that count as a spiritual doorway?

"No thanks, I'll take it."

After closing the deal with a slide of my credit card, I asked, "Can I come back for it later?"

"Sure thing. I'll wrap it up and keep it in back. Would you be interested in some of the mirror's history?"

"Oh yes, please."

"Consider it done," he said.

N N N

Over iced tea and club sandwiches, Morgan and I talked about our families, about work, and about life in general, but I didn't mention Cliff or the *Voice*. My problems hardly registered on the need-to-know scale when compared to Morgan's. He didn't go into details, but said he was posing as a photographer while searching for his sister, using one of her discarded cameras as a prop.

"Why are you posing as someone you're not?" I asked. "Do you suspect foul play?"

"Yes," was his disheartening reply.

"What makes you think she disappeared in Carmel Valley?"

"Her last letter was postmarked here. It's our only lead."

"Are the police involved?"

Morgan dropped his gaze to his half-eaten sandwich. "Yes and no."

I didn't ask him to clarify, wondering instead how he managed to cope during such a difficult task and what he drew on for strength.

When the conversation came to a natural stall, I asked, "Can I help in any way?"

"Right now, I'm just snooping around." Morgan's voice sounded calm and composed, but the deep grooves between his eyebrows and the way he clenched and unclenched his jaw gave away unspoken and deeply felt stress. "I'd like to see more of you though," he said.

All logic warned me to make an excuse as to why seeing him was currently out of the question. I was here to get my life back in order, not to reopen my heart. After my experience with Cliff, I was more susceptible than ever to Morgan's down-to-earth honesty and charm. No man had ever been able to sway me toward happiness this way. Like an antidote to burnout, he replenished me.

"I'd like to see more of you, too," I said.

Morgan escorted me to the antique shop to pick up my mirror and then drove me back to the Inn. Once there, he asked if I had plans for dinner.

I mentioned Bill's Dining House.

"I'll pick you up at six," he said.

And as simple as that, we had a date.

Chapter Thirteen

I HADN'T PACKED ANYTHING SUITABLE for a date. This hadn't been part of my plan. But if I hurried, I could make it to the Barnyard Shopping Village to buy something new.

Tucked between landscaped, brick-lined courtyards and mosaic paths, I found the perfect boutique and the perfect dress: gold and romantically chic. Actually, there wasn't much to it. It was more of a lined sheath; no belt; no waist; no fuss. A quick stop at a nearby shoe store for strappy heels and my outfit was complete.

Morgan's face lit up when I opened the door. I was aware that my hair fell full and smooth about my face, that my shadow-enhanced eyes appeared bluer than blue, and that the dress fit to perfection. It felt good to look good.

Morgan's skin was slightly weathered, his scent spicy like perfectly steeped tea.

I tore my gaze from his full lower lip and concentrated instead on his black turtleneck sweater and olive sports coat, casually unbuttoned. "Hello," I said.

"Hello to you, too," was his deep-toned reply. He reached around me to check if the door to my room was secure before guiding me to his Ford F250 diesel pickup truck—which translates to tall.

My silky sheath of a dress rose to mid-thigh as Morgan helped me into the passenger seat. I blushed, wondering if he had noticed. His broad smile confirmed that he had. I tugged, smoothed, and looked away.

"Nice dress," he said before closing the door.

"Jeez," I whispered, glad for the opportunity to take a deep breath before Morgan entered the truck on the other side. Even during the best of times, Cliff had never had such a powerful effect on me. In his own way, he'd tried, but in the end, he couldn't induce the weightlessness I was experiencing now. It wasn't just chemistry. I was defenseless against Morgan's selflessness, his depth of heart, his easy energy. Like the diesel truck he drove, Morgan was the kind of man I could depend on long past warrantable miles.

On entering the restaurant, we registered with the host and stepped into the bar. I ordered Sauvignon Blanc like a pro, thanks to Cornelio, and Morgan ordered a Scotch and water.

The bar, only half-full, hummed with a steady flow of conversation. According to the bartender, most of the patrons were locals. "During the holiday weekend, we'll attract more tourists," he said, "and the regulars will know to stay away or be in for a long wait. You've picked a good time."

We hadn't been sitting long before the host arrived to escort us to our table. On the way, we brushed against another couple preparing to leave. I glanced over with the intention of voicing a polite, "Excuse me," but the words never made it past my suddenly slack jaw.

The eyes I met were exactly like my own, except a colder blue than I'd ever seen in the mirror. The room melted away, leaving only me and someone who appeared to be my identical twin. Her hair was black instead of blonde, spritzed and volumized as if she had just stepped out of the glossy pages of Vogue, and she wore low-rise jeans with a short cashmere sweater, exposing a good three inches of tanned waist and belly.

I reeled and my soul took a breath, until Morgan, sweet Morgan, took the wine glass from my trembling hands and urged me forward while the world righted itself. The other couple moved on, but then, just for a heartbeat, the woman turned and aimed those cold blue eyes at Morgan.

"Dear God," I said, unable to tear my gaze from the beautiful, terrible apparition walking out of the restaurant.

When I finally reverted my attention back to Morgan, I noticed his face had grown pensive, his skin flushed. "Would you like a refill?" he asked.

"Yes, please." *More like the whole bottle.*

After guiding me to my seat, Morgan motioned for a waiter and said, "The resemblance is uncanny."

The resemblance was uncanny all right, enough to give me nightmares.

"It must be upsetting for her to discover she's not the only beautiful woman in town."

I suppressed an unladylike snort. My so-called twin, with her smoldering stare and supermodel moves—let alone her wide silver armband and show-stopping, ostrich-feathered clutch—was proof that any woman could appear beautiful given the right clothes, makeup, and attitude. I felt like the innermost doll in a set of nesting matryoshkas, the doll that you can't crack open, the one that carries nothing inside.

"For a few seconds, it seemed like we were linked in some way," I said. "Do you know her?"

"Yes."

A shiver shot through me like a spark plug firing. "What's her name?"

"Veronica."

Veronica wipes the face of Jesus. Oh God, what were the chances? I sat next to the Sixth-Station-of-the-Cross every chance I got while attending Mass as a child.

"When we first met, I thought she was you," Morgan said with a half-smile of remembrance. "I meant to give you hell for dying your hair black. But when I looked into her eyes, I realized you could never have mastered that cold expression. Otherwise—"

"I used to think it would be fun to meet my body double," I said, "but this wasn't fun at all. In fact, it was freaky."

"This is a small town. You'll run into her again."

My shiver was so intense Morgan noticed and frowned. "How about we change the subject?"

"Sure," I said. *For now.*

Our drinks arrived and we placed our order, but my appetite for grilled salmon had disappeared. I'd heard that encountering your doppelganger is a sign of bad luck, as it may be your evil twin. Evil or not, if Veronica was my twin, then . . .

I couldn't complete the thought. My bruised sense of identity wouldn't allow it.

✦ ✦ ✦

While preparing for bed, I reviewed the events of what should have been one of the most romantic evenings of my life. Morgan hadn't mentioned his sister, and I hadn't mentioned Dr. Mendez, Joshua, or the *Voice*. Neither of us had delved into the things we held closest to our hearts. We'd kept a safe distance, which was probably for the best.

The incident with Veronica was an event over which neither of us had had control. Although such helplessness wasn't new to me, familiarity did not guarantee mastery or acceptance.

My first reaction on meeting Veronica had been shock, which was now slowly turning into curiosity. Where had she come from? Why was she here? Something inside that bypassed logic signaled a warning: We would meet again, and this meeting would shake both of our worlds.

The phone rang. It was Dr. Mendez.

"Sorry for the late call," he said, "but something has come up."

"Yeah, tell me about it," I said, and then, due to being completely immersed in my own little world, I hijacked the conversation. "On my first day here, three people claimed they'd seen me before, which struck me as odd, at least until I ran into a woman named Veronica, someone who looks exactly like me. She scares me even more than the *Voice* does."

"Exactly like you?" the doctor said, with a rare note of surprise.

Good. I wanted my experience to rock his world. I wanted him to feel my shock, my confusion. A few strikes against his *id* might help him better deal with mine.

"Yes, exactly," I said and then sighed. Bet patients like me really made his day. Just thinking of the tediousness of listening to clients talk about their never-ending problems made me shudder. "How's Joshua? Is he okay?"

"He is the reason I called. Mona said that he had a disturbing dream last night and now will not respond to anyone."

The thought of Joshua, all alone and afraid, effectively wiped out my absorption with the high-flying events of the evening and my feeling of inadequacy. "What can I do to help?"

"Transpersonal psychotherapy rests on the belief that there is something bigger and deeper in the space *between* that operates upon us, which appears to be especially true between you and Joshua. Your image emerged in his drawing as a super hero, so it is possible that somehow, through you, he will be able to discover his own inner power, which is currently lacking. You said you needed time, but—"

"Sounds like Joshua can't wait until it's convenient for me," I said.

"He called out 'Sunwalker' during his dream."

"Jeez."

"It might be good for him to know that you are staying nearby. Would you mind if I picked you up for a visit?"

For the life of me, I was clueless as to how I could be of any help to the child, but Dr. Mendez wouldn't be asking if he didn't deem it necessary. "When?"

"Noon tomorrow?"

"It'll make things harder," I said. "I can't risk caring too much about anyone at this stage."

"Why not? What have you got to lose?"

My freedom, the freedom I crave more desperately than life.

"Okay," I said. "I'll be ready."

Chapter Fourteen

DR. MENDEZ WAS TO PICK ME UP AT NOON, and it wasn't yet ten. Rather than torture myself for the next two hours with fruitless worry about Joshua and the possibility that I might fail him, I exposed myself to another form of torture, that of diving into the cold pool of water just outside my room. A hollow, ocean-like roar surrounded me as I slid through the underwater world as if I were passing through a massive seashell in another dimension.

After coming up for air, I front-crawled and flutter-kicked from one end of the pool to the other, pushing against the resistance of the water until I ran out of strength. I pulled myself out of the water on trembling arms, only to find a towel dangled in front of my nose.

"You're one tough cookie."

I nearly dropped back into the pool. "Morgan!"

He wrapped the towel around me and rubbed my arms and shoulders vigorously until warmth seeped back into my muscles and bones. Then he lifted a lock of damp hair off my cheek and tucked it behind my ear. "Did I pick a bad time?"

"I'd say your timing's perfect," I said.

He led me to a chaise lounge and waited for me to sit down. "I'll grab another towel. Which room's yours?"

I pointed out the sliding door I'd left ajar.

With one towel wrapped around me, I was reasonably warm, but when Morgan returned and covered me with another, I felt downright cozy. He frowned at the clouds that blocked the sun before zeroing in on my quivering lips. "Not exactly ideal swimming weather."

I sank deeper into the padded chaise, enjoying the warmth of my makeshift cocoon. "You'd be surprised at how a little physical discomfort can subdue the mind."

"Does your mind need subduing?"

The same question coming from Cliff would have carried an undertone of criticism, but Morgan's tone conveyed interest and concern, which drew a part of me out of hibernation that I'd long thought dead. "What brings you here, Morgan?"

"I'm headed out of town for a few days to follow some leads on my sister . . ."

Footsteps.

I stood so abruptly that my towel hooked onto the chaise and I fell sideways into Morgan. He caught and held me until I'd regained my footing.

"Tony," I said. "You're early."

Dr. Mendez smiled, ignoring my slip of tongue.

Morgan held out his hand. "Morgan van Dyke. Nice to meet you."

The doctor took Morgan's hand and met his gaze with the calm non-reaction of a Buddhist monk. "Likewise, I'm Tony Mendez."

"You said you were heading out of town," I said, hoping that it wasn't too late to retrieve the information Morgan had been about to share.

He touched my cheek with the tip of his finger. "I'm not sure when I'll be back. Take care of yourself, okay?"

Where was he going? Would he be in danger? I hadn't yet told him about the doctor, Joshua, and the *Voice*. "You, too," I said.

As Morgan walked away, the sun buried itself even deeper beneath the clouds.

"You look like you've been caught in a polar vortex," Dr. Mendez said. "Better get into something warm."

"I'm sorry for calling you Tony. It just slipped out."

If his closed-lipped smile was meant to reassure me, it failed. He knew things about me that I'd rather he did not, even if that information might help him delve into my confused ego and id. He reclined onto the patio chair and closed his eyes.

"Be right back," I said.

On my return, Dr. Mendez was sitting up holding my cat.

"Gabriel!" I said, light-headed with relief. "Where've you been? There are coyotes and rattlesnakes out here. You could've been killed."

The doctor's eyebrows rose. "You have certainly made a lot of friends since your arrival here. When did this one show up?"

"Actually, he hitchhiked from home. He's my backyard stray, and he doesn't meow."

"Then he and Joshua have much in common."

At my blank stare, the doctor clarified, "They both need a home, they're both attracted to you, and neither of them speaks."

Yeah, right. Gabriel had a perfectly good home right outside my room, yet the igloo remained immaculate and unoccupied. And if the past few days were an indication of the cat's attraction to me, I wasn't impressed.

"Joshua isn't progressing well," Dr. Mendez said. "But I already told you that." He paused and studied the cat on his lap. "Are you aware that cats are sophisticated communicators?"

"Not this one," I said.

"Cats communicate through the subtle twitch of an ear and quick switch of the tail, as well as telepathically."

It was an effort not to roll my eyes. "I assume this relates to your universe as a hologram theory, the interconnectedness of all things and resonating tuning forks? A few weeks ago, I would've thought you were crazy, but with all that's been going on lately, I don't know what to believe anymore."

I stared at Gabriel. Gabriel stared back—no ear twitch, no switch of tail. If my stray was trying to communicate, our tuning forks weren't resonating.

"Would you be averse to taking Gabriel along?" the doctor asked. "He may be good for Joshua."

I shrugged. More chance of the cat's doing the child some good than of my doing so. "Sure, why not?"

◢ ◢ ◢

"What are we doing *here*?" I asked when we pulled into the Carmel Mission parking lot. Memory of the *Voice* speaking to me here during my Ash Wednesday visit with Cliff caused my blood to pump in an exaggerated way.

"Joshua goes to school next door and is currently in the Basilica with Mona, which seems to have a positive effect on him, as I hope you and Gabriel will."

The doctor's words did not slow my out-of-control heart. If anything, they accelerated its erratic beat. "Oh."

"I am not expecting miracles," he said. "Just be yourself."

We found Joshua kneeling in front of a statue of Our Lady of Bethlehem, next to which stood an iron frame supporting a multitude of white, flickering candles. "He enjoys lighting votives and praying to Mary," Dr. Mendez said. "For his parents, I assume."

Gabriel tensed and twitched his tail before leaping out of my grasp and running to the child's side. With my arms empty and my mouth open, I was clueless what to do next. I couldn't call the cat's name or race after him. We were in a church, for heaven's sake. Joshua turned and began stroking the cat, and by the time I'd crossed the distance between us, the child was sitting on the floor with Gabriel on his lap.

"Hello, Joshua," I said, figuring the cat, at least, was doing his job. "I see you've met my friend."

Joshua didn't respond, unless a blank stare counted as a response.

What happened to the friendly kid I'd met in the doctor's office, the one who'd given me his treasured mouse totem? And why had he called out 'Sunwalker' in his sleep, only to ignore me now?

Dr. Mendez signaled for me to accompany him outside. We took seats around the gurgling fountain until Mona, Joshua, and Gabriel joined us. In an attempt to remind Joshua of our former friendship,

I took the mouse totem from my pouch and held it out in my open palm.

The child let go of the cat with one hand to grasp the opal ring dangling from the chain around his neck. Likely prompted by Joshua's sudden movement, Gabriel leaped to the ground and, in his usual free-spirited manner, padded toward a fenced area next to the Basilica.

"Looks like the cat is headed for the cemetery," Mona said, and before anyone thought to stop him, Joshua followed.

Dr. Mendez shrugged and I shook my head, wondering yet again at my purpose for being here.

We found Joshua and Gabriel facing a gnarled tree, its base overgrown with ivy. The tree gave off a musty, black pepper smell, which I inhaled as though it were part of some healthful mist therapy.

"Even with such heavy limbs, it still manages to look graceful," Mona said, "probably due to all the droopy side-branches sprouting all over. Too bad there's no other marker for the woman buried here."

"A woman's buried here?" I asked, thinking maybe I'd misheard.

"It's probably just local myth," Mona said. "There's a plaque commemorating her husband, Manuel Butron, inside the Basilica. He was a Spanish soldier."

If the woman had been married to a Spanish soldier honored with a plaque inside the Basilica, why was *she* buried under a tree with no marker? "So, did the wife of this illustrious soldier happen to have a name?" I asked, my anger on her behalf evident in my sarcastic tone.

"Well, of course she did. Margarita Maria Butron."

"Spanish?" I asked.

"Rumsen, otherwise known as Ohlone/Costanoan. Father Serra encouraged intermarriage between the Spanish soldiers and mission Indians baptized into the Faith. Spanish land grants were sometimes offered as an incentive."

I looked at the mound of ivy beneath the tree and crossed myself. "God bless you, Margarita Maria Butron."

Gabriel's head jerked up, and he regarded me fixedly for several seconds before dashing back the way he'd come.

"I can't believe this," I said, summing up the day's oddness with an eye roll before reseating myself at the courtyard fountain. Joshua sat next to me, and Gabriel resumed his position on the child's lap. "Traitor," I said, addressing the cat.

Joshua stroked his new friend behind the ears—and continued to ignore me.

My consciousness wasn't transcending any boundaries as far as I could tell—no shared states of awareness, no interconnectedness, no fusion of memory. Total blockage. "I've never heard Gabriel meow," I said in a last feeble attempt to capture the child's attention. "He's the quietest cat I've ever met."

No response.

"Would you mind if Joshua borrowed your cat for a while?" Dr. Mendez asked.

"He's not *my* cat," I said, which was true, though it felt wrong saying it.

"You told me he was *your* stray," the doctor persisted.

Darn that man. If Gabriel preferred Joshua to me, so be it.

"I'm sure Joshua will take good care of him," Dr. Mendez said.

I shrugged, a gesture embarrassingly indicative of an immature brat.

"I've made arrangements for you to visit Joshua at the group home while I'm gone," Dr. Mendez said. "That is, if you want to."

The child didn't need me. If it hadn't been for Gabriel, this trip would have been a complete waste. I was surprised at how hollow this made me feel. Heck, maybe I needed Joshua, instead of the other way around. He and the cat had done quite a number on me, so subtly that they'd caught me unaware. "I came here to find myself, remember?"

The doctor smiled. "I remember."

Chapter Fifteen

AFTER DR. MENDEZ DROPPED ME OFF at the Inn, I was at a loss at how to spend the rest of the day. After pacing the room at least five times, my attention shifted to the mirror propped against the entry wall. Had the store clerk included its history as promised? I removed the bubble wrap and found a plain white envelope tucked next to the mirror, with two sheets of paper filled with hand printed text inside.

I curled up on the bed to read.

Although this mirror came to California from Spain, it is not Spanish in style. Furnishings of this period in Spain were based on imported French and Italian examples. This mirror is Rococo, a delicate and playful style that makes strong usage of creamy, pastel-like colors, asymmetrical designs, curves, and gold. Although there is no written proof, some believe this mirror was presented to Margarita Maria, a 15-year old Carmeleno Indian woman, on her wedding day. Her marriage was one of three intermarriages that occurred at the Carmel Mission in 1773. She married Manuel Butron, a 46-year-old Spanish soldier. Margarita had been baptized Catholic, and Father Serra, himself, officiated over the ceremony.

Margarita Butron? No way. Only an hour or so before, I'd been standing next to her supposed gravesite at the Carmel Mission. This was beyond crazy, coincidence to the hundredth power. Dr. Mendez would probably call it intuitive synchronicity, universal guidance, or some other such metaphysical term. I just called it weird. I closed my eyes and made the sign of the cross, unsure if I was expressing a sign of faith or warding off evil. "God bless you Margarita Maria Butron. God bless me."

A voice, a new voice—not *the Voice*—responded. *A wealthy guest attended our wedding. He gave us this pretty mirror as a gift. Beautiful things were rare in our crude mission, a mirror like this even rarer. It looked out of place in our humble home, but I treasured it, and I cleaned and polished it every day.*

I bolted upright. My heart felt twice its size, ready to explode with its next chaotic beat. Margarita had lived over two hundred years ago and, as far as I knew, could only speak Costanoan and a smidgen of Spanish. How could I understand her, let alone hear her?

Hands shaking, I read the rest of the store clerk's notes. *The mirror's last home was near the Tassajara Hot Springs, where members of the Esselen tribe had lived before their transport to the Carmel Mission. The last person to have owned the mirror was a member of the Ohlone/Costanoan Esselen Nation, who traced his ancestry all the way back to Manuel and Margarita Maria Butron of the Mission San Carlos Borromeo. The executor of the estate put all up for sale at public auction. Our store took delivery of this mirror only days ago.*

"Jeez!" I slid off the bed and paced the room with the disorganized self-talk of a lunatic. "I'm crazy. There's no other explanation. I see the grave of someone dead for maybe 186 years. Then my mind, already fertile for the impossible and the weird (disembodied voices, give me a break) attracts more weird stuff. Yeah, like a magnet, making me think I'm hearing Margarita, which is impossible. She is dead. She didn't speak English, but then what about the mirror and the shopkeeper's notes?"

Fear for my sanity had me grabbing my belted pouch and heading for the door. Time to learn more about Margarita Butron and the Rumsen Costanoan and Esselen tribes.

At the Carmel Valley Library, I searched through *Local History* until I found two Monterey County guidebooks, plus a thin volume on the Salinan Indians of California and their neighbors, including the Esselen, Chumash, Costanoan, and Yokut tribes. After checking them out, I headed for the restaurant next door to get dinner out of the way so I could return to my room at the Inn to read.

Over Meyer Lemon pizza with prosciutto, arugula, and

mozzarella, I paged through the library books, only to find one small reference to Margarita—that she was of the Rumsen Costanoan tribe and married to Manuel Butron—which added little to what I already knew. She appeared like the blip on a radar screen and was gone, though there promised to be some interesting reading about her tribe at the Mission.

※ ※ ※

At 2:30 a.m., I was still reading.

Life in the Carmel Mission had been hard for the Indians. Fifty crude, straw-thatched huts had housed over 740 natives, and the Padres had ruled their lives. The sounding of a bell signaled time for work, church, and exercise, with the Indians working seven hours and praying for two, six days a week. On Sunday, the time for prayer increased to five hours, with the remainder of the day devoted to rest.

Both sexes received corporal punishment for an assortment of crimes, using stocks, irons, and whips. Women were whipped in an enclosed, somewhat distant place, so their cries wouldn't cause the men to revolt, but the men were punished in full view of their fellow citizens.

When baptized, Indians pronounced a vow for life. Attempts to escape frequently resulted in lashes with a whip on the runaway's return. Indians had no civil liberties and were often no better off than slaves.

I wondered about Margarita and how she had adjusted to this strange world. Had she married the Spanish soldier by choice or had their marriage been arranged? The culture shock must have been enormous. Manuel, at least, would have been free to continue socializing with his friends, but Margarita had probably been cut off from her family and tribe, with little choice as to how to spend her days.

I dozed off and, while in a dream state, heard the voice again. *I look into the mirror and see who I am.* My eyes shot open, and for a while, I had the strangest feeling I wasn't alone.

My phone registered 4:00 a.m., too early to get up, so I prayed the rosary as I had as a child, using my fingers as markers in place of beads. The repetitious words stilled my mind and lulled me back to sleep.

I woke at a more reasonable hour and the temptation to call Dr. Mendez proved too difficult to resist. I told him about the voice I'd heard and repeated what she'd said, then explained about the mirror and its history and how I'd been thinking about Margarita when I'd drifted off to sleep.

"Maybe your mind just wants to give the voice a name," Dr. Mendez said.

"No, this wasn't the *Voice* I've been hearing, the one that speaks directly to me. In this case, it seemed more like Margarita's world and mine had overlapped, somehow, and that I was overhearing her thoughts. What concerns me . . . what really blows my mind . . . is how a spirit can cross over from another dimension and make its presence known to me, if only indirectly. This destroys my concept of what's real and what's not. I can no longer ignore the invisible."

"Our current understanding of reality is incomplete," Dr. Mendez said. "The tangible reality of our lives is a kind of illusion. You may have entered a state of consciousness through which you penetrated the hologram created by the accumulation of humanity's psychological states and experiences. In other words, you may have tapped into the holographic labyrinth that connects all."

A labyrinth that is doing a pretty good job of sending me over the edge. "Is there a way to control when and how I enter these connective states?" I asked.

"There is a technique that combines accelerated breathing with evocative music to induce altered states of consciousness, but it is best done in a controlled setting."

I didn't want to *induce* these altered states but *prevent* them. Anyway, I hadn't been doing any fancy breathing or listening to music when Margarita came to call.

"In the meantime, I suggest you continue to write everything down," Dr. Mendez said, "including the events that trigger your vi-sions and the voices. Who knows where this may lead?"

⁄ ⁄ ⁄

In my research and the notes included with my mirror, I had learned that some of the Esselen that intermarried with Margarita's Rumsen Costanoan descendants may have originally come from the Tassajara Hot Springs area in the Cachagua Valley, about four and a half miles east of Carmel Valley Village. So, after breakfast, I decided to take a drive in that direction. If nothing else, I'd get a glimpse of the sun-drenched, ochre-and-green-quilted hills I'd been reading about.

I fueled up at the Village station, picked up a sandwich and bottled water at the deli, and, following the map in my guidebook, set off.

Cachagua Road turned out to be little more than a paved path, so winding and narrow that I feared what might happen if a car approached from the opposite direction. Steep cliffs plunged to unknown depths, so I didn't dare take my eyes off the road. If I drove off the pavement, there was no way of knowing how far the Jeep would plunge before coming to a stop, or if I would live through it, let alone find my way back.

Eventually, the panoramic view of folding and faulting ridges and valleys numbed my fear enough to risk stopping and stepping out of my car. And what met my eyes nearly made the treacherous route worth navigating. I couldn't tell if I was looking at large hills or small mountains, studded with hundreds of trees. The light and shadow-enhanced landscape was bathed in silence—no wind, no traffic, no birds.

As I drove through wilder curvy country, hitting my brakes and feeling like I was carving a new path out of the rocky walls to my left, I lectured myself about never coming this way again. I passed a mailbox, several rustic buildings, and a tall fence that ran on for miles before I came across a sign with the name of a winery. I pulled into the narrow entrance only to encounter a closed gate. I slapped my hand on the steering wheel. "Damn."

No sooner had I backed out of the entrance than a Toyota pickup with a woman behind the wheel pulled up alongside me. The blue-mirrored lenses of her sunglasses shimmered in the way of guardians and messengers who appear at just the right moment to guide the way. She lowered her window. "Can I help you?"

"I was hoping to visit the winery," I said, trying not to sound as disappointed as I felt.

With her eyes hidden behind the sunglasses, I focused on her nose, which was slightly curved with a perfectly defined tip, as though great care had gone into sculpting it. She introduced herself as Marianne and explained that the tall fence and closed gate were there to keep out hungry deer, not humans. "Would you like a tour?"

"Absolutely."

I'd read about this winery in my guidebook. In addition to its Cabernet, Sauvignons, and pristine vineyards, it was famous for its twelve thousand rose bushes.

"Okay then, follow me," she said.

Without Marianne as a pilot, I would have gotten lost. Roads veered in all directions, weaving in, around, and between fields of budding grapevines, blooming roses, wildflowers, and ancient oaks. At the peak of a hill, we pulled into a lot next to two barn-like buildings painted a startlingly crisp white, presenting an aura of neatness and cleanliness.

Marianne's bleached-denim shirt, Wrangler jeans, and cowboy boots and the way her brown hair hung in a long single braid down her back, indicated that she had work to do, yet she treated me like a valued guest.

We passed a grape press outside one of the barns, and I could almost hear the squish, swoosh, and splash of juice separating from the fruit. In one of the whitewashed barns, Marianne pointed out a wall of stainless-steel tanks. "This is where the liquid grapes begin their transformation into wine." Then she indicated the wooden barrels stacked nearby. "Following fermentation, the wines to be barrel-aged are poured into oak barrels."

Although Marianne's mini lesson on the wine production process fascinated me, the information she shared about the roses interested me more. "The roses are cut and sent all over the world as fresh bouquets," she said. "At the end of the season, we pick the remaining flowers and use their petals for events such as weddings and concerts, where they're scattered on tables, bridal paths, and dance floors."

"The amount of labor involved in the wine-making and rose-growing process is mind boggling," I said. "What do you do around here for fun?"

The echo of Marianne's laughter bounced off the barn walls and wine barrels like a gift. "Sometimes we actually take time off for play. In fact, Saturday night we're hosting a Western barbecue with live music and dancing. This particular event is open to the public rather than restricted to club members, so you're welcome to come. No need to RSVP."

"I appreciate the invite," I said, "but no way will I navigate that long, winding road I took getting here ever again, especially at night."

"You must've taken the long way in," she said, "enough to test the nerve and patience of even the locals. There's another road leading here from the opposite direction, without the cliffs and sharp turns. The concert starts at six-thirty. Just say I invited you, in case anyone asks."

Before heading back to the Jeep, I asked Marianne if she knew anything about the history of the local Esselen. "A bit," she said, "but not nearly as much as my friend, Ben Mendoza. I'll give you his number." While scribbling the digits on the back of a wine label, she said, "Most people around here know Ben by his Indian name, *Gentle Bear*. He's an eighth-generation descendant of the Esselen tribe and guides trail rides when he's not busy on his family's cattle ranch. I'm sure he wouldn't mind talking to you." She then instructed me on the alternative route back to town, and, after a warm thank you, I was off.

Not far from the winery, I spotted a small general store tucked into a clearing on the right side of the road. Since the bottled water

I'd brought along had run out about halfway through the mouth-drying, throat-swelling drive up, I pulled in to buy another.

The entrance to the store was locked, but a neon sign next door flashed *Open*. After my eyes adjusted to the dimness inside, I realized that I'd entered a country bar with rickety tables and plastic folding chairs, arranged haphazardly, in a space no larger than a storage room. Three men pinned me with their stares—not especially friendly, not hostile either. They gave off an aura of suspicion and annoyance at the intrusion, hardly conducive to business from outside visitors. "What can I do for you?" the bartender asked.

I ignored the rude leers of the two men sitting at the bar. "Bottled water, please."

He reached behind the counter and said, "That'll be a dollar."

I paid the bartender, thanked him for his time, and headed for the door in quick retreat.

"Did ya know you got a double in these parts?" one of the stool-straddling strangers asked.

I glanced back, not about to snub these men and fuel a misunderstanding. "So I've heard."

The speaker was handsome enough, but his eyes were unpleasant in their vacancy. And the uninviting patches of stubble on his face—hardly the perfect five o'clock shadow—made it plain that he hadn't bothered to groom himself in a while. I managed a smile and was nearly out of the door when he said, "Could be Vonnie's twin, huh, Tommy Boy?"

Something about the men in the bar put me on edge and weighed on me all the way back to the Inn.

Chapter Sixteen

THANK GOODNESS FOR FITNESS CENTERS, I thought as I programmed the treadmill for a thirty-minute workout. No better way than exercise to work off the depressing after-effects of last night's dream. The two men from the bar had been chasing me through the woods, barking out my name. I was searching for a place to hide, heart ramming in my chest like an out-of-luck game animal, when Veronica stepped into my path. I woke up drenched in sweat. What was it about those men that bothered me so, and how in blazes did Veronica fit into the picture?

Even now, the fear still lingered.

I began with a brisk walk on the treadmill until confident enough to close my eyes and block out all other activity in the room. Minutes passed, and just as I was beginning to feel my dream-induced anxiety decrease, a raspy voice startled me out of my reverie.

"Who are you, my damned conscience come to life?"

I opened my eyes to seek out the speaker and nearly lost my footing.

Veronica stood at the treadmill next to mine, wearing shorts and a tank top that barely covered her flat belly. Didn't she ever get cold?

Though my mind remained clear, my body shut down as if it had taken a liver punch during a boxing match. Why was this woman, this replica of myself, acting like a bitchy Disney queen, and why was she directing her bitchiness at me?

"What are you hiding beneath those baggy pants?" she asked. "Hairy legs?"

I ignored her and continued my walk, though at a slower pace.

"My hair was blonde once," Veronica said. "But I didn't much care for the way it made me feel. Fortunately, it only took a little *L'Oréal Black Sapphire* to repair nature's mistake. Going black was easy." She stepped onto the rotating platform and went straight into a maximum-speed run—no panting, no heavy breathing. Who was she, Jane Fonda? "Couldn't do anything about the color of my eyes, though."

I sighed, hoping this strange one-sided conversation would end soon, but even before she'd worked up a sweat, Veronica continued, "You know, blue eyes can be traced back to a single mutation, in a single person, along the coast of the Black Sea."

The girl was missing a few screws in her head.

"So, how do you deal with your blondness, Marjorie?"

The question came so unexpectedly and sounded so ridiculous that I didn't respond. As far as the color of my hair and eyes was concerned, Mom was Dutch, Dad Italian. I took after Mom. Period.

"Cat got your tongue?" Veronica asked.

I was hallucinating, caught in a nightmare, looking into a fun house mirror. "How'd you know my name?"

"Morgan told me. Wonder what color he prefers."

Another comment that didn't warrant a reply.

"It's like looking in the mirror," Veronica said, "except you're so squeaky-clean. I'd have to ditch the losers I hang out with before I'd be taken for a nice girl."

Her mention of looking in a mirror brought back my father's words only weeks before he died. "Let the mirror broadcast the feelings you feel, my precious one. Let it help you look past the mask you hide behind."

I had all the signs of a dangerously high heart rate, thanks to Veronica rather than an intense workout: excessive sweating, shortness of breath, dizziness. "You consider Morgan a loser?"

"Oh no, not Morgan."

Comments about mistakes of nature and nice girls and losers? Why wasn't she addressing the important stuff, like how the exact same genes had combined in the exact same way at nearly the exact same time to produce two, nearly identical people? I mean, what were the chances?

"Okay, twin stranger," Veronica said. "Who do you think was adopted? You or me?"

Her question came like a slap—swift and with perfect aim.

"Well?" she said with amazing calm. You'd think the issue of adoption was no big deal, instead of a gut-wrenching topic that made me want to throw up. "We're identical," she said. "What are the chances we're not related?"

I hit the stop button on the treadmill console. "My mother's name is Truus. My father's name is Gerardo."

"Your *birth* parents?"

"Of course."

"You sure?" Her voice was pitched low, almost kind.

"Damn right, I'm sure." They would have told me otherwise.

Veronica presented me with a you've-been-had smile.

"I've got to go," I said, stepping off the treadmill platform.

I sensed her watching me as I picked up my bottled water and draped a towel around my neck. "I know you're curious," she said, "because I sure am."

I headed for the locker room on weak knees.

"I've already texted Pop," Veronica called after me. "If you don't get an answer, I'll clue you in on mine."

The steady stream of water cascading over my body helped soothe the big ache inside. If Veronica was my sister, either my father and mother had put one of their daughters up for adoption, or, just as hard to believe, they weren't my biological parents.

What could I hold on to? What was real?

Back at the Inn, I called my mother.

She answered after the first ring. "Marjorie, is that you?"

"Hi Mom."

"Thank God you called. I've been trying to reach you but keep getting a message that your cell number is no longer in service. I never got a chance to apologize for what happened at church."

I imagined her pacing the kitchen, wiping countertops, and rinsing stray glasses and cups. "Mom, I just met a woman who looks exactly like me."

An intake of breath from her end of the line.

"Her name is Veronica. Do you know her?"

"Oh my God, oh my God."

"Am I adopted?"

Silence, except for a mewling sound, like a kitten in distress.

"Mom?"

"I knew it would come out some day."

"Mom?"

"We'd been married for over five years and were desperate for a child. The doctors couldn't explain why I hadn't gotten pregnant. I'd tried ovulation prediction kits, conception kits, herbs, even Robitussin . . . Maybe I was just trying too hard."

So, here's where I should have expressed sympathy for the pain my mother was going through by telling her that I understood and how much I loved her, but I was too freaked out by what she was telling me to offer that kindness. Her over-protectiveness made sense to me now but understanding with the mind doesn't translate into understanding with the heart.

"We found a woman in Monterey," she said. "A midwife, who knew of a baby for sale."

For sale?

At my intake of breath, she paused. "Are you okay?"

"Yes." *No.* "Go on."

"The moment we saw you, we fell in love. Your eyes were such a startling blue, so full of love and trust."

Mirror, mirror, on the wall . . . "Am I a twin?"

"Yes."

"Then why didn't you adopt us both?"

"We would've jumped at the chance, but your sister had already been adopted by a couple on the East Coast. Maryland, I think."

Something about this wasn't right. A midwife, with babies for sale, who allowed the separation of twins? "Mom, were Veronica and I adopted *legally*?"

"From what I was told, your birth mother put Veronica up for adoption before she died and kept you."

Died?

"I don't know why you were put up for adoption later."

My birth mother was dead. I'd never get to know her, love her.

"Your mother must have had extended family willing to take you in."

I'd never get to know my birth family.

"Fortunately, you were too young to understand."

How convenient, an infant too young to question what was going on. But I had plenty of questions now, starting with, "Why didn't you tell me?"

"The midwife warned us to keep your adoption secret. If anyone found out that you were part Native American, you'd be taken away from us because of the Indian Child Welfare Act."

Native American? Jeez. Not Dutch? Not Italian? It felt like I was melting and re-solidifying into a person I didn't know. "But I have blonde hair and blue eyes."

"Exactly. You don't look a bit Indian. But the woman was firm about it. You're a descendant of intermarried Rumsen Costanoan and Esselen of the Mission San Carlos Borromeo, otherwise known as the Ohlone/Costanoan Esselen Nation."

Ohlone/Costanoan Esselen Nation? A uniting of Joshua and Margarita's tribes. No way. "Did she provide you with the identity of my birth parents?

"She only told us about your Native American ancestry and how important it was not to tell."

"Half? Quarter?"

"She didn't say, dear. Does it matter?"

Of course, it matters. "I can't believe Dad was party to this."

"He knew how much I wanted a child and that I'd make a good mother."

"You should have told me." *Damn it, you should have told me.*

"I know that now, and I'm sorry, but I couldn't risk losing you. Will you be okay?"

I wanted to reassure her but couldn't. "No."

I'd come to Carmel Valley to find myself; did this count? The puzzle pieces were scattered all over the place, and I had no idea how they fit together.

Through a haze of regret and self-pity, I ended our call, relieved that my mother hadn't noticed that I'd used the hotel landline, blocked by *67. I couldn't remember the last time I'd cried, but I was crying now.

Instead of calling Dr. Mendez, I followed my own counsel for a change by writing everything down in my journal, sentence after angry sentence, punctuated with question marks, dashes, and exclamation marks. To hell with interconnectedness. To hell with shifts in consciousness and parallel realities and holographic models of the universe. I hated what was happening here, what was happening to me. Bet Doctor Mendez would say I was getting exactly what I needed.

Chapter Seventeen

THE CONCERT AT THE WINERY WAS TONIGHT. I appreciated Marianne's invitation to attend, but didn't relish the thought of driving that long, lonely road back home after dark. The two men I had encountered during my first trip to Cachagua Valley still weighed on my mind, and I never wanted to cross their path again. I didn't ask myself what they had done to deserve this fierce aversion; I didn't need a reason. For once, I allowed my gut to tell me all I needed to know.

Fortunately, I found a more pleasant subject to dwell on, *Ben Mendoza*. According to Marianne, he was a descendant of the Esselen tribe and would therefore be familiar with its history—a history of even more interest to me now that I knew they were possibly my ancestors, too.

Time to give him a call.

The man who answered hesitated on hearing my voice. "Who's speaking, please?"

I told him my name and how I'd gotten his number.

At the mention of Marianne, his tone changed from a clipped pulling back to clipped politeness. "Sorry. You sounded familiar. What can I do for you?"

"I'd be interested in anything you can tell me about the Esselen and Rumsen Costanoan, especially a Rumsen Costanoan mission Indian named Margarita Maria Butron."

"Why the interest in Margarita?"

"I bought a mirror at an antique shop in the Village. Supposedly, it's over 200 years old and was a wedding gift to Margarita, which got me curious about her and her tribe."

"I know a bit of Margarita's history," Ben said, "but the person in charge of the Ohlone/Costanoan Esselen Nation's genealogy would be a better source. I'll look up her number and get back to you."

"That would be great, thanks."

I was about to hang up when he asked, "Can you ride?"

"A horse? Umm, yes, I did enough riding as a teen to stay on a horse's back without falling off."

"Then how about an equestrian intro to the Ventana Wilderness, homeland to the Esselen tribe?"

Marianne had told me that Ben provided guided trail rides when he wasn't busy on his family's cattle ranch, so I jumped at the chance. "When?"

"Today at noon."

"Where?"

"At the Ventana Ranch. The turn off is about seven miles down Tassajara Road. You can't miss the sign."

No problem; I'd passed Tassajara Road on the way back to the Inn, using Marianne's new and much improved directions. "How will I recognize you?"

"I drive a silver Dodge pickup."

"And I'll be in a green Jeep."

◢ ◢ ◢

The drive took longer and covered bumpier miles than I had anticipated, so I was relieved to spot the silver Dodge pickup parked in a clearing next to the road. A pickup that had been worked hard, judging by the mud splattered all over its backside and tires. It looked dependable, though, like the thirty-something man leaning against it.

Ben Mendoza was a big man. "Gentle Bear," I said to myself. The name fit. His black hair was long and straight and held back by a navy, bandana headband. He wore the practical trappings of this untamed country, jeans and well-worn cowboy boots; except in place of a denim shirt, he wore a black tee.

His rugged face was set in a smile. That is, until he neared my Jeep and got a good look at me. He halted and shook his head. "Is this your idea of a joke?"

Before I could do more than drop my jaw at his question, he said. "What'd you do to your hair?"

"Excuse me?"

He glanced heavenward and blew out his breath. "Might as well get out of the car, Veronica, and give your legs a stretch."

Veronica?

I gave him my brightest smile. "I'm Marjorie Veil. We talked on the phone."

His eyes widened.

"Veronica's my sister."

His expression settled somewhere between disbelief and guarded curiosity.

"We met for the first time yesterday, at the gym of all things," I said. "She doesn't like me much."

"Oh, I can imagine," Ben said, the corners of his lips edging up a bit.

"I assume you know her."

He said nothing, though his focused stare suggested unvoiced questions.

"I just found out we're twins and were separated at birth, which came as quite a shock, if you know what I mean." Emptiness ballooned in my chest, leaving little room for air. "I'd like to learn more about her . . ."

"Not from me, I'm afraid," Ben said. His chest expanded like Paul Bunyan as depicted in exaggerated cartoons, minus the blue ox and MacGregor tartan, of course. "Let's start over, so I get it right this time. Hello, I'm Ben Mendoza. People around here call me *Gentle Bear*. Nice to meet you . . . *Marjorie*."

"Nice to meet you, too," I said, all for second chances.

We headed for an old barn with tie stalls where two saddled horses stood waiting. Ben gathered up the reins of his mount and swung into the saddle. I approached the remaining horse with caution. It had been years since I'd ridden. No use in rushing things.

"She's a great trail horse," Ben said. "Calm and not easily spooked."

I ran my hand along the mare's golden neck and scratched beneath her white mane. "I've admired palominos since watching Roy Rogers and Trigger," I said.

The horse snorted and shook her head, then stretched her neck around and nuzzled my shoulder. "What's her name?"

"Blondie."

Of course.

I grabbed the saddle horn, put my foot into the stirrup, and pulled myself onboard, feeling the years slip away and my old confidence in the saddle return.

Ben's mount was more spirited. He tossed his head, signaling his eagerness to be off. His coat was predominantly white with a variety of chestnut colored patterns, his legs dark, and his head—also dark—splashed with bold, white markings. "What kind of horse is he?"

"An American Paint," Ben said, "descended from the horses brought here by the Spanish conquistadors. Native Americans revere this breed."

We rode from the yard in silence; and soon the silence turned into peace, as if we were on the edge of a new world, a world of ancient lands and untamed wilderness. As I took in the unfolding meadows and valleys of pine, I experienced a renewed appreciation for the sun, the wind, and the texture of the earth. Questions that had seemed so important to me only moments before dissolved like unremembered dreams.

To the right of the trail, I spotted a red-tailed hawk perched on a tree stump. Instead of taking off in flight as we drew nearer, the stocky bird remained still and perfect as a decoy.

"Why doesn't it fly off?" I asked.

"It knows we mean it no harm."

The hawk opened its hooked beak but made no sound. I reined in my horse and stared, never having been this close to a bird the size of a small dog.

Ben rode on, and I urged my mount forward, but not before taking a quick backwards glance. The hawk flew up and kited into the wind, wings spanning at least two feet on either side. Within seconds, it was flying overhead and circling back.

"I think the hawk's following us," I said.

"Possibly, but it's not the wildlife that should concern you as much as the smallest change in the landscape and weather, which can turn ugly in the blink of an eye."

The hawk flew in close with a raspy, steam-whistle scream, *Kree-eee-ar*. The rush of air created by its massive wings caused goose bumps to rise over my skin. I ducked out of instinct rather than fear, though a scene of attacking birds from a Hitchcock film did flash through my mind.

"When a hawk appears in your life and communicates with you, it may signify a warning," Ben said.

"Are you trying to scare me?"

"The hawk's warning shouldn't be taken as a negative sign, but as an opportunity to keep your eyes open and be aware."

"*Be* aware rather than *beware*. Okay, I get it."

In time, Ben halted, and when I reined my horse at his side, I saw something I'd never expected to see on this earth. Towering rocks plunged into a crater-like valley, and far below ran a river, only to end in a waterfall that, even at this distance, conveyed nature's power when allowed to follow its own true course. To further spotlight an already over-the-top display of nature's ability to impress, rays of light shimmered through blinding white clouds. And we were all alone to capture this miracle, two travelers on the planet peace.

"This is where the story begins," Ben said. Then he proceeded to tell me about the Esselen, the first inhabitants of the Santa Lucia Mountains, of their close ties to nature and their reverence for the spirit of this land. "They thrived in this rugged environment and were content."

Ben squinted at the sky. "I brought bottled water. Want some?"

"Yes, please." I tried to imagine my ancestors clustered near the doors of dome-shaped, thatched houses, arranged in wagon train fashion, around plaza-like clearings.

We dismounted, leaving the horses to feast on the grasses growing lush at our feet. Ben chose a smooth boulder as seating and continued his lesson. "The Esselen were healthy and free, rich in all that mattered. They didn't need to farm or labor ten hours a day. The women gathered food, cooked, and wove baskets, which sometimes took a year to create. The men hunted with bows and arrows they'd made themselves. All in all, they lived off the land and their simple system worked."

Until the missionaries came along, I said to myself, not wanting to destroy the moment or interrupt Ben's story. I took in my surroundings and realized that what I was seeing and touching had been seen and touched by the Esselen. Some may have sat on this very rock, which felt warm, as if alive. I imagined men talking and laughing while repairing their fishing nets, women grinding acorns, children playing hide-and-seek, and elders napping in the sun.

Ben went on to talk about the tribe's customs, their play, and their way of life. Occasionally, I'd ask a question, but mostly I listened, enjoying the sound of his voice and the stories he told. He talked about the Esselen ceremonies and about their creation story. He talked about the coyote, the hummingbird, the hawk, and the mouse. He talked about the earth, the sacred path, and the four directions, and how the Esselen had a profound understanding of the mysteries of life, the purpose of existence, and the forces of nature.

"If you want to visit some of their ancient ceremonial sites or check out their pictographs on boulders and in caves, there are tours available," he said. "Guides share tribal tales and songs and play drums around the campfire while you camp beneath the moon and the stars."

"That sounded like poetry, Ben."

"I've heard the tour promotions so many times, I've got them memorized. Let me know if you're interested and, even though it's the off season, I can arrange one for you."

I thought of Joshua. Camping beneath the moon and the stars would probably be right up his alley. "Could I bring a young friend?"

"Depends on your friend's age."

"Seven."

"Tour rule is seven or older. Is your friend from around here?"

"Yes, his name is Joshua Alameda."

"Alameda?" A smile crossed Ben's face. "Last I saw Joshua he was five years old and a regular chatterbox. It was tough him losing his parents the way he did. How's he doing?"

Just thinking about Joshua alone in his silent world curtailed my pleasure in our surroundings as effectively a velvet curtain drawn between my overly stimulated senses and an earth-shattering Broadway show. "He's under a doctor's care, but his progress has been slow."

"Poor kid," Ben said. "He's more than welcome to join the tour, but you might want to clear it with his doctor first. He was found wandering alone not far from here after the death of his parents, and he's bound to experience some traumatic memories."

"It's a miracle he survived," I said. "He experienced something beyond terrible."

Ben's eyes appeared suddenly moist. "Let's head back," he said. "I'm hungry."

"Me, too."

I was hungry, all right, but for something food wasn't about to satisfy.

Chapter Eighteen

T ALKING BECAME DIFFICULT as the trail narrowed and Ben and I rode single-file instead of side-by-side. But the ensuing silence gave me time to appreciate—if not understand—the calming effect this complete immersion in nature was having on me both physically and spiritually.

When the trail widened again, Ben reined his horse to a halt and crossed his hands on the horn of the saddle, signaling, to me at least, that he was open to a few questions from an inquiring mind.

I touched my heels to Blondie's flank and urged her forward until I reached his side. "Ben, what can you tell me about the Native American Medicine Wheel?"

His lips twitched. "Now what brought that on?"

Encouraged by what appeared to be amusement in his eyes, I said, "I'm seeing a psychologist, the same one who cares for Joshua. Actually, that's where Joshua and I met. In the waiting room of all things. Anyway, the doctor's name is Tony Mendez, and when I asked him about the framed illustration of the Medicine Wheel on his office wall, he told me very little."

Ben chuckled. "Tony's a friend of mine. He follows the four directions teachings and integrates them into his practice of transpersonal psychology. He probably figured you weren't ready."

"So, are you going to hold out on me, too?" I kept my tone light not wanting to reveal how eager I was for knowledge outside of the belief system that currently defined my spirituality. It felt like part of my mind was cracking open, maybe even my world.

"The indigenous people on the west coast didn't follow Medicine Wheel teachings," Ben said. "The sacred teachings of the Medicine Wheel originated with the plains native people."

"But the Plains and Esselen tribes must've shared some common spiritual principles and themes," I said in a voice that sounded like a plea. I longed for the type of spiritual healing and reaching of one's potential Dr. Mendez had hinted at in his office.

Ben's nod was barely perceptible. "Earth Medicine may not be the right path for you."

My mount sidestepped, tossed her head, and snorted. "Calm down, girl," I said, stroking the mare's neck, though I was referring to myself.

"I don't have the permission or training to be a spiritual leader," Ben said, "plus you won't know how to interpret the wheel teachings or apply them to your daily life."

"Maybe the parts I *could* interpret and apply to my life would help me broaden my world view."

Something flickered in Ben's eyes, which gave me the courage to press on. "Please. I'd really like to know."

He repositioned himself in the saddle and patted his horse. "I'll share with you the little that has been passed on to me. Stop me if I lose or bore you."

I nodded. *No chance of that.*

Ben's chest expanded and released, a sight I found comforting. Such a big man, so at ease with the world. "The Medicine Wheel symbolizes the great circle of life, with no beginning or end, always moving, always continuing, always teaching us new lessons and truths. Its teachings are about walking the earth peacefully, in harmony with nature, and seeking a healthy mind."

Ben glanced at me, apparently to see if I was following.

I was. In fact, I was hanging on to his every word, with an eagerness that would have been embarrassing if I hadn't been so focused on drawing out every bit of information he was willing to share before cutting me off.

"Different cultures interpret this tool in different ways," he said, "so the Medicine Wheel includes sacred symbols that cross many First Nation belief systems and are adapted to modern times. Because of this, the Medicine Wheel contains medicine more powerful than drugs."

Silence followed—a complete silence—no wind, no birds, nothing. Ben looked off into the distance, as if he'd forgotten my presence.

"Don't stop, please," I said.

He smiled, and I sensed his gentleness and felt a deep appreciation for what he was doing. *Thank you, Gentle Bear.*

"For the wheel's medicine to work," he said, "you need the faith, openness, and curiosity of a child. You have to believe that everything and anything is possible."

"I think I understand," I said. "So many things have happened to me lately that I can no longer dismiss as coincidence."

"Things will happen on your path to self-discovery that may seem coincidental, but in fact happen for a reason."

"I'm not an atheist, Ben, I believe in God."

Ben shook his head. "We're not talking about religion here. The Medicine Wheel and its teachings contain no dogma, only harmony and connection."

"A philosophy then?"

"Or a unique life science," he said.

"So, Earth Medicine doesn't necessarily conflict with my current beliefs?"

"That depends on what you mean by beliefs. The Great One created all."

The horses paused to graze on the wild grasses, moving forward every now and then for better pickings, which only added to the serenity of the ride. My gaze swept over the invigorating and aromatic terrain of white sage, chaparral, and oaks. "I'm only part Native American."

"This isn't about genetics, but choices."

The talk of truth and faith combined with the sun seeping through my jacket caused my defenses to melt away, and I found myself saying, "I've been hearing voices, Ben, coming out of nowhere."

"Then your time has arrived," he said.

"So, you believe that I'm hearing something—someone?"

"Possibly one or more Spirit Keepers are revealing themselves to you. They often appear in visions or dreams."

I thought of my vision of Joshua and the fire and wondered if I'd been led here for a reason. All seemed so unreal.

"Today men and women alike want scientific proof of the spiritual," Ben said. Which about summed up my attitude until lately. "The key to the spiritual is faith, common to all religions and philosophies"

"Will you help me?" I asked.

"Of course, but, more importantly, you need to help yourself."

"How?"

"I can introduce you to the Medicine Wheel, but it'll be up to you to discover something of value in its teachings, a clue, a direction, a path."

"When can we start?"

Ben's brows furrowed in a way that signaled for me to slow down as effectively as would a yellow light at an intersection. "This isn't a quick fix, Marjorie. No two people walk the same path to spiritual truth."

I tapped my internal brakes like the rule-following citizen I'd been trained to be, though my gut impulse was to do just the opposite—run the light while there was still time. I'd been holding back and proceeding with caution for so many years that it felt like I was now only beginning to live. "Do you think I'm ready?"

"Maybe your power has been transferred into the hands of others for too long. You might need to head out on your own for a while and find your own power."

"Then we're right back where we started," I said.

"Not quite. You're making room for the spiritual."

"What if I don't discover what I need to know before I leave?" I

110

asked, thinking, *time's a wasting; I need to get on with it.*

"You have the rest of your life."

◢ ◢ ◢

Over ham sandwiches and bottled water, I couldn't resist asking Ben a question that had been nagging me since we met. "What do you have against my sister?"

His body stiffened, and it took him a while to answer. "At times, she's bad medicine, but I sense good in her."

"Then you don't *dis*like her?"

Whatever he read on my face made his eyes narrow. "Watch out, Marjorie. She can be cruel. Her only soft spot seems to be for animals and children."

"She must know by now we're sisters. That should help."

"Or make her mad as hell," Ben said.

I hoped not. Veronica was possibly my only living blood relative.

"You said you're part Native American," Ben said. "How do you know?"

"My parents were told when they adopted me, though I wasn't let in on the news until after I'd run into Veronica and called my mother on it. Veronica said that blue eyes are the result of a genetic mutation, but she didn't say anything about being part Native American. I wonder if she knows."

Ben glanced at my hair and looked away. "It's rare, but not unheard of for Native Americans of mixed ancestry to have light coloring."

After a short silence filled only by horses snorting, birds calling, and wind rustling brush and trees, Ben said, "Marianne's hosting a western barbecue tonight at a winery close by. Care to go?"

"I'd love to, but I'm not too keen on driving an unfamiliar road after dark, especially after meeting two strangers at a nearby bar, who I'd prefer not to meet again."

"Why not go from here, and I'll follow you home? I can't promise that you won't run into those strangers, but with plenty of people around, including me, you'll be safe enough. Did you happen to catch their names?"

"I heard one call the other Tommy Boy."

Ben blew out his breath. "Then I know exactly who you're talking about. Tommy's sidekick is Jake. Veronica considers them friends."

"You've got to be kidding." No way could I see my exotic, larger-than-life sister associating with two guys who preferred brooding in dark bars to shaving or taking a bath.

"Can't say your sister has good taste in who she hangs out with."

"Will she be there tonight?"

"She wouldn't miss it for the world."

I looked down at my raggedy jeans and nylon jacket. "I'm dressed like a slob."

"Believe me, you'd rather be comfortable than fashionable," he said. "Unless" —the look he gave me made my face burn— "you're in competition with your sister. She gets all decked out for these affairs. Part of her mask, I assume. Anyway, she's got her eye on a new chap in town."

I wondered if Ben was jealous. If so, I felt sorry for him.

Chapter Nineteen

ON MY FIRST VISIT, I had considered this an odd place for a winery, and as I followed Ben's truck onto the grounds, I still thought so. Marianne had explained that the area's soil and climate were perfect for growing quality grapes, but I shivered at the memory of the narrow and lonely road I had navigated getting here.

As I drove my Jeep down the unpaved road, I admired the endless rows of grapevines running off into the rolling distance, bare, but neat and orderly like braided cornrows on a stylish head. Hybrid tea roses flanked the fields of grapes, all filled with shiny new growth. To my left, I spotted a pond with two weeping willows drooping over its edge, their slender, pliant branches lacing the landscape in light and shadow. Groups of people had gathered on an expanse of lawn nearby, set up with white-clothed picnic tables, red umbrellas, and a portable stage.

The winery barns on the hill above stood out like white paper cutouts against the darkening sky, and, even though clouds blocked the horizon, the vision of color and texture twilighting the hill and tree-studded horizon was nothing less than miraculous.

I quickly discovered that Ben was well known and well liked in the community. Many greeted him as *Gentle Bear*, others called him Ben. While he laughed and joked and introduced me to his friends, I tried not to cringe under their speculative stares.

"You're causing quite a stir," Ben said. "First, everyone thinks you're Veronica, gone blonde and they're surprised to see us together, since they've witnessed some explosive episodes between us.

Then, when I introduce you as Marjorie, they're blown away by the resemblance. This is going to be an interesting night."

✳ ✳ ✳

As the evening grew darker and the air cooler, I became increasingly grateful for Ben's advice about dressing for comfort rather than style. That is, until Veronica showed up. She wore a slinky halter-top and tight jeans, revealing all the curves that my jeans and jacket so effectively concealed. Her hair was shiny and full, her eyes made up to cat-eyed perfection.

And her escort was Morgan.

My insides twisted into a sailor's knot known for holding fast no matter how hard the strain. Ben nudged me, apparently no happier to see Morgan and Veronica together than I was. "There's the newcomer I told you about."

The band burst into, "Dream River," and I focused on the couples paired on the dance floor, willing my insides to do the job they were supposed to, rather than serve as my emotional radar. Ben accepted two stemless glasses of wine from a passing host and handed one to me. "A toast to our friendship," he said, tapping his glass to mine. "In spite of a bad start."

"To our friendship," I said, my voice thick with gratitude for this big, gentle man.

Veronica materialized at our side as if drawn by the ping of our glasses. "Hey white Indian. You move fast."

Though her white-Indian arrow had been directed at me, her attention was focused on Ben.

"Hello Veronica," I said.

"So, your mother confirmed it did she?"

"Yes. We're sisters." I wanted to pull my newfound sibling into a hug and make up for all the years we'd missed being together, but the chilling, non-glow of her eyes indicated that this wasn't the best in my trove of brilliant ideas.

Veronica zeroed the full force of her cobalt gaze on Ben and ran

114

her red-tipped finger along the crease next to his mouth with the audacity of an Odysseus siren. "Miss me?"

Ben straightened, grew taller, but said nothing.

Before I could process the undercurrents of this strange communication, someone touched the back of my arm. "What are *you* doing here?"

Blood rushed to my head, followed by a vision of my ex-fiancé with his shoulds and should nots and I-know-what's-best-for-you glares. I whipped around and thrust out a flat hand, anticipating— no welcoming—a confrontation with Cliff.

Instead, I met widened green eyes.

Morgan!

His simple question had created a powerful association in my mind—and triggered an explosion. *Calm down. Re-boot*, I told myself. *You've identified the trigger, now choose the response.*

Before I could attempt to explain, however, Veronica wedged between us. "Whoa, girl, someone's really done a number on you." Then she took Morgan's hand— "Dance with me, darling." —and led him away.

"Care to dance?" Ben asked. The invitation came as a surprise. Ben didn't strike me as a dancer. But even if awkwardness and complete lack of rhythm caused him to stomp on my toes, I'd be better off on the dance floor than standing there feeling sorry for myself.

Ben turned out to be an excellent dancer. The music, though not quite the "Honky Tonk Stomp," was too loud for conversation, which suited me just fine. I wasn't in the mood for talking, and apparently neither was he.

On the verge of spacing out to the Willie Nelson number, a prickling awareness brought me back to full alert. I scanned the perimeter of the dusky dance floor for the cause and caught sight of Jake and his sidekick, Tommy Boy, guzzling wine as though it were beer.

"Are you okay?" Ben asked.

"It's the two men from the bar. They give me the creeps."

He followed the direction of my gaze and frowned. "They can't do much harm in this crowd. Just stick with me."

The band chose that moment to announce an intermission and, darn, if we didn't run right smack into Veronica and Morgan. Bad break number two.

I looked away, embarrassed to meet Morgan's eyes and unwilling to endure another chilly reception from my sister.

"Can we talk?" Morgan asked—without touching me this time—as if approaching a skittish horse that might buck and run. At my nod, he escorted me past the umbrellas and picnic tables to a secluded spot near the pond. "What are you doing here?" he asked again.

I didn't answer, though now that I knew who was doing the asking, the words didn't send me into a tizzy fit or turn my mood sour.

"It isn't safe for you here," he said.

I almost laughed. Not safe? Escorted by Ben and surrounded by a crowd of maybe two hundred people.

"Is something wrong?" he asked.

I shook my head.

"Did you come here with Ben? I need to know that you'll be okay."

I knew Morgan wasn't Cliff, yet a list of what-ifs raced through my head, threatening to crush the feelings that had started to re-grow with such promise. Was it happening all over again? Would Morgan's concern for me turn into another form of suppression if I allowed him into my life? I dared not risk it. Not yet. Maybe never.

He frowned. "Marjorie?"

I had to say something but couldn't figure out what that something might be without sounding like a fool. How could I explain that I dreamed about being able to let down the walls I'd built up around myself and letting him in; about cradling my forehead in the curve of his shoulder, giving and receiving, but that the chance of building a successful relationship between us was doomed? At this point, anyway. It would mean giving up my search, my freedom. Not an option. "I thought you were headed out of town."

116

"I was. Still am," he said, treating me to a dimpled smile.

Okay, I would allow him his secrets, but I was entitled to mine. "Don't worry about me, Morgan."

Another smile, this time sheepish. "Can't help it."

I turned toward the strobe lights that pulsated above the stage and dance floor like the thoughts in my head. For too long, self-doubt had kept me paralyzed. I'd always taken the path of least resistance, allowing others to run my life. Well, it was time for a change. Time to set my own goals. And claim them. Starting tomorrow, I would concentrate on my number one priority, Joshua. According to Dr. Mendez, the child needed me and that's what mattered most right now. More than Morgan. More than me.

The *Voice* came as a whisper. *Do not be content with littleness. Love is not little.*

I shivered. "Goodnight, Morgan, and don't worry, Ben has offered to follow me home."

I started back for the populated area alone but didn't make it far before Tommy Boy stepped in front of me.

Bad break number three.

"Hey, you're the bitch from the bar. Damn, if you ain't the spitting image of Vonnie."

I barely heard him over the blood pumping in my ears. I barely saw him through the haze blinding my eyes. But I smelled him. Vinegar and rotten eggs. A regular compost heap. I tried to step around him, but he anticipated my move and blocked my path.

"Back off!" Morgan said from behind me.

The coward in me welcomed Morgan's interference. Yeah, the more commanding the better.

Tommy Boy backed off all right and quickly disappeared into the crowd.

"I thought you could take care of yourself," Morgan teased, which had me bristling all over again. If he hadn't hauled me off into a secluded spot, I wouldn't have been in a vulnerable position.

"Thanks for the rescue," I said before turning away again, this time heading for the only person who offered safe haven on this evening of bad breaks: Ben Mendoza.

Ignoring Veronica, who stood at Ben's side, I asked, "Could you escort me home?"

He glanced over my shoulder—at Morgan I assumed—and gave a slight nod. "Sure."

I turned to my sister, met her eye-to-eye. To hell with forever playing the wimp. "Just for the record, Sis, you look fantastic tonight, but it's getting cold, and I'm heading back. What you need is a warm coat."

Veronica's eyebrows rose and her mouth curved into a smile, but before she could formulate a comeback (which would probably have been a doozy), I took off my jacket and tossed it to her.

Then I locked arms with Ben and led him away.

When we were out of earshot, he said, "You and Veronica are most definitely sisters."

Chapter Twenty

IT WAS SUNDAY, APRIL FIRST, and I prayed that my plan wasn't a foolish one. Last night, I'd made up my mind to help Joshua. Becoming involved with the child had been the furthest thing from my mind when I'd first met him in Dr. Mendez's office only eleven days before, but so much had changed since then. It was time to ignore all the reasons for staying away from him, time to start thinking with my heart. And my heart told me I was doing the right thing.

Dr. Mendez had already gained approval with the group home for me to visit Joshua during his absence, so it took little coaxing to convince Mona to allow me to take the child to Mass at the Basilica and on a picnic afterwards.

My spirits lifted. A stepping forward rather than a retreat.

The phone rang. It was Morgan.

My newly lifted spirits dove back into the dry well inside of me. Could just the sound of his voice do that?

"I'm not sure what happened last night," he said.

I caught my reflection in the bathroom mirror, a sketch on white canvas—no contour, no color.

A sigh came from the other end of the line. "Guess I had no right butting into your business the way I did."

The pounding of my heart reminded me that I was still alive and well.

"You're upset," Morgan said.

It felt as if I were walking a slack line over Niagara Falls without a harness. My legs started to shake, and I leaned against the bathroom vanity for support. "I understand you're trying to be helpful, Morgan, but, really, I don't need a bodyguard. You've already got your hands full looking for your sister."

"Under normal circumstances, I wouldn't have questioned you like that," he said.

Normal circumstances? Nothing, no matter what the circumstances, gives one person the right to dictate to another. Nothing makes it okay. "I need a little time alone," I said.

"Do you really mean that?"

I didn't answer because I wasn't sure. I should have been, but I wasn't. I wanted to be understood as a person, a person trying to sever her dependence on systems and rules, someone trying to find her own voice.

"There are a few things I need to share with you," he said. "Give me a chance to explain, and I think you'll understand."

Let go. Take a chance, I told myself. After all, wasn't that what Dr. Mendez had encouraged me to do? "I'm meeting a friend for twelve o'clock Mass at the Basilica. Would you like to join us?"

Morgan didn't answer.

"He's seven years old," I said.

An intake of breath. "I'll be there."

✘ ✘ ✘

Joshua stood next to Mona in front of the Basilica. He was dressed for adventure in athletic shoes, jeans, and a hooded, fleece jacket, but he looked more like a brave little soldier than someone anticipating a good time.

No sooner had I reached Joshua's side than Mona greeted me and hurried away, her exit too quick for my taste. Shouldn't she have lingered a little longer, fussed a bit more? Sadness burned a trail from my throat to my belly. This kid needed the love of a mother, not the ministries of a caregiver. No wonder he appeared so . . . not sad, really, just not whole. I took his hand. "Come on sweetie. Let's go say 'Hi' to Jesus and Mary."

We dipped our fingers into the font of holy water and crossed ourselves before entering the sanctuary. We were early, so I took Joshua to the Belen Chapel to light a candle to Our Lady of Bethlehem and pray for his parents as he'd been doing last time we met. The icon of the Blessed Virgin Mary held the Christ-Child in her arms, and I wondered if seeing the loving bond between mother and child was what Joshua found so appealing.

After Joshua had finished praying, I led him up the tiled walkway to the front of the church, our footsteps sounding like drumbeats throughout the hallowed chamber. We genuflected and entered the third pew, where Joshua knelt, folded his hands on the edge of the wooden bench in front of him, and stared at the ornate altar with what appeared to be longing.

I heard footsteps, the lowering of kneelers, whispers, and coughs while the church filled with parishioners. And just as the organ launched into the entrance hymn and the priest and altar servers started up the center aisle, Morgan slipped into our pew. "Sorry, I'm late. It took some doing getting here."

Joshua leaned back and peered at him, then straightened and refocused on the altar, but not before I'd caught the look of curiosity that lit up his eyes.

During the organist's rendition of "Amazing Grace," I sensed a presence, as though my body had developed a second skin only inches from my own. Experience had taught me not to tense up or be afraid. I closed my eyes and let the presence speak.

The white men look at the statues . . . so stiff and cold, and the Padres imitate the statues, but my tribesmen and I fear them. We are captives . . . made to sit for hours, talking to their silent God. The Son is nailed to a cross. The Mother Mary is full of sorrow. Sad eyes are everywhere, looking up. I look up, too, but see nothing. Only the music vibrates with life. It enters my blood and flows through me. It makes the hours of prayer bearable, as long as I do not look at the statues. The organ moans, 'Why, why, why?' Through music, these people seek to understand. It helps them as nature helps me. It is the substitute . . . quite lovely in its own way. The composer must have come very close to God.

Whose thoughts was I hearing? The newly baptized mission Indian Margarita? But I didn't speak Costanoan or Spanish. How could I possibly understand what she was thinking?

Joshua touched my arm. Mass was over.

I took the child's hand and put the voice out of my mind.

"Joshua, this is Morgan," I said after we'd stepped outside the church and into the bright sunlight.

Morgan offered his hand. "Hello, Joshua."

They exchanged handshakes, but the child said nothing.

Morgan's eyes met mine, and with the uplift of brow and pursing of lips, he communicated that he knew something was wrong. "Do you two have plans for lunch?"

I nodded, thinking fast. Should I keep our excursion private or invite him to come along? Both prospects felt right, felt wrong. I flipped a coin in my head. *Heads.*

"We're picnicking at Garland Ranch Park. Care to join us?"

Morgan's eyes glinted like sunlight reflecting off emerald glass. "It's a great place for horseback riding."

His words appeared to lift Joshua from a state of lifelessness to full attention. His head jerked; his lips parted.

Morgan spotted the change in him. "Do you like to ride?"

Joshua nodded.

"How about today?"

He turned to me for an answer.

Horseback riding? What kid wouldn't jump at the chance? An outing on horseback would also provide the perfect opportunity for me to discover if he could handle a guided trail ride into the Ventana Wilderness. "Sounds good to me. What do you say, Joshua?"

His head bobbed up and down.

"I've got a picnic basket in the car," I said. "There should be plenty of food for the three of us."

"Perfect," Morgan said. "Mind if I drive?"

There he goes again, taking over. "Sure," I said, not about to ruin Joshua's day with another disagreement.

"Wait!" It was Mona with Gabriel in a pet basket. She covered the distance between us with a speed that left her panting. "I'm glad I caught you on time. The cat was getting fidgety, started tearing things apart."

I had missed my stray and reached for him, but Joshua beat me to it. With the speed and confidence of ownership, he claimed his pal.

Morgan watched the exchange, his expression thoughtful.

"I'll go get the picnic basket," I said.

What was it with me and the cat? You'd think I'd mothered him from birth the way he tugged at my heart. I sent out a silent message into the so-called collective consciousness. *I love you Gabriel. You're doing a good job.*

Morgan hoisted Joshua and Gabriel into the backseat of the pickup. My self-propelled hoist was more of a struggle, but at least, this time, I wasn't wearing a thigh-revealing dress to hinder my progress. Before he drove off, Morgan called a friend and arranged to have three horses delivered to the park. I silently wondered at his easy access to such resources after only a short stay in Carmel Valley, but kept the thought to myself. The diesel engine vibrated reassuringly, like the purr of a contented cat, and in less than fifteen minutes, we reached our destination: 4,500 acres of forest, chaparral, and grassland.

I slid out of the truck and turned to help Joshua do the same, but he had already managed on his own. Morgan retrieved a blanket from the back of the truck as if he'd known in advance that he'd be taking part in just such an occasion.

We picnicked in a clearing next to the Visitor Center, only a footbridge away from the parking lot, so Morgan could keep an eye out for his friend and the horses. No sooner had we finished our meal than a pickup truck pulling a gooseneck horse trailer entered the parking lot.

"That's Jeff with the horses," Morgan said. "I'll get them saddled."

I nodded, my attention focused on Joshua. He shifted from foot to foot, his gaze riveted on the horses about to be backed out of the trailer.

"I could use a little help, Josh," Morgan said. "Care to give me a hand?"

I'd never heard anyone call the child Josh before, so I held my breath and waited for his response.

If eyes are windows to the soul, Joshua's soul appeared suddenly joyful.

"Come on, cowboy," Morgan said, "the horses are waiting."

Chapter Twenty-one

MORGAN GAVE JOSHUA A BOOST onto a small, heavily muscled horse not much taller than a pony. The horn bag provided a perfect pouch for Gabriel, whose furry head stuck out comically like a papoose as he waited for the action to begin. I mounted my horse—a Quarter Horse by the looks of him—and tried to keep my expectations at bay, afraid to hope that Joshua would have the time of his life.

The high meadow grasses parted smoothly as we rode along the ascending park trail, giving us the appearance of ships floating on water. Each time we paused to take in the view, our mounts snorted, tossed their heads, and snatched bites of the wild grass, but all it took was a gentle tug on the reins and a nudge to their flanks with our heels to get them moving again.

We walked our horses single-file through sloping passes, thick stands of chaparral, maple-filled canyons, and dense oak woodlands. We rode across the willow-covered banks of the Carmel River and through the cottonwood-sycamore stands of an old floodplain. Sometimes the trails dipped steeply, and I worried about Joshua's safety, but he appeared confident and well in control, suggesting that he'd ridden many times before.

At junction points, where we halted side-by-side, Morgan pointed out reminders of Carmel Valley's past: Rumsien habitation sites, homestead remains, and livestock trails. Joshua followed Morgan's every word, his eyes radiating awareness and full participation, giving him the appearance of a normal, inquisitive seven-year-old.

Too bad, he didn't speak.

"It's like this land has been here forever," I said, when we reached Snively's Ridge with its view of the sweeping vista of Carmel Bay, Moss Landing, Santa Cruz, and Salinas. The air was cool and heavy with mossy fragrance, the landscape lush with wild flowers in rainbow colors and a quiet so soundless it seemed nature had put its volume on mute.

"Kind of puts things into perspective, doesn't it?" Morgan said, before turning his attention to Joshua. "What do you say, kiddo?"

Joshua smiled, but said nothing.

Morgan glanced at me and frowned. I could almost hear his unvoiced question: *What's wrong with him?* Instead, he said, "Time for a rest."

Although I was more than happy to sit on solid ground for a while, Joshua wiggled with restless energy and shifted from foot-to-foot, which, as far as I was concerned, was a good sign. Little boys were supposed to be fueled and ready for adventure. "Run along with Gabriel," I said. "But stay close."

After a quick smile in my direction, Joshua and the cat shot off like stray bullets.

My laugh sounded strange in this place of birdcalls and echoes.

Morgan sat next me, his forehead creased. "Why doesn't he talk?"

"He lost his parents over a year and a half ago in the Los Padres fire," I said, "and he hasn't spoken since."

"Poor kid. How old is he?"

"Seven."

"So young . . ." Morgan cleared his throat as if the emotional passageway between his head and heart had become blocked, making it hard for him to speak. Then he shifted his weight and changed the subject. "Remember I told you there were some things I needed to share?"

I nodded.

He stretched out on a patch of grass and closed his eyes. "Guess now's as good a time as any." His chest rose and fell while he geared up for his promised revelation. "As you know, my sister was a free-lance photographer, which means she traveled a lot. She stayed in one place just long enough to earn enough money to head off for another. She carried all she owned in her backpack, claiming she loved being light and free."

Light and free. Those two words alone gave me a sense of connection to Morgan's freelancing sister—no possessions, no obligations, no personal commitments.

"Then Teri met someone. She wasn't specific on the details, only that he was part Native American and lived in Carmel Valley. We don't know if they married. Teri is so anti-establishment and anti-authority she probably believed they were married in the eyes of God, which would have been enough for her.

"Anyway, I don't think Teri had a clue as to how much she was hurting our parents by not keeping in touch on a regular basis. She is hopeless at writing and claimed she couldn't afford long-distance phone calls. Mom offered to send her a cell phone with a pre-paid calling card, but she refused. Between work and her new friend, she was content and apparently didn't need anyone else.

"This went on for about five years. Then suddenly, all communication stopped. No letters, no phone calls, nothing. Mom nearly freaked out and wanted to hire a private investigator. Teri's last letter came from Carmel Valley and her boyfriend's ancestors apparently originated from there, so I asked Mom to hold off until I had a chance to do some investigating of my own. I've been here for a month now and have come across some promising leads."

"How can Teri have disappeared in a town the size of Carmel Valley?"

"Don't forget, Carmel Valley Road leads to the Ventana Wilderness, a 236,000-acre portion of the 1,750,000-acre Los Padres Forest, eighty-eight percent of which is public land."

"Where just about anything can happen and nobody would know," I said.

"Exactly."

"Which in a roundabout way leads to last night, I suppose."

"Yes. Besides pretending to be a photographer, I've been assisting as a guide, which has given me the opportunity to poke my nose into other people's business. By keeping my mouth shut and my camera focused, I've discovered some nasty goings-on in the Ventana wilderness. I can't go into detail right now but seeing you at the winery shook me up. I wanted you nowhere near what could be a dangerous situation."

"What about Veronica?" I asked.

"Veronica can take care of herself."

I closed my eyes, shook my head.

"Try to understand," Morgan said.

"Oh, I understand all right. You're trying to protect me. I'll give you that. But in the future, please remember, I'm a grown woman, level-headed to a fault."

His smile was kind, caring, and nearly impossible to resist. "I'll try to control that nasty urge to shield you from harm, but it won't be easy."

"I came to Carmel Valley to sort things out," I said, trying desperately not to cave in to Morgan's agenda—no matter how well intentioned—as I'd caved to Cliff's too many times to count, and nearly suffocated in the process. "Which no one can do for me, not even a caring man with a need to protect."

"How about your friend, Tony?" Morgan asked softly.

"Tony's my shrink."

Morgan's eyebrows rose and his lips curved in what appeared to be relief.

"Maybe, now, you'll understand that I have some personal issues to attend to," I said.

Gabriel sprang between us, and during the split second it took me to process that Joshua wasn't with him, my heart gave a massive leap and my breath locked in my throat. I took in our surroundings through a new lens—that of fear—and saw hundreds of fascinating hiding places and dangerous pitfalls for a seven-year-old on adventure.

The outlying area contained trees of endless personalities, able to fulfill the fantasies of any child on excursion, some with upright branches full of luscious green growth, others, dead or dying, with broken and leafless limbs pointing skeletal fingers in all directions. Chest-high brush grew between trees and around clearings. Had Joshua followed a tunnel into a secret place? I called his name, frightening birds into flight and startling hidden creatures into scurries for safety. All that had earlier calmed me now wrought uncertainty and dread. "Joooshua," I called between cupped hands. "Show us where you are."

Morgan touched my shoulder. "I'm sure he didn't go far. I wouldn't be surprised if he climbed one of the trees."

I scanned the tall grasses, searched behind bushes, circled oaks, maples, and redwoods, all the while calling the child's name. Morgan searched, too, but was quieter about it, hardly as bedraggled and panic-stricken as I. He was a country boy after all, knowing the way of the woods and what a child, free in such a place, might do.

The *Voice* said, *He is like the mighty oak, strong and secure.*

"If you're so smart and all-knowing," I said back, "tell me where Joshua is."

Silence. *Of course.*

"Over here," Morgan called.

He stood below a large oak with a branch leaning to the ground, a perfect ramp for a young boy about to start a climb. The cat sat on the reclined branch and stared at Morgan with eyes that appeared to say, *Now what?*

"Is he okay?" I called back, sprinting through the tall grass and uneven terrain like a wild animal instead of a klutzy human with a breakable neck.

"He's fine."

Although the sunlight streaming through the branches was blinding, I managed to spot a small figure halfway up the tree. "Oh God, oh God," I said, my breath coming in pants.

"How does it feel to love someone enough to break your heart?" Morgan said softly.

Without waiting for my response, he walked up the ramp and extended his hand. "Let's go."

"Go where?"

"Up the tree."

I eyed the ramp and the branches above. "I don't think so . . ."

"Come on. Do it for Joshua."

With a start, I realized how a mother must feel when protecting her child—strong enough to take on the world. Adrenaline pumped through me as I took his hand.

Morgan led me up the ramp and showed me how to use the tree's sturdy branches as a ladder. I grabbed the limb he stood on and pulled myself up, using the branch below as support. The branches were the size of elephant trunks and spaced closely together, making the ascent easy, even for a tenderfoot like me. "When I was Josh's age," Morgan said, "I climbed trees even taller than this one. Instead of worrying about the danger, I experienced freedom. Joshua may have found his spirit in this tree. You don't want to deprive him of that now, do you?"

Before I could answer, the *Voice* spoke again. *Like an otter, he's full of joy.*

Yes. Joshua was as joyful as an otter at play. Wasn't that exactly what I'd hoped to accomplish today, provide him with an opportunity to be as carefree as a normal child?

A cool breeze brushed through my hair and billowed inside my shirt, its caress nearly as intoxicating as the view. When I finally came face-to-face with Joshua, he grinned. I shook my head and grinned back. "You gave me quite a scare, buddy." I took in the area below us, giving my senses free rein, and suddenly, I didn't want to go down.

"This tree's perfect, Josh," Morgan said. "You sure know how to pick 'em. We'd better head on down though. Marjorie might slip and hurt herself. She's never climbed a tree before."

Joshua's face crinkled with what appeared to be a combination of disappointment and concern, which Morgan, to his credit, noticed. "We'll come back another time, Josh, I promise, but first I need a little help getting Marjorie back down. I'll lead, so I can catch her if she falls. You watch her from behind. What do you say, pal?"

Joshua nodded, his jaw firm.

I had to admit—grudgingly—that Morgan had done a good job in handling the situation. In him, Joshua had found a friend who not only understood his tree-climbing discovery, but had also joined in. Back on solid ground, Morgan and Joshua broke into smiles.

Gratitude for Joshua's safety had me softening toward Morgan, but darn, if he didn't turn and point to a weed. "Can you name that flower?"

"It's a weed, not a flower," I said.

"Flowers are weeds. Weeds are flowers. Do you know what it's called?"

I did but wasn't in a game-playing mood.

"A dandelion," Morgan said. "It flowers nearly nine months out of the year and then turns into a puffball of seeds. Did you ever pick one as a kid and blow its seeds into the wind?"

Of course, I had, but didn't say so.

He plucked the flower and held it to my nose as if it were a fragrant hothouse plant. "The dandelion represents the celestial bodies, the flower symbolizing the sun, the puffball the moon, and the seeds the stars."

No man I knew, except maybe my father, would even consider relegating such importance to something as insignificant as a weed.

"See how the flower head is made up of hundreds of ray flowers and how it looks like a pompom."

I took a closer look, realizing that Morgan had captured Joshua's attention with his dandelion lesson, which had probably been his intent all along. The game, and the dandelion, therefore took on new meaning.

"What color is it?" he asked. "And don't say yellow."

"Dandelion yellow," I said.

"What color are the leaves?"

"Grass green."

Morgan handed the flower to me and winked. "Every part of the dandelion is useful, for food, medicine, and as a dye for coloring."

I'd seen the weed growing along roadsides and in fields all my life but had never inspected one up close. I ran my finger over its smooth, moist surface, impressed in spite of myself. "The leaves have pointed lobes that shoot out like arrowheads stacked on top of one another," I said.

Morgan picked another dandelion, taproot and all. "See this dead leaf? It's a mixture of tumbleweed brown and burnt sienna."

I laughed. "Sounds like you memorized all the colors in a box of crayons."

"Of course. How else could I describe the assortment of colors out there? He turned to Joshua. "Isn't it good to hear Marjorie laugh?"

Joshua nodded, and then he, too, laughed. And with the laugh came a sound. I was certain Morgan heard it, but he continued talking to me as if he hadn't. "You've enjoyed the company of educated and sophisticated people but have missed the closeness of nature. Today you've had a chance to look around."

I was too absorbed in Joshua and the sound he'd just made to process Morgan's message.

"Are you happy, Marjorie?"

"I'm no Pollyanna, if that's what you mean."

"I'm not asking you to deny reality, just to acknowledge the wonder of nature all around you. Hey, Josh. Does Marjorie need to spend more time climbing trees?"

Again, the child nodded.

"That's not fair, Morgan. He'd agree to anything you say."

"Fair? I'd break all the rules of fairness," Morgan said with stone-faced intensity, "if that meant making you happy."

Chapter Twenty-two

NEXT MORNING, thinking back over the picnic, I realized that Morgan could seriously block my path to freedom. It would be too easy to let him take charge of my life and too easy to put my future and my chance for fulfillment into his capable hands. But then where would I be? Would I end up resenting him as I had resented Cliff? I couldn't do this to Morgan. Or to myself. Fortunately, I still had the power to prevent this from happening.

Since Joshua was in my life to stay, I renewed my vow to help him. And my gut told me, that a horse ride into the Ventana Wilderness of Los Padres National Forest would provide the perfect opportunity for him to escape the group home for a while. Maybe even have some fun.

However, if Dr. Mendez didn't agree, the plan would be off. I was too new at this trust-your-gut thinking to push my inner wisdom too far.

I phoned Ben to check if such a trip were even possible.

"My friend Pete is an excellent guide and wouldn't turn down a few extra bucks," Ben said, "though it's the off season. I'll check with him and get back to you."

I had barely put down the phone, when Ben returned my call. "How does Saturday through Thursday sound?"

"This coming week?" The man sure worked fast.

"Yep."

"I'll call Dr. Mendez, and if he has no objections, we're on."

"Okay, let me know if it's a go, and I'll set things up."

Before closing the call, I asked, "When can you introduce me to the Medicine Wheel?"

"Tomorrow would work," he said, "but it'll have to be early. I have appointments later in the day."

"What time?"

"Seven."

"Where?"

"Meet me at Los Padres Dam off Cachagua Road. There's parking at the trailhead."

"I'll be there!"

I called Dr. Mendez to share my plan, only to be met by silence.

"Do you think it's a bad idea?" I asked.

He sighed in a way that filled me with doubt. "To bring back his speech, Joshua may need to return to the scene of the fire that so tragically took his parents. His traumatic memories need to be unearthed and dealt with or they may haunt him for years."

My hope had been that a guided tour into the Ventana Wilderness would be therapeutic for the child, but in a pleasurable way. What the doctor was suggesting sounded scary, even dangerous.

"I will need to accompany you on the first leg of the journey to observe how Joshua adjusts to the change in environment and also to continue his meditation and breathwork if necessary."

Regret swept over me. I should have known better than to stick my nose into the child's business. He needed the help of professionals, not do-gooders like me. "You're teaching him how to breathe?"

"The conscious control of breathing helps bring to the surface unfinished traumatic issues that need addressing. Joshua's inability or unwillingness to speak is a crisis of personal transformation. We need to support his silence and recognize it as a form of self-healing, rather than treat it as an illness."

"So, you use breathing as a form of meditation?"

"Transformational breathing facilitates the natural healing process. It also leads to the experience of liberation on many levels."

Natural healing and liberation. Right up my alley. Anyway, I couldn't back down now. "So, you're coming, too?"

"I will need to clear my calendar first."

This time, I sighed. The responsibility of taking Joshua on such a tour on my own would have been a huge one. Now, I wouldn't have to face it alone.

"For some reason, Joshua has chosen you as his special guide," Dr. Mendez said, "and your ring as his instrument of power."

"Jeez," I said.

"With the support of people who care about him, the tour could offer a safe place for him to look deeply into his process and find what he's lacking. I will pick Joshua up at the group home and meet you at the Inn around eight Saturday morning."

"Okay," I said. "And I'll drive us from there."

Phone still in hand, I made another call, to the genealogist Ben had directed me to. Her name was Heather Garcia, but I didn't make the connection until I heard her voice.

"Carmel Valley Inn, Heather speaking."

"Heather? This is Marjorie."

"Hey, what's up?"

"Ben Mendoza gave me your number. He said you studied genealogy."

"Genealogy is, like, my hobby," was her upbeat reply.

"Can we talk?"

"Sure. Meet me in the dining room in ten minutes flat."

N N N

Over continental breakfast, Heather shared what she knew about genealogy, which happened to be a lot. Her initial interest had started while researching her own family tree in an attempt to prove that the members of her tribe were indeed descendants of the Esselen, one of the least populous of California Indian tribes and now believed to be extinct. Like Ben, she was of the Ohlone/Costanoan Esselen Nation.

When I mentioned my interest in Margarita Butron, Heather asked, "Which one, the original or the one born in the 1900's, five generations later?"

"The original," I said, noticing the rapid display of emotions on Heather's face. This bubbly woman, with her mass of chestnut curls, didn't fit my idea of a genealogist. She looked more like a high school cheerleader, her hands as expressive as pompoms.

"My mother and I are descendants of Margarita's," Heather said, ignoring the buttered croissants and rapidly cooling coffee in front of her, "which includes hundreds. Plus, we're discovering more each day. How a couple with only two sons ended up with such a huge family tree is a mystery to me."

Unlike Heather, I found it impossible to ignore the fresh fruit and pastries assorted like artwork at the center of the table. Between bites of blueberry streusel, sips of dark roasted coffee, and Heather's enthusiastic revelations, I wondered about my own ancestry. Heck, I wasn't even privy to the identity of my natural parents, let alone any distant aunts, uncles, or cousins.

At least you have your sister.

It was the *Voice* again, raising the hair on my arms, along with questions in my head. I had always sensed something missing in my life, but a sister like Veronica? Not in my wildest dreams. Then again, I never dreamt I'd be hearing voices either.

"I'll download a generation chart of my mother's family genealogy," Heather said, "starting with Manuel and Margarita as generation two. The first generation originated with Manuel Butron's parents in Spain, but we'll leave that for later. As yet, I haven't been able to find out much about Margarita, other than that she was born in 1759 at a former Rumsen Costanoan settlement called Tukutnut, also known as Santa Teresa, about three miles upstream from the mouth of the Carmel River. She survived an Indian attack that killed her parents and arrived at the Carmel Mission a very sick girl. She was Christened and married at the mission in 1773 and died in 1815. I'll see what else I can find out."

I got up to refill my coffee and, on my return, told Heather about the mirror I'd purchased at the antique shop in the Village.

"If it belonged to Margarita, it was likely passed down through the generations five or six times before ending up with you," Heather said. "Of course, with so many family members in the mix, the likelihood of tracing a direct route between Margarita's ownership of the mirror and the antique shop will be like zero."

Heather's passion made me want to share my new find, so when she said, "I'd love to see the mirror," I was happy to oblige.

"If an ancestor of mine once owned it," she said, in a voice I equated with heart-felt, thirsty wishes, "I'd like to hold it in my hands. Would you mind?"

"Are you kidding?" I said. "Because of you I'm beginning to feel a connection to a family I never would've known. I just found out that I was orphaned as a newborn and that I'm part Native American and have a twin sister." My voice cracked on *twin sister*, so I expected an expression of pity on Heather's part, but her response was just the opposite.

"How exciting. Where does she live?"

"In Carmel Valley," I said, the words, *how exciting*, bouncing around in my head like an acoustic echo. "I met her by accident. It was a shock for us both."

Heather's eyes widened and she hit the side of her head with the palm of her hand. "No wonder you looked so familiar when I first met you. Does she have black hair by any chance? Like, duh! Excuse me if I seem a bit overexcited. Things get a little dull around here and you, oh my gosh, this is so . . . I'm sorry. Am I embarrassing you?"

I hadn't laughed in a while, not in this throaty way. "Heavens no. Actually, you're helping me see the situation from an entirely different perspective."

"Um, clue me in if you make any new discoveries," Heather said. "Cause if your family is of my tribe, I could be of some help." She paused, blew out a breath. "Guess you can see I eat stuff like this up.

I get so excited when I stumble across a mystery. Your story should keep me going for a while. Wake up this town!"

Without realizing it, my friend had made me feel grateful for what I had and who I was. And she wasn't done. "In 1870, a couple of ancestors of mine left their children as orphans because of harsh times. One of those orphans was also a twin and ended up marrying a farmer and having a big family of her own. Of course, this was before your time, but the story of your ancestors may be similar."

"I'd like to hear more about her," I said.

"When were you born?" Heather asked.

"July 8, 1973. At least from what I've been told."

Heather grabbed a napkin. "Do you have a pen?"

I dug one out of my purse and handed it to her.

"Okay, that gives me a starting point. Now, for the fun part, which I call the excavation, you know, all those hidden pieces of information ripe for discovery if someone bothers to do a little digging."

"Do you still want to check out the mirror?" I asked.

"What kind of question is that? Let me get Pop to relieve me."

"Cornelio's your father?"

"Yeah. He owns the place."

"You're lucky."

"I know. He's the greatest. It's been tough for him since Mom died. She passed when I was just a tot, a car accident at an intersection less than three miles from here. The other driver failed to yield to oncoming traffic while making a left turn and, just like that, she was gone. Dad's never gotten over it. He wanted a big family, you know, all nine yards. But all he got was me, which is actually a good thing, because his left side is now paralyzed due to a stroke and he's got expressive aphasia. Words don't come as easily as he'd like, although he does a darn good job of making his wants and needs known when he puts his mind to it. Anyway, that's why I'm still here instead of pursuing a career as a genealogist. Circumstances clipped my wings, if you know what I mean, but . . . Oh, listen to me, running off at the mouth. Sorry, I tend to do that when someone offers me a listening ear. So, where were we?"

"We were going to check out the mirror," I said.

"Okay," Heather said with a wave of her hand. "What other secrets have you been keeping under wraps when you could have been making my day?"

"I think Margarita has been communicating with me," I said, though I had planned to keep this information to myself.

"And you expect me to be shocked, right?"

"Well, yeah . . ."

"Hate to disappoint you, my dear, but I don't find that hard to believe."

"Why would a woman who lived over 200 years ago still be sticking around? And why mess with me?"

"You might be on the same wave-length, you know, sort of tuning into each other's thoughts. Maybe all those years ago, she experienced similar feelings to yours."

"But her problems were different from mine. How could we possibly have anything in common?"

"Okay, bear with me here," Heather said, "because this may sound kinda weird. What if in the world of the spirit, there's a universal language and a universal emotion that you both understand? Then again, maybe my theory sucks and you'll have to be satisfied with living the question."

Living the question? What a thought.

Chapter Twenty-three

HEATHER APPROACHED THE MIRROR propped against the wall of my room as if it were a priceless treasure exhibited in the National Museum of the American Indian at the Smithsonian. She knelt and stared at the thin, wavy glass that fooled the eye into seeing flaws where there were none and sensing beauty deep beneath the mirror's silvery surface. "Just think," she said in a whispery voice. "Margarita may have looked into this very same mirror."

"It could have been the first time she'd seen herself other than in pools of water," I said, wondering what she'd looked like. Had she worn her hair loose or had she braided it? Had she painted her face, tattooed and pierced her skin? Had her clothing been made of deerskin, tule grass, or woven rabbit fur?

Heather traced one of the pink garland-like ribbons carved into the oak frame with the tip of her finger. "Wish I had a picture of it."

"No problem," I said, grateful for the opportunity to share a piece of her ancestor's past. "Stay put while I grab my camera."

Shooting from her side, I was able to catch Heather's profile as she looked into the mirror plus her full reflection looking back.

"This ol' mirror has, like, a gray look to it," Heather said, "and it's kinda wavy, don't you think? See the ripples and bubbles in the glass and, like, all those tiny, blotchy spots around the edges? No offense, girl, but it makes me look kinda old."

It did appear as though an older version of Heather was looking back, but my guess was that it had more to do with the lack of lighting in the room than the age or oxidation of the mirror.

"Yeah, makes you look like a regular old crone," I said, taking another shot.

"Your turn," Heather said, reaching for the camera. "I'll take a picture from the same angle you took mine. Kinda weird, how I can get the side and the front of your face all in one frame."

I found my gaze drawn to the eye of the camera reflected in the mirror, thinking of the many cultures that believed a photograph, like a mirror, could steal one's soul.

"Okay, now, one of the mirror by itself," Heather said.

As I scooted out of the way, I focused on the mirror's tinted and mottled outer surface. The Mayans believed that mirrors opened portals into the Otherworld, allowing ancestors to pass through, and at that moment, I believed it.

"I'd better get back to work," Heather said with a note of regret in her usually cheerful voice.

I ejected the memory card from the camera, slipped it into the side pocket of my purse, and followed her out of the room.

◢ ◢ ◢

My pictures would be ready for pickup in an hour, which gave me the chance to expand my initial exploration of the Village. I peeked through shop windows and watched people go about their business until I caught sight of my sister entering a boutique across the street. Though it would be wiser to stay away, I caved to a greater need: that of discovering what made my sister tick. What was it about her, for instance, that drew the eye? What gave her such vitality, such pizzazz?

Veronica was sorting through a rack of designer fashions labeled *New Arrivals* when I walked in. She wore black leather pants, a leopard print top, and spiked ankle boots; but what set her apart and shouted *Wow!* was her red lambskin jacket. It was cropped and simply hung there, supple as silk, and, with Veronica's every move, its zebra print lining peeked out impressively. Like a classic Vegas showgirl, her image flashed glamorous, unattainable, and too big for this town.

"Hi, Veronica," I said, primed for battle.

She turned and, for an instant, the expression on her face appeared innocent, almost vulnerable.

"I saw you from across the street," I said, "and wondered if you'd like to join me for coffee? My treat."

She stared at me as though shocked at the very idea of accepting my invitation, before visibly drawing herself together. "Now why would *you* want to treat *me* to coffee?"

"Because you're my sister."

"So?"

"I don't know about you, but I could use a friend."

"Seems to me you've befriended the whole damn town. Haven't you heard? I'm bad news."

"You're my sister," I repeated, "and that makes you important to me."

Her face, like that of an airbrushed mannequin with secrets I wasn't privy to, suggested the joke was on me. "Marjorie dear, you have no idea what you're getting into."

"I'm inviting you out for coffee, not to move in with me," I said, poking at my sister's armor like a quixotic fool.

Leave me to my misfortune, I imagined her response.

Instead she laughed. "Your treat, right?"

✗ ✗ ✗

The coffee shop was only a few doors down and free of other patrons, which was a good thing, considering the open-mouthed stare of the teenage girl behind the counter.

"Don't mind her," Veronica said, her armor solidly in place. "I've got a nasty reputation around here."

"So what?"

"Oh, dear sister, when you learn more about me, you'll stay clear all right. But, in the meantime, I might as well enjoy your company."

The scent of freshly ground coffee, crisping croissants, cinnamon buns, and apple fritters made my taste buds tingle and my stomach churn. But they didn't detour me from my mission of *fighting windmills and sheep.* "So, what did your dad say?"

"Coffee, black," Veronica directed the barista, delegating me—and my question—to no more than an annoying fly she'd just as soon swat as listen to. Then she headed for an outdoor table with the possessive familiarity of someone who came here often.

I selected a vanilla latte and paid for our order.

On joining Veronica with our drinks, I repeated my question with stubborn determination. "What did your dad say?"

She smiled as one smiles at a dense underling. "That he loved me."

"Mom, too," I said.

"And?"

"I asked her why she hadn't adopted us both," I said, realizing that the conversation might run smoother if I allowed Veronica to take on the role of interrogator.

She snorted. "So, what's her version of the story?"

"That you'd already been adopted." I didn't share the rest of what my mother had said—that our birth mother had put Veronica up for adoption *before* she died—though, considering the snotty way my sister was acting, she deserved a vengeful slap in the face.

Veronica shot me a look that sent prickles down my already tingling spine. So much for allowing her to take the lead.

"What else did your dad say?" I asked.

"Believe me, you don't want to know."

But I did want to know. I bit my lip to keep from pleading.

"You've got to trust me on this one," she said.

Trust my *Color Me Bold* sister? Not going to happen. "I'll find out sooner or later."

She smiled almost kindly. "You know what they say about curiosity."

Curiosity didn't begin to describe the urgency building up inside of me.

"I can tell by the sorry-assed look on your face that you haven't told me all you know, either," Veronica said.

Sorry-assed? I wasn't poking *her* armor. She was poking *mine.*

143

"Tell me about your dad," I said, desperate to discover what made us so different. Did life's circumstances override genetics to such an extent, or did we have traits in common, hidden behind makeup, clothing, gestures, and bravado?

"I'm not very happy with him right now," Veronica said, "and prefer not to dwell on him."

"You sound angry," I said.

"I am."

"How long have you felt this way?"

"A long time. Do you have any siblings?"

"One sister."

Veronica grinned. "Besides me?"

"No."

"What brought you to Carmel Valley?"

She'd gained the upper hand again, in what was turning into an odd conversation. "I'm on retreat."

Veronica tapped a perfectly manicured fingernail against the side of her mug. "How'd you meet Ben?"

I glanced at my own nails, short, unpolished, boring. "Marianne at the winery gave me his number when I asked her about the Ohlone/Costanoan Esselen."

"The Ohlone/Costanoan Esselen? Whatever for?"

"At first, I was interested because of a mirror I bought that supposedly belonged to a Margarita Butron back in 1773. She was Ohlone/Costanoan."

"You like old stuff, do you?"

"Not necessarily, but this mirror is special."

"Okay, so what else do you find so interesting about the Ohlone/Costanoan Esselen?"

"I found out that we were part Native American and that our mother was part Esselen and Rumsen Costanoan."

"Yeah, Pop told me," she said in a yawny voice. "Did you tell Ben?"

"Of course, though I don't look or feel Indian." I paused and took in Veronica's long black hair, how it hung loose about her face as I imagined Margarita's had when she was young. "At least, you've got the hair color right."

Veronica sipped her coffee, her hands steady, unlike mine, which were shaking as if I'd consumed too much caffeine.

"I think I heard Margarita speak," I said into the silence.

Veronica pulled in her breath mid swallow and began to cough as though choking.

I jumped out of my seat and patted her back, her lambskin jacket rippling like silk beneath my hand. "Are you okay?"

"You're hearing a voice, too?" she sputtered between hacking coughs.

"Yes, but—"

"Holy shit. We're both going crazy."

Veronica appeared sane to a fault, the very opposite of crazy. "We're just able to hear what others can't," I said.

Veronica pinned me with her cobalt gaze. "I think we're both losing our marbles."

"I took pictures of the mirror," I said. "I had prints made. Get yourself a refill. I'll be right back."

Without waiting for Veronica's response, I dashed down the street to the pharmacy and, in less than ten minutes, returned, a bit winded, but happy to see that Veronica hadn't ditched me. I sorted through the photos with the agility of a poker dealer shuffling cards until I found one of Heather looking into the mirror and her muted reflection.

Veronica glanced at the photo and back at me. "So?"

"Here's another," I said. And then we both saw it at once. Where the reflection of my face should have been, was the fuzzy image of a stranger.

"Holy shit!" Veronica said. "How'd that old Indian gal get into the picture?"

My arms, neck, and scalp turned into a mass of gooseflesh. When Heather took that shot, my attention had been focused on the camera reflected in the mirror, but what the camera *saw* was not me. "The picture I took of Heather turned out okay," I said. "Her face is a bit gray and muted, but that's definitely her. I wonder what happened to mine."

"This is too weird for my taste," Veronica said, harshness replacing the former hollowness of her voice. "If I didn't know better, I'd say you had it photoshopped."

"Do you think it's Margarita? Maybe she's trying to tell us something."

"Don't include me in your paranormal adventure," Veronica said, pushing back her chair. "I said I was hearing a voice. I didn't say anything about Margarita."

"You've got to admit she plays a part. This picture is proof."

"Got to go," Veronica said, standing. "Nice visiting with you." She took a deep breath and grinned as if our shared time together and the resulting conversation had been no more than a joke. "Good luck with the ghost, kiddo."

She started to leave and then turned. "By the way, I'm not returning that deliciously warm and practical coat you lent me Saturday night. So here, take mine." She wiggled out of her lambskin jacket and tossed it to me before sauntering off as if nothing out of the ordinary had transpired.

Chapter Twenty-four

THE AIR WAS CHILLY and the sky overcast, hinting at showers, but for me the morning promised to blossom into a day of remarkable beauty. I appreciated the warmth of the coffee in my insulated mug as I waited in my Jeep for Ben to arrive. I also appreciated the extra padding provided by the thermals underneath my clothes and the wool socks on my feet.

Ben drove up a few minutes past seven and greeted me with arms spread wide as I slid from my Jeep. "Want to start with a lecture or a hike?"

My heart ached in sweet anticipation as though I were joining a dear friend for an evening of intriguing mentalism and sleight-of-hand miracles. "A hike, I guess."

"Okay. A hike it is, while you search for your personal marker stones."

I glanced at the blue-gray, silver-tipped clouds and inhaled the sage and pine-scented air. You'd think I was about to climb Mount Everest, the way my heart pounded and my temples throbbed. As we walked through the trailhead gate and followed the unpaved dam road, Morgan's words played in my head like unappreciated parental wisdom. "You've enjoyed the company of educated and sophisticated people but have missed the closeness of nature. Today you had the chance to look around."

I had liked sharing the closeness of nature with Morgan. A lot. As I liked Morgan a lot. But my mission in Carmel Valley did not include getting involved in a romantic relationship, not so soon after

Cliff. Open doors and wide-open spaces were what I needed, as Ben now offered in his generous, undemanding way. I wanted to laugh. I wanted to dance. This was crazy.

We passed stately, twisted oaks to a large open flat with forking side roads on our way to the reservoir above the dam. "Before you can construct your Medicine Wheel," Ben said, "you'll need five marker stones. Four about the same size, the fifth, larger."

"Okey-dokey," I said, straining like a puppy on a leash.

"But there's a catch," he said, holding back a smile. "You'll need a *yellow* stone for the *East*, a *red* stone for the *South*, a *black* stone for the *West*, and a *white* stone for the *North*. Plus, the larger stone for the *Center* has to be *green*."

Whoa. Hold it. I thought of the amount of time it would take to find five colored stones, considering the area through which we were walking alternated between shady forest and open chaparral. "That could take hours."

"You'll definitely need to do some hiking," Ben said as we reached the intersection between the Carmel River and Big Pine trails. We took a right and headed up a narrow hillside path and side canyon. The trail leveled and split again—left this time—and zig-zagged down a steep hillside to an attractive campsite in a creek side meadow. We'd traveled a good three miles and I was ready for a break. However, Ben walked on.

I studied my surroundings with the caution of a city girl accustomed to pavement and street signs. The trails, at least the few I detected at this point, were unmaintained and overgrown. They rambled in no set direction, except maybe the path of least resistance. I saw signs of a fire in a mosaic of burned, less burned, and completely untouched areas. No surprise. Fires were frequent here. What did surprise me, though, were the green shoots sprouting out of the charred stumps of surviving parent trees, with woodpeckers and bluebirds nesting in their cavities and lush understory growing underneath. Pine, tanoak, twisted oak, and meadow. Where would I find five stones? "When do you want me back?"

"You can't pick just any rock," Ben cautioned, "even if it's the perfect size and color. Each rock has to draw you in some way."

"You're kidding, right?" I'd be lucky to find even one rock in this patchy post-fire terrain, let alone one that drew me in some mysterious way.

"When you find a stone you feel attracted to," Ben said, as if certain I understood and accepted that this stone-finding excursion was not a game, "put it into your left hand and tell it you want to use it for your Medicine Wheel. Then, wait to feel its consent."

Talking to stones? Waiting for their consent?

"Any questions?" Ben asked.

Yeah, what am I doing here? "I don't think so."

He tossed me a compass. "Keep track of the route you take and stay close to the trails, so you don't get lost or tangle with poison oak. I'll be back in three hours."

He was leaving me here? Alone? For three hours?

"Oh, and watch out for hitchhiking ticks," he said, before he headed back toward his truck.

I was alone, surrounded by trees, brush, poison oak, and ticks. *You asked for this,* I reminded myself, *so get going.*

A breeze whipped through the ponderosa pines and the scorched, fire-stiffened branches, causing them to sway as if waving me on.

I wandered through islands of tall grasses, rocky passes, shady forest, and open chaparral, scoping for mice, snakes, and ticks, and praying for stones. Each time I found what appeared to be a likely candidate—Igneous? Metamorphic? Sedimentary? —I tested it according to Ben's instructions and ended up with no stones at all. When I stopped to ground myself, I was amazed at how far I'd traveled. Just to be safe, I used a massive oak, as well as the compass, to keep myself oriented.

After what felt like hours of navigating paths through brush and deadfall, I finally found my first stone: white, almost transparent, smooth as a sparrow's egg. I held it in my left hand and whispered, "I

149

want to use you for my Medicine Wheel." At first, nothing happened. All I felt was frustration. The stone was perfect; I'd hate to put it back. Then the stone grew warm like a cherrystone heated in a microwave. I palmed my prize, pressed it to my lips, and when I spread my fingers for closer look, it appeared to glow from within. "I take that as your consent to represent North on my Medicine Wheel," I said before dropping it into my pouch next to the mouse totem.

Motivated now, I continued my search and could hardly believe my luck when I spotted a red stone. I thought of Morgan's box of crayons and decided to call it brick red. It wasn't smooth like the white stone. In fact, it looked more like a small turtle. I cupped it in my hand, expecting it to grow warm, but it remained cool. Just as I was about to toss it back and continue my search, the stone changed from brick red to red-violet to magenta and back to red. I rolled it in the palm of my hand while sunlight danced off its surface. "I consider this your consent," I said, and slipped it into my pouch.

An hour and a half left and I still needed three stones, but where would I find a yellow, a black, and a green? The sound of rushing water reminded me that rocks often congregated under flowing streams. Sure enough, when I came upon a shallow creek and tiptoed to its slumped, crumbling edge, I spotted a green stone similar to a small frog. I scooped it out of the water, and when I cupped it in my left hand, it pulsated along with the beat of my heart. Three down, two to go. Time for a rest.

Running water always calms me, but this site, grotto-like and hedged by dense ferns, exuded another kind of energy—something healing, something sacred, something flowing in a deeper dimension, as if a sensitive and protective spirit resided there.

This is where the earth plays. A powerful place. Too bad I can't stay.

A soft rustle alerted me to a doe and fawn emerging from the underbrush no more than six feet away. Unaware of my presence, they approached the creek with agile confidence. I adjusted my position for a better view, and a stream of pebbles cascaded from beneath me, sounding to my ears like gravel sliding from a dump truck.

The animals' heads shot up and froze, their eyes as unblinking as garden statuary. I held my breath, and, for a moment, they appeared to be holding theirs, too. Then in a quick, smooth motion, the doe shot back into the brush, and the fawn followed.

I didn't want to leave this place, but only had forty-five minutes left to find two more stones and make my way back to the Jeep. When I stood, I incited another avalanche of rocks. They formed a small pile at my feet, and on top, lay my yellow stone for the East, clear as topaz and brilliant as a diamond. *Consent or synchronicity?* I wondered, before settling on consent.

On my way back to the point of rendezvous, I canvassed my surroundings for my last stone—black for the West—with no success.

I sighted Ben leaning against my Jeep. He checked his watch. "What's the matter, three hours not enough?"

I shook my head, relieved to have found my way back, but disappointed at having failed my mission. "I only found four stones."

"Quite impressive," he said. "It took me weeks to find mine."

"Weeks? Why didn't you tell me?"

Ben's slow smile almost matched Morgan's with its heart-stopping intensity. Almost. "Show me what you've got."

The way I held up the stones in my cupped hand, you'd think they were precious gems found during a successful mining expedition. "This one's shaped like a frog, and this one looks like a turtle."

Ben nodded, straight-faced. "Could be significant."

"Really?"

"You'll have to wait and see," he said, reminding me of Morgan when he'd asked me to name the color of dandelions and experience the texture of their petal-like flowers. "What about the white one?"

"Actually, that's the first one I found. It gave off heat when I held it in my hand."

Ben gave a soft whistle before saying, "You'll have to wash your stones in water when you return to the Inn."

"Wash? Okay." How ridiculous finding and washing stones for a Medicine Wheel would sound to Cliff and my mother or, heaven forbid, my no-nonsense boss and technologically gifted friends. "Anything else?"

"You'll need four more stones for the outer circle of your Wheel."

I glanced back the way I'd come. Another three hours wouldn't be so bad, though I doubted Ben would be keen on waiting for me again. "Why didn't you tell me? I could've searched for them, too."

"The next four stones should be gemstones."

"Gemstones?" Who did he think I was, Christy Walton?

"They don't need to be *precious* gemstones."

"Oh goody," I said.

Ben smiled, apparently not the least bit bothered by my sarcastic tone. "The best stone for the *Northeast* is an *opal*."

I thought of the fire opal Joshua now wore on a chain around his neck.

"You'll also need *rose quartz*, *topaz*, and *obsidian*. Again, go for the stones you feel drawn to. Then wash them under cold, running water, put them into fresh water, and place them in sunlight for twenty-four hours to rid them of negative energies."

Negative energies, right. "Okay."

"Call me when you're ready, and we'll set up your Medicine Wheel."

"Thanks, Ben. I mean it. Thanks so much."

I was surprised, almost embarrassed, by the passion in my voice, though Ben seemed to take all in stride. "No problem."

"I'm a bit nervous about how my search here in Carmel Valley will end," I said.

"Every end is new beginning," he replied.

N N N

On my return to the Inn, I called Heather to let her know the photographs of the mirror were ready. I didn't mention the image of the Indian woman in the picture she'd taken of me. That would have to wait until we met face-to-face. Next, I told her about my search for marker stones, not bothering to curb the excitement in my voice.

Heather, of all people, would understand the importance of walking the wheel of life and mastering one's own destiny. When I told her I still needed a black and four semiprecious stones for my Medicine Wheel, she mentioned several places in Carmel that likely stocked what I needed and then offered to serve as my guide the next morning. "First stop will be breakfast at The Tuck Box, to fuel up for our adventure."

That taken care of, I washed my stones in water and patted them dry.

Chapter Twenty-five

HEATHER DIRECTED ME TO A LOT with free parking at Vista Lobos on 3rd Street, between Torres and Junipero. It fronted a small park with views of Point Lobos State Reserve, allegedly the inspiration for Robert Louis Stevenson's *Treasure Island*. The warm, sunny morning was ideal for walking along the elegant and quirky streets of Carmel-by-the-Sea. We strolled down Junipero to Ocean in no particular hurry to reach The Tuck Box, two and a half blocks away. I'd read somewhere that one needed a permit to wear high heels around here, which made perfect sense, considering all of the cobblestone paths and walkways that skirted the properties lacking street addresses and worth millions.

We wandered through Devendorf Park—an open grassy area with benches, shade trees, and a statue of Fr. Junipero Serra—then skirted Wishart's Bakery, the smell of coffee and something hot, buttery, and cinnamony clinging to its exterior like perfume.

The Tuck Box English Tea Room was Hansel and Gretel cute, with its fairy-tale walls of adobe and stone, leaded glass windows, and red and white striped awnings.

"Hugh Comstock had a unique architectural style," Heather said, pointing out the restaurant's fanciful chimney and swooping faux thatched roof. "Not to my taste, but I understand the attraction."

We took a booth next to a bay window facing the street, and after making our menu selections—olallieberry scones and tea for me and omelet, toast, and milk for Heather—I took the photos of the mirror from the envelop in my purse.

"What's wrong?" Heather asked, with the keen eye of someone prone to listening and observing.

I slid the pictures across the table. "See for yourself."

"Uh oh, you're, like, making me nervous."

She studied the top photo like an aesthete looking for hidden images. "It's pretty cool the way this shot captures the mirror's details." She paused and looked at me, her head angled, her eyes probing. "Hey there, girl, looks like you're about to come apart at the seams."

I shook my head and waited.

She laid the photos out like a 5-card spread in a Taro reading, and then her upbeat expression turned into a frown. "Did you, like, have this one altered?"

Again, I shook my head.

"Okay, so that's you looking into the mirror, but . . . Who's that looking back? No way, oh my God, do you think it's . . . Oh my God, oh my God."

Yep, I mouthed, as the server brought our food.

"Marjorie, like, you now have proof that Margarita's trying to communicate with you," Heather whispered once the server was out of earshot.

"It wouldn't be hard to fake a picture like this," I said.

"But you didn't."

"No reason to, but who'd believe me? Thank goodness I finally have a witness to the strange things going on in my life."

Breakfast forgotten, appetite gone, I asked, "Remember how I told you about my twin?"

"How could I forget?"

"Well, she's been hearing a voice, too."

"What does the voice say to her?"

"My sister isn't much into sharing."

Heather drummed her fingers on the table. "There's got to be a connection between the voices you two are hearing and this picture."

"I was hearing a voice before coming to Carmel Valley and

155

before buying the mirror, but the second voice, the one I think might be Margarita Butron, isn't the same. Different voice. Different message. The original talks to me directly, the second one does not."

"Whatever, I'm excited to be part of it and all," Heather said.

I gathered up the pictures and handed them to her. "These are for you. I had extras made."

She pressed them to her breast. "Ooh, thanks."

"If only I had a picture of Margarita's gravesite."

"Word is, she's buried at the Carmel Mission," Heather said before taking a swallow of milk. "Let's stop by on the way back to the Inn."

I grinned. "We've hardly touched our breakfast."

"Oh." Heather gulped down the rest of her milk and held up her glass. All that was missing was the "Got Milk?" mustache.

I wrapped my scone in a paper napkin and slipped it into my purse as the server arrived with our bill.

"Won't taste the same once you get it back to your room," she said, "especially without the whipped cream and preserves."

"Yeah," I said, without regret. Our visit to The Tuck Box had been worth it, if for no other reason than for the pleasure of sitting in a storybook house straight out of my dreams. "Time to do some shopping."

Heather led me to a jewelry store on Ocean Street between San Carlos and Dolores at a pace that had me panting. "Low key, no hype, been around for over twenty-five years. Welcome to paradise."

Display cases of estate and contemporary jewelry bordered the store and crisscrossed its interior, up-lit and spotlighted with *buy me* sparkle, but nowhere did I see loose stones. A man who appeared to be in his late sixties approached after allowing us enough time to look our fill. "May I help you?" He had a glint of inspiration in his eyes, as if he'd just gotten up from a work in progress.

I told him what I was looking for and he led us to a workroom in the back of the store. Precious and semi-precious stones, as well as gold, silver, and platinum, glimmered in surprising disarray, alongside molds and jewelry parts with names unknown.

"We create most of the pieces sold here," the man said, "so we always have an assortment of stones on hand. Where would you like to begin?"

I asked for an opal and he brought out a sample tray for my inspection. Opals, ranging in color from white to light gray, dull yellow, blue-gray, and black, took up one side of the velvet surface and orange and scarlet-hued opals took up the other.

"It's claimed by some that the opal improves the wearer's vision," he said. "There's a wide range in quality here, so the prices vary."

"I'm partial to the fire opal," I said.

He used mini prongs to select a fire opal similar to the one I'd given Joshua, though a bit larger. "The common opal doesn't have the opal's characteristic iridescence but is still quite attractive. This one has splashes of color more vibrant than the others."

I held the gemstone in the palm of my left hand and told it that I wanted to use it for my Medicine Wheel. Its fire and brilliance appealed to me, as did the warmth throbbing from within, which I accepted as its consent. "I'll take it."

"What else would you like to see?"

"Rose quartz, please."

"Healer of heartache," the jeweler said, bringing out a tray of milky pink stones. "Rose quartz is inexpensive, so you can choose one of significant size without breaking the bank."

Though I considered them all equally lovely, I selected one about the same size and shape as the fire opal I'd just chosen. As I waited for its consent, I tried to picture the stone lying on the flattened earth in the Northeast position of the wheel. It would have to be large enough not to disappear into the background.

"By the way, my name's Mike," the jeweler said. "I don't usually man the store, but today my two assistants called in with excuses."

"I'm Marjorie and my friend here is Heather," I said, eyeing his casual attire, which consisted of khakis and a checkered shirt instead of a suit and tie. "Are you one of the artists?"

"Yes and no. When I first opened the store twenty-five years ago,

I did all the artwork myself, but, over time, I found myself accomplishing less and less. As the saying goes, 'The spirit is willing, but the flesh is weak.' Are you interested in seeing any more stones?"

I held the opal to the light, and it flashed its consent. "Topaz, please."

"To heal physical and mental disorders," Mike said when he brought out the tray.

My attention locked onto a honey-yellow stone, so clear and brilliantly faceted that it didn't need up lighting or spotlighting to market its worth. I pointed out my choice, marveling at how gem cutters determine which of the stone's facets become visible and which do not. *Thought creates form.* "May I?"

"Of course," the jeweler said.

I picked up the stone with what Ben called my left, receiving hand and scanned over it with my right, giving hand. *Are you the right stone for the Southwest point of my Medicine Wheel?* I knew by now the importance of seeking inner guidance in making my choice. It wasn't so much the stone's answer I was waiting for, but its help in bringing into manifestation within me the characteristics it symbolized.

"It's okay," I said when I saw Mike's eyes narrow. "I know this one's going to cost me."

"You definitely know what you want," he said. "Anything else?"
If only that were true. "Obsidian, please."

"Ah, to repel negativity and aid in letting go of the past."

I nodded, though I knew next to nothing about the qualities of the gemstones I was choosing. According to Ben, I needed to select from among the recommended stones by following my gut rather than concerning myself with the stones' so-called powers.

"I don't carry obsidian, I'm afraid," Mike said.

Heather hadn't spoken during the stone-selecting process and her eyes appeared as sightless as those of Fr. Serra's statue in Devendorf Park. "Are you okay?" I asked.

"Semi-precious stones for a Medicine Wheel," she said, rubbing her forehead with the fingers of both hands. "Wow. That kinda discourages us poor folk from giving it a try."

"I'm just being extravagant. The five marker stones for setting up your basic Medicine Wheel are simply rocks and don't cost a dime."

"Phew, that's a relief."

After I'd paid for my purchase, Mike escorted us to the door with the courtesy of a porter at a luxury high rise. "I've worked with gems and precious stones most my life and have become aware of their medicinal properties. They're truly gifts from our Mother Earth."

Well-dressed locals and tourists walked up and down the streets at a casual pace, apparently as enchanted as I was by this square mile of paradise. Fountains and flagstone paths; flowers and trees with lofty crowns; art galleries, secret gardens, and pubs. No wonder artists such as John Steinbeck, Robinson Jeffers, Jack London, Sinclair Lewis, and Ansel Adams had called it home.

Finding obsidian proved to be difficult. We learned a lot about its properties (how it's grounding and protective and used to clear away negative energies) but couldn't locate the stone.

"Did you happen to notice that the two markers you're still missing are both black?" Heather asked.

Her question hardly registered. My appetite was back. Small wonder, after our missed opportunity at breakfast. "Let's stop for lunch."

"No way, kiddo. Not until your mission here is accomplished."

We were back on Ocean Street near Devendorf Park. I eyed the benches with longing, but Heather tugged me into a science and nature store, which contained such an array of brain-teasing oddities that we could have spent hours caught under their spell.

I asked the clerk for obsidian, expecting another negative response. Instead, he said, "Sure, I've got one that's been collecting dust for as long as I've been working here, which has been a while, since I'm forced to supplement my career as an artist."

"Sold," I said.

Heather elbowed me. "You didn't even look at it. Each stone is supposed to be special, remember?"

"You heard the man." I handed him my credit card. "It's been collecting dust for a while, which translates into 'waiting for me.' Now, let's have lunch."

"But we still need a picture of Margarita's grave."

I felt like a recalcitrant student on a field trip. "Whose task is this anyway?"

"Sorry," Heather said, her upbeat tone belying her words. "I won't let you give up just because you're hungry."

N N N

"It doesn't feel right taking pictures of Margarita's grave," I said when we reached the mound of ivy under the pepper tree.

Heather pulled out a compact camera. "My take is that you're doing exactly what Margarita wants." She shot photos from at least four angles, and then said, "Look. There's something lodged in the bend of the tree."

Balancing on tiptoes, she reached past the ivy blanketing the gravesite and pried the object loose, "Ta-da," and held up a black stone, water-worn and bowling-ball-smooth.

I felt like a cat correcting itself midair. Something weird was going on here and all I could do was land on my feet and go along for the ride.

"I wonder what kind of stone it is," Heather said. "Let's go ask Mike."

N N N

"It's an Apache Tear," Mike said, "a translucent form of obsidian. It comforts grief, provides insight into distress, and removes self-limitations."

"Good job, Heather," I said, ignoring the synchronicity of finding the exact stone I had been looking for at what was purportedly Margarita's grave. "I really appreciate your help. I really do. But let's go eat."

On the way to Wishart's Bakery, Heather practically swelled with good cheer. "I'm having a ball today. How about you?"

In my experience, too much happiness, expressed too freely, usually leads to a fall, so I said nothing.

"Come on," Heather said. "You're practically trudging. Consider me a creative gift of providence. An *assister.*"

I punched her shoulder. "More like *a* sister."

Heather's eyes widened and her mouth gaped open, "Way to go, girl. You're actually playing. I knew I'd draw you out, given time."

"Word-play doesn't count."

"Turning words *insight out* counts in my book," Heather said.

I rolled my eyes. Insight out. Yeah. Let the party begin.

Chapter Twenty-six

FOLLOWING BEN'S INSTRUCTIONS, I washed my gemstones, put them into a glass of water, and set them in sunlight to rid them of negative energies. Next, I called Ben to share my shopping success. He listened patiently and, after I'd finished, asked what I was up to the following morning. At my admission that I was up to absolutely nothing, he offered to meet me at eight—same place as last time—and told me to bring my journal in addition to my marker stones.

"But my gemstones won't be thoroughly cleansed by then," I said.

"You won't need the gemstones for this part of the journey. Only the stones you found during your hike."

I felt out of control but didn't care. "Okay, I'll be there."

✗ ✗ ✗

I couldn't resist a smile when I saw Ben leaning against his mud-splattered truck. His casual manner contrasted sharply with that of the men I was acquainted with in Menlo Park. Try as I might, I couldn't picture any of them in this environment, nor would I trust a single one of them as my spiritual guide. Ben helped me appreciate rather than fear the gifts of nature and encouraged rather than ridiculed my quest for meaning. Most of my long-time acquaintances would be shaking their heads, looking up at the heavens, and saying, "Get real!"

"Did you bring your marker stones?" he asked.

"Sure did."

"How about your journal?"

"Yep."

"Good." He grabbed a small bag from the back of his truck. "Let's go."

As we followed a narrow trail that zigzagged and snaked, ascended and descended, Ben clued me in on the journey I was about to take. "Today, you'll experience the first of four paths of the Medicine Wheel. It can take months, years, even a lifetime, to complete them all." He stopped and studied my face in a way that brought no discomfort. "I want this clear from the start. The Medicine Wheel, as a mirror to your inner self, can't be explored in a rush. You need time to absorb the qualities each direction has to offer, which means you set your own pace."

I nodded, wondering if Ben meant to warn me that the walk could be disappointingly slow and that patience, which I often lacked, would be crucial.

Ben led me into a circular clearing, smooth as a pitcher's mound. Trees and shrubs blocked the wind and created a climate of seclusion, comfort, and safety. "The tasks I'm about to give you are meant to help you perceive, comprehend, and be more fully aware of your life purpose. Skip any of them and you'll miss out. Important lessons are learned in each direction, each building on the last."

"I'll do exactly what you tell me to," I said, and then caught my breath, remembering how very good I was at following other people's instructions. With this thought, came doubt. How could I believe, even for a minute, that performing a bunch of tasks in an outdoor circle would help me perceive, let alone comprehend, my life purpose?

"Don't expect too much right away," Ben said.

I looked at him bleakly, wanting to tell him that I expected nothing and that maybe I shouldn't be here and that this wasn't real. In the past, I mocked people attempting to find themselves in this way, calling them "Lost Souls" and "New-Agers." In my mother's youth, they were dubbed "Hippies" and "Flower Children." What made the search acceptable now, here in the woods with Ben? "What if nothing happens?"

"This isn't a test," Ben said. "If nothing else, appreciate the sense of being part of something mysterious, something that's hard to come by in our skeptical and technology-driven world."

"Is this a form of meditation?"

"The end result of the first path is for you to awaken."

"So, this is only the beginning?"

"The beginning and the end. Remember, the Medicine Wheel is a circle. On the other hand, if you're asking if this is the beginning of your walk, the answer is yes. Your first step will be in the direction of the East, the direction of far-sightedness, illumination, and clarity, where you'll observe through the eyes of the soul and seek a vision of your own true purpose. Now, show me your markers."

I lifted the stones from my pouch.

"When working in the easterly direction, you'll sit with your back to the East so you can *align* yourself with the flow of cosmic forces rather than *confront* them. Let's begin by putting your green stone in the center of your circle."

Go with the flow, I thought as I placed my green stone in the middle of my wheel.

"Now, put the yellow stone in the East."

I walked to the eastern point of my circle and put down my stone.

"No. Make the circle wider."

I moved my rock out a foot.

"Okay, now, put the black stone in the West, the white one in the North, and the red one in the South."

As I did so, he continued, "Each stone acts like a switch to trigger a response in you. Try to see your circle as the floor of an invisible dome and your directional stones as the outermost points of conduits running along that floor to the stone in the middle. Cosmic forces will flow along these invisible lines to the green stone in the center, which is also the center of your being. Ready?"

I nodded.

Ben brought out a stick, which, he explained, was made of sage, heather, and cedar, and stuck it into the ground. "Before you do any work with the Medicine Wheel, you'll need to perform a cleansing to get rid of negative energies and help open your inner ears. Do you know what I mean by inner ears?"

"Dr. Mendez talked about the ears that hear inner dialogue and can also experience special insights into other realms of existence."

"Which may include telepathic messages from unknown sources, as you've already discovered." Ben lit the stick and fanned it with a feather until it began to smoke. Then he directed the smoke toward me. "Don't worry, the smoke won't hurt you." He handed me the feather. "Keep fanning the smoke in your direction. Imagine it surrounding you and penetrating your body."

When I'd done as he had instructed, Ben said, "This is called smudging." He showed me how to smudge all the directions of my Medicine Wheel, including the above and below, then extinguished the stick, picked up the smudging tools, and handed them to me. "Yours for future cleansings." He smiled at my thoughtful expression. "Given time, you'll discover the presence of your higher self and the energies of the Great Mystery that surround and flow through you."

I tried to make room in my mind and heart for the mysterious energies he spoke of, and maybe in part, I succeeded, if the peace and contentment building inside were anything to go by.

"I jotted down what you need to do next," Ben said, "so I can get out of the way. You've got to be alone for your discoveries." He handed me a scrap of paper with some hand-written notes. "Follow these steps, then write whatever comes to you in your journal and move to the center of the wheel to rebalance yourself."

After Ben had disappeared into the scrub and trees, I read his notes. They directed me to take off my shoes and socks. I re-read the instructions, hoping I'd misunderstood. It was early yet—and cold. I shivered at the very thought of baring my feet.

However, I hadn't misread a word. Within minutes, the toes of my right foot were testing the ground. The sensation was pleasant, the earth warm and inviting.

With Ben's notes as my guide, I stood, faced east, and stretched out my arms. "Grandfather Sun, please guide me in my quest." I wondered if I should be sensing something besides an empty ache, then referred back to Ben's instructions. *Sit facing west.* I forced out all thoughts of failure. A link would be made.

Eventually, I fell into a meditative state.

My hometown of Menlo Park came to mind, the epicenter of the information age, a part of Silicon Valley, the brave new world in technological advances. Atomic scientists at Menlo Park's Stanford Linear Accelerator were able to dissect the tiniest particles of physical matter, yet they had no answers to the questions that were dearest to my heart and necessary for my sanity. Instead, here I sat, in the middle of nowhere, surrounded by trees, weeds, ticks, and poison oak—searching. Why couldn't I find wholeness in my hometown? Why didn't I have power over my life?

My thoughts leaped to my computer and the energy and travel that took place when I connected to the Internet. A path would lead from my computer to a machine maintained by my Internet service provider, then leap to a computer connected to a regional network, then to a major backbone network. From there the path would step down until it reached the computer that hosted the information for which I was searching. And all this traveling would occur invisibly, and within seconds.

In my Medicine Wheel, I, too, was surrounded by invisible energy, with my brain serving as the computer terminal, my feet the ground, and my arms the antenna. My entire body was equipped with receptors to sense the ever-changing environment around me: the warmth of the sun, the texture of the earth, and the shifting hue of the sky. If this was possible, why wasn't it also possible for me to hear voices, or, for that matter, see spirits from another dimension?

Maybe, my recent experiences weren't abnormal after all. Maybe Dr. Mendez's concept of the universe as a hologram meant that we

166

might be living in something like a computer program, where the stuff we touched and felt was mostly empty space and that reality as we consciously experienced it was not real.

Maybe I was just breaking through.

From close behind me, I heard a song that battered me with raw emotion. The song broke into a long, painful wail, followed by silence—a silence that seemed appropriate somehow, as if all God's creatures felt and shared the pain. I made no effort to think. I was here to see, accept, and heal. Not to understand.

I visualized a gate leaning in desolation and partially covered by the twists and tangles of vegetation. It stood ajar—an open invitation to my seeking mind. I drew nearer. Scrolls of intertwined ironwork, depicting vines with clusters of grapes, adorned this once proud-standing gate. Two angels, supporting a wreath, knelt in the gate's center. Inside the wreath lay a lamb on an altar, above which hung a chipped and mildewed cross on a background of faded blue.

The gate beckoned, *Enter*, and in my dream state, I did just that. A faint difference in the height of vegetation indicated where a path had once led. A path meant a destination, possibly a new discovery. My usual blinders dissolved and my mind experienced a new sense of freedom. If this spelled danger, so be it. Fear could no longer restrain me.

A statue blocked my path—one I'd seen before. The one in the architectural antique store that had reminded me of St. Peter, with his cloak wrapped furtively around him. Before I could explore further, the vision disappeared. I opened my eyes, grabbed my journal and pen, and began to write.

Words flow like blood from a fresh wound, but instead of resulting in weakness, new strength grows inside of me, making room for hope. I try to go forward without fear, but my head is full of shadows. Only when doubt strikes, when the soul is exposed and laid bare, do the shadows make themselves known. Only then do I shiver and peer into the darkness and sense their eyes upon me.

I crawled to the center of the Medicine Wheel, stretched out on the earth, and rested my head on my arms.

Chapter Twenty-seven

SOMEONE SAID MY NAME. I opened my eyes. It was Ben. "Are you okay?" he asked.

"Yes, just a little disoriented."

"Do you need to sit for a while?"

"No, I'm fine."

But I did sit, with my head down and my eyes closed. I massaged my neck, took a deep breath. "Where'd you go?"

"Just beyond the trees. Didn't want to leave you alone."

When I indicated I was ready, he guided me up and supported me until I'd regained my balance, then gathered the stones and picked up my journal, notes, and pen. "Looks like you did some writing."

"Can't remember."

Ben slipped the notes into the journal and handed it to me.

I unzipped the pouch, dropped the stones inside. "What about the smudging tools?"

"I'll carry the rest," he said. "Let's go, I'm hungry."

"Ben . . ."

"First we eat. Then we talk."

By the time we reached our parked vehicles, I felt stronger. Ben grabbed a cooler from the back of his truck, and we sat on the tailgate. He pulled out sandwiches, chips, and bottled water. Then he offered me a pocket-sized antibacterial wipe to clean my hands.

I stared at him, drop-jawed. "Wow, Ben, you're amazing."

"Just a quick stop at our local bakery café for chicken sandwiches on broche buns with avocado and bacon," he said.

Silence took over as we dug into our meal.

"The journey never goes according to one's expectations," Ben said after I'd downed my sandwich like a starved teen. "Your path reveals itself slowly, so you need to explore it slowly."

"Out here each time?"

"You can set up your Medicine Wheel anywhere, but before you move on to the southern direction, I want you to explore the East some more. The East is where you put out your questions and wait for answers." Ben reached into his pocket and handed me a folded scrap of paper. "Writing is a manifestation of the East. Through writing, messages hidden deep inside come to the surface."

"I heard a woman crying," I said, "and I don't think it was Margarita. Any idea what that might mean?"

"It could mean that you unconsciously invited someone else's spirit into your sacred space, someone who may have died before she had a chance to go through the process of seeking, learning, and experiencing. You may be reaching for enlightenment together."

This all sounded as improbable as Dr. Mendez's talk about the holographic universe and collective consciousness, but the idea of linking to someone in need and helping out in some way brought a pleasant, warm sensation to my stomach and chest.

"Remember, this is only a guess and, even if correct, just part of the answer. Only time will tell."

"Or, I'll never know."

"A risk we all take." Ben dropped our empty water bottles and discarded lunch wrappings into the cooler. "We better head back. It looks like rain."

"I'll do my best to honor what you're teaching me," I said, after a quick glance at the notes Ben had given me.

"Couldn't ask for more," he said.

N N N

On my return to the Inn, I sat at the small wrought-iron table outside my room and read Ben's notes.

169

The East is the place of sunrise, where you awaken and start a new day. The sun symbolizes your inner light. In the East, this inner light can grow brilliant and strong enough to guide you on your intended path. Access to the light can give you the courage to extend your horizons and consider the big picture—possibly even understand how everything fits together.

Would the puzzle pieces fall into place during my stay here? Would my path become clear? I found this hard to believe. Sure, I had extended my horizons by coming to Carmel Valley, but only by such a wee bit.

In the East, the Great Spirit reveals Himself to you if you learn to look. His face appears everywhere and in everything, be it man, rock, or tree.

"Please let this be true," I whispered.

The element of the East is fire. Fire penetrates, purifies, and consumes.

True enough. I'd seen signs of fire's penetrating and purifying qualities in the Los Padres forest, the way it had cleared away underbrush and caused seeds lying dormant within the earth to burst forth into new life. But fire had also brought pain and death, making it not only creative, but also destructive, its physical form only possible by consuming something else.

Yellow is the color of the East and the color of sunlight, cheerful, inspiring, able to expand the mind's ability to understand. The season of the East is spring, when the earth awakens and new life bursts forth. Don't fear life. Rather, embrace the chaos.

The color yellow reminded me of the dandelion Morgan had so playfully pointed out to me. Only after inspecting the weed closely, had I realized the true value of his gift. He had opened my eyes to the ordinary. The message about not fearing life echoed Morgan's words: "There's so much in life to be enjoyed, Marjorie. You've been surrounded by educated and sophisticated people and removed from the closeness of nature."

I had so much to learn.

◢ ◢ ◢

Next morning, I gave in to the urge to call Morgan. In spite of my determination to keep him at a safe distance, I missed his voice, his smile.

"Hey, stranger, what's up?" he said.

Skipping the not-much-how-are-you, I plunged right in with a message that I knew he wouldn't like. "Dr. Mendez and I are taking Joshua on a horseback excursion into the Ventana Wilderness. Our tour leaves Saturday and comes back Thursday."

"Why are you telling me this?" he asked, his words clipped. "You know how I currently feel about that area and how I worry about your safety."

"And you should know by now that I can take care of myself."

"Since when do they conduct tours during the off season?"

"Ben arranged a private tour."

Morgan's sigh signaled that surrender did not come easily for him. "You won't let me stop you."

"Joshua and I need to take this trip and it has to be now."

"I won't ask how you know that."

"Good, because I couldn't give you a satisfying answer."

"What else can I say, besides have a safe trip?"

"Thanks, Morgan." I pressed my fist against the ache in my chest in hopes that the outside pressure would make it easier to breathe. "See you when we get back."

Why had I called him? Had I secretly hoped he'd stop me? Was I still that weak?

The phone rang. I wanted it to be Morgan, calling back to say that I was doing the right thing and had his full support, instead of suppressing my feelings, aspirations, and dreams with disapproving sighs. I wanted Morgan to love me unconditionally, not hold me accountable to his own paradigms and expectations to qualify for his affection.

As Cliff had.

"Marjorie, this is Heather. I think I found out who your mother was."

The ache in my chest gave way to weakness in my knees. I lowered myself onto the bed.

"I accessed eight generations of Margarita's genealogy, which, as I told you, is also my mother's genealogy. The year you were born, an Antonia Flores gave birth to twin girls and died soon after. There was no mention of a husband, so she probably wasn't married. If Antonia was your mother, guess what that means?"

"That Veronica and I are bastards?"

"No, silly, that we're family. Many times removed, but family. Just think. We could be passing relatives every day without knowing it."

Had my mother's name been Antonia? Was her voice the one I'd been hearing since Ash Wednesday? If so, that would explain why Veronica was hearing a voice, too. Oh God, I'd been ignoring the *Voice*. What if I'd been ignoring my mother?

"Where do we go from here?"

"I'll continue researching. That's, like, how I get my kicks, remember?"

I blew out my breath. "You're a good friend."

"Hey, girl, I could be wrong here. Right now, all's just theory."

"I started my journey on the Medicine Wheel," I said.

"I've always meant to, like, give it a try," Heather said. "I've heard you've got to, you know, want it very much."

The Medicine Wheel wasn't the path for everyone. In fact, a year ago I would have been horrified at the very thought of being out in the wilderness alone communing with nature. Before I started hearing the *Voice*, I'd been more or less conditioned to my world and would never have rocked the boat as I was doing now. Many of my acquaintances were happy and well-adjusted without venturing on such a journey. They were finding themselves and contacting the Great Spirit via more mainstream methods.

"You're reaching a higher level of understanding in your own special way, Heather."

"Thanks, my friend. Even so, I'm open if and when the time comes."

Chapter Twenty-eight

DARN IT, GABRIEL. How do you do it? My stray had hitched a ride again, this time on Joshua's lap. I eyed the cat through my rearview mirror and met his blank stare, then scolded myself for believing, even for a minute, that this innocent animal had the ability to outmaneuver me. It wasn't Gabriel's fault that we couldn't coax Joshua into the Jeep without him.

Heavy clouds dominated the skies, and branches of oak and pine swayed in the chilly breeze with the vigor of feather dusters. What if it rained? Would the trip be canceled? I couldn't bear the thought.

"If they cancel the trip and send us back, the world will not come to an end," Dr. Mendez said, reading my mood.

"This trip is important to Joshua," I said.

The doctor smiled.

"Okay, I'll amend that. It's also important to me." I searched my mind for the reason I felt so strongly about this excursion but couldn't come up with a reasonable answer. I just knew.

We had to go back to the scene of the Tassajara fire, and it had to be now.

"Some things are beyond your control," Dr. Mendez said. "I thought you had learned that by now."

I gripped the steering wheel, willing myself to relax.

As we continued down Tassajara Road, I took in the austere landscape: no road signs, no graffiti-tagged concrete barriers or overpasses, and no promiscuous American Apparel billboards overhead. Instead, an unpaved one-lane stretch of dirt, gravel, and rock, with blind curves and drop-dead descents over a non-existent shoulder.

"Living out here must be terribly inconvenient," I said.

"It has its compensations," Dr. Mendez said. "Just think. Here, people schedule their lives around the rising and setting of the sun. Clocks, with their constant reminders of minutes ticking away and their blaring alarms, are not intruders in their homes. Experience is literal rather than virtual. Life is not put on hold to be lived later."

"Have you been here before?"

"I was raised near here."

His revelation caught me by surprise. "Then how? I mean . . . What inspired you to go into psychology?"

He chuckled, likely accustomed to this question. "I was an avid reader and had a teacher who encouraged me. As I grew older, I not only wanted to understand the way of the red man, but of the white man as well. I counted on the world of psychology to help me find answers to many of my questions."

"And?"

"With every answer, came another question."

"Why doesn't that surprise me?" My thoughts continued to wander, encouraged by the isolation of our surroundings. "Why wouldn't you tell me about Earth Medicine?"

Dr. Mendez didn't answer right away. Typical. In the brief time I'd known him, he didn't come across as a man who favored quick comebacks. "Earth Medicine can't be explained. It must be experienced."

"So, does that mean you'll never share what you know?"

"You might see pictures advanced beyond your understanding, challenging your access to their meaning. Who will be your guide if you practice it alone?"

Ben, Gentle Bear, Mendoza, of course. "What if I never find my way?"

"Doubt will get you nowhere."

It seemed like I was forever applying my brakes to maneuver the hairpin turns on this primitive road without guardrails. Thank goodness for four-wheel drive. "Don't you ever get scared? I mean, what if you never find the answers?"

"Most fears are imaginary."

"Now, that's a thought," I said.

"Little things are teachers. Pay attention to Joshua. He is always learning in his quiet way. He watches, listens, and examines. The journey is never over."

"I don't want him hurt."

"There is no change without pain."

I didn't expect—or like—this answer and frowned.

"Will you feel more at ease if I tell you that Joshua has an inner guide and that the Great Spirit is in his heart because he is not too busy to listen?"

"So why doesn't he speak?"

"Maybe silence is part of his path to wisdom."

I chanced a glance at Joshua's reflection in the mirror. He didn't appear to be following our conversation, but then again, I had no way of knowing what Joshua was and wasn't absorbing. He seemed occupied with the off-the-grid world unfolding around him, his eyes orbiting back and forth, his hands stroking Gabriel's fur.

The road was slippery due to a recent shower. When the Jeep's tires hit potholes, muddy water shot up and landed with splats on the windshield. My Jeep was being put to the test, as I would be soon. *Where the road ends, mine continues.*

I turned to Dr. Mendez. "Did you live like this?"

"Yes, and I loved every minute until I reached my teens. Then I wanted to experience the so-called real world. I thought I was missing out on something important."

"Were you?"

"In a way, yes. In a way, no. I am lucky. I had the opportunity to experience both worlds and the opportunity to compare."

"And?"

"I realized that happiness comes from within and travels with you no matter where you live. Inside, I carry what I learned here as a child, which provides me with a place I can go when I am laid low by life's complications and questions."

My face burned as something deep-felt surfaced. What was it about his words that bothered me? "In our fast-paced world, we do fine until we hit a snag." I said. "Then, when we stop to think and ask questions about the purpose and meaning of life, we have no place to find the answers."

"We have our churches," the doctor said.

"But for many, church only happens one day a week and, even then, is harried and full of deadlines. People get up early, feed the family, get dressed in their Sunday best, and before you know it, they're snapping at one another on the way to their spiritual experience."

"What a picture you paint."

My heart pounded as though I were jogging instead of driving down the muddy, pot-holed road. "My question is, where's the time for meditation and reflection?"

"Good point. I suppose something can be said for life close to nature, which provides the spiritual connect we often seek in churches, temples, and mosques."

"No electricity, no cell service. A little too rugged for me."

"You cannot have it both ways."

"I like my cozy home and my big tub."

"Which you have missed how much in the past week?"

"I haven't had time."

The doctor shifted his weight and stared out the window.

Once again, I caught Joshua's reflection in the rearview mirror. How I longed to hear him chatter and laugh like other children. "Everything okay back there, Joshua?"

Dr. Mendez turned and glanced behind him. "His smile cannot get any wider without leaving his face."

As we pulled into the ranch, I spotted Ben standing next to his mud-splattered pickup. I waved through the Jeep's now equally muddy windshield. He waved back and headed our way.

Dr. Mendez stepped out of the Jeep and, to my surprise, gave Ben a bear hug as if reacquainting himself with a long-lost friend. The doctor was a good five inches shorter and maybe ten years older, but otherwise the two men were built alike—compact and rock-solid.

"Doc and I go way back," Ben told me.

Dr. Mendez put his hand on Joshua's shoulder, drawing him into the conversation. "Marjorie and my little friend here are responsible for my return home."

Ben knelt in front of the child. "Last time we met, you were about so high," he said, raising his hand three feet off the ground. "I've picked out a horse for you. Want to meet him?"

Joshua peered toward the stables and nodded.

"Is that your cat?" Ben asked.

Joshua turned to me, and his eyes locked onto mine.

"Gabriel hitch-hiked his way into our lives," I said. "And he's become quite attached to Joshua."

"Then come on, sport," Ben said. "Let's go find a nest for your little friend." Over his shoulder, he instructed Dr. Mendez and me to transfer our gear to Pete. "He's the cowboy loading up the mules and will be your guide."

Pete looked like one of the bad guys straight out of the old Westerns my dad and I used to watch on TV. His hat, neither black nor white, was a dusty, sweaty brown. More bone than muscle, he had hollows below his cheeks and around his eyes. He looked tired and underfed, the kind of man I'd make room for if I met him on the street and would fear if I met him alone after dark.

No friendly smile of greeting from our prospective guide. Occupied with his task, he ignored us altogether.

Great. We've got Perfect Pete for a guide.

Undeterred by Pete's appearance and off-putting behavior, Dr. Mendez introduced himself and handed over his gear. I followed suit and listened with growing admiration as the doctor bonded with this intense man.

177

"Two more travelers'll be joining us tomorrow," Pete said, "plus another guide, but with the Doc's help leading the mules, I can handle the first leg of the tour on my own."

Two more travelers? Why hadn't Ben mentioned it? Did Pete need the extra money? If so, I would have chipped in more. This wasn't part of my plan, as just about everything else that had occurred since my arrival in Carmel Valley. For the sake of my peace of mind, I let it go.

We were about to become part of the Los Padres National Forest, 1.75 million acres of tranquil paradise and five hundred miles of riding trails, yet I felt excitement rather than fear. Was my Native American blood strong enough to identify with the surroundings in some way, or did the call come from outside? How would nature speak to me? How would I respond?

Dr. Mendez broke into my thoughts with an order to saddle our mounts. We walked to the old barn where the horses were stalled. Joshua stood next to a horse not much bigger than a pony, stroking its neck and forehead. The cat made do in a saddlebag on the horse's side. Most cats would be meowing, or at least clawing their way to freedom, but not Gabriel. He seemed perfectly content where he was.

Ben led me to the palomino I'd ridden before. I stroked her neck. "Hello, Blondie. So, we meet again."

Dr. Mendez approached a horse similar to Ben's paint. "I see Beauty is still alive and kicking."

"She's old," Ben said, "but still a great trail horse. Figured you'd enjoy riding her for old time's sake. Go ahead and saddle up."

I stood by, hands in pockets, until Ben took notice.

"I'll get what you need and show you how it's done," he said.

When he returned, he handed me a blanket. I spread it over Blondie's back as I'd seen Dr. Mendez do with Beauty.

Ben hoisted the saddle over the blanket with a warning. "Blondie expands her belly during cinching. Then, when you think you've got the belt good and tight, she deflates it, leaving the girth loose." Ben

178

poked the horse's belly and quickly tightened the belt. "Keep this in mind, or you and the saddle might slide off."

I swung into the saddle and caught up the reins. Then I reacquainted myself with Blondie as Ben made final adjustments to my stirrups. "Pete's been guiding around here for years and is one of the best. Loves the earth and protects it. He's a bit fussy for a cowboy, but you'll like him once you get past his porcupine exterior."

No chance of that. "Thanks for arranging this, Ben."

He smiled and waved me on. "Better get going. Pete's waiting."

"Later," Dr. Mendez said, lifting his hand in farewell.

Chapter Twenty-nine

NO SOONER HAD WE JOINED HIM than Pete began his orientation in a stern, no-nonsense voice. It was obvious that he took his job seriously and that his mission was to keep us safe. But was he capable of showing us a good time as well?

"If we get rain, the trails'll be slippery an' the streams'll overflow, which'll make it hard to get around. I don't expect any trouble, but we'll be in the wilderness, so keep an eye out." He directed his talk to Joshua and me, likely aware that Dr. Mendez was already familiar with the terrain. I listened to every word, not forgetting for a minute my greenhorn status. I didn't want to cause any trouble, especially since Ben had arranged this trip at my request, during the off-season.

"We're not go'n far today," Pete said. "First camp's six miles from here, only a few hours ride, but the spot'll be secluded enough for you to get the feel of things. You can set up the tents, and I'll cook us up a nice meal."

Pete, as outfitter and pathfinder, headed the line. Joshua rode behind him and I followed. Dr. Mendez brought up the rear, leading the two packhorses, his duty until tomorrow. "When the trail's wide enough," Pete said, "you can ride side-by-side, but on the narrow trails, I want you to ride single file like you're do'n now." He turned and looked at me. "Get what I'm saying?"

I nodded. *Killjoy.*

As time went on, our guide became quite entertaining and, to my surprise, friendly as well. "Check out them rock formations. Pretty awesome, huh? Like they've been painted by hand, with all them greens and golds and shadows. Them mountains hold the secrets of time."

Joshua sat in the middle of the saddle, heels down, chin up, adapting to his new mount with what appeared to be a deep understanding that demonstrated he'd ridden similar terrain many times before. I caught him peering at the bushy habitat alongside our path and wondered what he was looking for. That is, until a convey of quail exploded into rapid flight, with whirring wing beats and calling *pit-pit-pit* in alarm. His horse sidestepped and whinnied, but a gentle touch from Joshua distracted the horse from the perceived threat.

After we'd ridden several hours, Pete pulled off the trail and motioned for us to follow. We dismounted in a flat clearing on a slight rise near a dense stand of trees; a campsite, according to Pete, located in a spot once used by Native Americans. We unsaddled and brushed our horses, after which Pete set up the camp kitchen and Dr. Mendez and Joshua pitched the tents like pros. I, on the other hand, proceeded to pound my finger instead of a tent stake and trip over one of the tent's rope supports. When my male companions broke into laughter, I joined in. "Good thing I've got you strong, macho dudes to help me, or I'd be in big trouble."

A supply of logs had already been set up at the site, some positioned around the campfire ring for seating, so all Pete had to do was ignite sticks of kindling stacked tepee-style around a small pile of tinder to get a fire going. No portable potties, so I knew what I had to do, for once envying the men.

As I headed out, Pete warned about poison oak and ticks. "Oh, and I've got somethin' you might need." With a broad smile, he handed me a roll of toilet paper and a shovel.

I heard laughter as I made my way into the bushes, deciding there were limits to my love of the wilderness.

Later, as we sat around the fire, lulled by the sounds of crackling flames, Pete suggested we scan the trees for birds.

A pecking sound had Joshua pointing at a nearby oak.

"It's an Acorn Woodpecker," Pete said.

"How can you tell?" I asked. "I don't see anything."

"By the sound," was his reply. "And if ya get lucky enough to sight an Acorn Woodpecker up close, you'll see it has a red crown and white forehead."

He went on to share comical stories about the bird's habit of storing acorns in trees and poles.

Next, we spotted what Pete described as a Western Scrub Jay perched low and in the open. It was blue and crestless, with a white throat and brown back. We listened to its harsh, nasal *kweeah* sound and deemed it an extremely noisy bird.

"Prob'ly robbing acorns from the woodpeckers," Pete said. And so it went, Joshua and I enthralled and the doctor listening politely, making few comments.

Finally, Pete paused, only to continue in a voice meant to convey mystery and intrigue. "Now for the part ya won't find in Audubon books." His timing was perfect; it was getting dark, giving way to the sounds of crickets and croaking frogs. "The Red-Tailed Hawk is a large and magnificent bird, once revered by many Red Indian tribes. Its feathers were treasured and used in ceremonies, specially for healing."

Joshua and I strained forward, the perfect audience for the telling of magical tales with animals as teachers and healers.

Pete spoke in a voice so low it rumbled, "The hawk teaches ya to look and see, specially for ways out of tough situations."

Then, right on cue, Dr. Mendez joined in, causing me to wonder—at least briefly—if he and Pete had rehearsed their lines in advance. "Messages of the spirit are close at hand but obscured by the obvious."

Silence followed, except for the pop and crackle of the fire and the steady hum of crickets.

"If ya hear the ear-splittin' cry of the hawk during a journey, beware," Pete warned, his voice urgent, his eyes on mine. "Beware of a comin' event that'll knock ya off your feet."

Though he probably shared the same story on all of his tours, it felt like he had composed it especially for me. He was good, a storyteller, keeper of tomorrow, and he wasn't done. "Or the hawk's cry might be tellin' ya to stand tall and show some grit when faced with an unexpected opportunity."

Although voiced in different words, his message so closely matched Ben's that the beat of my heart kicked up a notch. A small hand gripped mine, and I tore my gaze from Pete's. Joshua smiled, and I marveled at his sensitivity. Once again, he had perceived my discomfort.

I glanced at Dr. Mendez, who had apparently noticed Joshua's action. For a moment, he appeared thoughtful—probably thinking about the interconnectedness of all things as predicted by the holographic model. Then he raised his brows in see-what-I-mean? fashion.

The fire crackled, an owl hooted, and for a while, no one spoke.

"Anyone hungry?" Pete asked.

"Yes," we all said at once.

✎ ✎ ✎

With a crude assortment of pots and pans, Pete orchestrated a meal that looked and smelled as if prepared by a gourmet chef. Eating around the campfire, under the stars, would be a new experience for me, and I couldn't imagine a more relaxed and down-home atmosphere for our supper.

Dr. Mendez conjured up a bottle of red wine and some collapsible wine glasses that popped into shape when he unpacked them.

"What's this?" I said. "Aren't we supposed to be roughing it?"

"Using silicone glasses *is* roughing it," Dr. Mendez said.

I studied the doctor and realized that I knew very little about him. Was he married? Did he have children? Did it matter? He was a good psychologist, a decent human being, and as farsighted as a hawk. I liked him and wished him well.

"This is great," I said as he poured the Merlot into the rubbery stemless glasses.

183

"I'll just have coffee," Pete said, "and'll get some soda for the kid."

Careful not to squeeze the flexible glass too tightly and spill the wine over the top, I raised my drink to the doctor's in a silent toast.

"May each of us succeed in our quest for clarity," Dr. Mendez said.

"Amen," I replied.

✦ ✦ ✦

Pete eyed the camp critically as if monitoring the damage wreaked by our meal.

I followed his gaze, feeling smug, certain that little had been disturbed. But when I looked at him for confirmation, his frown told a different story. I scanned the area a second time, attempting to see it through Pete's eyes. Still, all appeared neat and orderly.

Pete stood and began gathering the meal's remnants together. I offered to help, but he refused. "No kitchen duty for the one footin' the bill."

No complaints from me, especially in light of the delicious sense of listlessness that threatened to root me to the spot.

"Let's call it a day," Pete said, which was all it took. Dr. Mendez gathered up the wine glasses and half-empty bottle of wine; Joshua picked up the dinnerware, and I stayed put, sedated by the fresh air and the star-studded sky.

Minutes later, Joshua scampered toward his tent with Gabriel at his heels. Dr. Mendez winked a *good night* and followed. Without a television, computer, or other such diversions, I, too, was ready to retire.

On the way to my tent, I checked in on Joshua and sensed rather than saw two pair of eyes fixed on mine. I blew a kiss into the dark. Their response, silence.

I buried myself in my sleeping bag, made *Princess-and-the-Pea* comfortable by the self-inflating mattress below, and although invisible creatures abounded and were certainly aware of our presence, I felt no fear. Pete and Dr. Mendez knew this country and could deal with its dangers. I'd also noticed a rifle attached to Pete's gear. With these thoughts running through my mind like a steady stream of fence-leaping sheep, I was soon asleep, trusting as a child.

Chapter Thirty

THE CLATTER OF POTS AND PANS woke me the next morning, followed by the welcoming scent of coffee, bacon, and campfire filtering through the tent walls. I stretched and took a moment to relish the cold air on my sleep-warmed skin. Then I wriggled out of my sleeping bag, pulled on my clothes, and reached into my knapsack for a mirror. Makeup was out of the question, and without styling tools, the best I could do was pull my hair into a loose ponytail.

Now, if only I had some water.

I stepped out of my tent, and Joshua approached carrying a bucket. Yep, filled with water. "Thanks so much, my friend. How did you know?"

The child was either exceptionally observant, due to his silence, or there was another explanation for his ability to tap into, even anticipate, my wants and needs. An explanation I didn't yet have the tools in my spiritual arsenal to formulate into words. Without waiting for a reward, other than my heartfelt thanks, he scampered off, the cat close behind him.

By the time I reached the campfire, all three males—with the cat—were well into their breakfast of fried bacon, eggs, and hash browns. I joined in, sensing their eagerness to saddle up and move on.

Meal over, everyone pitched in to tidy up the camp and pack the mules. Pete ran a discerning eye over the site, determined to leave it undisturbed and unadulterated, as though our stay had been no more than an illusion.

We hadn't ridden far when I heard the thud of cantering hooves to our rear, a reminder that additional guests and a guide were about to join us. In spite of my misgivings, I was curious as to who they might be, so I stood in the stirrups and twisted around in an attempt to catch sight of the new arrivals.

First Ben and then—

Veronica!

"Hello, white Indian," she called as she cantered from behind Ben. She rode a chestnut Arabian with a high-spirited alertness that apparently matched her own: beautiful from afar, but liable to buck you off at the slightest provocation.

Suddenly numb to all but the sturdy warmth of my mount, I stared at the mirror image of myself on one of my most glamorous days. Veronica's skin had the airbrushed look of a Vogue model, and her designer jeans fit tight. Plus, she wore red cowboy boots. Red! And her blouse, though long-sleeved and modestly buttoned, still managed to look sexy. But what had me grabbing the saddle pummel to steady myself was Veronica's hair, trimmed to her shoulders and blonde. The exact style and shade as my own. Now, we looked truly alike.

I heard a sound somewhere between a gasp and a groan.

Joshua.

He stared at Veronica, slack-jawed.

Dr. Mendez drew his horse alongside mine, having relinquished the pack mule to the new guide. "No need to worry. Joshua will be fine."

Not about to admit that my own discomfort had for a moment taken precedence over Joshua's, I said, "Hope you're right."

Before Veronica could completely ruin my day, Ben called her name. He sat rigid in his saddle and glared at her in the way he had glared at me the first day we met. Having recently experienced his composed side, I marveled at the change in him.

He didn't look like *Gentle Bear* any more.

Veronica, however, appeared unfazed by Ben's obvious

displeasure. She flashed me an I-know-something-you-don't-know smile and then ignored me all together.

What was it that made my sister larger than life? When Veronica was around, she was the center. Then it struck me. Veronica had power. And she knew how to use it. She used her body, her face, her youth, and her femininity, which all added up to an irresistible authority over man, woman, and child. So why the mountain-sized chip on her shoulder? What was she searching for? What the hell did she want?

Ben rode to my side. "When Veronica heard you were taking Joshua on a horseback tour into the Ventana Wilderness, she invited herself along. I tried to talk her out of it, but she wouldn't listen. I sense trouble."

"She's my sister," I said. "Everything will be all right."

"Don't carry loyalty too far," Ben said. "I know her. You don't."

"Maybe I do," I said, looking away.

I sensed Ben's concerned gaze as he turned his horse around, but I refused to meet his eyes.

Pete rode to the end of the line to confer with the new guide and returned to the lead. "Line up," he said, "and no tailgatin'."

We positioned ourselves as before with a horse-length between us, except now, Veronica and Ben rode behind Dr. Mendez and the extra guide led the mules in the back. I leaned over as far as I dared to check him out, and then wished I hadn't.

It can't be!

I felt dizzy, as if I were part of some kind of inexplicable plan, formulated by mysterious forces beyond my control.

Jake was our new guide.

Ben knew how strongly I'd reacted to this man at the concert. Was this another reason he'd come along? I half expected Jake's sidekick, Tommy Boy, to pop into view, but, thank God, I was spared that final disappointment.

I turned my attention to Joshua and realized that, even together, we were still alone.

You need a mother's strength, said the *Voice* from out of nowhere.

"Welcome to the party," I said in return. "Where have you been? What took you so long?"

A vulture circled overhead, and I marveled at how a bareheaded scavenger associated with death could look magnificent at a distance.

The yellow-green lichen that dangled pendulously from the surrounding oaks was still moist from the early morning fog, which, according to Pete, meant we were in a valley since higher elevations don't experience fog. The dream-like setting reminded me of a fairyland with the invisible alive. And watching.

Although old-growth chaparral coated the south-facing slopes of the ranges like a carpet of green velvet, some of the hills appeared bald, which reminded me of the Tassajara fire that had killed Joshua's parents.

What had he experienced? What had he seen?

Dr. Mendez approached me as unexpectedly as the *Voice* often did, with a surprise of his own. "I will be leaving in the morning."

Hold it. What about Joshua. What about me? "You just got here," I said.

"Ben's here."

"Ben's not a psychologist."

"Joshua does not need a psychologist twenty-four-seven."

"But—"

"His treatment currently requires support rather than professional therapeutic help. He needs a safe place to look deeply into his own process You, Ben, Morgan, Veronica, and Pete are his tribe right now, facilitating a positive context for his experience. The rest we must leave in the hands of the Great Spirit."

"I wish you'd stay," I said to his back as he rode away.

Ben, Veronica, and Jake kept to themselves, and the rest of the morning passed uneventfully.

Around noon, Pete led us into an open meadow and called out like a head-'em-up-move-'em-out trail boss, "Dismount!"

Joshua swung his right leg over the rump of his horse, jumped to the ground, and landed on both feet like a pro. Something sheltered in the grassy vegetation had caught his eye.

I dismounted—city-girl fashion—and nearly landed on my rump when I saw the object of his quarry.

A jackrabbit.

We stood still, not wanting to scare the little fellow off.

It stared at us, long ears alert, whiskers twitching.

Someone came up from behind. I half expected whoever it was to destroy our moment, but this didn't happen. Veronica approached leather-moccasin smooth, and then she, too, appeared to slip into the world of the animal.

Our eyes met and a current of understanding flashed between us, but then Pete clanged a triangle, "Time for lunch," and the jackrabbit scampered off.

Without a word, Veronica started back for the camp. Joshua, however, nimble as the rabbit we'd just been observing, blocked her path and stared up at her like a friend reacquainting himself with a friend. I marveled at Veronica's reaction, or rather lack thereof. Face passive, body still, she permitted the child's silent inspection.

He smiled. She smiled back. And I experienced a moment of jealous protectiveness.

Then Joshua returned to my side and slid his hand over mine, reintroducing me to love outside of myself.

◢ ◢ ◢

Dinner was a quiet affair, each traveler apparently absorbed in some form of inner dialogue, which, with Veronica around, I hadn't expected possible. When all evidence of the meal had been cleared and packed away, Pete drew our attention to the stars in a night so dark they seemed close enough to touch. "Check out the Big Dipper."

"Oh goody, Girl Scout camp," Veronica quipped.

I laughed, picturing Veronica all decked out in a Girl Scout uniform, and concluded that, even in a solid white shirt, cadette sash, and khaki skirt, she'd manage to look sexy.

"Okay, smart aleck," Ben said. "To what star do the two stars at the end of the Big Dipper bowl point?"

"North Star," Veronica said.

"Also called?"

"Polaris. Any more questions?"

"Yeah." This time from Pete. "What planet outshines evr'thing 'cept for the sun and moon?"

Veronica took a moment to answer, and I almost applauded when she barked out, "Venus." She turned to me. "What about you? Any questions?"

I had a hard time keeping a straight face. "What's your sign?"

"Ha, ha."

"Cancer," Ben said softly.

Veronica awarded him with a half-smile before Pete got going again.

"The movement of the stars or planets and how they affect humans didn't hold much concern for the Red Indian. They were more interested in the Earth Walk."

"Speaking of which . . ." Ben said, eyeing Veronica. "According to the Indian, you and Marjorie were born under the earth influence of 'The Long Days-Time,' which is a time of testing and maturing."

"Testing, maybe," Veronica said. "But I'm as mature as I'm going to get."

"That's too bad," Ben said.

I coughed back a laugh.

"Your birth and animal totem is the woodpecker," Pete said. "The beat of its peckin' is similar to a person's heartbeat, and the pulse of the earth."

This was better than television any day, and I was enjoying every minute. Veronica, however, shrugged and stifled a yawn.

"The woodpecker sometimes drums just for the enjoyment of it," Ben said. "They also cling to things."

Finally, a full-fledged smile from my sister. "I won't ask what you mean by that, Ben darling."

"Woodpecker people also make good parents," Ben continued. "They're particularly responsive to the defenselessness of a child."

"Let it go," Veronica said.

"One last thing," Ben said. "Woodpecker people have to be handled carefully. They can be led but won't be constrained."

Pete cleared his throat. "Back to the stars."

Time was measured differently here, if measured at all. The sun moved, the trees moved, and the water moved, but time stood still. And tonight, time was gentle and generous. It did not slip away. Only my fellow travelers did. Starting with Joshua.

"Happy dreams, my love," I whispered to his sleeping form. Somehow, he'd ended up snuggled against me, Gabriel on his lap.

I glanced at Dr. Mendez and wondered if he was observing us through the eyes of a psychologist or a friend. From the gentleness of his gaze, I figured both.

"Let me give you a hand," he said, before lifting Joshua and the cat from my side and carrying them to their tent.

"Dear God," I said on reaching my tent. "Please let this continue."

For the second time that week, I prayed the rosary, starting with the *Sign of the Cross,* the *Apostles' Creed,* and the *Our Father,* surprised I still remembered the words. Next, I prayed three *Hail Marys,* followed by the *Glory Be to the Father,* calling on the spirits I had once known so well, especially the Blessed Virgin Mary, the Great Female Spirit, mother of Jesus.

Between the hoots of the Great Horned Owl and howls of distant coyotes, came the realization that it was Palm Sunday.

The day marking the beginning of Holy Week and the final week of Lent had come and gone without notice.

Chapter Thirty-one

I WOKE WITH A SENSE OF UNEASINESS in the place of my dreams. The clatter of metal utensils and the smell of coffee and bacon greeted me as they had on the previous morning, but today something was different. Instead of light chatter interspersed with laughter came heavy and hushed conversation.

Wariness addled with grogginess made dressing a slow process. I pulled my hair into a ponytail, twisted it, and clipped it to the crown of my head, then poured water onto a towel and pressed it to my face, hoping to dispel my apprehensive mood. When I raised the flap of my tent and stepped outside, cool air greeted me.

As did Morgan.

"Good morning," he said with a tip of his Stetson.

"What are *you* doing here?" I asked, remembering too late my less than favorable reaction to the same question, asked in a similar tone, by Morgan on the night of the concert.

Before he had a chance to answer, I looked away, distracted by the brush of something quivering against the leg of my jeans.

"Gabriel." The cat allowed me to pick him up, and I took the rare opportunity to hug him close before glancing back at Morgan.

His green-eyed gaze roamed leisurely from my clipped hair to the hands that cradled the cat. "Miss me?"

His boyish grin was a lethal weapon as far as I was concerned. *Look at me like that, and I don't have the strength to resist you.* "I haven't had time."

"Too bad," Morgan said.

I agreed. White lies—and omissions—usually lead to trouble, but I hadn't come this far to give in now.

Gabriel stiffened and leaped from my arms when Joshua stepped out of his tent. The child picked up the cat, and a word escaped, so soft and swift that I nearly missed it.

He'd said the cat's name.

My gaze darted to Morgan's, wondering if he had heard it, too. But my excitement turned to confusion when I caught the look of tenderness in his eyes before he turned and walked away.

Dr. Mendez stood next to the fire warming his hands. When he saw me headed his way, he grabbed a mug, and by the time I reached him, he'd filled it with coffee.

I wrapped my cold fingers around the enamelware mug and nodded my thanks. "I just heard Joshua say Gabriel's name."

"A good sign," he said.

Good sign? More like fantastic. "I wish you weren't leaving."

"Actually, I am not."

My sudden jerk caused the hot coffee to spill over my hand.

The doctor scooped up a towel and handed it to me. "Morgan asked me to stay."

"But—"

"He believes Joshua will need me."

"Of course, Joshua needs you. Why the sudden change in plans?"

"Ask Morgan."

I smacked my mug onto the fire pit ring— "I will" —and headed off. What was going on here? First, Veronica, Ben, and Jake showed up, and then Morgan, who, out-of-the-blue, asked Dr. Mendez to extend his stay.

Though fueled by questions and a growing sense of helplessness at my continued loss of control over a tour that *I* had organized for Joshua, I came to an abrupt halt on seeing Morgan and Veronica huddled together. Every bit of their body language implied secrecy, which only intensified my curiosity, sense of helplessness—and anger.

Watch your back, said the *Voice*.

"Okay, shadow person," I answered. "Whom or what for?"

Silence.

"You're a big help."

I made a U-turn back to Pete's camp kitchen. "A deluxe camper's kitchen," he'd called it when he first pointed it out to me. "Picked it up, used, for fifty bucks. Plenty of table space, removable hangin' pantries, lantern hooks, and even a hanger for my nifty 'chuck wagon' dinner bell. Whole thing sets up in five minutes and packs up so compact I can stow it on a pack mule, no problem. How's that for modern convenience?"

"Awesome," I'd told him, though right about now I was more interested in the gourmet meals he was able to concoct—Dutch oven potatoes, grilled Brussels sprouts, potato boat with ham, cheese, and bacon, campfire mushrooms—than the equipment he used doing so. What I needed was a hearty breakfast to calm me down and give me strength.

Too bad Jake had the same idea.

He looked up as I approached the fire and then looked away.

Refusing to retreat like my usual weak-kneed, lily-livered self, I took the opportunity to study him. What a contrast he and Pete made. Whereas Pete sought attention, Jake shunned it. Pete was energetic, full of stories, and eager to help. Jake's movements were slow, sly, and barely perceptible. He was as quiet as a shadow, and I feared him.

Instead of serving himself, Jake scooped scrambled eggs and beans onto a plate, topped them with bacon, and handed the steaming plate of food to me.

"Thanks," I said.

As though connected to me by an ethereal cord of energy, Joshua appeared at my side. Without a word, Jake filled another plate and handed it to him. Their eyes met. Joshua's hands went slack. The plate fell to the ground.

"Joshua," I cried, before directing the child to a flattened log.

195

"Come on, sweetie. Sit down." Back was his unfocused, thousand-yard stare, a gaze as blank as Gabriel's. Speaking of which. I scanned the area, but the stray was nowhere in sight.

However, Veronica was.

She called to Joshua as she approached, "Hi, handsome."

The child blinked and appeared to awaken from a deep sleep.

"How about some breakfast?" she asked.

He nodded.

I didn't understand what had just happened here but was glad that Joshua appeared less distant. Veronica presented him with a kid-sized portion of bacon and eggs and sat at his side with an expression of deep concern.

"Good morning all," Morgan said from behind me.

What was it with people coming up from behind unnoticed?

Ben also made an appearance and gave Morgan a manly slap on the back. "Hey, buddy. What brings you here?"

Morgan glanced my way before answering. "I was in the area taking pictures. Hope you don't mind if I tag along."

"The more the merrier," Ben said, as though we were one big happy family—uninvited guests and all.

Whose tour was this anyway?

Pete, forever the guide, called for everyone to eat up, clean up, and leave the place in better shape than we found it. "Hey, Marjorie," he said. "Hope you like water 'cause we're gonna be crossing some creeks and streams."

Instantly, I was on alert. "Isn't that dangerous this time of year?"

"Yep, but we're gonna do it carefully."

I glanced at Joshua, my heart hammering.

Pete continued. "Today we're pass'n though some of the most beautiful country on the face of this earth. Might even meet up with mule deer, tree squirrels, and rodents."

"Wonderful," Veronica said. "I love rats."

I reached for the mouse totem in my pouch, amazed at how much I'd come to treasure this smooth brown stone.

"Hey Morgan," Pete called. "Prep up that camera of yours for some great *National Geographic* shots."

"Will do," Morgan said, focusing on me. I tried to mask the hurt caused by his secrecy but knew I had failed when he frowned.

◢ ◢ ◢

Oaks and pines continued to dominate the woodlands as we resumed our ride. On the more exposed sites, the trees were widely spaced, giving the area the look of a grassland-tree savanna. Wildflowers popped up among the grasses and beneath the shade of the trees. Pete pointed out larkspurs, monkey flowers, fairy bells, violets, heart's ease, and California poppies, which created a mosaic of color in the shifting light.

Surrounded by hills, valleys, oak savannas, and deep ravines, it was hard to imagine that we were only a short distance from Carmel and Monterey.

Horses snorted, saddles creaked, hoofs plodded, and birds chattered. A whiff of horse sweat accompanied by the smell of sage, pine, and vanilla hung in the air.

Morgan rode up alongside me. "You okay?"

"Yes."

"Mad at me?"

"Yes."

"I don't mean to make you mad."

I faced him in a quick, jerky motion. "Why are you here, Morgan?"

He didn't answer my question, so I asked another, right off the top of my head—a great source for off-the-script moments and Mad Libs. "Do you think I'm selfish for what I'm trying to do?"

"Willful perhaps. Selfish, no." Intrigued by something up ahead, he urged his horse forward and galloped off the path.

Pete laughed. "Guess Morgan's already discovered one of my surprises."

Morgan dismounted and began setting up his camera, alerting

Veronica to something worth closer attention. She rode past me and halted next to him.

We had ridden into a valley, secluded by towering rocks. "For millions of years, this area was covered by ocean," Pete hurried to explain, "with sediments accumulat'n at the bottom. Over time, the sediments lifted up thousands of feet by the mountain-formin' process. That's what you're seein' now." He whistled with undisguised admiration, though he'd obviously witnessed the spectacle hundreds of times before. "Check out those colored bands."

I marveled at the panoramas of re-oriented rock formations that jutted from between trees and chaparral in gradients of color from light grey to dark brown. And just as I thought there couldn't be anything more enchanting, I heard the rush of water. As we neared, the rush turned into a roar. "A waterfall!"

"We're not crossing that, are we?" Veronica asked, pointing at what appeared to be a rapidly moving river.

"It's only a creek," Pete said.

"You call that torrent a creek?"

Diverted from the magnificent sight of the falls, I zeroed in on the rushing water and found myself agreeing with Veronica. "How deep is it?"

"Some places are only deep pools," Pete said. "Though the stream's higher than usual 'cause of the winter and spring runoff."

I studied Joshua's pony. It looked sturdy and was likely accustomed to crossing streams. Everything would be just fine.

Joshua jerked, and I thought my heart would stop, until he pointed at a deer standing nearby, ears erect, eyes unblinking, and muzzle quivering.

"I told you we'd see mule deer," Pete said.

At the sound of Pete's voice, the deer ran off with a stiff-legged gait.

Morgan snapped away from atop his horse with one of his sister's discarded cameras. Through its lens, he appeared to be awakening to a world different from the one he was accustomed to and recording beauty without the pressure of needing to do it perfectly—therefore, free to do it well. He looked toward the sky and his smile faded. I followed his gaze, but only saw clouds.

Nothing out of the ordinary.

"We're campin' on the other side of the creek," Pete said, pausing to allow his horse to dip its muzzle into the water and drink.

I wondered what it would be like to sleep with the sound of the waterfall in the distance and concluded I'd like it very much. Checking back on Joshua, I saw that Morgan now rode on one side of him and Dr. Mendez on the other.

I guided Blondie toward the creek. She stepped in and out several times before entering all the way. "Careful, careful," I said, urging her forward. She snorted and blew at the swiftly running water, then put her head down to take a drink and apparently check the sloping stream bed for footing. "Atta girl," I said, "take it slowly." A little slip, but she quickly regained her equilibrium, and soon we all arrived safely on the other side.

Morgan helped Pete and Jake care for the horses while the rest of us unloaded our gear and erected our tents. Veronica scanned the sky as Morgan had earlier, her look as sultry as the weather. I shifted my attention to the world above but could only make out some very tall clouds.

The towering rocks in the distance looked like spires and the water a huge baptismal font, but even surrounded by such beauty, I got the feeling everyone was just playing a waiting game.

Veronica came up on heavy heels to where I sat next to my tent. "This simplify-your-life bullshit isn't for me," she said. "My thighs hurt and I could use a hot bath."

This would have been a good time to mention that she'd barged in on a trip that I'd set up and paid for, which hardly put her in the position to complain. Instead, I said, "I agree about the hot bath, but about the sore thighs—"

"Don't even suggest lending me a pair of your baggy Wranglers. No way."

"Okay, but—"

"See those clouds?" she asked.

"Yeah, aren't they beautiful?"

"Beautiful, my foot! They're cumulonimbus clouds, common in the summer, not the spring. And even then, I've never seen them around *here* before."

"Bad?"

"They're also called thunderheads. Does that give you a clue?"

"Not good."

"Not good," Veronica agreed.

Chapter Thirty-two

AFTER DINNER, Pete announced that his friend, Ben *Gentle Bear* Mendoza, would perform Native American spirit-songs around the campfire, and I was hard-pressed to contain my excitement. Forever busy, I rarely listened to music back home. The ticking of the clocks, the hum of the refrigerator, and the faint sounds of barking dogs and sporadic traffic had orchestrated the rhythms and harmonies in my world, which had been enough. At least, so I'd thought at the time.

Since venturing into the wilderness, I was experiencing a new kind of music, sometimes calming, sometimes inspiring, and sometimes annoying. Birds chattered; animals rhapsodized in camaraderie; water trickled, telling stories and whispering secrets; wind enlivened the voices of trees.

And tonight, I would experience the music of the Indian.

Pete handed me a turtle-shell rattle, with small mammal vertebrae, horsehair, and feathers secured to its body with rawhide lashing. "To symbolize the rain," he said. "You'll know what to do."

He gave a cedar flute decorated with geometric symbols and dangling leather cords to Dr. Mendez. "Word has it you're pretty good at this."

"And Gentle Bear'll share the songs of his ancestors."

"Of course," Veronica said with an eye roll that would have made a querulous teen proud. But when Pete offered her a rattle, she shooed it away. "I'll sing with Ben."

"The drum represents the heartbeat," Pete said, presenting

Joshua with what looked like a hollowed-out log with tanned buck-skin stretched across the opening.

"With each beat of the drum," Dr. Mendez said, "you will be pulled from ordinary awareness to the opening in the earth leading to the Lower World of mysteriously beautiful landscape, formed of mountains, forests, and trees, all illuminated by a subterranean sun."

That, I thought, sounded like a description of where we'd already arrived, unless, of course, the doctor was describing the inner world of the unconscious, made accessible via the drum as a bridge.

Morgan sat facing me on the opposite side of the fire. Pete waved a one-stringed fiddle his way, which appeared to be made out of a hollowed-out vegetal stalk bound with sinew wrappings. Morgan shook his head and held up his camera.

"Did you bring your markers?" Ben asked.

I reached into my pouch and handed him five of my stones: *yellow* for the *East*, *red* for the *South*, *black* for the *West*, *white* for the *North*, and *green* for the *Center*.

Ben made a crude Medicine Wheel around the perimeter of the campfire and then asked Joshua to join him. They walked to each point of the wheel, where Joshua beat the drum with the palm of his hand to call on the powers of the Four Directions. Holding the green stone above his head, Ben cried out, "Great Spirit, we give thanks for our lives and for the gifts of the earth and the sky. Be with us on our healing journey."

After placing the green stone in the wheel's center next to the fire, Ben lit a smudge stick. The aroma of sweet grass and sage min-gled with the musky smell of burning wood and pine needles to pu-rify and bless each traveler in our group. As the blue light of late afternoon turned to the vibrant oranges and reds of twilight, Ben lifted his voice in song. "Nya Ho To Tya Ha."

Joshua settled next to me, closed his eyes, and tapped the drum with the pads of his fingers. He'd obviously done this before. But when? Had he joined his father in healing rituals and ceremonies?

At Ben's signal, I shook the rattle tentatively. At first, it sounded like beans shaking in a jar, but when I closed my eyes and imagined I was the rain, the rattle took on new life, blending seamlessly with the beat of the drum and Ben's powerful chant-like song.

Dr. Mendez blew into the flute, and the resonance of its plaintive call caused my heartbeat to slow. As the air blew out and re-entered the flute's chamber, I imagined the uplifting moan of the wind and the lonely howl of the coyote, and my body relaxed into—and united with—its pure melody.

Ben started to dance in circles in the ancient way. "Help me see the path with a heart," he cried. Our instruments served as backups to Ben's gripping prayer songs, and the blended sounds were so sweet that my chest ached and my eyes burned. The birds and animals became silent as if taking in, even understanding, our composite message.

Veronica's singing mimicked Ben's like an echo, "Oh Ho Mo Ne Me." Their voices melded, and for a while, they became one, sharing a common goal.

I entered a serene state of stillness, no longer sensing a separation between my body and spirit. Following the breathy sound of the flute and the hypnotic beat of the drum, I journeyed out of my body. The heavens united with the earth and a thin space opened between them. Something bigger and more powerful than I, something more optimistic, more loving, more beautiful, drew me to the other side.

Sunwalker . . .

The drumming stopped, but the flute and singing continued, and just as I was about to pass through the space between here and there, I felt a tug on my arm. At first, I resisted its pull, but a second, more urgent tug caused me to open my eyes. Joshua knelt next to me, and in his silent, knowing way, he took my rattle and clasped my hand.

I looked over Joshua's shoulder and met Morgan's eyes, but in the shifting firelight, it was impossible to read the expression on his face.

Dr. Mendez lowered his flute onto his knees just as Ben raised his hands and cried, "Thank you, Creator, for sending forth Eagle's gift of wisdom and healing."

A hoarse, two-second *kee-eeeee-arr* screeched from above, followed by silence.

The doctor picked up the drum and tapped it steadily. "I'll lead Ben home while he recalls his spirit."

✗ ✗ ✗

Next morning, I woke to the feel of warm breath on my face.

I opened my eyes, met Morgan's gaze, smiled.

Until comprehension set in. "What are *you* doing in *my* tent?"

His lips were so close to mine that I thought he was going to kiss me. And, darn, if I wouldn't have let him. Instead, he said, "To invite you to watch the sunrise with me."

"But it's still dark outside."

"Of course, it's still dark outside, sweetheart," he said with a John Wayne drawl. "That's why we need to set out now."

Was this man crazy?

"Don't say no," he said softly.

"Okay, okay," I said, directing him outside with the point of my finger. "Give me a minute while I get dressed."

He'd already seen me at my worst, so no use in primping now. I pulled on my jeans, sweatshirt, wool socks, and hiking boots, then snuggled into my hooded, down jacket and secured my hair under a beanie.

By flashlight, Morgan led the way to a spot some distance from the camp. Although sheltered by oak and pine, I sensed we'd soon be privy to a spectacular view of the eastern horizon, jutted with neck-craning red-rock spires.

Morgan spread a blanket for us to sit on and then turned his attention to the predawn sky.

"The sun won't rise for a while yet," he said, "which gives us a chance to talk."

Good. Now maybe he'd answer some questions, like what he was doing here and what was up between him and Veronica.

"Have you called your mother since you've been out here?" he asked.

Whoa. Hold it. What right did he have poking his nose into *my* business when he was so tight-lipped about his own? "You don't even know my mother, and you obviously don't know me," I said. "But just to set the record straight, she's very controlling and wants to live my life for me. Bet you wouldn't put up with her meddling, if she were *your* mother."

"Would it be that detrimental to make one call?" he asked.

"Yep."

We faced each other, his eyes warm and penetrating and mine likely shooting out sparks.

"Are you sure?" he asked.

"I already have a shrink, Morgan. I don't need another."

We hadn't seen or heard from each other in ten years, and now, within days of our re-acquaintance, he had the nerve to comment on my behavior. What was it about me that drew people's unsolicited advice? It couldn't be my appearance. Veronica and I looked identical, and I hadn't noticed anyone leading *her* by the collar.

"Are you punishing your mother because she wants to protect you or because she can't let you go?"

"Don't make me question myself, Morgan. I can do a pretty good job of that on my own."

"You think I'm picking on you?"

"Yes, and I believe I might understand why. I remind you of your sister, the way she's treating your mother and your family. But is what she's doing so wrong? Have you ever considered that maybe she needs a little space? A loving family can really cramp your style."

He ran his fingers alongside my cheek and under my chin, before cupping my face with the palm of his hand. For a second time, I thought he was going to kiss me, and in spite of my objection to his none-of-your-business questions, I closed my eyes, probably even puckered my lips.

Instead of a kiss came another question. "What is it you're searching for?"

The conversation had taken a new turn, even fuller of potholes than the previous one. I sighed and reopened my eyes. "I've come to the recent conclusion that I've been a little too proficient at following the say-so of others, including my family, my boss, and my church. Instead of freeing me to get in touch with myself and my reason for being, they've pressured me into conforming to rules and rituals."

"Rules and rituals are meant as aids, not hurdles," Morgan said, dropping his hand from my face and leaving the chill morning air in its wake.

Though part of me knew that the coldness of separation was a small price to pay for being able to speak my own mind, another part of me ached for the warmth of his touch. "I no longer feel connected to life . . . and to God."

"Has that changed since you've come here?"

"Almost. Last night with the chant-like songs, for instance, I felt something, really felt something."

"Ben calls them *vocables*, but I know what you mean. The Church has chants."

"No comparison, Morgan. And you know it. The Gregorian chants in church don't belong to the people. Only the priests sing them and usually only during High Mass."

"Indian ceremonial songs were led by tribal medicine men and lead singers," Morgan said, "not exactly ordinary people."

"The *vocables* I heard last night were simple and accessible, like outpourings."

Morgan wiped the moisture pooling under my eyes. And I didn't stop him. It felt good to release some of my pent-up emotions of late, to admit to having longings and desires.

"I agree they were beautiful," he said, "and that your intentions are good, but . . . When we get back to town, will you join me for Easter Mass?"

An image of Cliff and my mother, their trickery, their betrayal, had me shaking my head. "I tried going back to church with a different attitude and it didn't work out too well."

A blush of salmon glowed above and between the eastern ridge of rocks, turning the black horizon into an orange-blushed blue.

"You've definitely been a good influence on Joshua," Morgan said.

"He doesn't try to change me."

"Actually, I don't want to change you, either," Morgan said, covering my hand with his, "which is what I've been trying to tell you, though apparently not very well. You see yourself as a caterpillar, and I see you as a butterfly."

Tired of talking about me, I pulled my hand from Morgan's and changed the subject. "I can't get a grasp of Joshua's love."

"I'd say Joshua *is* love," Morgan said.

"You mean the way the Bible defines love? Patient and kind, bearing, believing, hoping, and enduring of all things?"

"God's message in a nutshell," Morgan said.

"So that's the answer? All one has to do is love? Morgan, tell me straight. What do you want from me?"

He didn't answer.

"Do you want my love?"

He stiffened, made no comment.

"I'd love you in a heartbeat," I said, "if that were the answer. Every bone in my body tells me you'd fulfill a need in me like no other man on this earth. I'd come so close to heaven, I'd be tempted to give up my search altogether, but then I ask myself, 'At what price?'"

Still no comment.

"That's why I can't give in, Morgan. When I look into your eyes, see your tenderness, your strength, I want—"

"Stop it, Marjorie."

"I just want—"

He grimaced as if my words were hurting him, and then he got up and walked away.

Too late, to retract my outburst of honesty, the truth I'd hidden for so long, even from myself. But I didn't regret what I'd said. Secrets come out eventually, and Morgan had asked for it. Too bad I wanted him more than I'd ever wanted Cliff, and too bad he presented such a big threat to my freedom.

Losing my freedom, yet again, was not an option.

I watched the sunrise alone, nearly blinded by the intense light.

Maybe, that's how it is with God. If I could actually see Him, I'd be blinded. Maybe, like the sun, the Great One is meant to be *felt*, not seen.

Maybe. Maybe. Maybe.

Chapter Thirty-three

O N RE-ENTERING CAMP, I caught Pete squinting up at the sky, his face set in a scowl that did not lighten my day. Morgan was nowhere in sight. Dr. Mendez stood at the campfire, as usual, drinking coffee. I joined him and reached for a mug. "Have you seen Morgan?"

Doctor Mendez took a long, appreciative sip before answering, which had me wondering if anything at all escaped or perturbed him.

I picked up the makeshift coffeepot Pete had made out of an empty coffee can and started to pour the black, steamy liquid into my mug. I'd get my answer when the doctor was ready.

"Swing the can around a bit," he said, "so the grounds concentrate on the bottom."

Holding the coffee can by its wire handle, I did as he suggested, pretending that my question about Morgan mattered less than it did.

"He packed up and left," the doctor said finally. "Said he wanted to take more camera shots and would meet up with us later."

I tilted the mug to my lips to hide my disappointment.

"Ready for a big day?" he asked, the silky baritone of his voice smoothing some of the morning's wrinkles.

I forced Morgan from my mind and stared at the towering clouds. "Yesterday, Veronica pointed out some thunderclouds."

"We may encounter rain."

"Are we still headed for the Tassajara Hot Springs region?"

"No reason to change the plan now, considering it brings us closer to civilization."

"Civilization?"

"Our next stop is about six miles from the Tassajara Hot Springs, which includes a Zen Buddhist monastery and a nearby camping site."

"I'm glad," I said, "just in case . . ."

The doctor nodded.

"What do you think about Joshua?"

"So far, so good. I have resumed his meditation and breathing exercises during our camp breaks, and his bond with you and Gabriel appears to remain strong."

"But today's the day we pass through the area where he lost his parents." Would Joshua's meditation and breathing exercises and his bond with Gabriel and me be enough to counteract the pain he might experience? Would our attempt to help him give full expression to his emerging emotions do him more harm than good? I searched the doctor's face for a clue as to his feelings about what we might encounter but perceived nothing—not a crease in his forehead, not a curve of his lips, not a shrug of his stocky shoulders.

"I fully agree that Joshua needs you," I said. "But I still don't get why Morgan asked you to stay."

"He must have had a good reason."

"That's what worries me."

"Worrying won't help."

N N N

Joshua rode ahead of me as usual, but this time, Dr. Mendez rode at his side, apparently watching for any signs of fear or discomfort as we neared Tassajara.

Thunder clapped and then rumbled in the distance, low, long. I turned in my saddle to check on Veronica, who, in my mind, served as the atmospheric barometer for our group and our surroundings. The frown on her face was hardly encouraging, nor was the way her gaze remained fixed on the horizon.

Signs of the destructive fire that had passed through the area two years before increased with each quarter mile we traveled. I saw boulders that had cracked due to intense heat, scorched earth, and erratic gaps between tall healthy trees, filled with misshapen branches denuded by the flames that had torched them. Intrigued by what Pete, as storyteller, might add to my understanding of the traumatic event, I urged Blondie to the head of the line.

"Mornin'," Pete said.

"Good morning, I think. Will we get rain?"

"Prob'ly."

"Will it be dangerous?"

"Uncomfortable, mostly." He surveyed the cloudy sky. "Been through a lot worse. It's you and the kid I worry about."

"So, you *are* worried?"

"Bad choice of words."

"What happened here with the fire?"

"Seems like yesterday," he said before releasing a long sigh. "Lightnin' sparked the Tassajara fire that ended up destroyin' over 87,000 acres of land."

"It must have been horrible," I said.

"Depends on who ya ask. Fires are actually good now and then to burn off litter and duff. Chaparral, for one, needs fire for growth and reproduction."

I took in our surroundings through new eyes and noticed the light green signs of sprouting new growth. "But the fire also caused harm."

"You got that right," Pete said. "It wiped out trails and campgrounds, a real bummer for members of the Esselen tribe, who make their livin' from pack trips and guided tours like this one. They also raise cattle in the area."

"Plus, lives were lost," I said.

"Only two that I know of."

Obviously, Pete wasn't aware that the two casualties were Joshua's parents, which was probably for the best. He had enough to worry about, considering the change in weather. As we rode on, I caught more signs of nature rebuilding itself. In places, the grass grew so thick and tall that it came up to our horses' knees, probably serving as shelter to a new crop of animals as well. Namely, mice. "What can you tell me about the mouse totem?" I asked.

Pete's eyes widened with what looked like surprise, an expression I hadn't expected to see on his wizened cowboy face. My original impression had been that nothing would surprise him, particularly anything coming from a tenderfoot like me.

"Accordin' to the stories we share on our wilderness-spirit expeditions, the Native American considers the mouse a great power and helper," he said. "Why'd ya ask?"

"Joshua gave me his mouse totem as a gift. It meant a lot to him and now means a lot to me. I was just wondering if maybe it had some kind of symbolic meaning."

"Well now, gimme a second to gather my thoughts."

Pete was a natural in his Mark Twainish ability to tell a tall tale, and he didn't disappoint me now. "The mouse is near-sighted, so can only see what's right in front of 'em. It teaches us not to look too far ahead or we'll miss out on what's already there. It also teaches us that we can't really experience anything unless we're touched by it. We've got to feel what we see . . ."

Pete threw a quick glance my way, apparently to see if he still held my attention, and then gave a slight nod and continued. "The mouse is the totem of the South, where folks like you and me get a stab at blossomin' and unfoldin' after awakenin' in the East. Though, to be quite honest, not many people I know of make it to the blossomin' and unfoldin' stage. They get bogged down, like sleepwalkers, to the point where they stop growin' altogether."

Saddles creaked. Hoofs struck stone and thudded on earth. We were following an old Indian trail, and each bend treated us to more signs of plant life bouncing back in abundance after the destructive fire: the baked-cookie smell of sappy pine warmed by the sun, the bracing scent of decaying vegetation, and the coolness of the moisture in the air. I couldn't get enough of the high, steep cliffs or the creeks cutting through them. I couldn't get enough of the silence and the peace. How long would it last?

ᴎ ᴎ ᴎ

Veronica's continued silence alerted me to a change in mood, like a malevolent fog drifting in the air. With enough room on the wide-open savannah to turn my horse, I circled back to check on her. "You okay?"

"Just hunky-dory."

Her lack of vitality had me eyeing her with suspicion, but I decided not to dig into what was wrong. Instead, I asked a question for which I was determined to get an answer, no matter what Veronica said about curiosity. "Tell me about your dad."

A loud shriek tore the heavens, and my heart somersaulted in my chest.

"Damn hawks," Veronica said. "Enough to give you the creeps."

The horses snorted, and Pete laughed at a joke he'd shared with the doctor. "About your dad," I said.

Veronica shrugged. "He told me I wasn't adopted."

Not adopted?

It took me several seconds to digest what she'd just said. Even then, my brain didn't fully comprehend what it meant. We were sisters, identical twins. If she wasn't adopted, then . . . "He's your *real* . . . I mean . . . *biological* father?"

"*Our* biological father."

I pulled back on Blondie's reins. She whinnied and came to a halt.

Veronica rode on. "His name's Bob," she said in a voice as toneless and tightly controlled as Rod Serling's in his chilling reminders of a world beyond our control.

Bob? Not Geraldo, as I'd believed for twenty-eight years.

No, no, no, I love you Daddy. I'll never forget you. You were the greatest.

"Finished asking questions?" Veronica called from at least two horse-lengths away.

Hell no.

I urged Blondie forward with the kick of my heels. I knew my birth father's name, but it conjured no pictures, no memories—no love. Was he tall? Was he handsome? Did he ever think of me or regret leaving me behind? What was his story? What was my story?

When I caught up with Veronica, she presented me with a sad smile.

"I can't take it all in," I said. "Bob. Oh my God." I thought my head would burst. My father was alive, and Veronica was my link. She could take me to him. He was only a six-hour flight away. "So, your mother is . . ."

"My step-mother."

"And our biological mother?"

"Is dead."

"Her name was Antonia Flores," I said.

"Yeah, Dad told me."

"Remember Heather, the one who took the picture of Margarita's mirror?"

Veronica didn't answer, looked straight ahead.

"While researching her family tree, she discovered an Antonia Flores here in Carmel Valley, who delivered a set of twins the year we were born and died soon after. She was a descendant of Margarita Butron, six generations removed."

"Pop was married to my step-mother when we were born," Veronica said, followed by a quick hiss through her teeth. "That makes him a cheat."

The prospect of meeting my biological father suddenly dropped to near zero on my to-do list. From deep inside, a tingling blossomed into knowledge. Something tragic had happened to our mother.

Before she died.

◢ ◢ ◢

Pete chose another indigenous ceremonial site with a stream running within earshot for our lunch retreat. "The land was part of the Esselen tribe's religious experience," he said. "Some spots, like this one, are known to have special powers. Pay close attention and the place'll speak to you."

I unsaddled and groomed Blondie, then gave her a carrot and some water for a job well done and handed her over to Jake. We didn't converse or make eye contact, an unvoiced arrangement, on my part at least, to make our coexistence tolerable.

Time to catch up with my journal.

I sat near the edge of the rapidly flowing stream and entered my private space, where anything was possible except for my ability to understand. Shadow shapes appeared and disappeared in the water that flowed over hundreds of colorful stones, sometimes cradling the bank and sometimes carving it. I thought about the undivided, flowing movement of consciousness, of how our thoughts and ideas unfold like ripples, eddies, and whirlpools in streams of water, some recurring and persisting, others vanishing as quickly as they appear.

I heard someone crying.

"Antonia, is that you?" I whispered. "If so, cry for us all."

I wrote without being conscious of what I was putting down, wondering if someone else was directing my hand. This went on for some time, and would have gone on longer, if Pete hadn't rung his 'chuck wagon' dinner bell and yelled, "Ya'll come eat or starve."

N N N

Only after our group had finished setting up camp and gathered around the campfire for dinner did Morgan rejoin us. I handed him a mug of coffee, a peace offering. He nodded his thanks but didn't meet my eyes. There was nothing rational about my response to this man. When I was near him, my emotions battled with my mind. So far, my mind had been the victor, but for how long?

With food came strength, and with strength came an easing in mood. Pete was determined to make this trip a success, which for him included entertainment. "Cowboy Night," he announced.

Before Morgan had a chance to bow out this time, Pete handed him a scaled-down travel guitar. "You're needed tonight."

"Sit by me, Sis," Veronica said while Pete distributed the rest of the instruments, "so I can braid your hair."

My face must have registered surprise at the sudden reversal from mean girl to caring sister because she added, "Humor me."

No sooner had I settled next to her than Veronica yanked the beanie off my head and pulled a comb and two rubber bands from the pocket of her fringed, rawhide jacket. The pull and tug of the comb through my tangled hair hurt, but I bit my lip and kept silent, determined not to whine like a baby.

"You've certainly done a number on Morgan," Veronica said.

My disastrous conversation with Morgan at sunrise had been replaying in my head all day. And now this?

"He loves you," Veronica said.

Love? Yeah, right.

"You've got the power to make him do just about anything."

I'd been trying to keep my mouth shut but insinuating that I had—or even wanted—power over Morgan was pushing too far. "I want power over my *own* life, not anyone else's."

She had finished combing my hair and started to braid it, not an easy task, considering my hair was only shoulder length. I'd probably end up looking like Pippi Longstocking, but at this point, I didn't much care.

"Something about loving yourself before you can love others?" Veronica asked.

She made my quest sound petty, but I refused to budge. I knew what was best for me—not my mother, not Cliff, not Morgan, and most definitely not my sister. No more relying on others to protect me or tell me what to do.

"Why don't you like yourself?" she asked.

Jeez, what was it with all the self-taught therapists around here?

"Don't try to psychoanalyze me, Veronica."

"Do you believe Morgan loves you?"

I didn't answer. Even if I knew what to believe, which I didn't, it was none of her damn business.

Abruptly, Veronica stopped braiding my hair and slapped my shoulder with her comb. "What are you, clueless?"

I didn't like where the conversation was going, but if I'd learned anything about my sister, she wouldn't stop until she was satisfied.

And satisfied she was not.

"Do you think *I'm* powerful?" she asked.

Dumb question. "Powerful *and* beautiful," I said.

"We're identical, for God's sake," Veronica said, drawing Ben and Pete's attention.

I waited for their gazes to drift away before saying, "It's not a case of genetics, but attitude."

"Yeah right, gets me into trouble every time."

"You go after what you want. You're free. You know who you are."

Veronica shifted from behind me and brought her face up to mine. "You think I'm free? You think I know who I am?"

"Dear God, yes."

"What a bunch of crap," she said, favoring me with another slap of the comb. "I have no clue who I am, Sis. But I do know what I want."

"That's good," I said.

She shook her head and her response came out soft as a deathbed confession. "I'm very needy."

Needy, my foot. "Veronica?"

"What?"

"I love you."

Her mouth curved into what looked almost like a smile, but she didn't return my endearment. At least not in words.

At this moment, I believe she softened toward me. It was the moment everything changed. "And just so you know," I whispered, "I can take care of myself."

She forced air through her nose in a good imitation of Blondie, minus the head toss and foot stomp. "Come on. Let me finish your hair."

ℵ ℵ ℵ

217

The flickering campfire highlighted the dabbler musicians like strobe lighting on a Nashville stage. Pete was testing the fiddle, Morgan tuning the guitar, and Joshua fingering the drum. I glanced at Ben, who sat eyes closed with a harmonica on his knee, and Dr. Mendez, equally reposed with the flute on his lap, and wondered what the makeshift band would do.

Morgan started by picking a wordless country tune on his guitar and the rest of the group joined in, hesitantly at first, and then with gained confidence. When the melody ended, Morgan asked. "Anyone know "Cattle Call?""

"Sure do," Pete said. "It'll take a bit of yodelin', but I've got it covered."

After singing about cattle prowlin' and coyotes howlin' and doggies bawlin', Pete yodeled. "Doo, doo, do do, do doo," reminding me of the cowboy reruns starring Roy Rogers and Gene Autry. And I loved it.

Morgan then sang "To Make You Feel My Love," and though he didn't look my way, I fantasized that he was singing it just for me.

During the next song, the doctor's flute took center stage, sounding like a bagpipe in its lonely call. Ben joined in on the harmonica, followed by Joshua on the drum, and I decided that the simplicity of the Grand Ole Opry songs of old were appropriate out here somehow.

Everyone, except me, joined in while Morgan crooned "South Wind of Summer." They sang of the wind singing through the trees and hanging low in the breeze and strong hearts flowing over, while my eyes filled with tears.

Veronica changed course by asking the crew to play "Powerful Thing." After she finished bellowing out the accompanying words, I said, "You have a beautiful voice, Sis."

"And *you* don't?"

"Actually, I don't know."

"What do you mean, you don't know? Are you saying that you don't, or that you can't, sing?"

I should have kept my big mouth shut. "Both. I think."

"And I thought I was screwed up," she said.

Veronica instructed the musicians to play "Paper Wings" and then poked my shoulder with her knuckled fist. "Join me."

Gillian Welch had performed this song in a movie I'd once seen, and it had affected me so deeply that I'd memorized the words. Now, as my voice blended with my sister's, I sang for the first time in as long as I could remember.

And it felt good.

More than good, actually.

It felt magnificent.

Morgan ended the evening by singing, "Red River Valley," and his voice touched me, as he touched me in so many ways.

For a long time, my darlin', I've waited
For the sweet words you never would say
Now at last all my fond hopes have vanished
For they say that you'r going away.

When he finished, all was silent, except for the crackling of the fire, gurgling of the nearby stream, and call of the night animals.

An owl hooted, *hoo-h'HOO-hoo-hoo*, and I whispered, "Amen."

Chapter Thirty-four

IT WAS LATE WEDNESDAY MORNING, April 11, and the tour was nearing its end. Having promised something special as a grand finale, Pete led us to an ancient cave. "A spiritual site," he called it, "with a surprise inside."

Jake stayed behind with the horses—and the cat, while Pete, Morgan, Ben, Dr. Mendez, Veronica, Joshua, and I trekked the last leg of the journey on foot. We stomped across tall grasses, around bushes and trees, over and between boulders, and through a small stream. "Hang in there," Pete said, his breathing heavy. "What you're gonna see is worth the trouble gettin' there."

The huge sandstone outcropping, which Pete referred to as a cave, revealed itself slowly, camouflaged as it was by a periphery of bushes and trees. Rays of sunlight filtered through a break in the clouds and highlighted the flattened soil in front of the rock shelter's rough, oval mouth, creating what appeared to be a massive welcome mat.

However, I felt more than welcomed. I felt drawn, hardly able to resist the urge to break from the group and sprint through the shallow cave-like opening.

The shelter's interior was in shadow, so it took several seconds for my eyes to adjust. Even so, I glimpsed only a dim and distorted view. Pete pulled out a pocket flashlight and flipped it on. Instantly a beam of light exposed details of the inner cave walls that incited a collective gasp.

"There they are," Pete said, "straight ahead, right in front of us."

Hands, a great family of hands, hands of all shapes and sizes, intertwined and pointing in all directions, were imprinted on the overhang's interior wall. As we approached for a closer look, Pete said, "It's an ancient mural created by the Esselen. Beautiful, huh?"

"Beyond beautiful," I said. We could spend hours here and not fully appreciate the significance of the archaeological treasure now exposed to our eager eyes.

I sensed Pete's excitement at sharing this ancient artwork as he pinpointed the white and ochre colored dots, lines, even modern graffiti, interspersed around and between the hands. "This rock art, painted back as far as 4,000 years ago, contains messages sent from the grave. The Esselen believed that ev'rything is alive, including rocks, and that ev'rything has a spirit. What I think they're showin' us here is their belief that the invisible world is full of mystical forces, prob'ly what scientists in modern times would call energy."

"Too bad about the graffiti," Morgan said softly, pointing out some recently imprinted initials.

"Yeah," Pete said. "Technically speaking, these rock art sites are open to the public, but the exact locations are usually kept secret to keep out looters and vandals. Once these caves get damaged, they stay that way forever. Anyway, the Esselen believed that rocks hold memory and that if ya put your hand over a hand carved or imprinted onto a rock, ya can tune into ev'rything that ever happened there. We're not supposed to touch the rocks 'cause the bacteria and oil on our skin causes the pictographs to deteriorate, but it's okay to hold your hand an inch or so away from the wall's surface, if you're into givin' the tunin' in thing a try."

He set the flashlight on the cave floor and held up his hands to demonstrate. Joshua and I walked up to the wall and, without touching its surface, swept our out-stretched hands over the ancient hands, each attempting to find a print similar to our own. Energy surged through my fingertips and palms as my hands hovered over the exact spot where an Esselen, possibly even one of my ancestors, had left his or her mark.

Joshua closed his eyes and started to tremble as if no longer in control of his arms, legs, and body. The sight disturbed me, and I turned to Dr. Mendez with the silent question. *What should we do?*

He shook his head and pressed a finger to his lips.

In an attempt to discover what Joshua was experiencing, I, too, closed my eyes, and almost immediately opened them again. "Mother!"

For a moment, I had imagined that the woman who'd given birth to me twenty-eight years before had come back and touched me through the hands on the wall.

I sensed rather than saw Veronica's jolt of surprise. "Who did you hear or see?"

"No one," I said, reaching for Joshua and pulling him close. "I heard and saw no one."

"No offense," Veronica said, "but this place reminds me of a huge, dark birthing chamber, with all the hands shooting out of what appears to be a Yoni fertility symbol, which would explain your reference to *mother*."

"I don't know," I said, unable to explain what I had just experienced.

"Come to think of it," Veronica said. "It would be kind of hard for a woman in labor to manage the long trek getting here. Even a strong Esselen woman used to such tough conditions."

"The reason the cave's mouth isn't lettin' in more light is 'cause of all the bushes and trees blockin' the sun," Pete said defensively, probably misinterpreting Veronica's comment and my reaction as criticism and disappointment, rather than appreciation of his big surprise. "It's big enough for a small tribe to hold a ceremony," Pete continued, "like bringin' in young men for fertility rites when they're goin' from boyhood to manhood. Guess we'll never know."

Dr. Mendez touched the small of my back, signaling that it was time to leave the large grotto-like shelter. "Come on, Joshua," I said. "Better head back to camp before dark."

If Veronica, too, had sensed something out of the ordinary, she wasn't showing it. My sister was, after all, an expert at masking her feelings and thoughts.

When Morgan came out of the cave, he took me into his arms and rubbed my shoulders and back. "I'm here if you need me. Always remember that."

Pete took off his hat and slapped it against his thigh. Dust misted out in a cloud of disappointment. "Might as well set up camp and call it a day."

He glanced at me and then looked away. "No entertainment tonight."

The lack of entertainment didn't bother me. I had other things on my mind, like what had happened to Joshua and me in the cave and how the clouds had turned dark and the air moist and chilly. Morgan and Ben exchanged glances. Veronica looked at the clouds and shook her head.

After dinner, Pete joined Joshua and me next to the campfire. "I meant for the hands in the cave to be a big surprise and that you'd get a real kick out of 'em the way I do." His lips moved as if he were talking to himself and then his face brightened. "Ever heard of Robinson Jeffers?"

"The poet?"

"He lived in Carmel. Built himself a house outa rocks and called it Tor House. Even though I didn't get much schoolin', I like his poems. Can't say I understand 'em all, but I like the sound of 'em. He wrote a poem about the hands in the cave."

"You're kidding," I said, glad that his mood had lifted.

"I tried to memorize the lines for my tours, but . . ." Pete paused and studied his hands.

"What would you say if I told you I've been hearing and seeing things?" I asked.

"You mean things other people don't?"

"Something like that."

Pete scanned the troubled sky. "Out here, a person can believe almost anything. I've heard some mighty convincing stories about spiritual sites and such. Some have scientific explanations like positive and negative ions, but not all."

If the collective consciousness theories Dr. Mendez had talked to me about bore any truth, it would be possible for some kind of energetic whorl of lingering memory to gather in such sites, consisting of the thoughts of all the people who'd previously visited or meditated there. Coherent memories of intense moments of like-mindedness would be available to tap into by anyone with the ability to do so.

"Joshua and I sensed something in the cave," I said. "Right, Joshua?"

I felt rather than saw Joshua nod.

"You mean somethin' bad?" Pete asked.

"Gosh no. The experience was exhilarating, like the surprise you promised as a grand finale. I loved the hands. They had energy and seemed to be sending a message from thousands of years ago."

"Did you like the hands, too? I asked Joshua.

He huddled closer to me before giving another nod.

I squeezed his hand— "I thought so" —and then turned back to Pete. "Tell me more about the poem."

Though Pete's smile was no more than a lipless slash, it clearly expressed his pleasure in sharing Jeffers's message. "The first two lines go like this:

Inside a cave in a narrow canyon near Tassajara
The vault of rock is painted with hands . . .

"Sorry, can't remember the rest."

Softly, as if carried by the breeze, Dr. Mendez recited the remaining lines of the poem, which spoke of a multitude of hands and questioned whether the brown, shy people who painted them intended religion or magic with the sealed message.

I savored the words, not wanting to let them go.

ℵ ℵ ℵ

Next morning, I woke to the rumble of distant thunder.

Soon after came a bright flash, as if a megawatt spotlight had flicked on and off, followed by a crackling sound and another long roll of thunder. Heart racing, knees shaking, I crawled out of my sleeping bag and grabbed my clothes. I heard that it's rare to experience a thunderstorm first thing in the morning, but when they strike, they pack a punch.

Rain pattered on the canvas walls, and while I dressed, the patter turned into a downpour. I opened the tent flap and peered through the sheet of rain. The entire force of men, dressed in rain gear, scrambled to load our supplies onto the horses. Morgan greeted me with a dimpled smile. "Pack up. I'll take care of your tent."

Pete tossed me a wrapped sandwich. "Best eat this now."

"Are we close to Tassajara?" I asked, my heart weighing heavy.

"Yep," Pete said. "Almost at the end of our journey."

Joshua stepped out of his tent, and I gestured for him to join me. He looked pale and listless, and I wondered if this was because of the storm. What an unfortunate thing to happen, just as we had reached the place I had hoped would incite Joshua to speak again.

While I rolled up my sleeping bag and gathered my belongings, I encouraged Joshua to eat part of the sandwich Pete had given me. He did so reluctantly, sharing portions of it with Gabriel, who would have eaten the whole thing, if I hadn't intervened.

Ben opened the flap of the tent and handed me two disposable ponchos with attached hoods. "I'll check Joshua's mount. Join us when you're done."

I slipped a poncho over my head and waited for Joshua to finish eating before helping him with his. By the time we reached the others, Ben had tacked up Joshua's horse, put his supplies in a waterproof bag, and secured it over the saddle horn.

Joshua mounted, and Ben handed him the reins, warning him to stick close to the doctor and me. Joshua nodded, his eyes unfocused. Even the cat, who Ben had nearly buried beneath the folds of a blanket inside Joshua's saddlebag, couldn't help the child now. This trip had been a bad idea.

N N N

By late afternoon, the rain had stopped and Pete found a suitable location to set up camp. Normally, we would have settled under the protection of the trees, but because of the continued threat of lightning, we opted for a low, open area, surrounded by outcroppings of rock.

"Tomorrow'll be our last day," Pete said. "We'll leave the horses at Tassajara Hot Springs and then I'll get someone to drive you back to your cars. By mornin', I'm hoping for better weather." He inspected the campsite with a wistful expression on his weathered cowboy face.

Ben, Morgan, and Dr. Mendez set up camp for the last time, and for once, Joshua didn't join in. Instead, he and Gabriel found a large, slick rock and planted themselves on top like newts. Veronica erected her tent without adding a word to the conversation. Jake fixed a pot of coffee and then built a fire to comfort and dry the wet and weary travelers. What an introspective group we'd become.

Once I'd erected my wet tent—which took me twice as long, with ten times as much fumbling as it had taken Veronica—I invited Joshua to join me next to the fire for a game of cards. The only game I knew was solitaire, but that didn't matter. At this point, nothing would have interested the child, except, maybe, the miraculous return of his parents.

Even Gabriel seemed out of sorts. Instead of winding his body around Joshua in his usual cat-like manner, he roamed the camp in an aimless circle. Morgan and Ben checked the horses with extra care, making sure to hobble and tie them securely.

"We're goin' to combine lunch and dinner," Pete said, "so we can have evr'thing packed away come dark."

He motioned to Joshua. "I could use a little help serving the meal. You game?"

Joshua nodded and trudged to his side.

"We're only havin' campfire beans and cornbread," Pete said. "Nothin' fancy, but it'll have to do."

Jake piled more wood on the fire, and Dr. Mendez volunteered the last of his wine. All but Pete accepted gratefully. Jake scooped large portions of beans onto our plates, and Joshua followed balancing a platter of sliced bread.

I watched the child for signs of distress, but he seemed pleased with his new role as camp server. He waited patiently while each person took a slice of Pete's last supper offering.

"This'll be our last meal together," Pete said, " 'cept for a quick breakfast in the morning. The storm wasn't part of the plan, but that's how it goes."

The Rolling Stones' lament, *You Can't Always Get What You Want*, flooded my mind, which spoke to my current disillusion with the trip and its therapeutic value for Joshua. But then I recalled the last part of the lyrical hook, which sounded a lot like something Dr. Mendez would say to me about now—that I might just get what I need.

"Funny you mentioning this being our last meal together," Morgan said softly, "today being Holy Thursday and all."

Lent was almost over. Two more days until Easter Sunday.

Chapter Thirty-five

I WOKE TO THE CRACK AND ROLL of thunder. Again. But this time it was night instead morning, and the crack sounded nearer and the ground rumbled beneath me like the landing of a beanstalk giant. Lightning flashed, lit up the tent. I counted the seconds before thunder cracked and rumbled again and only made it to five, which, divided by five, meant trouble. The strike was only one mile away. Successive lightning strikes often jump two or three miles. That meant we were sitting at ground zero. I tried to remember what I'd heard about safety during a thunderstorm. Nothing came to me except staying away from anything that conducted electricity, including tall trees and bodies of water. Did tent poles conduct electricity? I wasn't about to hang around and find out.

I pulled on my jacket and rushed into the electric dawn, surprised that it wasn't raining. I crouched low, at least remembering not to touch the ground with my hands. There was no wind, yet my hair lifted into the air. I knew instinctively this wasn't good.

Another flash of lightning lit up the sky and I noticed smoke coming from one of the tents. "Pete!"

Morgan charged out of his tent, flashlight in hand. "Damn!"

"Pete's tent is smoking," I screamed.

Within seconds, Ben and Dr. Mendez joined us, and we rushed to our guide's aid. Lightning struck again, this time hitting an oak tree nearby.

Sparks. Smoke. How often did lightning strike in one place?

Morgan handed the flashlight to Ben and helped Dr. Mendez pull

Pete's unconscious body out of the scorched and smoking tent. The doctor tipped Pete's head back and listened at his nose and mouth. "We need to move him onto his side."

No sooner had the doctor repositioned Pete's head and arms for the turn than Pete opened his eyes and howled.

"Thank God," Ben said.

I eyed Ben as if he'd lost his mind.

"It means he isn't suffering from cardiac arrest," Ben qualified. "If the lightning had struck him directly, he'd need CPR to jumpstart his heart. The lightning must have hit a tree nearby and traveled underground through the roots of the tree and underneath his tent."

"But he's in pain." I said.

The acrid smell of burnt tent and singed clothing coated the inside of my nose and throat with a sooty layer that made it hard to breathe. I blinked away tears due to the combination of wet, itchy smoke and the heaviness in my heart.

"By the looks of his clothes," Ben said, "he may have some superficial thermal burns. It'll hurt like hell, but he'll live."

"Poor guy," I said.

"Actually, he's quite lucky. By the looks of it, the lightning didn't go through his heart or any other vital organs. Plus, Tony is an experienced wilderness doctor as well as a psychologist, so he's trained to handle things like this."

"God, I hope you're right," I said, not feeling as upbeat about Pete's condition. "Should I get Joshua out of his tent?"

"Let him sleep. He's safe for now."

"Are you sure?" I'd read somewhere that the most dangerous period in a lightning storm was at its end.

"The storm is over," Ben said.

I wondered how Veronica and Jake had managed to sleep through all the commotion, but let the thought go. Right now, Pete's welfare took priority.

"Marjorie," Morgan said. "Do you have your phone handy?"

"Yes." Thank goodness, my battery still had a charge, since I'd decided to turn it on only in case of emergency. "Hope we get reception out here."

"Have an ambulance sent to Tassajara Hot Springs. We can have Pete there in less than two hours."

I rushed to my tent for the phone and on my return, handed it to Ben. "They'll need to know exactly where we are."

"Right," he said, tossing me the flashlight.

"Marjorie," Morgan called. "Pete wants to talk to you."

"Darn," I said when I got to Pete's side. "That was close. Are you okay?"

He took a ragged breath and reached for my hand. "Just listen, okay?"

At my nod, he continued, "Remember our talk about hearin' and seein' things?"

"You bet, especially after you told me about the poem."

"While I was unconscious, I had a vision," Pete said, squeezing my hand. I leaned in closer, barely able to hear him. "It had to do with you and Joshua and the cave." His grip on my hand loosened. "The cave is sacred. A good place."

Dr. Mendez touched my shoulder. "Pete needs to get those burns taken care of, plus just to be safe, he needs to be checked for internal injuries. I did what I could with what I had on hand, but we need to get moving right away. I will keep him company while you and Joshua gather your stuff."

I turned back to my wounded friend and said, "When I first met you, I thought you were stern and boring. I actually called you 'Perfect Pete.' Little did I know how apt the nickname would be. You are perfect, Pete, and I mean it with all my heart. I'll never forget you or this trip."

One last squeeze and he released my hand. "Don't go broadcastin' it to the entire camp. Next thing you know, the nickname'll stick for good. Now get. I've got an important date and don't wanna be late."

The wilderness no longer appealed to me. I no longer felt safe. Thank God, Pete hadn't lost his life. I opened the flap of Joshua's tent, anxious to get out of this area before anyone else got hurt. "Hey kiddo."

No response.

Empty sleeping bag.

Empty tent.

My knees barely supported me as I backed into the open.

Oh my God, oh my God. "Morgan! Joshua's gone!"

I was tempted to give in to the weakness that threatened to turn me into a trembling mess, tempted to rely on Morgan's strength, his counsel, his calm reassurance, but something inside warned that this was not an option. I had to clear my head, make use of the personal strength and ability I had never called on before.

Morgan peered into the tent and cursed under his breath before calling for Ben to search the camp.

"Where could he be?" I asked before clenching my teeth to keep them from chattering.

"Probably with Veronica."

"Dear God, I hope so."

"Me, too," Morgan said.

"It was my idea to bring him on this trip," I said. "I shouldn't have let him sleep by himself in a tent, but I thought with so many of us close by and with Gabriel in the tent with him, he'd be okay. If anything happens to him—"

"Jake and Veronica are missing too," Ben said, his forehead creased, his body tense, nothing gentle about him.

I looked at Morgan for reassurance, anything to calm my raging heart, give me hope, but the scowl on his face didn't reassure me at all. "Let's go," he said.

"Go where?" I asked.

Morgan looked at me blankly for a second or two, then said, "Go back to Tassajara Hot Springs with Tony and Pete. You'll be safe there."

For a second, I thought I hadn't heard him correctly. Did he have such lack of faith in my ability to help in a crisis? Okay, so my voice wobbled a bit, and I was fighting the shakes. No surprise. I was scared for Joshua, worried about how he was feeling. But that didn't mean I couldn't contribute something of value.

Take me with you. I pleaded silently. *I'm not staying behind.*

Morgan hesitated, and I clung to the brief hope that the light of understanding would flare up in his eyes. Instead, he touched my face with fingers that trembled slightly. "Ben and I will search for Joshua. My bet is that he's with either Veronica or Jake. Don't worry, we'll find him."

I glanced at Ben. His eyes narrowed. "Morgan . . ."

I shook my head. Ben meant well, but this was between Morgan and me. Morgan had to grasp the situation himself, or it meant nothing.

"Yeah," Morgan said.

With his eyes still on me, Ben said, "Never mind."

"Then, let's go."

Morgan and Ben saddled their horses and rode off, leaving Dr. Mendez, Pete, and me behind in the deserted camp.

Conflicting emotions coursed through me. Sadness. Disappointment. Anger. The anger, however, fizzled out quickly, giving way to determination. It was high time I started listening to my own counsel for a change, which meant acting instead of reacting, leading instead of following. Would Morgan just sit back and do nothing if the situation had been reversed? Hell no. And I wouldn't have respected him if he had. As I wouldn't respect myself if I hightailed it out of here with Dr. Mendez and Pete instead of taking part in helping Joshua. I was responsible for getting him into this mess, so it was my responsibility to help get him out of it. No matter if my contribution would only be a small one.

"Do you need my help with Pete?" I asked when I'd rejoined the doctor.

"He is tough and able to ride without assistance," Dr. Mendez said. "You do not intend to go with us, do you?"

I studied him, allowing my resoluteness to build. His fitness became him, the ponytail, boots, and jeans, his tanned face. "Not if you don't need me."

"You're not familiar with the terrain. You may get lost."

"Then draw me a map."

"To where?"

"Pete told me he had a vision about the cave. I can probably remember how to get there, but a few directions wouldn't hurt."

"I would oblige, but, around here, there are no street signs."

"Then I'll retrace our path."

"It will not be easy—"

"Morgan's wrong. I *am* needed, and I *can* help."

Dr. Mendez didn't respond.

"What'll you do when you get to Tassajara Hot Springs?" I asked.

"Once Pete is situated, I will return with the authorities. Ben has already contacted them about Joshua's disappearance. They will know what to do." Dr. Mendez shook his head. "Life can change with such startling abruptness."

I thought about Joshua and then cleared my mind. The pain was too intense. "I know."

"There are invisible forces at work here," Dr. Mendez said. "Make use of them."

"Have you seen Gabriel?"

"The cat is the least of your problems right now."

"I was just wondering . . ."

The peach glow of sunrise had transitioned into a startling combination of light and dark blues. Under normal circumstances, I would have paused to appreciate the wondrous shadings of nature, but not now. If I stalled much longer, I'd lose my nerve.

"What about the tent and stuff?" I asked.

"Pete has an emergency crew that comes out for situations such as this. All will be cleared up and packed away in no time."

"When Pete has recovered enough to start worrying about Blondie," I said, "tell him I'm paying him double the rate he normally charges for the tour."

"He is currently fixated on his missing rifle."

"Maybe Ben or Morgan took it."

"That is possible. Now, go. There is no security in playing it safe. Listen to the quiet voice within, which is calling you to do more."

My ability to saddle a horse, almost habit now, came in handy. It also helped calm my nerves. *On with the saddle pad. Lift the saddle, girth, and cinch over the horse's back. Cinch down. Girth on. Tie front cinch. Snug it up. Tie back cinch loosely.*

"I would go with you," Dr. Mendez said, "but—"

"Not necessary," I said. "Just glad you understand."

We said our farewells and I didn't look back, welcoming the indefatigable energy that fueled me. You're finally free, I told myself. Free to succeed and free to fail.

The pendulum paused. For an agonizing moment, guilt and fear rooted me to the spot, but instead of resisting these emotions, I surrendered to them. Fighting would only make them grow stronger. Time to move forward into the uncharted terrain of the next moment. Every ounce of my being, every instinct, told me to head for the cave. The directive was so intense that I had no choice.

Even in semi-darkness, the way was clear.

Chapter Thirty-six

HOW I WISHED FOR Morgan's calming presence now. He would have proved a strong ally at my side. For once, we wanted the same thing, and for once, we could have worked together. I didn't object to his desire to protect me. In fact, I craved that kind of security. However, I wanted my sense of self protected, too. I refused to be a doormat ever again. Cliff had cured me of that. He had wanted an obedient servant, which had left me feeling suppressed, smothered, and used. Were equitable relationships the exception rather than the rule? Was I searching for something that didn't exist?

Where was Morgan anyway? He had been in a hurry, almost as if he'd known something I did not, which suggested there was more to this situation than met the eye. He had told me during our picnic in Garland Ranch Park about something suspicious going on in the Ventana Wilderness and how he didn't want me anywhere near there. Why hadn't I paid more attention, asked more questions? Then again, why had it been necessary for me to ask for information that Morgan should have offered freely? Why the mystery?

Okay, so what *did* I know?

I knew that Joshua's parents had died here and that the child had experienced something traumatic enough to rob him of his speech. I also knew that Joshua was afraid of Jake. The poor kid had spilled his breakfast and had become limp and unresponsive when he encountered our reclusive guide at the campfire. Jake hadn't missed the child's reaction yet had proceeded to clean up the mess and slip away.

Looking back now, Jake's actions seemed more than a little odd.

And what about Veronica? Joshua wasn't afraid of *her*. In fact, they seemed to share a special bond, which had fueled a bout of jealousy on my part. If she wasn't involved in Joshua's disappearance, where was she? In my heart, I trusted her and believed that Joshua trusted her, too; but I didn't trust Jake. Oh no, not Jake. From the start, he had signaled bad news.

So now what? I was unarmed and alone. Well, not completely alone. I had the *Voice*. Whoever and wherever she was. I'd already surrendered to my fear; why not surrender to her as well?

"Tell me what to do," I said—half in jest, half with an allowance for hope. And for the first time, she responded, as if I'd finally spoken the magic words.

Soon you will understand the true purpose of your journey.

Even though the speaker existed in a realm invisible to me—one that defied all logic—her words brought comfort. With her assurance came hope, a conviction of something not seen.

Blondie snorted and tossed her head, alerting me to the dangers of my surroundings. I had to be nearing the cave. So where was it? Countless shades of green surrounded me, some dappled with sunlight, some draped in shadow. Water trickled in a hidden stream. Wind whispered through shrubs and trees. Everything looked familiar, smelled familiar, and sounded familiar, but the connection I had felt to the cave was lost. What had been so clear minutes before and had brought me this far was gone. I struggled to recapture the energy, the determination that had given me strength. I came here to help Joshua, damn it. Pete's vision—and the *Voice*—would lead me to him. I had to believe that.

A hawk screeched overhead, followed immediately by the stench of evil. It closed in on me; it poisoned my lungs; I saw its unholy face.

"Jake!"

He bowed and swept his arm into a wide arc as if welcoming me to the gates of hell.

"Where's Joshua?"

The heat of anger pumped up my muscles and pumped down my fear. I needed to rein it in, before I did something stupid.

"How'd you find us?" Jake asked.

"Us?" I yelped.

"Dang, you look like Vonnie," he said.

Though Ben had told me that Jake was my sister's friend, I couldn't visualize Veronica hanging out with him. My smart, savvy sister? Never.

"Vonnie's one hot and powerful bitch," he said, "very controlling. But you. Same face, same body, but your eyes tell a different story."

So, Jake had turned into Mr. Talkative all of a sudden, now that he had me alone. My mind raced, crashed against a wall. "I asked you a question," I said.

"I heard you."

"Where's Veronica?"

I detected a flicker of life in those dull, indifferent eyes. "She doesn't like you much. Says you're on a friggin' journey."

Did Veronica talk about me like that? The thought hurt.

"Don't you know?" Jake said, "Everybody's on a fuckin' journey. What makes you so different?"

Where was Joshua? Where was Veronica? They had disappeared at the same time Jake had. Were they his prisoners?

"You use your colored rocks. My customers use white pills. If you want to go on a mental journey, I sell something that'll transport you first class. You'll cry tears of joy."

When I shook my head, he said, "Don't knock it till you've tried it. I can help you get real close to the Source."

Had I misjudged Veronica? Could my sister be dealing drugs? That would explain her association with this bottom-dwelling loser.

A gray figure hobbled up from behind Jake, only to be illuminated by the mid-morning sun. It seemed inappropriate somehow—sacrilegious even—for Tommy Boy to be honored in this way. "What's *he* doing here?" I said.

"He's come for your horse."

"Unless you can tell me where Joshua is, I'm not staying."

"Get off the fuckin' horse and I'll show you," he said.

The rhythmic swishing of blood in my ears and debilitating ache in my chest signaled that I was terrified half out of my wits; but damn if I'd give up now. Joshua needed me, and apparently, I had succeeded in finding him before anyone else had. Yippee for me. So how was I going to get the two of us out of here without getting killed? I stepped down from the saddle, welcoming the feel of solid ground in my suddenly un-solid world. When Tommy Boy took hold of the reins, I regretted having stored my cell phone in my saddlebag. I might have found an opportunity to press 911, though the reception out here was likely zero.

Jake led me to a crude shelter almost completely hidden between rocks, bushes, and trees. Enough was visible, though, to surmise that it consisted mainly of scrap wood and tin, bringing to mind shelters used by the homeless, which barely served as protection from the elements.

As we stepped inside, the foul odor hit me like a slap. Switching so suddenly from inhaling clean air to its complete opposite caused me to stifle a gag. If death had a smell, other than rotting flesh, this was it.

"Sorry," Jake said. "We're all out of air freshener."

"You'll get used to it," Tommy Boy said from behind me.

I felt his breath on the back of my neck, which triggered a swelling of goose flesh. I hoped I'd never get used to the smell of hell, or to the filth I was encountering now. Animals kept their dens cleaner than this.

"Come along, sweetheart," Jake said.

For the first time since my arrival, I almost balked. Hearing Morgan's endearment coming from this man made me nauseous. My face must have registered my revulsion—if Jake's reaction was anything to go by.

"Don't," he said. "I'm a lot nicer when I'm in a good mood."

We crossed the first trash-filled chamber only to enter an equally wretched space. And there on the filthy floor sat Joshua, with his hands and feet tied and his back pressed against the wall. The look of relief on his face when he saw me made me forget about my own discomfort and become completely absorbed by his. I rushed to his side and dropped to my knees.

"My sweet, precious darling, what have they done to you?"

"Lucky kid," Jake said.

Tommy Boy sneered. "Not so lucky."

I started to untie Joshua's hands, until a sharp pressure on my shoulder brought me to a halt. "No," Jake said.

Out of the corner of my eye, I saw Tommy Boy hand Jake a rope. I jerked around and directed a gaze of pure hatred their way. If I'd been the super-hero Joshua had mistaken me for, the beam of energy emitting from my eyes would have neutralized the enemy. As it was, it only seemed to egg them on.

"Why'd you tie him up?" I asked, my only defense, apparently, words. "He's only a kid. What has he ever done to you?"

"Nothing yet," Jake said, reaching for my hands.

I slapped at his grimy paws. "What are you? Crazy?"

When Tommy Boy attempted to grab me from behind, I jammed my elbow into his midsection, twisted around, and slapped his face.

"Bitch," he screamed, covering his cheek with both hands.

"Coward," I said.

For the first time I understood the urge to hurt someone, I mean, really hurt someone. If I'd been holding a gun, I think I would have pulled the trigger. "What kind of monster are you, picking on a woman and a child?"

"Are you sure she ain't Vonnie?" Tommy Boy squealed.

"Fights like her," Jake said as he pulled my hands back from behind.

I started to struggle, but he jerked my arms up, sending a jolt of pain to my shoulders that temporarily disabled me.

"Why?" I asked, the one word covering so many questions. Why did Jake deal in drugs? Why did Veronica associate with him? And most of all, why had they kidnapped Joshua?

Instead of giving me an answer, Jake dealt me a swift shove. I landed on my knees next to Joshua, and when I looked into his eyes, I almost cried. Instead of seeing fear, as I'd expected, I saw an expression of hatred. Directed at Jake. The child had already been introduced to this dark and destructive emotion.

I didn't hear Jake and Tommy Boy leave the room.

Chapter Thirty-seven

TOMMY BOY HAD BEEN RIGHT about one thing. I did get used to the smell. Would I also get used to the fear? Occasional stirrings in the adjacent room confirmed that Jake and his sidekick were still hanging around but gave no clue as to what they were doing. Whatever, I was grateful that, for now at least, it didn't include Joshua or me. I was also grateful that the child was sleeping, releasing him, if only briefly, from this frightening ordeal.

About to drift into that welcome state of ignorance myself, I was startled back to awareness by a woman's angry voice. "What the hell have you done?"

"Hey, Vonnie. Where've ya been?" Tommy Boy said.

"What are you two smoking?" she demanded.

"What's up babe," Jake said, his voice sluggish.

"Where is she?"

"In the back with the kid," Jake said.

"Are you nuts?"

"Caught her snooping around," Tommy Boy said.

"So, why didn't you just send her on her way?"

" 'Cause she caught on to us," Jake said.

"She was looking for Joshua, for Christ's sake."

"Too late now," Tommy Boy said brightly. "What're we gonna' to do with 'em?"

"You know, Tommy, if you weren't either drunk or high most of the time, maybe you'd use your brain once in a while. But what's your excuse, Jake? I thought you at least had some smarts."

"Back off, Vonnie." Jake was yelling now. "Since when do *you* get spooked about anything?"

"Since right about now," she said. "God, it stinks in here."

"Lighten up," Tommy Boy said. "You used to be fun."

"Quit whining," she snapped.

"You've got a real problem," Jake said.

"*I've* got a problem?" Her voice was pitched high, not Veronica-like at all, causing chills to trail through me like a tribe of marauding army ants. "You kidnap the kid. You kidnap my sister. You've got a shack full of pot. And *I've* got a problem?"

For several moments, all was quiet. Then Tommy Boy said, "We had no choice."

"You always have a choice," Veronica said softly.

"When Pete asked if I wanted to earn some extra cash," Jake said, "he didn't say anything about guiding a kid. Of all the rotten luck. Then the twerp recognized me. I just needed a little more time."

"To get rid of the grass?" Veronica asked.

"We've got to keep the kid out of sight for a couple of days," Jake said, "so he doesn't spill the beans."

"Yeah," Tommy Boy said. "Till we sell the goods and split."

"Without telling me, right?" Veronica's voice sounded amazingly calm. Bet she was mad as hell.

"You've been acting weird ever since your sister showed up," Jake said.

"He don't trust you anymore," Tommy Boy added.

Jake didn't correct him.

"So now what?" Veronica asked.

"We didn't figure on the cops," Jake said.

"So, what *did* you figure on? That Morgan, Ben, Marjorie, and the doc were just going to leave the kid behind? Come on. You can't be that stupid."

"We're only talking a day or two," Jake said.

"So, what's everybody supposed to do in the meantime? Take a nap?"

242

"Shut up. I need to think."

"Think about what? Just let them go!"

"Can't."

"Says who?"

"The boss," Tommy Boy stated.

"You mean someone who scares you more than the law does?" Jake didn't answer.

"Now why, I wonder, would your boss want you to keep the kid?"

"For a hostage," Tommy Boy said.

"Wow, I'm impressed." Veronica's voice sounded closer as if she were headed our way. "You've really outdone yourself this time." When she entered the room, I sagged in relief. Her eyes narrowed when she spotted Joshua and I huddled on the filthy floor. "Crazy fools."

Joshua—awake now due to the yelling match next door—smiled. I didn't question the child's faith in Veronica. Light-headed relief replaced any questions I harbored about her presence in this god-forsaken dump.

Veronica untied Joshua and rubbed the circulation back into his hands and legs. "You okay, little guy?" She wiped his face with the tip of her shirt.

Jake entered the room without making a sound. Quite a talent, really. Too bad, he'd picked the wrong side of the law. Some kind of cigarette dangled from his lips, and I was willing to bet it didn't have a brand name.

Veronica's full concentration remained on Joshua. "Are you hungry, my friend?"

The poor kid probably hadn't eaten since Thursday night.

"All we have is booze," Tommy Boy announced.

He apparently didn't mean this as a joke, demonstrating that the state of his mental health was worse than I'd originally thought.

Veronica snorted, an apt assessment of the ridiculousness of the situation. "I brought food and water, which I'll even share with you fools if you can force something nutritious down."

She untied my hands and feet and helped me stand.

"What's wrong with you?" Jake asked.

Veronica stared at him with what appeared to be pity. "All you two do is sit around and blow smoke. At least, when you're not selling the stuff." She blew out her breath as if she, too, were doing a bit of cannabis puffing. "One of these days . . ."

"One of these days, you're going to miss me, baby," Tommy Boy sang. Off key to boot.

"Been drinking, too?" Veronica said.

Jake's usually languid face turned into a portrait of anger and disgust: his eyes became slits, his lips stretched over clenched teeth. "The breakfast of champions."

"More like embalming fluid."

"And your berry juice is better?"

Another snort from Veronica. "Come on, sweetie," she said, helping Joshua to his feet. "Let's get some fresh air."

Once outside, I pulled air into my lungs as though emerging from a forced dip into a toxin-filled slough. So many questions competed in my head for attention. You'd think I'd suddenly developed ADD.

Anyway, Jake had followed us out. "What's the plan?" he asked.

"We're surrounded by people searching for the kid, including the cops," Veronica said. "If they find this place, you're screwed."

"I suppose your hotshot friend's still asking questions about his sister?"

"He knows she disappeared around here, which sort of leads to reasonable curiosity on his part."

"Has he figured out about the kid?"

Veronica glanced at Joshua and didn't answer.

"About him being her son?" Jake said, directing his cruel gaze at the child.

My head spun with sick realization, a realization I dared not put into words in front of Joshua.

Tommy Boy, who had joined us outside, now asked, "Does he suspect us?"

"What do you think?" Veronica said.

Tension continued to build, feeding on fear and frustration. I wasn't the only one scared half out of my wits. Everyone was scared. Except maybe Joshua. He was currently too full of hatred to be scared.

"Sober up and listen," Veronica said. "I've put up with a lot of your screw ups, and I've covered up for you because—"

"Blah, blah, blah," Tommy Boy said, too drugged or plastered to recognize the desperateness of their situation.

Jake slammed his fist into Tommy Boy's chest. "Shut up, you dumb fuck, this is serious." His eyes met mine, kicking my heart rate up a notch or two and making me wonder what went on in a mind such as his.

"I should let you crash and burn Tommy," Veronica said.

"Can you get us out of here?" he asked.

As Jake watched Veronica, I half expected to see a forked tongue flick out of his mouth. For snakes, the tongue serves as an organ of smell, for people an organ of taste, which Jake obviously lacked.

"You might try doing a disappearing act," she said.

"What about the kid and your sister?" Jake asked.

"Joshua can't speak. Remember?"

"Oh, yes, he can." Jake glared at Joshua with the eye of a brawler in an amateur boxing match. "He said the cat's name. I heard Marjorie tell the doctor about it. And that means he can identify me. We've got to do something."

"Like you did with his parents?" Veronica asked softly, her words confirming the worst of my fears. I looked at Joshua. His eyes glinted with even more hatred, if that were possible.

"Tell me," I said, unsure if I was talking to Joshua or Jake.

Jake stared past me, his hands opening and closing.

"You might as well fill her in," Veronica said. "I get the feeling you're not going to let her go anyway."

He didn't blink, didn't move a muscle.

"It was an accident," Tommy Boy whimpered.

Jake's face twitched. "Shut up, you stupid shit."

"We put them on some *stuff* to settle them down," Tommy Boy continued, "but we didn't kill 'em. The fire killed 'em."

Joshua moaned, and although it came out no louder than a sigh, it sounded so sorrowful I feared for his sanity. I sank to the ground, drawing the child with me. "My baby. My precious baby."

Veronica's face was set in a mask of aloofness. "If you can prove that, you won't spend the rest of your life in jail."

"Was Theresa Alameda Morgan's sister?" I asked, already knowing the answer.

"Yes," Veronica said. "Around here, Teri was known as Theresa, and when she married Paul, she became Theresa Alameda, though I think Alameda was an assumed name." Veronica glanced at Joshua, likely trying to gauge how this information was affecting him. "Joshua is Teri's son, therefore Morgan's nephew."

Joshua trembled in my arms.

After the many tragedies he'd already suffered, to discover out-of-the-blue that Morgan was his uncle was probably beyond his capacity to absorb. I wondered if Morgan had been clued in on the details by Veronica, and if so, how she had learned of Morgan and Theresa's relationship.

"If you kill the kid, or my sister, you'll get the death penalty or life," Veronica warned.

"*If* we get caught," Jake said.

"The authorities are all over the place!" she said.

"What about you?" Tommy Boy asked. "Are you going to jail?"

Veronica glanced my way, didn't meet my eyes. "I'm sure they'll reserve a special place for me."

"Are you going to turn us in?" Jake asked. Something I was wondering about, too.

"If you play your cards right, you might still be able to get out of this."

"We're listening," Jake said.

"First, you've got to get rid of the weed."

"So we're not caught with the evidence. Right?"

Veronica nodded.

"You could help us smoke it," Tommy Boy suggested.

I couldn't believe the verbal garbage coming out of his mouth. Booze and drugs had severed the connection to his brain, if there had ever been one.

"Might do your sister and the kid some good," Tommy Boy said, apparently warming up to his less-than-brilliant idea. "Looks like they could use a little cheering up."

"Joshua doesn't need drugs," I snapped. "Maybe, if you looked really hard, you'd see a very brave young man. Unlike the two of you."

No sooner had the words come out than I regretted them. Up until now, Jake and Tommy Boy had focused little attention on the child, and I'd been the only one aware of the animosity in his eyes. Now they noticed it, too. Tommy Boy seemed to repel backwards. A flicker of worry crossed Veronica's face. I broke into a sweat.

"It's not the marijuana I'm worried about," Jake said, "but the ecstasy."

Veronica didn't even attempt to hide her shock. "What?"

Jake's mouth curled. "Our little secret."

"He didn't think you could handle it," Tommy Boy added.

Tommy Boy's childishness and undeveloped conscience, coupled with his lack of responsibility, equaled a dangerous combination. A combination obviously not lost on Veronica. Her face paled in the semblance of Morticia Addams, which might have been comical in another situation, but now filled me with dread. "You've been selling it around here?"

"Didn't get a chance," Tommy Boy whined. "We just got it."

Jake tolerated Tommy Boy, his attention on Veronica. "10,000 tablets, about a week's supply on the street."

"How—" Veronica began.

"Our source in San Francisco gets it directly from the 'Cook,'" Jake said.

Veronica sagged to the ground and dropped her head into her

hands. "Crap. That makes you a Class A supplier, which means fourteen years in jail."

"That's why we didn't tell you," Tommy Boy said, shifting from one foot to the other.

"If we slip up and don't pay our dealer, the cops won't need to arrest us," Jake said. "We're screwed either way."

Which meant they were desperate. It didn't matter if they now committed murder. They were already in too deep.

"Why?" I asked, addressing Jake.

"How would someone like *you* understand?" he asked.

"I probably won't, but try me.

He met my eyes, and I wondered how he could possibly care what I thought. "If *we* don't distribute it, someone else will. You'd be surprised at the law-abiding citizens using it."

I made no comment; certain this was true.

"Did you know that ecstasy started out as an appetite suppressant? Then it became a treatment for Parkinson's disease. Pretty legal stuff, wouldn't you say?"

I nodded, feeling sweat trickle down my back.

"Our good old government even considered it as a possible weapon for the army. I was never clear on what kind of weapon—maybe they thought they'd make the enemy all soft and cuddly. Marriage counselors used it to reduce hostility between spouses. Nice, huh?"

Again, I nodded.

"All of a sudden, the Feds decided it was a controlled substance and made it illegal. Do you think everyone just stopped using it?"

"But why take the risk?" I asked.

"The money!" he blurted. "Why else?"

I waved my hand at our surroundings, brows raised.

"This was our chance to get out of this hell hole," he said. "Our last chance."

"Until *you* came around and brought the kid," Tommy Boy said.

Jake's eyes grew hard. He glared at me as if *I* rather than he was the cause of his misfortune.

A question still nagged at me. "How did Joshua get away during the fire?"

"We've been wondering about that, too," Jake said, eyeing Veronica.

"They found him wandering in the woods," Tommy Boy said.

A quick glance at Jake confirmed that he was still looking at Veronica. What did he suspect?

"Tell you what," Veronica said. "I'll stay with Marjorie and Joshua, while you two find a place to hide your wacky weed and Scooby Snacks."

Tommy Boy grinned. "Sounds good to me."

Jake didn't agree. "How do we know you won't let them go?"

"You don't," Veronica said. "Can you come up with a better plan?"

They stared at each other, calling to mind a standoff in an old TV western. I should have been scared, but something kept me calm, almost as if a comforting hand rested on my shoulder.

"No!" Jake said. "You're coming with us. Tommy, tie them back up."

Tommy Boy was happy to oblige, and in a ridiculously pompous manner, he escorted us back to the small, stinking room and tied up our hands and feet.

Veronica helped her friends load their bounty, and after some shuffling, the three of them left the shack together.

Chapter Thirty-eight

I LOST TRACK OF TIME. Once or twice during the long night, I had dozed off; my dreams plagued by imagined endings to our plight, each more dreadful than the last. Completely awake now, the full force of the possibility that Joshua and I might die washed over me like a tsunami. What difference had my life made to anyone, except maybe Joshua? Because of me, he might die.

My desperate thoughts turned to my mother. I should have called her as Morgan had suggested. He'd known that I was hurting her and had tried to warn me. He knew because his sister, Teri, had done the same. I could hear Morgan's words as if he were sitting right next to me. "Why are you punishing your mother? Is it because she loves you too much or because she won't let you go?" Yet, in spite of my regrets, something inside still refused to give in. If I got out of this alive, I'd continue my search.

My journey would not be over.

I would, however, contact my mother.

My main concern right now was for Joshua. I would protect him with my life, if it came to that. But would my life be enough?

Although mad as hell at my sister, I refused to judge her. Unless, of course, she posed a threat to Joshua. So far, that hadn't been the case. Joshua trusted Veronica, and for now, so would I.

It had to be past lunchtime, maybe even late afternoon, considering the rise in the room's temperature and the accompanying rise in its stench. Footsteps sounded in the next room. My insides twisted with the knowledge that, with my hands and feet tied, I couldn't shield Joshua from harm. He was awake, his eyes calm and hate-free. Thank God.

Veronica rushed into the room, her face uncharacteristically flushed. "Hurry. We don't have much time."

"Time for what?"

She untied my hands and feet. "Quick, take off your clothes."

"What?"

She dropped to the floor and yanked off her boots. "Close your eyes, Joshua."

He didn't need a second telling.

"Veronica, are you crazy?"

"Shut up and strip. Jake and Tommy are stoned. Idiots. They can't even keep it together when their world's falling apart. I was able to convince them that I needed to check up on you, but even in their semi-wasted state, they'll get suspicious soon."

I unlaced my boots with shaking hands.

"Hurry, damn it!" Already down to her bra and panties, Veronica got up, rushed to the doorway, and peeked into the next room.

I removed my belted pouch and stepped out of my jeans.

Veronica grabbed them and pulled them on.

"My totem," I said.

"Belonged to me first."

"What?"

"Give me your shirt and put on mine."

Time slowed to a crawl. I felt stuck in slow motion, unable to move.

"Damn it, Marjorie, when did you turn into such a klutz?"

"Okay, okay." Adrenaline rushed through me like a performance-enhancing drug. My movements quickened. "Darn, your jeans are tight."

"Wait till you put on the boots. Now, talk like me."

I opened my mouth to argue but stopped when I saw what appeared to be fear in her eyes. I thought of all the powerful moves my sister made and the powerful way she talked. "Go to hell!"

"I can see the transformation already," she said.

I'd already noticed that Veronica's hair was braided like mine, but only now did I begin to suspect why. "So that's why you cut and bleached your hair and nixed the makeup."

"We needed to look *exactly* alike."

I wondered how my sister could have planned this in advance. Usually so cool and calm, her agitation attacked me like a virus. "Can't we just run for it?"

"You, my little sister, are going to walk out of here."

"And how am I supposed to do that?"

"As me."

"Where will I go?"

"You'll walk into the trap the police have set for Jake, Tommy, and me, then tell them what's going on and to send back help."

"I can't leave Joshua behind."

"I'll take care of him. Like before . . ."

"What do you mean, like before?"

"Walk like me."

"Veronica, this is crazy."

"I said walk like me!"

I took a few steps, swaying my hips as I'd seen her do, trying to replace terror with resolve.

"A bit overdone," Veronica said, "but a good start."

I eyed the red boots on my feet.

"Like them boots, do you? Would look perfect with a red jacket."

This was unreal, a bad dream. I wasn't about to risk my life in an escape attempt. Me. The person everyone was always trying to protect and tell what to do. "I'm not going," I said.

"If you want Joshua to live, you will."

"No, Veronica. Jake can tell us apart."

Veronica opened her eyes wide and frowned. Her face took on an entirely different expression. "I've been trying to tell you. Power is all in the mind."

Then I sensed it, too. I felt stronger, taller, more powerful.

"Now tie me up," Veronica said.

I did as instructed. Voluntarily. Because it was the right thing to do, not because someone was telling me to. "What if they hurt you?"

"As me, I have power, but as you, I'll have more."

I shook my head, confused.

"Those two losers are actually impressed with you. Your naivety fascinates them. In their eyes, you're a rarity. You remind them of their mothers."

Being called naïve and motherly wasn't exactly an ego booster, but at this point, ego didn't much matter. "They're desperate, Veronica."

"It'll be okay."

"God, you'd better be right."

"I'm staking my life on it," she said.

And with those words, I knew I couldn't leave either of them. "I'm not going."

I caught a look of relief in Joshua's eyes and reluctant admiration in my sister's. And for once, my face showed no expression, which was a good thing, because Jake chose that moment to re-enter the room.

Veronica sat next to Joshua, eyes wide, and thanks to all the chemicals Jake had inhaled into his system, he didn't seem to notice the exchange.

Unfortunately, he was carrying a rife. Pete's rifle.

"We're taking them to the cave," he said, addressing me with an unfocused smile. "Untie them."

Chapter Thirty-nine

THE CAVE HAD BEEN CLOSE AFTER ALL, within walking distance of where Jake had intercepted me and taken my horse. It was getting dark. A tall cliff, plus bushes and trees walled the area, further blocking the sun. Lightning flashed in the distance, followed by the rumble of thunder.

"Not again," Tommy Boy whimpered.

I nearly whimpered, too. This location had attracted me during my first visit, and I'd been more than eager to enter the cave's interior, but now it terrified me. The atmosphere rated right up there with misty graveyards and haunted mansions as an ideal setting for mischief, and I had no inkling of what steps to take next. After such a delicious taste of freedom since coming to Carmel Valley, this renewed sense of helplessness rubbed me raw. Using Veronica's vernacular, it sucked.

Jake cursed the shadowy darkness inside the cave. Tommy Boy's small lantern did little more than illuminate the tomb-like quality of the area directly in front of us.

"Let's leave 'em," Tommy Boy said, his voice echoing back like a cold draft. "With us guarding the exit, they can't get away."

"I'll stay," I said quickly.

Jake shrugged. At this point, he didn't seem to care what I did. I was grateful that with the faint light cast by the lantern there was little chance he'd recognize that I wasn't Veronica. Tommy Boy treated me to a blank stare, reminding me of monkeys at the zoo with their empty eyes, resigned to their fate.

"Tie them back up," Jake ordered.

"We left the ropes behind," I said.

"Fuck."

"We could use our shoe laces," Tommy Boy said.

Jake looked at Tommy Boy for several seconds before shaking his head. "Forget it. They're not going anywhere."

Then, side-by-side, our captors walked out of the cave and disappeared through an opening in the surrounding bushes and trees, which might as well have been a moat, given our change of getting through it alive.

"Okay, Veronica," I said. "We can't walk out of here with Jake and Tommy Boy armed and blocking the trail, so what's the plan?"

"Plan?"

Unable to make out my sister's face in the semi-darkness, I couldn't tell if she was serious or just pulling my leg. "You're the one who forced me into an identity switch, like some *Parent Trap* scheme. Call me crazy, but I thought you might have a plan."

She didn't reply.

"You do, don't you?"

"You mean like pulling out a gun and shooting our way out?"

"Yes, damn it!" What was the matter with her? It wasn't like Veronica to be so passive.

"What do *you* suggest?" she asked, her tone snarky.

"Me?" I hissed. "You're the strong one. I'm just—"

"You're just what, Sis? We're identical in more ways than you think. What I can do, you can do, maybe even better. It's hard to step forward if you don't believe in yourself."

"You missed your calling, Veronica. You should be peddling advice instead of drugs."

Silence.

"I'm sorry," I said, though I wasn't.

"Feeling better?" she asked.

"We exchanged clothes, not personalities," I snapped, deciding to keep talking to hide my fear.

"You could have fooled me," she said. "You've become bitchy

enough to pass for me, though I'd like to believe I'm not such a coward."

"Ouch."

"Listen, Marjorie, back at camp you said you could take care of yourself. I suggest you stop whining like a Tommy Boy clone and prove it."

No answers. No road maps. No directions. What now?

"Anyway," Veronica said. "You're the one wearing the ruby slippers."

"Boots."

"Minor difference."

"So, I'm supposed to just whack them together three times and make a wish?"

"Unless you happen to have some pepper spray or a loaded Taser in this fanny pack of yours," she said, indicating the belted pouch that was now strapped around *her* waist.

My heart jumped as if trapped inside an inflatable bouncer. I wanted to punch something—someone. We had to stop bickering and come up with a plan.

"Let's get this straight, Marjorie. You had a chance to get away and didn't take it. That took courage, but I could use a little help here."

"Mommy will help us," Joshua said.

I sensed Veronica's surprise, which matched mine. Joshua's words had come out so naturally, as if he'd been speaking all along and we just hadn't been listening.

"Look at the hands," he said.

"I can't see them in the dark," I said.

Veronica unzipped the pouch and pulled out the smudge stick and matches Ben had given me the day he'd introduced me to the Medicine Wheel. "How about these?"

"Smudge sticks don't burn, they smolder," I said. "And matches don't stay lit."

"Smudging is supposed to get rid of negative energies, right?" Veronica asked.

"And penetrate the barrier that separates us from the Spiritual realm. Why?"

She lit the stick and waved it in the air until it started to smolder, then handed it to me. "Go for it."

"You want me to smudge the cave?"

"Unless you've got a better plan?"

She called this a plan?

For lack of anything better to do besides worry myself sick, I started to walk the perimeter of the cave—one timid step after another—waving the smudge stick up and down, left and right. My boot kicked something solid. It propelled forward with a metallic clang.

"What was that?" I croaked.

Joshua dropped to his knees and skittered after the sound.

I nearly passed out with relief when he flicked on a flashlight and pointed it at the pattern of hands.

"Pete must have left it behind during our visit," I said.

In the eerie luminescence of the light's beam, I saw enough of the child's face to witness the wonder that had replaced the fear in his eyes. "You okay?" I asked.

He nodded, his gaze fixed on the wall of hands. The tension appeared to drain from his body, only to be replaced by a faint smile. He closed his eyes and started to breathe at an increased rate."

"What's he doing?" Veronica asked.

"Some kind of breathing exercise Dr. Mendez taught him as part of his therapy. It helps him relax and loosens his psychological defenses, which supposedly leads to the emergence of the unconscious and mystical connections to other people."

"Sounds more like he's hyperventilating to me," Veronica said.

"Yeah, it's kind of scary, but Dr. Mendez seems to know what he's doing."

Almost as if instructed to do so, Joshua said, "Sunwalker."

I stubbed the smudge stick on the cave floor to extinguish it and then crawled to Joshua's side and pulled him close. "My precious."

We cuddled in our earthen tomb to wait, and while we waited, I realized that following day would be Easter Sunday. How appropriate. Buried in a cave on Black Saturday, the day the soul of Jesus descended into the underworld of departed souls.

"Mommy!" Joshua said, which jerked my attention back to the pictograph with its long flame-like fingers.

A pale outfall of light radiated from the wall as if its rocky surface were lit from within. The word *Mother* formed in my mind as well. How strange. I sensed only one presence, yet Joshua and I were both calling it *Mother*. Had my sister sensed it, too?

"Tell me I'm not crazy," Veronica whispered from directly behind me.

"Our mother's spirit is here," I said. "I know it."

"Okay, so let's say I've been hearing her, too," Veronica said, settling next to Joshua and me. "What's her purpose? Why should we care? And what are we supposed to do about it?"

"I've been asking myself the same questions and haven't been able to come up with any satisfying explanations. Just knowing I'm not alone and that you and Joshua are hearing something, too, gives me the strength to keep asking questions and listening for the answers."

"Glad to help out," Veronica said, her tone implying otherwise. "So, who else do you think we're hearing?"

Here was my chance to put into words what I'd only been journaling about until now; to put forward the questions journalists ask, attempt to answer, and, more often than not, get wrong. "Spirits . . . their thoughts."

Veronica pulled in a slow, controlled breath and released it in a way that would have made a yogi proud. "You're making me nervous."

"Bear with me now," I said, mimicking Heather as she'd try to explain the unexplainable not all that long ago. "Because this is going to sound kind of weird. I think . . . Actually, I know . . . that our mother has been talking to me since I visited The Lone Cypress on Ash Wednesday."

I glanced at Joshua. He continued to stare at the wall with the alertness of someone consumed by whatever had originally attracted his attention. His intense breathing also continued, and I tried not to let it worry me. I should've listened more carefully when Dr. Mendez had discussed the therapy work he was doing with the child, but it was too late now. At least Joshua wasn't twitching and trembling or passing out.

"Listen, Veronica. Joshua's hearing his mother, too. What are the chances that all three of us are going crazy? And you can't blame a faulty gene because Joshua's not related to us. My guess is that we're tapping into some kind of collective unconsciousness. Heck, maybe we're tapping into ourselves. How long have you been hearing voices?"

"Since coming to Carmel Valley two years ago and finding the mouse totem." Veronica's voice relayed strain almost beyond endurance, and I marveled that she hadn't sought professional help.

"You've got to understand with your heart, not your head," I said, quoting Dr. Mendez, though with less confidence and not nearly as soothing a voice. "Otherwise none of this will ever make sense. Joshua hasn't been able to speak the truth, and we haven't been able to hear it."

Veronica chuckled, but not in a positive way. "So, because we weren't listening, these so-called spirits decided to smack us over the head?"

"Something like that," I said.

"So, what's our mother trying to tell us?" she whispered.

"I don't know but hope to find out one way or another."

"When we get out of this mess, I'll help you do just that," Veronica said.

"Okay," I said, grateful that she'd said *when* rather than *if*.

Joshua whispered something under his breath, which drew our attention. We waited, but nothing else happened.

"Is your mama here?" I asked.

"Yes," he said, so clearly and sweetly that it brought tears to my eyes. I prayed that he'd live to chatter like other children his age.

To keep my fear at bay, and to keep from falling apart in front of

Joshua, I resumed quizzing my sister. "What do you think Jake and Tommy Boy are up to?"

"They're probably at a stalemate," Veronica said. "They don't dare leave you and Joshua behind. You know too much. But they don't want to come right out and kill you either."

I shivered. "They probably hope someone else will do the job for them."

"Or *something* else, like the fire did with Theresa and Paul. A perfect solution for two low-level criminals."

"This might be a good time for you to tell me what's going on."

"God, Sis. I couldn't do anything for Joshua's parents. They were drugged and unconscious when I ran across them on one of my mind-clearing hikes. I wasn't strong enough to carry or drag them to safety. Besides, I didn't have time. A fire had started nearby. I tried calling 911 but couldn't get reception. Thank God, I managed to untie Joshua. But he didn't want to leave his parents. So, I bribed him with my mouse totem."

"You were going to tell me about that."

"As I said, I found it on a hike soon after my arrival in Carmel Valley. When I gave it to Joshua, I told him it would bring him good luck. I left him as close as I dared to the monastery at Tassajara and told him to go for help. Then I went back for Paul and Theresa. But the fire blocked me. No one could have saved them. Not at that point, anyway."

"What else?"

"All I know is that Joshua and his parents came across Jake and Tommy's camp unexpectedly. Probably on a hike or a picnic. They found the shack and, unfortunately, the marijuana. I figure Jake and Tommy panicked and fled, because they left Theresa and Paul behind, drugged and at the mercy of the fire. They also left Joshua to die, not knowing I had freed him."

"So why didn't you turn them in?" I asked incredulously.

"I wasn't aware of any of this back then. Only that I'd saved a child and not his parents. I was pretty shaken up, wondering if I could've done anything differently."

"But you're still hanging out with those losers, calling them friends."

Veronica continued as if she hadn't heard me. "So, you can imagine my reaction when I discovered Jake was going to be one of the guides on your tour. Ben wasn't too happy when I invited myself along. Actually, he was pissed. Then he insisted on joining the party, too. To protect you from me. Can you believe it? With Jake being the dangerous one. Sure, Ben knew you didn't like the man, but he had no idea . . . Anyway, when I told Morgan about Joshua and his parents, we put our heads together and figured out that his sister, Teri, and Theresa Alameda were one and the same. I give Morgan credit. He moved quickly after that. He managed to show up on the trip and convince Dr. Mendez to stay in case you or Joshua needed him. At first, Jake thought he was safe. Joshua showed no signs of regaining his speech and didn't seem to be aware of Jake's presence. But then . . . Well, you know the rest. When Pete was injured in the lightning storm, Jake got the diversion he needed to kidnap Joshua and split. As soon as I noticed Jake was gone, I followed him, curious as to what he was up to. I didn't know he'd taken Joshua, though I should have. What was he thinking? How could he believe he'd get away with this?"

"So, Joshua knew you all along," I said, "which explains why he took such interest in me at Dr. Mendez's office. He thought I was you and that the mouse totem was mine."

"Actually, there's more to it than that," Veronica said. "He wasn't surprised when he saw me again, as if he already knew there were two of us. There's something else going on between the two of you, but what that something is, I can't begin to imagine."

For a while, we sat in silence, but before I could give in to despair, Joshua said, "Let's pray."

The three of us scooted forward, and when we reached the wall, we bowed our heads and joined hands.

I led us in a prayer of faith, thanksgiving, and acceptance, closing with, "Not our will but your will."

To which Veronica and Joshua responded, "Amen."

Chapter Forty

SOMETHING WARM AND FURRY WOKE ME. I froze; didn't dare move. There were raccoons and skunks in this area. Raccoons could be vicious, and often had rabies. Skunks had rabies, too. Plus, their spray . . . Oh my God.

It emitted a vibrating purr, so quiet and low I felt more than heard it. I tried to keep my body from shaking, my breathing steady, hoping that whatever it was would soon leave the way it had come.

Then came a meow.

Not a raccoon.

Not a skunk.

"Gabriel," I said. "Is that you?"

I turned on the flashlight and there he was—my stray. I stroked his quivering body, so happy to see him I momentarily forget the predicament we were in. "Where did you come from? How did you find us?"

Joshua sat up and rubbed his eyes.

"Joshua. It's Gabriel. He meowed."

"Hi Gabriel," Joshua said, and the cat lunged onto his lap.

"Happy Easter," Veronica said.

"Already?"

She pointed at the lighted dial on her wristwatch. "Yep, two a.m."

Easter Sunday, a day of celebration, commemorating the resurrection of Christ. Jesus had stepped out of his tomb and restored faith to his followers. Peter, for one, would never deny Him again. Yet, here we sat—in our own tomb of sorts—waiting. *God, help us.*

I aimed the flashlight at mural of hands and took slow, deep breaths, reminding myself to reach into the state of mind where solutions were possible. I imagined myself inhaling molecules exhaled by my ancestors, giving and receiving in a web of love.

"Sunwalker," Joshua said again, like a one-word mantra, and I reached for his hand. Courage, I realized, wasn't the absence of fear, but knowing there was something—someone—else more important.

I had to stay strong for Joshua.

"It's time we put some of Dr. Mendez's breathing and meditating exercises to work, little man," I said. "And since you're more advanced than we are, you start, and Veronica and I will join in when we get the hang of it. Okay?"

Joshua nodded.

"According to Dr. Mendez, we're beings without borders and that means everything, and I mean everything, is a seamless extension of everything else. Even this cave is alive and part of the whole. We're like strands of a spider's web. Touch one and affect all."

"I suppose that means Joshua's ring, my mouse totem, and your red boots are also alive and part of the whole," Veronica said.

"Actually . . . yes."

"Maybe a fella ain't got a soul of his own, but on'y a piece of a big one," Veronica said, quoting Steinbeck.

"That about sums it up," I said. "Our totems are our symbols of faith and power, our access to our deeper selves."

Joshua lifted his ring and pointed it at the wall of hands.

"Great," Veronica said. "Now, he thinks the ring has special powers."

"Who says it doesn't?" I said, tapping my red boots together. "Every thought, every act has its image stored in the mind of nature, so it's possible that images of the thoughts and actions of past visitors are stored here, maybe even in the wall of hands."

"And we see these images how?" Veronica asked.

"Not we. Only a few people, like Joshua, have the ability to bypass the limited range of their senses and tap into the parallel Universe that surrounds us."

Veronica blew out her breath. "Joshua looks like he's in a drugged daze, and his lips are moving like he's talking to someone."

"He's probably in a meditative state. We were supposed to join him, remember?"

"Go for it, Sis. I'll stay on the alert for those two loose cannons outside who are probably about to do something stupid."

"Where do you think they are?"

"Just beyond that screen of bushes and trees, our only way out of here, unless we suddenly turn into mountain goats."

"Do you think they can hear us?"

"I doubt it, since we can't hear them. Although, at this point, they probably don't care what we're saying or doing as long as we stay put."

I closed my eyes and matched Joshua's breathing, breath for breath, and just as my mind started to quiet and my thoughts to clear, the silence was broken by sounds coming from outside the cave. I turned off the flashlight and got to my feet.

Tommy Boy came in first, holding a lantern. Jake followed, carrying a rifle. His face, up-lit by Tommy Boy's lantern, looked like a floating mask. His lips twitched. His eyes gleamed. I half expected a smile to burst forth on his face, followed by crazed laughter.

Instead, he said, "We've come for the kid."

I glanced at Joshua. His breathing was slow, rhythmic, his gaze focused on the wall of hands, giving no sign he was aware of the mess we were in.

I should have left when I had the chance. What had my staying behind accomplished besides cutting off all chance of getting help? No way would I let Jake and Tommy Boy take the child. They'd kill him this time, or, at the very least, drive him over the edge. I had to do something. But what?

I focused on the wall of hands and again matched my breathing to Joshua's. *Reach into the state of mind where solutions are possible.*

"What the fuck's the matter with the kid?" Jake asked.

"He's connecting with the spirits of the departed," Veronica said.

"This fuckin' cave gives me the creeps," he said.

Waves of energy pulsed around and through me as though I were inside a giant womb rather than a cave made out of cold, hard rock. The hands on the wall began to throb, causing a disturbance that traveled longitudinally like a crowd-wave at a sporting event. I felt disembodied, almost dispassionate, as though observing a scene performed on a distant stage with actors who'd rehearsed their parts *ad nauseam* for the climax of the story—the point of no return. *Help me. Show me what to do.*

"Let's grab the kid while he's all docile and freaky," Tommy Boy said.

"Or shoot him and let him out of his misery," Jake said with a sick laugh.

A flickering light bathed Jake and Tommy Boy in a shimmering mist of gold. It was beautiful to behold, them standing below the glowing cathedral-like ceiling of the cave. I thought I heard singing but wasn't sure.

"No," I whispered, drawing on the hurt and pain they had caused and allowing it to fuel my resentment and fear. "They're criminals. They're scum. They don't deserve the light. It isn't fair."

They are your brothers, a voice said, *my beloved sons.*

No, no, no, I thought, trying not to cry.

Then calm as you please, Gabriel padded up to Jake and rubbed against his legs.

Jake kicked him aside. "What's the retarded cat doing here?"

As if in answer, my stray headed for the wall of hands.

I glanced at Jake. He was eyeing me strangely.

"You're not Veronica," he said.

I didn't say a word, didn't have to. He'd read the answer on my face in the flickering eerie light.

"Bitch."

Every hair on my body seemed to stand on end, followed by a buzzing in my ears. *He's going to kill me. I'm going to die.*

Jake smiled as if he knew exactly what I was thinking, then he cocked the rifle and pointed the barrel at my chest.

From deep inside, I whispered, "Not my will, but your will."

In a sudden, fluid motion, Jake turned away from me and aimed the rifle at my sister. "I should have done this a long time ago."

Oh, dear God, not Veronica. My heart pounded, drew the blood right out of my veins.

You of little faith, a voice said.

Looking at my sister, my chest swelled as if to make room for her inside. I loved her so much.

You must love your brothers as well.

I thought my heart would split due to the pulsing pressure building inside. Time stilled, or ceased all together. The weight of anger, mistrust, and doubt lifted from inside of me and wisped through the cave like a mini tornado.

I looked at Jake from behind different eyes. A voice I didn't recognize as my own said, *Jacob Neil Tritsman. What have you done?*

The rifle jerked in Jake's hands as he turned and aimed it back at me. "How'd you know my name?"

By this time, I had lost control of what I was saying. I was just a vessel channeling words through the unconscious. *My precious, precious child.*

"Shut up or I'll shoot."

Your papa can't hurt you anymore. He has found peace. So have I.

"Momma?"

I've always loved you, my little hero. My protector.

"I've done bad things," Jake said.

Yes.

"I'm a loser."

No.

"What do I do?"

Free yourself. Start over.

"I'll go to prison," Jake said.

Enrichment will come back to you. Control your destiny.

"Too late," he said.

It's never too late.

"They'll put me in prison," he repeated.

The expression of fear and lost hope on Jake's face made me want to reach out in compassion, as if he were Joshua, as if he were my own son. Who was I channeling? Jake's mother? My mother? All mothers? *You're already in prison, Jake.*

"I'll be there for a long time," he said.

You didn't intentionally cause Paul and Theresa's deaths.

"The drugs."

The authorities will go easier on you if you share what you know.

"Why can't I pull the trigger?" he cried.

Slowly, I came back to full consciousness, as if waking from a lucid dream. *Jake is just a swirl of energy*, I reminded myself, *condensed, solidified. He and I, Tommy, Veronica, Joshua, and the cave, are all part of a whole, connected like strands of a spider web. Touch one strand and—*

"The hands," Tommy Boy shouted, pointing at the mural.

Everyone, including Jake, turned to face the wall. A mysterious form of energy highlighted the design of hands and refracted into the cave, flashing and whirling. The hands appeared to pulsate and cycle, giving the illusion of movement.

What were we seeing, hearing?

"Who's there, Tommy Boy?" I asked.

"My mother."

Joshua's ring shot a lantern-like beam toward the wall of hands, and just like that, Ben's Medicine Wheel teachings and Dr. Mendez's quantum theories clicked into place as an unreal reality unfolded around me.

Creation is the transition of the invisible to the visible. In a universe where all things are interconnected, all consciousness is also interconnected and has an effect on the subatomic world. Each of us is the consciousness of mankind. We can tap into the consciousness of those who've been here before us.

Jake's face no longer appeared crazed, as if he were sensing something, too.

I blinked, shook my head, and took command of the conversation between us. "Your mother was a blessed person, Jake."

"She was," he said, staring at the wall of hands.

"She wants you to put down the rifle and approach the wall," I said with confidence, as though Jake's mother were still channeling through me.

"I'm no Indian," he said.

"We're all linked to the unseen," I said. "We're all equal in our potential for love and forgiveness."

Tommy Boy put down the lantern, edged forward, and pressed both hands against the mural. He closed his eyes and whispered, "Mama, Mama, Mama."

"Accept the gift, Jacob Neil," I said.

"My mother's dead," he cried. "My father hurt her."

"And with her, part of you died, too," I said. "Honor your mother by turning yourself in."

"Do what she says, Jake," Tommy Boy cried. "My mama's here."

"I'm a failure," Jake said.

"Set yourself free, and you'll never want to go back to the way you're feeling now."

He turned and stared at me, the rifle slack in his hands. "Where's the light coming from? What is it? What's happening?"

"All I know is that it exits," I said. "And it becomes available to heal and generate happiness and joy. The answer will come, but it takes courage to let go and face the new."

"It's not that hard to hurt someone," Jake said, his voice soft, almost kind. "Even kill someone. All it takes is one split second, one false move. And then, after billions of seconds of being a good, upstanding citizen, you become a felon. One split second. One false move. And then you're in too deep and there's no turning back. How close have you come to giving someone a little shove when standing next to him on a cliff? Would you pull the trigger if you were holding a gun? Would you kill me now if you had the chance? Would you kill me to save Joshua? Your sister? Yourself? Would you pull the trigger?

If you're honest with yourself, you'll admit that you're only one split second, one false move away from becoming a criminal. We're not that different, you and I."

Like the fire that had blazed through the Los Padres National Forest, Jake was burning the frameworks that imprisoned me—my limiting beliefs, my old patterns of thought—transforming them into blackened snags, a perfect habitat for the seeds of awareness buried deep inside to burst into life.

We're not that different, you and me.

What, I wondered, would we do without our enemies?

"Did you kill your father?" I asked, prodded by an inner knowing.

"Why are you asking," Jake said, "when you already know the answer?"

I said nothing.

"Just a little push was all it took, and just like that, he fell into the Pacific and was gone. Mom covered up for me, but I knew. I knew I was a criminal at ten years old"

A criminal at ten years old. What chance did he have?

"What's *your* daddy like?" Jake asked suddenly. "I mean your real daddy, the one who left you behind to be raised by a total stranger. Bet he's a real winner, your old man."

We're not that different, you and me.

Jake closed his eyes and dropped his head back. "What should I do, Mama. What should I do?"

"What does your heart tell you to do?" I asked, wondering yet again where the words were coming from.

"Jail."

"A stepping stone to building your new life," I said. "Even Jesus descended into hell for a time."

Jake tucked the butt of the rifle under his right arm, made a half turn, and pressed his left hand against the hand of an ancient.

Before the possibility of doing so even crossed my mind, Veronica rushed forward, grabbed the barrel of the rifle, and yanked it from under Jake's slackened grip. If I live to be one hundred, I'll never forget the look she threw my way, one of relief, gratitude, victory—and love.

Then out of nowhere and from everywhere, disembodied voices reverberated within the chamber, blending into one emphatic cry. *My children!* The sound was high, weird, and powerful, like that of a hurricane-force wind. On hearing them, Jake seemed to lose all strength, or maybe the will to fight. He sank onto the cave floor and covered his face with his hands.

Veronica walked to the mouth of the cave, pointed the rifle into the air, and fired three shots. The sharp cracks of the discharges sounded through the rock shelter like the cracks of a bullwhip. And then came silence, a silence so complete that my ears ached as if caught in a vacuum.

When I looked at Veronica in stunned amazement, she winked and gave me a thumb up. "That should do the trick." Then she pointed the rifle at Jake and Tommy Boy, who offered no resistance.

New voices, men's voices, some familiar, many not, screamed orders and called names from outside the cave.

We're safe now.

I drew Joshua onto my lap, too dazed to question who was comforting whom.

"Are you okay?" Veronica asked from her position at the mouth of the cave.

I didn't respond, didn't dare move, didn't dare hope. Instead, I started to laugh.

The cave filled with men in DEA jackets armed with searchlights, handguns, and rifles. The excitement was over, but the work had just begun. For one thing, arrests had to be made.

I heard someone call my name but couldn't answer.

Veronica knelt beside me. "Hey, Sis."

"They'll arrest you," I managed between giggles.

"Nah. I'm working with the DEA. Plan on making it my career. If they'll have me."

I laughed even harder.

"They sent me here to chum up with Jake and Tommy Boy, a little test to see if I pass muster."

"Oh my God, I can't believe this," I stuttered.

"You were wonderful," Veronica said. "I'm glad I was here to witness the awesomeness pouring out of you."

I grabbed my stomach, leaned forward, but couldn't stop laughing. Veronica grasped me by the shoulders. "Don't whack out on me, Sis."

"Josh!" Morgan called from the mouth of the cave.

"In here," the child called back.

At the sound of Joshua's voice, I stopped laughing and burst into tears. *Get hold of yourself. Breathe,* I told myself. But I couldn't. It was okay to let go now. It was okay to laugh and cry as I'd never laughed and cried before.

Joshua wiggled out of my grasp and collided with Morgan as he entered the cave. Morgan crushed the child into an embrace that spoke more effectively than words the emotions he felt on holding his sister's son for the first time.

Joshua, too, appeared to understand that Morgan was family, given the way he hugged his uncle with a fierceness I'd never seen him express before.

Then to my surprise, Morgan, with Joshua at his side, headed straight for Veronica, his gaze radiating concern. He kissed the top of her head, asked if she was okay, took her into his arms.

With my cheeks wet and sticky with tears, I started laughing again, wondering if I'd live through the pain.

Veronica's bark of amusement made me wonder if we'd both gone insane. "Morgan, I'm Veronica."

Morgan pulled back, frowned.

She pointed at me. "I know she looks like hell, but that's Marjorie over there."

Joshua grinned as if he found the situation highly comical after what we'd just been through, but Morgan stiffened and came toward me in what appeared to be slow motion, crossing the longest, short distance in the world.

No matter how hard I tried, I couldn't stop laughing.

Of course, Morgan hadn't recognized me, wearing these god-awful skinny jeans and red boots. He ran his fingers through my hair, rubbed my arms, kissed my face, all the while whispering words of comfort. My laughter turned to giggles, then sobs, and while Morgan rocked me like a child, the sobs slowly ceased.

"I'm a farmer, not a hero," he whispered, "an expert at working up and planting the ground, but a failure at fighting evil or protecting you from it. When I heard you'd headed out on your own, I thought I'd lose my mind. Ben and I should've taken you with us. What was I thinking?"

"You were trying to protect me. Understandable, but I told you—"

"Yeah, that you could take care of yourself. You don't know how many times I've reminded myself of that over the past forty-eight hours."

The DEA agents had handcuffed Jake and Tommy Boy and were now leading them out of the cave.

"Your sister's been helping the authorities," Morgan said as he helped me to my feet. "She's been working undercover."

"I know. She just told me," I said, finding it hard to talk with my throat raw from laughing and crying and my teeth chattering like a *Yakity-Yak*-talking-teeth toy. I tried to stand and my knees buckled. If Morgan hadn't been supporting me, I would have slid to the ground. "How long have you known?"

"We've been working together for weeks," he said. "You walked into a volatile situation. I tried to warn you, but you were drawn like a magnet."

"Morgan. Your sister . . ."

"I know . . ."

"So, what took you so long?"

"You mean to go after Jake and Tommy Boy? Let's get out of

here. Then I'll explain." He turned to Joshua. "Let's go, buddy." Morgan took hold of one of the child's hands, and I took the other. With Gabriel in the lead, we penetrated the veil between darkness and dawn and stepped out into the light.

Only when Joshua let go of our hands to retrieve the cat, did Morgan answer my question. "By the time I found out about Jake and Tommy Boy, it was too late to save Teri. Anyway, thanks to Veronica, they were already subjects of a larger investigation. As it turned out, they were only small fry."

"Dangerous small fry," I said, thinking of the damage they'd done.

Morgan nodded. "The DEA was just 'shaking the trees.'"

"So, Jake and Tommy Boy would have been arrested one way or another," I reasoned.

"That's how I figured it. Either way, justice would be served."

"Morgan. Joshua is your . . ." My voice caught and I could get no further. Tears welled in my eyes and threatened to blind me.

"I know," Morgan said again. He bent and peered into the child's eyes. "Josh, I'm your momma's brother, your Uncle Morgan."

It was surprising that I had any tears left, having cried more in the past few weeks than during my entire lifetime.

"I live on a farm," Morgan said. "We've got cows, calves, bulls, and dogs. Would you like to come live with us?"

Joshua started to nod, but caught himself and said, "Yes."

If surprised at the sound of the child's voice, Morgan didn't show it. "Good. Then you can also meet your Opa and Oma. That's Grandpa and Grandma in Dutch."

"I don't have to go back to the group home?" he asked.

"Only to say goodbye to your friends and get your stuff."

"What about Marjorie?"

Morgan looked at me with those arresting green eyes, and my knees weakened again. "You'll have to ask her about that."

"Will you come live with us?" Joshua asked, testing the little strength I had left to deal with all the emotions I hadn't been aware I possessed. I couldn't smile due to the hurt in my heart.

"I don't think that's what your Uncle Morgan meant, honey, but I'd love to come and visit you."

Joshua's expression turned thoughtful.

Until now, I hadn't had time to face the fact that I'd be losing him. I knew this happy beginning for Joshua marked a sad ending for me. He'd gained a new family and would eventually forget about me. How could I go on without him?

Not my will but your will. I had to do what was best for Joshua and that meant letting him go. I looked away and met Veronica eye-to-eye. "Someday I'll forgive you for keeping this from me," I said.

Veronica's smile suggested a deep-rooted sadness. "Confiding in you would've been too risky. You would've given all away with that amazingly expressive face of yours. Never, I mean never, play a game of poker. Unless you plan to lose."

I laughed, though not in the crazed way as before. "I'll remember that, though I've learned a thing or two by watching you."

"You mean, like how to fail?"

"You didn't fail."

"I miscalculated, Sis. I hadn't counted on the rifle. It wasn't even his."

"All was as it was meant to be, Veronica. I was forced to stand up for the ones I loved."

"It must have been the red boots," she said with a full-fledged smile. And what a transformation. I had considered her beautiful before, but now she was stunning.

I'd received help in the cave, part of a mystery I would likely never be able to explain.

"Hey Vonnie," Tommy Boy called. "Tell these guys we didn't kill anybody. Tell them we're your friends."

"Poor bastards," Veronica said under her breath. "I'll see what I can do."

Jake looked at me, then back at Veronica, and I pitied him. A lump formed in my throat and my eyes burned as I recalled the words of one of the voices in the cave: *They are your brothers, my beloved sons.*

"Don't," Morgan said, as though sensing my thoughts. "Because of them, Joshua lost his parents and couldn't speak for nearly two years."

One split second, one false move. We're not that different, you and me.

"Yeah," I said, silently vowing to pray for them.

Without warning, Joshua left our side and headed for Jake and Tommy Boy. I tried to stop him, but Morgan pulled me back. I held my breath and braced for words of accusation and hatred to spill forth by way of his newly awakened voice. Instead, Joshua said, "Mommy told me not to hate you anymore."

Neither man spoke. Nothing more needed to be said.

"He's not very good at hating," I said, turning to my sister. And this time, I caught tears streaming down *her* face.

Up to this point, Ben had stayed in the background, but on seeing Veronica's tears, he stepped forward and placed his hands on her trembling shoulders. "Good job," he said.

She smiled, turned, and melted into his arms.

"You're not going to leave us for Washington, are you?" I asked.

Veronica focused her cobalt gaze on Ben. "I've got some mighty good reasons for sticking around. Anyway, I promised to help you figure out what our mother's trying to tell us. I think we'd make a great team."

Morgan hugged Joshua to him with one arm and me with the other. "Let's go."

"Where's Dr. Mendez?" I asked.

"After he informed us that you were headed for the cave, he decided to stay behind with Pete, said you'd know where to find him if you needed him."

He'd always be needed, if not as a counselor, then as a friend. Instead of reducing my spirituality to the mind or to some meta-psychological theory, he had helped me heal and grow. He had guided me without killing the mystery, without closing the question.

Chapter Forty-one

THE ONLY EXPLANATION WAS that I'd been exhausted, too exhausted, until now, to question how Morgan had managed to get me back to my room at the Inn so quickly. Where were my supplies? Where was Blondie? And how on earth had I gotten back in less than three hours, when it had taken days to get to the last campsite of our abruptly terminated tour?

While I soaked in the tub, I thought back to what Dr. Mendez had told me about our final stop—that it had only been five miles from the Tassajara Hot Springs. We'd been closer to civilization than I had realized, and for this, I was grateful.

It felt good to be back.

In spite of all that happened, I would never regret my journey into that wilderness of mystery. For one thing, I got to know my sister. And what a remarkable sister she'd turned out to be. Despite her badass appearance and attitude, she was smart, strong, and working with the DEA. I recalled my suspicion and jealousy on seeing Veronica and Morgan together at the concert and again during the Ventana Wilderness tour. Of course, they'd been together. Of course, they'd been secretive. All made sense now. Each had been shouldering an enormous responsibility, complicated even further when Joshua and I arrived on the scene. They'd been trying to protect us, while I'd been busy harboring and feeding my doubts.

Yet in spite of suspecting my sister of dealing drugs and befriending criminals, I'd never stopped loving her. Thank goodness, I'd never stopped loving her. Had Ben been included in Veronica's undercover ruse? Something told me he'd been in the dark, too. And, like me, he had loved her unconditionally.

My thoughts drifted to Joshua, which, as usual, inspired an inner softening. He was able to speak again and would have a family now, a good family, a loving family. My precious Joshua was going home.

I pulled a large towel from the bathroom rack and rubbed myself dry before making my way to Margarita's mirror. I had lost weight since coming to Carmel Valley, but appeared surprisingly fit. I searched my reflection for a trace of the power I'd felt while pretending to be my sister. I didn't know how to define that power. Still don't. Only that it exists and becomes available after you figure out what you want and are determined not to quit until you get it. For an instant, the image of Veronica stared back at me, and I pulled in my breath, pleased. The mirror revealed a new self that no longer caused me to turn away.

Like a fairy tale mirror, it had also revealed to me the man I loved and a family for which I hadn't known I'd been searching: Margarita, Heather, and a fusion of Veronica and me—possibly even our mother. I had finally found the perfect mirror to fill the void above the mantel in my home.

◊ ◊ ◊

Morgan was waiting, gorgeous Morgan, with his penetrating green eyes and hypnotic gaze. But so much more. I knew that now. I had discovered that he was as strong and enduring as an oak, able to provide comfort and stability, as well as nourishment. He was self-less, sensitive, willing to adapt, and able to sacrifice something of value in order to attain something of greater worth. In only three weeks, I'd learned all these things about him, and now he was waiting. For me. When I entered the Inn's dining room, our eyes met, and when he opened his arms, I stepped into them. And stayed.

Bliss.

But the bliss didn't last.

Barely had I settled into his embrace, and barely had I formulated the words to define how I felt—safe, comfortable, loved—when he broke the contact and tore his vital spirit from my grasp. "Let's go," he said.

"Go where?"

"To get Joshua."

"Why?" All I wanted was to be back in his arms.

"It's Easter Sunday."

"So."

"Remember the morning of the sunrise?"

"Yes," I said, looking anywhere but at him. "How could I forget?"

He grinned. "Me, too."

My face burned as I recalled the unfiltered stream of words that had unmasked my secret longings. But, apparently, that's not what he was referring to. "I asked you to join me for Easter Mass."

"There are no Masses at this hour."

"There is now. My brother's here."

"Father John Phillip?"

"The one and only. I called him as soon as I was sure you and Joshua were safe, even before I called Mom and Dad."

"He must have left Sacramento lickety-split," I said.

"He was eager to meet his new nephew . . . and reconnect with you. He figured we'd meet sooner or later, but never guessed we'd get into such mischief."

"How did your family deal with the news about Teri?"

"It was tough, but not unexpected. We'll finally have the chance to say good-bye." Morgan paused, understandably shaken, but composed himself quickly, something I'd come to love about him. "What they hadn't expected was the gift of Joshua. Through him, Teri lives on. One reason for the special Mass.

"Another reason for the Mass is to give thanks for the miracle of you showing up in Joshua's life at just the right moment, and for your safe return. We acknowledge and honor the part you played in finding our nephew and also for helping him speak again."

"I exposed the child to danger. What if—"

"Let's go," Morgan said. "By now, Joshua should be rested and waiting."

⚡ ⚡ ⚡

Joshua sat between Morgan and me in the front pew of the Basilica. Mona, Heather, Veronica, and Ben occupied the pew behind us. Father John Phillip lit the altar candles and readied the holy table before exiting through a side door. A minute or two later, he reappeared wearing white vestments and carrying a covered chalice. In place of a hymn, he began Mass with an antiphon. "I have risen; I am with you once more." When he made the sign of the cross and said the prayers of greeting, all my pain—internal and external, real and imagined—receded. I had no recent memory of such relief, peace—liberation—and wondered if I was experiencing a piece of heaven.

I allowed myself to open to the inspired message offered by the Mass. My skin seemed to vaporize as if nothing were holding me together. Even my bones felt soft and elastic. Nostalgia welled in my throat as Father John Phillip recited the opening prayer, ". . . raise us up and renew our lives by the Spirit that is within us." And then finally, as though a neural pathway had opened in my brain, I understood.

The Spirit was within us—within me.

A nudge to my side forced me to open my eyes and turn to Joshua. A glow of knowledge streamed from his eyes as if he'd opened a wisdom door and shared my new discovery.

He, too, understood.

"Please be seated," Father John Phillip said, and although he proceeded to read comforting words from the Epistle and Gospel, when Morgan's thigh brushed against mine, *his* presence took complete hold of my mind.

As if sensing the change in me, Joshua, too, edged closer. To my surprise, and relief, I didn't feel constricted or confined. The motive, the intention, the impulse of my two companions, wasn't one of control or ownership. This was different, this innocent yearning for warmth and understanding, this inexplicable urge to share comfort and love. I couldn't fight what I'd been unconsciously hungering for all my life.

Was giving and accepting love the missing piece to life's puzzle? Was life's mission to create rather than to fit in? Maybe what I needed was to wake up, rather than break free.

Father John Phillip stepped down from the altar and approached his nephew with a serotonin-inducing smile that no *Twilight, My Space*, or *Ace of Spades* drug could duplicate. "Joshua has found his family and found his voice, thanks to the Lord." He blessed the child's forehead with the sign of the cross and said, "May our Father in heaven speak through you, and may you never forget the power of silence. May you continue to watch and perceive, and may you continue to express your love by being a good listener." He leaned forward and hugged the child. "Welcome home, Joshua."

Father John Phillip then turned to me. "We give thanks for your safe return. May the Almighty continue to work through you in freeing others as you have freed Joshua." He winked in typical John Phillip fashion before turning to the other participants in the Mass. "Now let us join in prayer for our sister, Teri, and our brother, Paul. May their souls rest in peace."

"Amen."

Father John Phillip returned to the altar, and we stood for the *Profession of Faith*. Later, when I approached the altar for Communion, I not only partook of the bread— *". . . which earth has given and human hands have made. It will become for us the bread of life."* —but also the wine— *". . . fruit of the vine and work of human hands. It will become our spiritual drink."* Something I'd resisted doing for too long as just another thing church authorities were telling me to do. After experiencing the mysteries of Medicine Wheel in my search for understanding, I now appreciated the importance of fully experiencing the rituals offered by the church of my upbringing as well.

Bread *and* wine, symbols of forgiveness and love; mysteries to give our lives new purpose.

After Mass, Veronica and Ben joined hands, lifting this Easter Sunday up another notch on my perfect-day meter. I liked and respected Ben and would never forget his kind, gentle way.

𝒩 𝒩 𝒩

"This will be your last night at the group home, Josh, so you need to say good-bye." Morgan's brows furrowed as he waited for his nephew to respond.

The adults and children at the home had been all the family Joshua had known until recently. Would it be hard for him to leave them behind?

Joshua dove onto his bed and plowed beneath his covers. "Do I have any boy cousins?"

Morgan laughed. "So much for saying good-bye."

He knelt next to the bed and rested his arms on both sides of the child. "Yes, you have two cousins, Todd and Jon, and they're eager to meet you."

"Mom and Dad used to call me Josh," Joshua said.

Morgan's brows shot up in mock surprise. "Umm . . . seems to me I've already referred to you as Josh a time or two."

"Can I use both names?" I asked. "Sometimes I need to call you Joshua."

"I like it when *you* call me Joshua."

I tucked the blankets around the child as best I could and sat at the foot of the bed. "Do you want your mouse totem back?"

He shook his head, his eyes solemn in his former non-speaking way. "I have Gabriel and my new family, but you're all alone . . ."

The cat purred, evidencing a marvelous expression of contentment he'd never expressed before.

"Mommy said to be patient," Joshua said, "but does that mean you'll be gone for a long time?"

I couldn't answer.

"You're the only one who heard me when I couldn't talk," Joshua said. "And you gave me your magic ring."

I'd gotten so used to his silence that I had some adjusting to do. "Not magic, exactly," I said, although if he believed the ring had special powers, it probably did and would likely continue to do so as long as his faith held.

"You also gave me my best friend ever."

The cat, no longer mute or one of the homeless, purred his loud contentment. After our escape from the cave, Morgan had told me that Gabriel had sneaked past Jake and Tommy Boy and entered the cave—sort of like a canary in a coal mine to check for danger—and when he didn't return, Morgan knew for certain Joshua and I were inside. "The hardest thing I've ever had to do," he'd admitted, "was to wait for an opportunity to come to your rescue. When I heard the shots, I thought I was too late."

"I have a family now," Joshua said, "but I still love you best."

While the two most precious men in my life waited for me to pull myself together, I struggled for words. "I'll never leave you, Joshua, not in my heart, but I will be gone for a while."

His eyelids dropped, and he stifled a yawn. "That's okay, I'll wait."

"Time to go," Morgan said.

"I don't think I have the strength to leave him."

"You have to," Morgan said.

I hated those words, upset with Morgan for saying them, but knew them to be true.

"Marjorie?" Joshua whispered, barely able to keep his eyes open. "Mommy said your real name is *Sunwalker*. It's the name *your* mommy gave you . . ."

We both stared at the child, at a loss for words.

N N N

The day of celebrating the resurrection of Christ was almost over. As I walked into the night with Morgan, I realized that Joshua and I had been resurrected, too. We'd been freed from the cave, but also from our greatest limitations. Joshua could now speak, and I had learned to listen. Listen so I could hear.

I reached for Morgan's hand and wondered if he would also be capable of listening—and hearing—when I shared my plans with him the following day. And even if he did listen, and even if he did hear, would he understand?

Chapter Forty-two

I HAD INTENDED TO CALL HIM LATER, after I'd had a chance to eat and build up my strength. I had intended to fix my hair, apply some makeup, wear something nice. But most of all, I had intended to forestall—as long as possible—my meeting with Morgan van Dyke.

Morgan, however, had other plans.

"I'm parked outside," he said when I answered his morning call.

I glanced at my watch. "It's only eight o'clock."

"We're going for a drive," was his calm reply, followed by a chuckle that caused my toes to curl.

"Where?"

"To the mission. To see Margarita's grave."

◢ ◢ ◢

So, Morgan knew about Margarita.

I'd never gotten around to telling him about her or the voices. I'd been afraid to. Because I loved him. And that gave him the power to hurt me. As Cliff had hurt me. It also gave him the power to block my path, now that I was finally free.

We paused in front of the pepper tree that marked Margarita's grave, and Morgan fixed his intense green eyes on mine. "Talk to me."

I hesitated, surprised anew at the force of his gaze, the way it cut through my heart like a green diamond. "I'm going home for two weeks to sort things out."

Morgan showed no surprise. "And?"

"I'm going to have a long talk with my mother."

"Glad to hear that."

"And share my journal with Dr. Mendez."

Morgan turned his attention to the gnarled and burled tree, his gaze following its up-stretched branches into the marshmallow-clouded sky.

"After that, I'm heading for Big Sur," I said.

He stiffened. "So, your search isn't over?"

"Not yet." My voice caught on these two simple words as if I were presenting a eulogy at my own funeral. I wanted desperately to allow him to shield me and protect me, but he couldn't shield me from the voices, and he couldn't protect me from myself.

He touched my cheek with fingers that trembled. "Ben told me about Margarita."

I started to lift my hands and then let them drop. "I should've been the one to tell you about her, but I was always too mad . . . and afraid."

"You're hearing another voice as well?"

My cheeks burned. "Yes, Antonia, my birth mother." I took a breath that sounded like a gasp for air. "I never got around to telling you about her, either."

"No. But it explains a lot. Like why you consulted Dr. Mendez and why you came to Carmel Valley. Pretty scary, huh?"

"When I first started hearing Antonia's voice, I'd never been so scared in my life, except maybe in the cave with the rifle pointed at my chest."

Morgan winced, and I hurried on, in an attempt to keep a swell of grief from stealing my voice. "I need more time, Morgan. I don't know if Antonia will continue to talk to me, but, regardless, I have more discoveries to make."

"Such as?"

"I need to know what Antonia wants. I think she needs me."

He cradled my face with his calloused hands and looked so deeply into my eyes it felt as if he were entering my mind. "And?"

"I need to discover who I am and what I can give."

He passed his thumbs over my wet cheeks. "Do you need to be alone for that?"

My heart fisted, anticipating the giving, and receiving, of an unrecoverable punch. There was no way I could avoid hurting him, although he was the one I loved above all. "Hopefully, not for long."

"When you disappeared a few days ago," Morgan said. "I realized that by trying to protect you, I'd been trying to control you, which almost led to disaster." He dropped his hands to my shoulders and bowed his head.

"I'm not asking you to change," I said.

He chuckled low in his throat. "You'd give me up in a heartbeat before you'd give up your freedom."

"No," I said. "At least I've learned that much. To be entirely free, I'd have to stay single all my life, which isn't an option. I want to marry and have a family. With you."

For a few seconds, Morgan said nothing. He swallowed, looked up at the sky, and closed his eyes. "You've accomplished so much here," he said finally, his eyes moist.

I should have pulled him into my arms to show him that I, too, was capable of deep love and demonstrating it, but I knew this opportunity to talk might not come again, at least not for a while. "I've been a catalyst, true. I'd have to be blind not to see that, but all I did was walk into situations. Things happened, and I reacted. I have to do my part, too."

"Which sometimes means being acted upon," Morgan said. "And giving in to a higher power."

I broke contact with Morgan's gaze and concentrated instead on bulky clouds floating across the heavens. "You mean submit?"

"In order to receive."

"I think I already did that while alone in the forest and again while trapped in the cave. What a paradox, Morgan. I had to surrender in order to be free."

"Hard to swallow, isn't it?" Morgan said. "Realizing that we're not always in control."

"It's humbling and scary," I admitted.

He pressed his forehead to mine. "So, Big Sur beckons."

Dear God, how could I make him understand? "Hopefully in the land of my mother's people, I can close the door on what caused me pain and disappointment and move on."

"Cliff?" he asked.

"Not Cliff as much as what he did to me. If I don't learn to trust again, we don't stand a chance. But that's not all. I need to learn to say *no* to what hurts me, so I can say *yes* to love. I crave security, but something inside still needs to be born."

"I'd love to see you dance and hear you sing," Morgan said. "I'd love to watch you heal."

I pulled back in surprise, looked him straight in the eye.

"But, I know, you're not ready," he said. "You don't want to be courted, but to be understood, and I love you exactly as you are."

"You don't know how much I want to believe that . . ."

"Maybe this'll help." Morgan touched his lips to mine.

Shivers of delight stunned me into submission. But not for long. I opened my mouth and spoke to him in the new language I'd learned since coming to Carmel Valley: the language of love, the non-possessive kind, the kind that heals, that soothes, that comforts—the kind that sets one free.

And Morgan understood every word.

He kissed the corner of my mouth, my cheek, my forehead, and stroked my back. "You've just told me all I needed to know."

A ripple of cool, cypress-scented air whispered past us, and we both shivered.

This is only the beginning, the *Voice* said.

Morgan's head jerked up.

"Morgan?"

He stood completely still, and I waited. Whatever he had experienced, he would need time to absorb it. I, of all people, should know. He lowered his eyes to mine, and in doing so, tears spilled down his bronzed cheeks. When I touched his face, he drew in a ragged breath and shook his head, as if unsure of how to proceed. "I just received a message too strong to ignore. That you love me and will come back to me and that all is well." He buried his face in my hair, and I thought I heard a sob. "Joshua and I will wait for you as long as it takes."

A gust of wind swooshed through the pepper tree, and sunrays streamed through the spaces between the branches to illuminate the ivy over Margarita's grave. Morgan whistled softly. "The world of the invisible surrounds us."

"And I hope we never lose our connection to it," I said. "I pray that we don't."

"Someday, my love, we'll have to settle somewhere in-between."

"Yes," I said. "Between the visible and the invisible, between the ordinary and the sacred, between will and surrender."

A Word from My Protagonist

Dear Reader,

My name is Marjorie Veil Sunwalker. Margaret Duarte, the writer of this novel, believes she has created me. She believes she has made up the events and details of my journey. What she doesn't realize is that I have been with her for a long, long time. She was only an instrument, my interpreter.

Margaret first felt my presence during a visit to the Monterey Peninsula in California. It was August of the year 2000. She was on the 17-Mile Drive and had stopped at the landmark of the Lone Cypress. There, I gently touched her, beckoning her for the first time. At her next stop she saw what remains of The Ghost Tree, bleached white by wind and sea. As she stood entranced, I nudged her again. Finally, at the Carmel Mission, I set the trap, and she was caught. She didn't know the how or whys, but she knew she would write a story.

From then on, I've been her invisible guide. I've whispered my thoughts and experiences to her, lifting the veil a bit at a time. It was her job to put all the pieces together. She was to make sense of all the twists and turns that appeared along my path. She was to be my voice.

Another thing Margaret does not know is that this was also her journey. We traveled the road of my quest together. Often my surprises were her surprises, my trials became her trials, and my awakening helped her to awaken.

I give Margaret credit for taking on this large project. She was obsessed and stubborn enough to carry it through. She kept unraveling, sorting, and weaving until the invisible threads of my tale were connected into an intricate web, ready to preserve between the covers of her book.

Margaret has learned to receive my message with the single eye of her heart, instead of the eyes in her head. That's the eye that sees inner reality and the world of Spirit.

However, she still doesn't think I'm real. I say it all depends on one's definition of real. The membrane between Margaret and me is very thin, and the crossing over is easy.

The path we walked together was a sacred one, not bound by space and time. Because you are alive, you may find yourself on a similar path one day, trying to open your eyes to the Sacred Mystery. We may have more in common than you think. If this novel happens to get into your hands, I hope you can join us in our dance of discovery.

By the way, Margaret is still unaware of one last thing. The circle of my life and hers is not yet complete. We have only reached the opening stages of our journey. We have only been awakened.

Our story is not over.

Acknowledgments

MY DEEPEST THANKS TO:

My husband, John, who has been patient with me over all the years I've been writing and promising, "I'm almost done, just one more revision, that's it, I promise." Well, it's finally true (for this book anyway).

My first readers for their faith in my story: Anne Van Steyn, Sandra Van Steyn, Kay Hardesty, and Kathy Simoes.

My critique partners for their valuable suggestions: Jo Chandler, Lee Lopez, Dorothy Skarles, Natalia Orfanos, and members of *Amherst Writers and Artists' Group* directed by Gini Grossenbacher.

My line and content editors: Judith Reveal, Christine Van Steyn, Moira Warmerdam, and Marianne Chick for their helpful input and encouragement.

My sisters, brother—and friends—for reading my work and standing by me when I was ready to give up: Theresa Adrian, Vicki Van Steyn, and John Van Steyn.

My cover artist, Clarissa Yeo of *Yocla Designs* and Jonnee Bardo of *Gluskin's Photo Lab and Studio* for my author photo.

And to my family for their love and forbearance: John, Todd, Martina, Jon, Angelina, and Tessa. Maybe now you'll understand what I've been up to all these years.

Many books were helpful in researching for this novel, especially *Earth Medicine* and *The Medicine Way*, by Kenneth Meadows, *Dancing the Dream* by Jamie Sams, *The Holographic Universe* by Michael Talbot, *Spiritual Emergency*, by Stanislav and Christina Grof, *The Natural History of Big Sur*, by Paul Henson and Donald J. Usner, *Salinan Indians of California and their neighbors*, by Betty War Brusa, *The Ohlone Way*, by Malcolm Margolin, and *The Carmel Mission*, by Sydney Temple.

About the Author

Margaret Duarte's parents immigrated to the United States from Holland (the Netherlands) with her two older brothers the year before she was born. She grew up on a series of dairy farms in California into what became a very large family—seven brothers and two sisters.

When she entered high school, her fascination with creative writing began. She was fortunate to receive excellent instruction, plus a great deal of encouragement from her English teachers.

Scholarship in hand, Margaret entered California State University, Sacramento, where she earned a degree in English and a secondary teaching credential. Then she did something she swore she would never do—married a dairy farmer.

Over the following thirty years, she helped on the family farm, raised two sons, taught at a local middle school, and dabbled in an assortment of hobbies but did little writing other than in her journal. It wasn't until her sons were grown that she finally returned to what her teachers had encouraged her to pursue while in school—writing.

Though it delayed her career as a writer, she never regretted her decision to marry and raise a family. Her years as wife and mother taught her about love and selflessness and fueled her for the years of writing that lay ahead. They also uncovered what would become the driving force behind her work: the call for spiritual and emotional freedom. Through her novels, which synthesize heart and mind, science and spirituality, Margaret hopes to inspire people to activate their gifts, retire their excuses, and stand in their own authority.

Book two of the "Enter-the-Between"

Visionary Fiction series

Marjorie Veil is running again. But this time, she's not running from herself. She's running to embrace her past so she may move on with her future. A future that includes a man and an orphaned boy who both love her. But in order to build a life with them, she must have the strength to defy the expectations of her over-protective adoptive mother, and she must be steadfast in deciphering the veiled messages coming from the Native American woman who died giving her birth. Marjorie's quest is the story of the soul trying to break free of its conditioned restraints to live a life of freedom, courage, and authenticity, and focus on what is really important in her precious present moments.

Book three of the "Enter the Between"

Visionary Fiction series

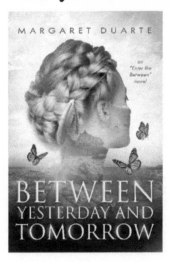

When Marjorie Veil takes refuge at a friend's Victorian mansion in Pacific Grove, otherwise known as Butterfly Town USA, she seeks answers to two burning questions. Why had her biological father abandoned her at birth? And why is her mother sending messages from beyond the grave, shedding light on agonizing secrets she took with her when she died?

Despite plans to enjoy Pacific Grove's quaint bookstores, ocean views, and butterfly sanctuary, Marjorie's stay is anything but replenishing. She senses something disturbing beneath the mansion's outward calm. Soon she begins seeing and hearing things that cause her to question her sanity, and she unearths a backyard labyrinth that reveals its own powerful secrets.

A psychological-supernatural tale of an ordinary woman in extraordinary situations which she resolves in remarkable ways.

Book four of the "Enter the Between"

Visionary Fiction series

Medicate or nurture; reform or set free? These are quandaries rookie teacher Marjorie Veil faces when she takes on an after-school class for thirteen-year-olds labeled as troublemakers, unteachable, and hopeless. Faculty skeptics warn that all these kids need is prescribed medication for focus and impulse control. But as Marjorie quickly discovers, behind their anti-conformist exteriors are gifted teens, who are sensitive, empathetic, and wise beyond their youth. They also happen to have psychic abilities, which they have kept hidden until now. Can Marjorie help them do what she has been unable to do for herself: fight for their spiritual and emotional freedom?

Lightning Source UK Ltd.
Milton Keynes UK
UKHW031543010622
403836UK00004B/901